SAVING Eagle One

Col. Lee Martin

McGowan Collection Series, Book 5

Also by Col. Lee Martin:

- The Third Moon is Blue
- Starbright
- The Six Mile Inn
- The Valiant
- Ten Minutes till Midnight
- Wolf Laurel
- Provocation: Return of the Weatherman
- A Hateful Wind
- The Justice Club
- Killing the Viper
- Southern Psalms
- Palisades

First time readers of my novels are encouraged to read the earlier books in the Bruce McGowan Collection Series as well. Perhaps you will then appreciate Saving Eagle One all the more. The series is in this order:

Wolf Laurel

Provocation: Return of the Weatherman

A Hateful Wind

Killing the Viper

Acknowledgements

Thanks to my good friend, retired FBI Special Agent Dave Parker, for his technical advice on Bureau and Secret Service standard operating procedures, weapons and organizational structure. Dave, with his stellar history of government service, represents the best of our country's federal law enforcement.

To the rabid fans of Bruce McGowan who are always looking for the next in the series...Andy Black, Bruce Kolleda, Bob Deitz, Duff Smith, Jane Justice, Dave (above), and of course my kids, Adam Martin and Miranda Martel, just to mention a few. Contrary to popular belief, McGowan is *not* my alter ego, but I have enjoyed creating him.

Ah yes and of course, to the charming ladies of the Lake Sinclair Book Club in Eatonton, Georgia, my appreciation and admiration.

And to my favorite author whose captivating novels have always inspired me to be a better writer, a fond farewell. The South's preeminent wordsmith, Pat Conroy, was a man of uncommon words, unforgettable characters and an uncanny genius for storytelling. The world will sorely miss you.

CONTENTS

Col. Lee Martin

Saving Eagle One

Prologue

A miserable night. Damn miserable. Icy rain blowing sideways and pelting the Lincoln like liquid shrapnel. Parked well into the shadows, we did our best to stay out of sight of the chopper's sweeping searchlight. It was likely an FBI helicopter, but could have been a city or state bird as well. No way to know since it was night and I couldn't make out any markings. But its pursuit had been relentless over the last two hours.

I knew the chopper had not been dispatched upon any information the feds might have elicited from my brother, Joey. He had told me on the phone that some feds, identifying themselves as the FBI, had swept in not ten minutes after we left his place. They looked and sounded legit, he said, having badges and credentials. But as we also knew for sure at this point that a terrorist infrastructure was in fact embedded within federal law enforcement, we had no idea *who* could be trusted.

Whoever the terrorists *and* the feds were, they had already done their homework about the McGowan brothers. They not only had information about me at Wolf Laurel, but Joey and the McGowan Funeral Home. It was interesting that the two actual terrorists who swept into the funeral home had gotten there ahead of the FBI; therefore, their Intel on us was just as good as the government's...maybe better. But maybe they were one and the same. When the federal officers arrived later, Joey denied having seen me or even being in touch with me. As he had grown up all those years with the likes of me, both of us learning to be convincing misinformers of the truth when necessary, there was a chance they might have even believed him.

But whoever was now zeroing in on us had done so quickly. After we had lit out and were on the road something less than two hours, they had by then learned I had Joey's Lincoln. And with license plate readers on top their cars, all they had to do was sit on I-81 and wait for us to go by. I thought we might lose them by ducking off into Winchester and finding concealment down one of the alleys. If they were the *good* Feds and were close to taking us down, I was sure they weren't going to resort to gunplay. And I wasn't going to shoot at *them*. However, if they were the *bad* Feds, all bets were off.

But then again if they *were* the good Feds, they believed that I was of all things both a murderer and a kidnapper. I guess I can't blame them for thinking that, considering

several of their people lay dead back at Wolf Laurel. Their VIP was also missing and possibly being held captive and I hadn't stuck around to convince them that I was just an innocent victim of it all. There were at least four vehicles of pursuers on my tail. Maybe one of their snipers would eventually put his sights on me, careful not to hit the man beside me. I figured it would not be long and the entire town would be cordoned off. One way or the other, I'd be nailed. A matter of time.

All the while, parked briefly in that dark alley until the chopper moved away, for some odd reason I found myself thinking about what I was doing only fifteen hours before in my warm kitchen, sipping Adriana's robust coffee at the table waiting in anxious anticipation the arrival of our honored guests. My mind trails off like that sometimes. Maybe it's some kind of defense mechanism that subconsciously takes control of my brain when I'm in dire situations. But then I looked over at the man riding shotgun with me. Having not said much over the past hour, he appeared to be in deep thought as well. I'm sure he was pondering not only his own safety but also that of his wife. Was there any way the bad guys could get to her? My hope was that she along with my wife were still well hidden back at my fishing camp.

After a few moments, I eased from behind the wheel of the Lincoln to peer around the corner. The bird in the air finally did move on, focusing its penetrating beam on a vehicle similar to mine parked a street over. I watched for a couple of long minutes while one of the vehicles that had been on our tail converged on the car. But because in no time at all I was soaked and shivering from the bitter cold rain, I jumped back into the car.

Pulling out slowly, I kept the headlights off and made a right turn onto Loudoun. I had no idea where we'd go from there, but now we needed to get out of town somewhere out in the wooded countryside. However, we had not covered more than two blocks when suddenly on our left approaching from a side street a black SUV came barreling down on us. Immediately, I knew these people were not feds. What gave me a clue was the man I spotted on the passenger side of the vehicle pointing a shoulder-fired RPG out the window directly at the Lincoln. Sphincter pucker time.

Chapter One

I never thought I would get there, but I finally did it. I actually retired...fully retired. Not only was I no longer a full-time *or* even part-time badass, but no longer a contractor available at the government's beck and call. And believe it or not, I've not been going through any D.T.s. This is not meant to sound egotistical, but I was very good at what I did. Many say the *best*. I bagged a lot of bad guys over the years and I have no doubt that America is a hell of a lot safer because of my skilled handiwork. But, again, I'm not one to boast; it's just the God's truth. That was then...this is now. My license to kill has officially expired.

My wife Adriana and I have never been happier in this stage of our lives. I'm knocking on the big six-0 and she's flirting with the five-0. We still run that quaint country inn called Wolf Laurel off Seven Bridges Road in Eastern West Virginia, a homey, Victorian B&B that these days seems to be even more popular than ever. Perhaps it's because it's advertised in the back of a number of magazines as one of the Top Ten get-a-ways in America. But just maybe it's more about what went down here last fall. People do have a natural sense of curiosity and I'm sure a lot of them wanted to experience the place where it all happened. A place one may even now find in the history books.

Adriana is the hostess here like always and I am the caretaker. I fix stuff and keep the yard looking nice. Sometimes I even give our guests tours of the county's historical sites and cultural venues. We both love our jobs and positions in life, and even after all we've been through together, no thanks to me, we're still in love. Like a couple of teenagers in heat.

In my final mission with CTT, I experienced what I've come to realize as the most gut-wrenching event in my life. I call it the *Hateful Wind* event. My wounds, both physical *and* emotional, have long since healed. Mostly, anyway. A good part of my soul is *still* lamenting. I guess I never will fully get over seeing my boss and compadres lying in pools of their blood, dead upon the orders of the man who in that upcoming election might have become President. However, when I think back about it, I *was* able to ease my pain just a tad by putting that well-placed bullet in the bastard's head. In my book, it was not murder. It was justice. A righteous damn kill if you will.

What I later learned was that Team Zulu along with the Chicago and L.A. Teams Yankee and X-ray, no longer existed. Actually the entire counterterrorist program which had been covertly imbedded within the Department of State had been scrapped. This had to have been a decision made by the President himself.
Why...I didn't know. Could have been budgetary issues or perhaps the Secretary of State somehow found out the unit actually existed...camouflaged somewhere within his bailiwick under another section's title. Could also have been because there was now reliance more so on teams fielded by the National Counterterrorist Center (NCTC) and the FBI. However, wasn't my concern any longer.

A few days after that last mission, at the invitation of the President himself, I found myself sitting in the oval office listening to him tell me to not be surprised one day if he and the First Lady took a little needed R&R at our fanciful little retreat. He thought our place sounded nice. I didn't think much about it at the time...that he was actually serious. Something else was on my mind. I was just glad he wasn't having me investigated for the congressman's murder. Oh, I'm sure he knew I was the guy who did it, even though I had become his trusted man in the field. His ace terrorist hunter on Team Zulu. I was willing to answer for the killing, if it came to that, but he never accused me. And if he *had* done so and sent me away, I then wouldn't have been available on his orders a few weeks later to pull in America's most cunning sniper to take down the world's most dangerous terrorist since Usama bin Laden. I guess I owed the Prez for my freedom and he knew it. That's one reason he kept me on his string. I think they call that blackmail. But I was glad to do the mission, extortion or not. The world is indeed safer because I successfully hatched the plot that took out a deadly terrorist snake. So, it all worked out for the both of us. He's finishing out his term as a hero for saving American lives and I'm living out my life as Bruce McGowan, private citizen.

Well, it was the Sunday after Thanksgiving last year...the afternoon following church service when Adriana and I were putting away her china that had embossed on it colorful images of pilgrims and horns of plenty. While she was working on the inside of our inn, it was my job to remove all remaining Thanksgiving decorations outside to include the front door fall arrangement that she had hand-crafted from dried brown and rust colored flowers. But that being accomplished, I was further tasked to retrieve from our storage shed all of the boxes and boxes of Christmas decorations. At Wolf Laurel it seems that one holiday's end kicks off the next. Anyway, as to the Christmas stuff, how one woman can accumulate so many tree ornaments, snowy globes, wreaths, collection of angels and holiday what-nots to display is beyond me. It took me over two hours to bring it all in.

The next day I then found myself feeling like Clark Griswold, driving the old 300 horse Suburban sleigh out on Mountain Road to chop down that perfectly-shaped Douglas fir that would grace our B&B sitting room. No artificial or fiber optic, sacrilegious trees in *our* house. Adriana has trusted me with that mission for the past five years and I haven't failed to deliver yet. But this was going to be a special year. Wolf Laurel would officially be 75 years old come December 12th. And that tree had to be *extra* special.

As though she hadn't already accumulated enough decorations over the years, she said there were a few other items she needed for the tree. I asked her what more could go on that tree as opposed to what I remember about last year's tree. She said it was important that there be a different theme each year and this year's would have a more classical, Old World theme. A theme for a tree? I thought *Christmas* was the theme. Well anyway, since we were also celebrating the birth of Wolf Laurel, the tree needed to be decorated in an early to mid Twentieth Century America style with mauve and blue antique globes, swags of colorful, various-shaped beads and other vintage-looking knick-knacks. And for sure, there would not be one fat-bellied Santa or any reindeer with red noses anywhere in *our* house. She showed me some photos in a magazine of trees in living rooms decorated back in World War II that she wanted to duplicate.There were a couple of antique stores downtown where she had seen what she needed to make it all happen.

Late Monday afternoon the gray-white sky looked as though it could produce snow at any time. As it loomed ominously above the sweeping farmland, it cast a kind of 'Christmas is coming' aura. Downtown, a couple of shops had already set up in their storefront glass displays of holiday items like Santa in his sleigh, a lighted manger scene, a wooden toy train and a gingerbread house covered with artificial snow. Red and green wreaths with white lights garnished the lamp posts while classical Christmas music emanated throughout a few of the quaint little gift shops. And if *that* was not enough, Adriana had found a local station on her car radio that played twenty-four hours of Christmas music beginning well before Thanksgiving which had already contaminated my brain to a point where the music of The Nutcracker's Sugar Plum Fairies still danced through my head for thirty minutes after it hit the pillow at night.

When we were finally through shopping that Monday evening and after we had stayed up half the night decorating inside and out, it was all too apparent that Wolf Laurel had suddenly been transformed into something resembling a Thomas Kincaid Christmas cottage. But with four more weeks before Christmas, I had the feeling we *still* weren't done. As long as more decorations existed out there, my lovely wife would find them. However, I just wasn't sure how much more the cottage could take in.

That Tuesday afternoon about four-thirty our land line rang. I picked up the receiver.

"Mr. McGowan?"

"Yes."

"Please hold for the President."

My eyebrows narrowed. "President? Of *what*?"

"Of the United States."

"Right. Okay, who is this?"

"The White House Chief of Staff. My name is Arnold Kessler."

"Hello, Mr. Kessler. How do I know it's you and not my brother Joey pulling another dumb ass practical joke? You can give it up now, Joey."

"Umm...I'm not your brother Joey, Mr. McGowan. Believe me, my name *is* Kessler."

Adriana was frowning and quietly mouthing, "Who *is* that?"

I smiled. "All right, I'll play along. Put the President on."

There was a long pause. I smiled again and nodded. Apparently Joey was now going to try imitating the President's voice. I knew I was right about this.

"Bruce? Are you there?"

Check that. I was *wrong*. I'm very good at voices and I'll never forget *that* one. Not too long ago I sat for about fifteen minutes listening to the man who owns it.

"Mr. President. What a surprise."

"How're you doin,' my friend? Havin' fun these days?" He called me his friend.

I don't know how these stupid little barbs come out of my mouth, but I replied, "As much fun as a tornado tearing through a Mississippi trailer park." I clinched my teeth as soon as I said it.

He chuckled, then said, "I shouldn't laugh at that you know, considerin' what happened last summer out in Oklahoma. But I know about that sense of humor of yours. Mr. Byrd said you kept crackin' him up."

I don't remember that. Lionel Byrd never cracked a smile when I came out with my asinine quips. Of course just hearing the name of my former boss, God rest his soul, always causes a sheet of gloom to fall over me.

"Yes, sir. Anyway, it's good to hear from you, Mr. President. Uhh...is there something you need me for?"

Adriana, who was still eavesdropping, squinted her eyes at me. If I *was* standing there talking to the big guy and was so eagerly volunteering for another covert assignment, President or not, my derriere was grass and she was going to be the lawn mower.

"Yes, as a matter of fact I need you *and* your lovely wife to do something for *us*."

"*Anything*, sir."

"Do you have room for the First Lady and me there at Wolf Laurel the second weekend of December? Adriana painted my wife a right lovely picture of your place and after you all left, we started talkin'. We thought maybe we might kick off a little Christmas spirit by comin' there for a visit."

The sudden shot of adrenaline firing through my arteries shouted 'Holy Crap.'

"Absolutely, sir. We don't have any guests booked until the *third* weekend. We'd love to have you."

Adriana's eyes widened. She mouthed, "What? The President actually coming here?" Just the thought of having him and his wife as guests prompted a grin on her face that showcased all thirty two of her perfect teeth. If that grin lasted as long as I thought it would, we might have to have it surgically removed.

"Excellent, Bruce," said the voice on the other end. "We'll look forward to it. Now as to the particulars and some of our protocol, I'll turn you back over to my Chief. Goodbye, sir. See you soon."

How about that? I'm not only his friend, but a 'sir.'

After a moment, Kessler was back on the line. "Mr. McGowan, I'm sure you didn't expect this kind of news today." He then chuckled.

"Got *that* right."

"Well, anyway, tomorrow, Wednesday, the head of the White House Secret Service will be arriving at your place around eleven in the morning to go over all the details and requirements. You and your wife are not to tell anyone about the President's visit. As a former Federal agent and until recently enjoying a Top Secret clearance, you are sworn to secrecy on this. If there is a leak anywhere and at anytime before they arrive there, the event will not happen. Are we clear on that?"

"Crystal, sir."

"Fine. Do you have any questions or concerns before our agent arrives?"

"No, sir."

"Then have a good day, Mr. McGowan." The call ended.

Adriana then grabbed me by the shoulders. Her eyes appeared as large as shooter marbles. *"They're coming here!?"* she exclaimed. "Wait till I tell..."

"No, sweetheart. We can tell no one. For security purposes as well as the First Family's privacy, this has to be the biggest kept secret of your life. No one...not your parents, not Joey, not your hair dresser."

It was like her balloon had suddenly deflated. "Well *crud*." That's the worst anybody will ever hear her swearing. But then the sun came back into her face. "Anyway, we'll have them as our guests. *Our* guests. They could vacation anywhere and they chose *us*."

"You must really have sold the First Lady on Wolf Laurel. She apparently talked the President into coming here."

"When *are* they coming?"

"The second weekend of December," I replied.

"That's in what...two weeks. How long are they staying?"

"Don't know yet. I was only told they'd be here that weekend. I can't imagine more than three days."

Adriana then began ringing her hands and looking around the room. "Okay, let's think this out and not panic. We've got to get this place in shape. I'll make a list of everything we need to do and put us on a schedule."

I grinned. "You'd *like* to be somebody's boss, wouldn't you?"

"Well, you're the one who always jumps out and says what goes around here, being the macho man decision maker you are. But remember, I was in charge of this place long before you came aboard with that commando take charge attitude of yours. You'll be following *my* lead on *this* mission, Mr. McGowan."

"Yes, ma'am," I said with the click of my heels, giving her a faux salute. And I knew she would organize things to a tee. All I had to do was stay the hell out of her way and fall in line.

* * * * *

I've lived a lot of places in my nearly six full decades of life. Growing up with Ma and Pa McGowan and my younger brother, Joey, in the old homestead, I told myself when I left home I'd never again live in an old house where the cold wind blew through the walls, the floors creaked and gave, and some part of its rickety structure always either needed repaired, repainted or rebuilt. Then I met the lovely Adriana, the owner and proprietress of Wolf Laurel. She's the very essence of beauty. A woman in her mid-forties, but looking ten years younger with that Victoria's Secret body. A woman with a soft glow in her eyes, skin as flawless as a diamond and a heart so impeccably pure, God has to be smiling every time he looks down on his creation. We fell in love, got married and suddenly I'm back in my old childhood home...or a place pretty much like it.

Although we haven't had to fix a lot of stuff around the house, at my begging, she did allow me to put in a modern heating system so that our guests wouldn't be found frozen to death in their beds. I actually had to show her the online reviews from former guests who wrote comments like..."beautiful inn, elegant and stately, but I'd rather stay some place where I didn't see my breath in the morning when I brushed my teeth..." She eventually got it. However, we do still keep a crackling blaze going on the large hearth primarily for the sake of ambiance.

When guests enter the house from the wide veranda, they step into a short hallway, actually a kind of a foyer, that connects a large sitting room on one side and a separate den on the other. The sitting room empties into the dining room which then bleeds into the large country kitchen. Through a side doorway, after making a right turn off the sitting room, another hallway begins which leads to the five guest rooms. Again off the sitting room there is a magnificent set of wooden stairs that leads to our upper living quarters which contains another sitting room, smaller kitchen and the bedroom where a good amount of begging often takes place. The chopped up, L shaped design of the old inn does allow us and our guests to enjoy privacy, but I am thoroughly convinced the architect who built the place had to have been a fall-down drunk.

We've entertained everybody from famous writers and actors to NASCAR drivers and university chancellors, besides of course ordinary people like us. We've even had foreign and domestic terrorists staying here, which are stories for another time. But never the President of the United States.

* * * * *

Government types are notoriously prompt, anally so. If they're running late for some reason, they'll make it anyway on time even if at a break-neck speed they have to run over people in their way. But if they're running *ahead* of time, they'll purposely lolly-gag or stop for a pee break until they're able to arrive at their objective at the very minute promised. At precisely 1100 hours on that

Wednesday a black Crown Vic pulled into our driveway. Two men in black suits exited. And being the anal government man *I* used to be, at precisely 1100 hours I was waiting for them on our veranda.

The taller man, a 40-ish Joe Friday looking guy with salt and pepper hair, walked briskly toward me like he had a corn cob up his dump pipe. The second, a younger dark-complected man with curly black hair, followed behind him along our walkway and up onto the steps. Besides the corn cobs, I think they were also wearing what were supposed to be smiles, but I couldn't be sure.

The first man held out his hand and greeted gruffly, "You Bruce McGowan?"

"That's me."

And again in that matter-of-fact Joe Friday tone he said, "I'm Special Agent-in-Charge Bill Clayton, Secret Service. This is Special Agent Joachim Nazer. I believe you spoke with Mr. Kessler on the phone."

"That I did. Good day, gentlemen. Your identification?"

"I beg your pardon?"

"Your badges and IDs." I could be anal too. After all I had a lot of practice over the years.

They glanced quickly at one another and then pulled from their coat pockets the official wallets containing their credentials.

I added, "One can't be too careful."

"Uh, right," Clayton replied.

"Would you like to come in?" I asked very nicely.

"We will. We'll follow." Still all official like.

To lighten them up, I offered, "Coffee or a soft drink?"

Clayton continued to supply the answers. "No, no thanks. But we *would* like to sit and talk a while. Later, if we can look around, we'd appreciate it."

"Certainly."

Adriana then came into the sitting room where I had parked the men. I introduced her. "My wife and proprietress of our B&B, Adriana McGowan. Dear, these gentlemen are Agents Bill Clayton and Joachim Nazer."

Each stood, clicked their leather heels and dropped their heads sharply like Nazi stormtroopers, then shook her hand. "Ma'am. A pleasure," Clayton said.

She smiled that hypnotic smile of hers. Her radiant beauty obviously disarmed them because they both actually smiled back which caused their laser-like government eyes to soften a bit.

"Gentlemen, please have a seat," I said. "You're sure you don't want something to eat or drink?"

Nazer was the one who spoke up this time. "We're fine, sir. We'd like to just go ahead and open a dialogue with you and Mrs. McGowan about the President's and First Lady's visit."

Clayton sat in the leather sofa chair while Nazer took the one with wooden arms. Adriana and I settled in on the couch.

"Good," I replied. "We're all ears."

They both took out small notebooks and ball point pens and looked around the room. "Beautiful inn," Nazer remarked. "How long has it been here?"

Adriana said, "Wolf Laurel is actually about ninety years old, but the house became a wayside inn for travelers exactly 75 years ago this December. The place was in my first husband's family all that time, but I assumed control about a dozen years ago when he passed away."

I added, "And she's *still* in control. I just live here and do what she tells me. But she feeds me and keeps me alive. Great arrangement." I was just breaking the ice. They didn't appear amused. The only time they smiled was when *Adriana* spoke.

"And you've already decorated for the holidays. Nice looking tree...well-shaped, all trimmed and everything," Nazer added.

Adriana grinned. "Thank you. I do look forward to this time of year."

I added. "Yep, I'm pretty proud of that tree. I went out in the woods a couple days ago and killed it," sounding like I had just bagged an eight pointer. "Drug its carcass in here and nailed it to that stand." A bit corny I agree, but still breaking the ice.

Adriana pinched my thigh...a kind of warning she gives me when I come out with frivolous crap like that. Clayton was all the while giving me a puzzled look. "Okay, then. Just to let you know, as per protocol we performed a background check on you both. It would be a requirement in cases like this. I'm sure it's no surprise to you that we found nothing concerning, ma'am. Now Mr. McGowan, you are former FBI and later worked for the Department of State. However, we're at a loss to determine exactly what you did for State Department. It seems a lot of your file information is missing. Can you help us out here?"

"I'm not sure what you believe to be missing, but in essence I performed national security work. I'm just not at liberty to go into the details."

They gave each other bewildered looks again. "I'm afraid you must, sir. We have to know..."

"Only two or three people know what my responsibilities were, Agent Clayton. The President himself is one of them. My wife here doesn't even know the total scope of my work with the government. Just know that I was on the right side of the playing field when I discharged my duties."

A scowl came over Clayton's face. "Then you're not going to tell us anything more."

"Not a whole lot."

"And just how can we go back and recommend to the President this is a safe place for him and the First Lady to stay? We have to know *everything* about the people who will be boarding them."

"This is not by any means meant to sound pompous or self-important, Agent Clayton, but the President knows very well who I am and what my government background is.

There's nothing he does not know when it comes to my service history."

"You sound like you were either some sort of spy or have a *personal* history with the President. What were you...CIA?"

"None of the above, Mr. Clayton."

He sighed and gave Nazer one of those looks. One of resignation. "Okay, may we then have a look around? We'll need to scan your inn for security purposes...both the inside and the grounds."

"Sure," I said. "We'll show you the rooms first."

"Are there guests here now?" Nazer asked.

"Not until tomorrow," Adriana responded. "Actually we will have two sets of guests...two couples. One couple is scheduled to check out Saturday afternoon while the other will stay till Sunday morning."

"How about the weekend or the week days before the President's arrival?"

"Three lady cave explorers from North Carolina have booked for the 3rd through the 5th. But no one else until the 19th."

"Good. That works with the timeline," Clayton said. "How many total rooms do you have? We'll need places to bunk for three agents and of course your best room for the President."

Adriana replied. "We actually have five guest rooms downstairs. The upstairs are *our* quarters. We would suggest putting the President and First Lady at the end of the hallway, last room on the right. It's a large suite complete with a king size poster bed, a 42 inch screen TV, a sitting area and a microwave. It also has the largest bathroom of any of the rooms. There is a room straight across the hall for one of your agents as well as a nice room next door to the suite."

After we had escorted the agents through all of the rooms, we then returned to show them the kitchen and dining areas.

Clayton asked, "As this is a Bed and Breakfast, I assume you'll be *serving* a breakfast. What will that be?"

Adriana shook her head. "I'm not sure, Mr. Clayton. Sometimes we'll serve our very popular cheese and ham quiche with fruit and English muffins while I may instead prepare my cinnamon French waffles with country bacon."

My stomach then gurgled as my brain digested that tasty bit of information. And Clayton said, "Hmm, I think I'm suddenly hungry. I'm sure the First Family will enjoy the place. Don't take this the wrong way, but one of our agents will first need to sample the food."

Like we generally poison our guests. They check in, but they don't check out.

"Now Mr. McGowan, we'd like to walk the grounds to do a site survey?"

I then jerked my head in the direction of the door and replied, "Follow me."

I took them over nearly every square foot of our two acres of gardens and woods. They jotted down notes as we went and chose strategic areas where the grounds agents would be positioned, paying particular attention to the back yard near the windows of the President's suite. "I see that you have no neighbors breathing down your necks. It's good that you're off the beaten track and appears the next house is beyond that pasture over there. There's good visibility of most of the grounds from the house. So, here's how we'll set up. There'll be three agents in the house at all times the President is on site. Two roving agents are to be stationed at strategic places on your property's perimeter while the other two sit in ready posture in the police unit. Each agent will be equipped with automatic weapons. Don't take this the wrong way, McGowan, but I need you to stay out of the way of operations as much as possible."

"You don't have to worry about me, Agent Clayton."

"Somehow I kind of believe that, McGowan. I know that for some reason the President considers you 'somebody special.' By the way, do you have any weapons on the premises?"

I laughed, "You're kidding of course."

"Where inside the house?"

"None down on the main floor, but if you guys need anything special from my upstairs, let me know."

Clayton scowled. "I need to know what you have and where they are."

"You're not *taking* them, Agent Clayton."

"I don't *want* them...just tell us what and where."

"A Glock 39 caliber .45 in my nightstand, a Colt revolver .45 between my mattress and box springs, a Springfield XDM that I always carry...don't worry, I have a permit...a Bushmaster ACR in a case under my bed, two loaded shotguns and a .30-30 in my locked gun case in the upstairs hallway. I have a SIG Sauer P238, a Walther WA 2000 and a Remington 700 .308 in the floor compartment of my SUV out there. My wife has a Kahr .380 in *her* nightstand."

Nazer let out a low whistle. "Expecting trouble?"

"Not with *my* toys."

"I don't know," sighed Clayton. "I personally don't have a comfort level with the President staying here and that arsenal laying around under the same roof."

"My weapons are not just laying around where anyone could find them. And all that firepower is only as deadly as the operator."

"And I have a feeling that's what their operator *is*."

"I'm retired, Agent Clayton. Just an ordinary citizen now. And my firearms? Nothing but tools of my former life now stored in mothballs."

Clayton shook his head and sighed again. "Damn. I've *definitely* got to talk about this with somebody. Hell, it might even come down to sending you and your Mrs away on your *own* vacation while the President and First Lady are here. Anyway, I guess that's it for now. The day before their arrival, we will be back to set up. We'll have a K9 with us to sniff around for any IEDs or other explosives."

"Like we always keep stuff like that on hand," I said.

"Merely security protocol. Somehow I think you know that."

I nodded.

Nazer then said, "We have a couple more things to visit with you about, sir. Can we go back inside?"

"Sure. Come on."

We sat again in our same spots. I re-offered coffee and they again declined.

Clayton began. "Okay, Mr. and Mrs. McGowan, the Chief of Staff said he made it very clear on the phone that you were not to divulge to anyone that the President and First Lady were planning to stay here. Moreover, while they are here, you are not to allow any family, visitors or guests to come on the premises. If they press you for a reason, tell them *anything*...the place is being fumigated or you have no heat. We don't care what you tell them, just keep them away. We're only talking two full days. Are we understood?"

Adriana frowned. "How about our maid Juanita? She's like a member of our family. She's here most days remaking beds and cleaning. And she's not an illegal, if you're wondering."

Clayton shook his head. "No maid. She's not to be here those days; neither is she to know about the President."

Both of us nodded. "Understood," I said. "But sometimes my brother or one of Adriana's friends might stop by unannounced."

"However you can keep that from happening, you need to do so. Tell your friends and family in advance you'll be away for a couple of days."

I shrugged. "We'll work on that."

"You see, only a handful of people besides our agency will know the President and First Lady are staying here. Because this is not a sealed off resort or a Camp David, security is always a concern. Don't worry, the Press Secretary will send out a communique to the public about the First Family's stay here after their return to Washington. You'll get all the attention for your B&B you want after that."

"Are you at liberty to tell us who that handful of people are?" I asked.

"That would not be your concern. But you already know about Mr. Kessler and there'll be six other Secret Service agents here with me. Two of them plus me will be in the house and four positioned outside on the grounds. My SAC, Special Agent in Charge Tyson, will be situated at a strategic location here in the county.""

"Any Marines?" I asked.

"There will be five of them stationed with Marine One at the airport...two aviators, a mission officer, who is a Navy Commander, and two Marine NCOs. They will remain inside the VH-3D Whitehawk through Sunday. It's totally self-contained. They can bed down, shower and mess. If there is any emergent need for them, I'll make the contact with their commander."

"And the Vice President and National Security Advisor would know about the President's retreat, correct?"

"No more guesses, Mr. McGowan," Clayton said.

"Any press?"

"No. Again, that's all I can tell you. And I think we've covered everything. Any other questions?"

Adriana and I shook our heads. "We're good," I said.

"Fine. Then we'll be off. Thanks for the tour and your hospitality. If all goes to plan, we'll see you on Thursday the 11th. The President plans to arrive sometime between noon and one o'clock the next day. He and the First Lady plan to leave here Sunday afternoon." Clayton then paused. "That is if we recommend to him this is a secure place."

I guess he was waiting on a response from us, but all we did was nod. I then showed the agents out onto the veranda and we shook hands.

"Goodbye, McGowan," Clayton said. "Careful not to shoot anybody."

I smiled. "Just bad guys, Agent Clayton. Be seeing you."

When they left, Adriana asked me, "They actually won't require us to leave because of all your weapons, will they?"

"We aren't going anywhere and my weapons are staying put. President or not, I'm not making any concessions or adjustments in my life just so he and his Mrs can have a little R&R here. He and his troupe will accept things the way they are or they can go to...uh, to the Greenbrier."

Chapter Two

I can't begin to count the times Adriana interrupted her sleep those last few nights before the advance party was set to arrive. First, she would just lie there tossing and turning for a few minutes, then finally get up and go sit at the desk in the living room to add something to her list...or should I say *one* of her lists. She was not only a perfectionist when it came to planning for guest arrival, but a worrier. Room readiness, menu preparation, creative decorating, ordering of fresh flowers for the vases...everything thought out in minute detail. Everything spit and polished. And that was in anticipation of *ordinary* guests. I couldn't imagine what she would put herself through the night before America's royalty arrived. And put *me* through.

Our late November and early December guests came and went. I remember as a cadet at the military school just down the road preparing for what we called a GI Inspection where everything got the white glove treatment. That was nothing compared to what Adriana had Juanita and me doing. I spent two days alone scrubbing down the kitchen and waxing the hardwood floors throughout while Juanita covered every inch of the interior doors, window sills and bathrooms with sponges and oil cloths.

"I do not know why she require theese," Juanita said to me in her broken English. "Eat is not spring yet and I not ever work theese hard on the place." She was getting suspicious. There was a moment she stopped what she was doing and approached me while I was on my knees in the hallway. "You always do the outside, Meester McGowan.

Why are you doing the inside work?" And then after a bit of contemplation, her jaw dropped. "You and Meese Adriana are going to sell Wolf Laurel and you are getting ready for the sale."

I stood and took her by the shoulders. "Not to worry, Juanita. We're not selling out. Mrs. McGowan..." I had to think up a good one. "...is just going through her change. I think you know what I mean. This is her way of dealing with it. Some women get cranky and some get moody. She wants to *clean* everything."

For a moment Juanita just looked at me and then gave me an understanding nod. "I have been through that. I get real hot and sweat very much. And then I yell sometimes at my husband. He almost leave me twice."

Well sure. It was a stupid lie. But I thought that was going to be the end of it. An hour later, however, when I went to the kitchen for a Diet Coke, Adriana cornered me. "Okay, Skippy, what was it you told Juanita about me going through the change of life? You couldn't think up any other explanation for all our cleaning?"

She flicked me on the forehead with her thumb and index finger and then gave me a peck on the lips. "Next time, cabbage brain, be a little more creative, okay?"

* * * * *

Thursday, December 11th. The phone rang just before noon. The call we were expecting.

"Mr. McGowan, Agent Clayton here. We're just getting off I-64 and will be at your location in one-five." Government term for fifteen minutes.

"We'll be waiting. Have you had lunch?" Being hospitable again.

"Sandwiches on the road."

"So, we don't fix you all anything?"

"No." Short and sweet.

"Fine." I can be short and sweet as well. The call ended.

This time *two* black cars pulled up to the house. The first one was an extended limo Cadillac driven by a young woman. I thought it might be the Presidential limo they call "the Beast", but I couldn't be sure. What threw me was the fact that it didn't have flags on its fenders that contained the Seal of the President of the United States. However, the President wanted his visit to be secretive...no flags, no flourishes. Clayton was the front seat passenger and another male agent sat in the back. After they exited their car, the doors to the trailing Crown Vic opened and four other men got out. I felt like I was in a Men in Black movie, plus one woman. She was wearing a black suit as well.

Clayton led the agents up onto the veranda and just as Adriana stepped out to join me, he began the introductions. "Bruce McGowan, Adriana McGowan, this is Special Agent Joanie Smithers." Adriana and I shook her hand. Her grip was firm just like the rest of her. I saw immediately from the agent's nice smile she was not as anal as Clayton. Not to be sexist, but she was also a looker...a hundred fifteen pounds, petite frame, full, inviting lips and blonde, tightly coiffed hair. I didn't much check out the other agents, but Clayton introduced them anyway. "On my right is Special Agent Howard and these gentlemen are Special Agents Franks, Davis, Hunyh and Bartow. This is the Secret Service team that will be with you from now through Sunday. Do you have rooms ready for us?"

"We only have five rooms including the one to accommodate the President and First Lady," I replied.

"Sorry, I wasn't clear. Agents Smithers, Howard and myself would be staying here. Just for tonight, the other agents are booked at a motel in town."

"We look forward to having you with us," Adriana said. "I can show you your rooms if you like."

As we walked inside, I commented, "I see Agent Nazer is not with you."

Clayton replied, "That's correct. He came down with the flu. Sounded hoarse on the phone yesterday."

"Too bad. Well, Adriana will get you settled and then we'll be available for any discussion you need to have."

"Fine. After we freshen up, I'd like all of us to sit down somewhere and go over our agenda as well as what the President's plans are."

I nodded. "How about something to drink for you all? My wife made a fresh pot of coffee. We also have tea, hot *and* cold, and soft drinks. I assume a cold Heineken is out."

Clayton looked at the others. "Coffee okay?"

They all nodded. No takers on the brewskis for obvious reasons.

With steaming cups of coffee in our hands, we all retired to the veranda. Just enough porch chairs and rockers to go around. Considering it was early December, it was a pleasant day to be out of doors...fifty-five degrees and plenty of radiant afternoon sun. But, a cold front was scheduled to come in on Friday at midday, bringing with it near freezing rain.

One of the agents, Donald Bartow, asked, "Do you mind if I have a cigarette?"

I did mind. Don't like the smell, the smoke or any butts lying around. However, being the accommodating host that I am, I replied, "Whatever." I think my one word answer and voice tone told him 'hell, no,' so he changed his mind. He said, "Second thought, I guess I won't. Need to quit anyway."

I was sure that by Sunday afternoon I'd be finding his nasty little fags all over my yard.

"Well, here's our schedule, McGowan," Clayton began. "The rest of the day we get acquainted with Wolf Laurel, inside and out. Smithers, Howard and I will go back through the President's room to see that everything is in order. I'm sure it is. My roving agents here will spend the better part of the afternoon canvassing your grounds and ultimately assign themselves to sections for which they will be responsible. Don't be alarmed, but you will see them carrying either Uzis or MP5s."

And I would be alarmed why?

"Tomorrow, the President is scheduled to arrive in Marine One at the Greenbrier Airport. There will actually be two identical helicopters in the air coming in. This is SOP to throw off terrorists or anyone else with subversive intentions. No one except the Secret Service and Marine crew will know which chopper the President is on. Both will land and when security is properly established and the environment is deemed safe, the subterfuge will depart. The President's helicopter will set down on the Greenbrier tarmac well away from the terminal and our vehicle will then pick him up. All that the airport officials know is that a government helicopter is scheduled to land at 1200 and unless someone spots the markings in the distance, no one will know it's the President. If anyone figures it out, they'll think he's going to the Greenbrier for either a meeting or some kind of retreat. We intend to avoid any press and have taken steps to assure there is no fanfare. In essence, as I told you the other day, no one but us and those few people I mentioned know what the President is doing this weekend. Also mid-morning tomorrow in advance of the President's arrival, we'll do a final sweep of the house and grounds with Bacon."

"Bacon?"

"Remember the K9 I told you about? It's the dog's name. He is so named because that's what he eats."

"Have you not introduced him to Alpo or Purina? All those nitrates and fat are carcinogens. I'd say you need to get the dog a physical before PETA gets onto it."

"Uh, I'm...not his handler."

And I'm only kidding, Agent. Lighten up.

Clayton then continued. "Smithers here will be attending to the security and general needs of the First Lady. I will shadow the President. Feel free to engage them in conversation when they are in the sitting room or out here on the porch, but their privacy must be respected otherwise."

Now you're their social director?

Adriana asked, "Will they be here at the inn the entire time or touring the area? I can suggest some cultural and historical settings. And I would be glad to take her to some of our wonderful antique shops."

"From what I know, they just want to relax here at Wolf Laurel. As both seem to be anxious to see you two again, I'd say you may have the pleasure of their company quite often."

"Any special things they prefer to eat or drink?" Adriana asked.

"The President likes an occasional beer and both might enjoy some red wine in the evenings. Knowing this is a Bed and Breakfast, do you ever prepare dinner? If not, I'll arrange with one of your fine restaurants in the area to have dinner brought in for them."

"We have a damn good pizza parlor a couple miles away," I said.

Adriana gave me a sharp glance. "Don't listen to him, Agent Clayton. We'll cook dinner both evenings. I anticipated doing as much. We'll make a hearty pot roast with some nice vegetables tomorrow and a chicken dish on Saturday. I have already baked both a cake and a pecan pie for dessert. Would you and your team be joining us?"

"On these short retreats, the President often invites us to dine with them. Can you accommodate all of us? If not, we can scrape up some of that pizza Mr. McGowan was jesting about."

"Nonsense. We have a large dining table and plenty of food. We'd be glad to have you."

We then heard the first words from Agent Smithers. "Mrs. McGowan, I may be a hardened federal officer trained to discharge the most important duties in government service, but I am also a domesticated woman who loves to cook. Besides protecting the First Lady, I would be delighted to help you with the meals."

An obvious intellectual besides coming across as a woman of refinement and culture. After hearing her talk I guessed that she might be an Ivy Leaguer with that Boston brogue, perhaps Harvard or Brown. The full package: cute, tough, smart and well-spoken. What was she doing wasting her time as a Secret Service agent?

"I'd love that. When you get settled and are done with duty, let's sit and talk. And please call me Adriana."

Clayton jumped in, "While we're here, Agent Smithers will never be 'done with duty', Mrs. McGowan. However, there will be some down time this evening. But for now, let's get cracking."

A control freak if I ever saw one. And from the get-go, he wanted everyone to remember that he was in charge. But I knew he was a confident, demanding personality, good at his job, and didn't get to his position by being unassertive. He was the kind of agent who would lay down his life without batting an eye to protect the President.

The agents were thorough in their examination of the premises. Several times Clayton actually apologized for his consummate inspection...checking of the beds, digging into closets and drawers and even wriggling into the crawl spaces inside and underneath the house. But I had to give it to him, out of respect for his hosts, he didn't allow his agents to enter our quarters on the upper floor. He handled the inspection of our suite himself. I showed him every weapon and where the ammunition was located. He seemed very interested in my Springfield Armory XDM with which he admitted he wasn't all that familiar. And I thought I saw a bit of drool in the corners of his mouth when he fondled my Bushmaster.

Now don't get excited. A bushmaster is a very expensive assault rifle.

But then I received from him a word of caution. "Keep your arsenal locked up and do not carry when downstairs in the company of the President and First Lady. I'm enamored with all your hardware, McGowan, but still not sure about *you*."

Like I care.

After returning to the main floor, I went outside and watched out of curiosity the four agents who were assigned to the outer premises look over the grounds and communicate with one another by talking into their wrists and bringing their fingers up to touch their ear buds. Tomorrow morning after Bacon arrived, they would then put *him* to work. I would be sure to have Adriana fry up some good old thick Gwaltney for the canine.

At just before six, the agents reconsolidated on the veranda and began comparing notes. As the clock in my stomach told me it was supper time and Adriana and I had not discussed what we'd be eating, I finally broke in and asked them what they intended to do for dinner. Clayton actually smiled and said that the pizza sounded good. Would I mind ordering three or four pies. The government would pay. I didn't mind that at all. And he asked if that offer of beer still stood.

Over the dinner table, even though their Sig Sauer .357 pistols were still visible in their shoulder holsters, the agents finally showed signs of relaxing. Mostly they talked shop to one another, careful not to discuss anything that required Adriana and I to have clearances. Nor did they speak of the First Family. I found out that John Huynh was second generation Vietnamese, born here in the states. His father, a South Vietnamese Army Tu Ta (Major), was allowed to leave the country in 1975 and ultimately became a naturalized citizen. He passed away three years ago.

Jefferson Howard, a tall, articulate Black agent who would remain in the house with Clayton and Smithers during the President's visit, was sure he had met me. He looked familiar as well, but if we *had* met, it was only in passing. Maybe it was when I was summoned to the White House to receive from the President himself the offer to replace Lionel Byrd as the director of all covert counterterrorist operations. Now that I think about it, we might have said a few words to one another as I was standing there waiting outside the door of the Oval Office.

As Clayton had done on his earlier visit, I started getting asked about what I did for the government. I basically capsuled my twenty plus years as an FBI agent then gave them only cursory information about my job at the State Department. They learned only that I did some Intel work, mostly profiling, and that seemed to satisfy them. I was neither going to boast of my record nor give them any particulars of my service. Clayton and I kept trading glances while I was talking. His eyes told me he knew more about me than I was letting out, but I knew he *didn't*. However, his knowing I had been the President's man in the field on more than one occasion, I was for sure some kind of government badass. But, he didn't explore it any deeper in front of his team so as not to put me on the spot. But somehow I knew he would have his keen eyes on me a lot over the next couple of days.

After the ravenous team of agents had wolfed down the last of the pizza, smoking man Bartow pulled on his coat and excused himself to the veranda. Diminutive agent Brent Davis accompanied him. Maybe he was also a smoker. *Something* had sure stunted his growth along his way through life. I guess there's no height requirement for Secret Service agents. Howard and Clayton moved to the sitting room with their Heinekens to review tomorrow's protocol as Agent Steffen Franks, a very quiet and studious-looking man with horned-rim glasses announced he'd be taking a power walk to work off his dinner. Huynh was going to call his wife and children.

That left Smithers to hang out with Adriana in the kitchen. She might have been thirty, but no older, and I had the impression Clayton closely scrutinized and limited her duties given her neophyte status on his team. As we were talking at dinner, I also noted some of Clayton's chauvinistic attitude toward her on a couple of occasions. I had the impression he was not good with women in the Secret Service. A little later this was reinforced by Smithers herself as I overheard her conversation with Adriana.

"The Secret Service is of course a tremendous experience for me. Being this close not only to the First Family but to the very nerve center of American politics is immensely exciting. I started with the Service straight out of college seven years ago and after punching all the tickets, finally got assigned last year on the First Family's protection detail. But Agent Clayton still treats me like a greenhorn. Sometimes I think that I am just relegated to being a personal assistant to the First lady. I'm also not given any heavy duty where it comes to protecting the President himself. Mostly I'm attending library events and socials with the First lady, but otherwise detailed to the White House. Granted, I could be in Detroit or Los Angeles investigating counterfeit operations or protecting visiting foreign dignitaries, but I otherwise feel a bit unchallenged."

It seemed to me that Agent Smithers was giving Adriana, a civilian, a little too much information about her under-utilization. If Clayton overheard the conversation, he probably wouldn't like it and might eventually take steps to get rid of her. But it appeared she needed to get some things off her chest. Maybe because she didn't always have an empathic female ear in her environment, she felt a degree of comfort talking with Adriana, the wife of a long-time government agent. However, she merely wanted more action out of her job. And in watching her and taking note of the intensity in her eyes, I knew she could be a tough little philly if the moment ever came for her to utilize her skills. And she *definitely* wanted to be placed in a venue where such an opportunity might occur. At a quarter till nine, Clayton reassembled his team and said, "At first light we'll do a cursory sweep to assure nothing has changed during the night on the premises and then head out to the airport to recon the LZ. We'll be back here at 0900 to meet Jim Cabella, driving from the Charleston field office, who should then be on site with his K9. Again, the chopper will touch down at noon. Agent Howard and I will pick up Eagle One and the First Lady and then cart them back here to Wolf Laurel. The rest of you will follow in the Crown

Vic. Agent Smithers, you will remain here to assure continued security. I have already coordinated with the local State Police detachment, one Captain Harlan Williams, to stand by with troopers in case there are any problems with traffic or something misfires, causing the President's visit to go south. Williams only knows there are a couple of Washington VIPS coming to the area and he needs to have his units ready to roll out at any given notice."

"I know Harlan Williams," I said. "We've done business together and he's a friend. *Good* friend. You can depend on his support."

Clayton continued. "As to the military types remaining at the airport, here's the plan. A camo tarp will cover Marine One so that the Presidential markings will disappear. The chopper and its Marine crew will remain on site those three days.

"Now, agents on the perimeter. Here's how it will go down at night. It'll be cold...freezing by midnight. I want you bundled up and rotating between the grounds and the Crown Vic every two hours so that nobody ends up a popsicle. Roving agents will concentrate on the east side of the property where that trail comes in from the woods and the heavy vegetated garden area. The Crown Vic will sit back in the tree line by the entrance to Wolf Laurel. Continue to scan using night vision. Any questions?"

Everyone shook their heads.

"All right then. Have a good evening and get a good night's sleep. Tomorrow is a full day."

When they broke up, Clayton and Howard retired to their rooms. Smithers joined Adriana in the sitting room for a glass of Shiraz and some additional conversation. Agents Bartow, Davis, Huynh and the be-speckled Franks departed for the Hampton Inn. I then excused myself to my Big Easy upstairs where I communed with some old friends...the Pittsburgh Steelers on Thursday Night Football and Samuel Adams.

Clayton was good at what he did. A seasoned agent who knew how to cover all the bases when protecting the most important figure in the world. The kind of professional I would have welcomed on my team. All business, always focused and always prepared for the worst case scenario. He was mandated to perform his required meticulous threat assessments, even in sleepy little counties like this where trouble would not be expected. However, it's possible he might have learned somehow about the terrorist element I discovered staying on these very premises a few years ago. But this trip for Eagle One was a small mission for him, although more of a covert operation to ward off media hounds and to escape the public eye. An operation with only a little tax payer money spent just so the Prez and his Mrs could have a needed weekend of rest and relaxation. And by the way, Adriana and I were not charging the government one dime for their stay............

Chapter Three

Friday, December 12th. I heard the floor squeaking downstairs at 5:15 and knew at least one of the agents was already stirring about. Probably checking to see if there was coffee. Adriana had set the timer on the Brewmaster the night before; therefore, the piping hot nectar would be flowing in another fifteen minutes. As four or five mornings a week I take a run out into the Greenbrier countryside, I hit the toilet, brushed my teeth and then threw on my heavy jogging clothes. Adriana quickly dressed and went on down to the main kitchen to prepare the cinnamon buns for baking. There would also be oatmeal with apples and brown sugar, toast and bacon for any of the agents who'd rather go that route. I reminded Adriana to put aside an extra slab of the bacon for the pooch when he arrived.

When I finally went down, I heard voices in the kitchen, subsequently finding Adriana and Agent Smithers having a laugh about something. Being the paranoid that I was, I was hoping it wasn't about me. Smithers was also in *her* reflector-lined jogging suit getting ready to go out.

"Ah, I see you like to start your morning the way I do," I said.

"I can't get my body *or* my mind going for the day until I do my two miles."

"Do you mind if I join you? I usually run a course I've laid out that keeps me away from the traffic."

"That would be good. I like running with someone to help with my pace."

I then heard footsteps in the hallway. Clayton and Howard were also up. However, when their faces appeared in the kitchen doorway we saw that they were fully dressed for the day in their Men in Black suits and Sig Sauers.

"Good morning, gentlemen," Adriana greeted. "I'll have breakfast ready for you in a few minutes if you'd like."

"Whatever you're baking sure smells good," said Howard.

Mornings were obviously not Clayton's favorite time of the day and it appeared his gruff demeanor was even further exacerbated. "Just some of that coffee for me is all, ma'am." He then eyed Smithers in her warm-up clothing. "Make sure you get back here to do our ground sweep at daylight. Then we're rolling out for the airport recon."

Make it a *large mug* of coffee, Clayton.

Smithers and I did our stretching routines and then hit the thirty-one degree air. The sun wasn't going to lighten the horizon for at least another hour, so I took with me my LED mini-light. My usual jogging course was a secondary farm road that began on Seven Bridges about five hundred feet from our driveway and continued for almost three and a half miles.

We were both bundled up warmly wearing multiple layers. She had pulled on her NorthFace Triclimate coat with reflector tape and I had on an old ski parka. Steam began spewing profusely out of our mouths as our breaths deepened. For the first quarter of a mile, however, we did what we used to call in Jump School the Airborne Shuffle, short steps on the balls of our feet that served to warm us up. But then her strides lengthened and I knew immediately she was an endurance runner.

"I usually run a couple marathons every year and a dozen or so 10Ks in between," she said. "But on most work mornings I only have time to go no more than two miles." Considering our speed, I was impressed she could say that without huffing and puffing out her words like I was doing.

"Well, up until a couple of years ago, I was religious at going five miles every morning; however, if I tried that now it'd kick my ass."

"You still look to be in good shape for your age."

That was the ultimate ego deflater. Did I actually look that old for her to make a comment like that? I guess to a child like her I *was* ancient.

She apparently thought about how that last comment sounded and laughed. "I'm sorry. I didn't mean it that way. You don't look as old as you are." She paused a moment and smiled. "And *that* didn't sound right, either. But you know what I mean."

"All too well, Agent Smithers."

The remainder of the jog was just small talk here and there. When I'm running with someone, especially in freezing weather, talking and laborious breathing don't mix. Our goal had been two miles, but then suddenly I realized that we had actually *gone* two miles and were not yet on our way back. "This is a good turn-around point if you're good with that."

She looked at the luminous dial on her watch. "We went a little further than I had planned. But I've been enjoying the run. This good country air obviously agrees with me."

When we finally reached the gravel road leading into our B&B, I was surprised that the four miles had not led to any system breakdowns. I actually felt good. Of course it also didn't bother me jogging that distance on a cold winter's morning with that delightful breath of spring air running beside me.

As twilight was now giving way to an ever brightening morning, I saw the Crown Vic in the driveway. The four off-site agents had returned. There was no one in the car, so I figured they were inside having some breakfast. But Clayton was waiting for Smithers on the veranda alongside Howard. "Did you have a good run, Agent?"

"Absolutely, sir," she answered.

"Good. We're burning daylight here. Let's take that sweep around the grounds." He then stuck his head inside and called for the rest of his team to finish their meal and get out there.

While the Secret Service team walked the grounds, I snagged a cup of Joe and pinched off only a small piece of a cinnamon bun, then went up for a shower. I don't generally have a huge appetite just after a long run. Adriana, who had already showered, was still finishing up in the bathroom when I rid myself of my sweats and went in. But seeing my beautiful bride's svelte body in her pink bikini underwear with no bra, I was starting to work up different kind of appetite. However, when she noticed that my appetite was suddenly expanding, she promptly said, "*Forget it!* Take your shower...and make it a cold one."

After the agents had completed their walk of the Wolf Laurel grounds, I watched from our bedroom window as Franks and Huynh continued canvassing the landscape outside our grounds with their field glasses. Smithers returned to her room to shower and change into her black suit and at 0750 left with Clayton and the others for the airport. I finally went back downstairs and partook of the oatmeal Adriana had made up along with a couple pieces of buttered toast, a second cup of coffee and the morning paper. I would enjoy the quietude around the place for an hour or so until they returned.

I was sitting on the veranda at 0905 finishing up the *Messenger* when Bacon, the Federal K9, arrived with his handler in a black Tahoe. Clayton driving the Town Car with Howard and Smithers aboard pulled in beside them. This time the Crown Vic agents were not with them. The handsome German Shepherd, Bacon, was a lively, healthy-looking specimen. The fur on his back, face and ears was a combination of black and white and the rest of him, a light brown. Once he entered our yard, he immediately hiked up his leg against a banister and then quickly ascended the steps to our veranda, stopping at the front door as though he knew what was required. Or was his snout picking up the scent of the breakfast Adriana cooked a few hours before? *Yes, there's a slab in there with your name on it, fellow.* I laid my paper down and walked over to greet them. His handler, Jim Cabella, a uniformed FBI agent, then attached the leash to the dog's collar and waited until I opened the door. Before doing so, I introduced myself and asked if I could pet the pooch.

"Let him smell your hand first," Cabella said. "If he's good with you, he''ll either lick your hand or put his nose between your legs."

"And if he's *not*?"

"Then his *teeth* might go between your legs. You could lose some things."

I took a step back.

Cabella laughed. "I'm just messing with you, Mr. McGowan." A man with a sense of humor. I liked him, but there are things you don't joke about. A guy's manliness is one of them.

Bacon, of course, led them directly to the kitchen. "Is there anything in here that the dog might be interested in?" Cabella asked. "Anything you want to tell us about?"

"Maybe nothing *you'd* be interested in. However, I'm sure your dog would."

"What."

"Bacon."

"Yes, that's his name."

"I *know* that's his name."

"Then what scent would he be picking up in here?"

"Bacon."

"Come on, Mr. McGowan. Why do you keep saying the dog's name?"

Why do I feel like I'm in an Abbott and Costello *Who's On First* skit?

"Your dog is smelling the bacon my wife cooked this morning."
Cabella smiled sheepishly. "Sorry about that. Again, just making a joke. I'll move him out of the kitchen. Can you now show me where you'll be bunking the President and his wife?"

I nodded and led him and the dog down the hallway. Clayton, Smithers and Howard followed.

"Again, this is only a procedural thing, McGowan," Clayton said. "Bacon is trained to sniff out bombs and contraband like drugs; but that doesn't mean we suspect anything like that is in here. I think I made that clear to you before."

"Yeah, and I have no problem with it. Let him be as nosy as he wants."

After entering the President's room, Bacon made short order of things in less than two minutes. He had stuck his nose up to every door, drawer and floor board before making his way back out. *Clean*, he snorted. Cabella then allowed him to enter the other four guest rooms and the result was the same. But as Bacon was led back along the hallway toward the sitting room, he stopped and scratched at the door of a small hall closet. Cabella pulled him back as Clayton opened the door. He asked, "Is there anything that we need to know about in here, Mr. McGowan?"

"I don't even know what's in there, but I don't think so."

Clayton saw that there was a box on the floor along with a pair of my old boots and a stack of board games such as Trivial Pursuit, Scattergories and Monopoly. He pulled out the box, finding only a loose mess of old photographs, mostly of Adriana's dead husband Mason's family.

Satisfied with that, he then rifled through the pockets of some hanging coats and jackets that also belonged to her former husband. Standing there, I was hoping Mason hadn't been a druggy and had left in any of the pockets a pouch of angel dust. I meant to take those rags to Goodwill two years ago. Obviously, *something* had piqued the dog's interest. Clayton, however, didn't find anything but a little pocket change, a pack of twelve year old chewing gum and a snot-crusted handkerchief.

He then saw a couple of boxes on the upper shelf and pulled each of them down. The first one was large and contained only some sheets and pillow cases. But when he opened the second one, his eyes narrowed. He then gave me about a four second look after which he reached down into the box. To my surprise, he pulled out a 19th Century revolver, what looked to be a .44 caliber black powder pistol. But that wasn't what the dog had sniffed out. The next items he unloaded from the box were two leather black powder flasks and a large coffee can inside a clear plastic ziplock bag. He then opened the bag, pulled out the metal can and allowed about three ounces of the black powder to pour into his palm. The can was still half full.

Clayton turned back to me and said, "No firearms downstairs you say."

I shook my head. "I had no idea that gun or the powder were up there."

"Whether you did or not, McGowan, a potential threat to the President's life has been found within only feet of his room. How do I know these items weren't hidden there by someone who might be planning..."

"You'd better think about what you're about to say, Agent Clayton." My voice had increased a few decibels.

"Again, you had told me there were no guns down here...that your entire arsenal was upstairs, which has also in fact given me a shitload of concern. How do I know I can now trust you." He had raised *his* voice as well.

"Come on, Clayton, do you really think I'm some kind of subversive?"

"*I actually don't know what or **who** you are, McGowan,*" he yelled. "You haven't told me shit about your...quote 'exploits'...after the FBI years and there is a hell of a lot information missing in your State Department personnel shield."

Agent Smithers wisely placed herself between us to defuse the situation. "Gentlemen, please. This is not good. The President will be here soon and what you are doing threatens our very service to him and the First Lady."

"Stay out of this, Smithers," Clayton barked. "You have no say in this conversation."

I think I had now totally changed my opinion of the pompous ass. Go take some Ducolax, pal.

A new voice behind us then broke in. "What *is* all this yelling about?" Adriana stood at the end of the hallway, hands on hips.

"Agent Clayton found a pistol and some black powder there in the hallway closet and apparently thinks that you and I are plotting against the President."

"I didn't say that, McGowan. I'm just making the point that we were not told about a firearm and gunpowder in proximity to where the President is sleeping."

Adriana walked slowly toward the senior agent and bore down on him with her steely blues. "Agent Clayton, the gun and powder belonged to my former husband who died over a decade ago and they have been in that closet untouched ever since. Mr. McGowan here I'm sure knew nothing about them. As a matter of fact, I had long since forgotten about them myself."

I then placed my face within inches of Clayton's. In a softer tone of voice, I said, "Perhaps you should call off the President's retreat, Agent Clayton, if we are not to be trusted."

He in turn backed his face away from mine and nodded. "Yeah, maybe I should."

"Nonsense," remarked Adriana. "You know darn well you can trust my husband. The President himself has on several occasions had opportunities to do so. So get any notion out of your system to the contrary. You've made a hell of a lot more out of this gun matter than necessary." She then looked down at the antique pistol in Clayton's hand. "As I remember, Mason couldn't even get the damn thing to fire."

My pure-hearted wife actually said the words 'hell' and 'damn' which pretty much shocked the shit out of me. I don't think I had ever seen her that pissed. There. All the penny-ante cuss words were out.

Clayton dropped his head and allowed the revolver to hang limply at his side. "All right. Let's catch our breath here. McGowan, you're the president's hero for some reason and this thing..." he brought the pistol back up. "...is little more than a toy. Take it and the gunpowder upstairs to add to the rest of your collection."

I guessed that we were now good again with one another and the President was still coming.

I turned to the K9. "Come on, Bacon. I've got something in the kitchen for you."

Chapter Four

It had already been an eventful day. For one reason or another, my heart rate had been up most of the morning. The agent team had another short meeting out on the veranda, out of our earshot, and then Clayton stuck his head back in to announce they were heading out to the airport. "We plan to return with the President and First Lady around 1230 hours or so. It would be nice if you could have some refreshments waiting, Mrs. McGowan." Ever the social director.

"It will also be the lunch hour. Should I have some sandwiches and soup prepared?"

"No, ma'am. My agent who will accompany the President has already advised that he and his wife are currently having brunch with Mr. Kessler and his staff. They won't be needing anything. I'm leaving Special Agent Cabella here with the K9 to assure nothing has changed before we return with the VIPs. As soon as we do arrive, he'll be released back to Charleston."

"Then I'll have some coffee, hot tea and cider along with homemade ginger cookies waiting for everyone."

"I'm sure they will like that on this cold day."

No sooner had the agents departed for the Greenbrier Airport, my undertaker brother Joey called. "Brewster, what's going on this weekend?"

"Just per usual...taking care of guests."

"That's Adriana's job. For the first time in a month *I ain't got no body*...pardon the pun...and thinking about meeting up with Jake Lanham to go snag a buck. I was talking with Junior Brooks yesterday and he said the deer have been all over woods down by the river."

"As much as I'd like to, Joe Boy, I really need to be here this weekend."

"Bruce, Bruce. You've gotten too domesticated there, man. Untie the apron strings and break away. We haven't been down to the camp since early summer. Hey, I'll come over there later this afternoon. We can have a beer and discuss it."

"No, don't do that. We'll have a house full of people and Adriana's going to need me to be here."

"*I* can't even come over? I've been there before when you've had guests."

Somehow I needed to keep him away and at the same time not make him feel he was getting the old brush-off. "Tell you what. Meet me for lunch about 11:30 down at The Outpost. Then I need to be back sometime before 12:45 to help Adriana make some preparations."

"No can do, brother. I have a lunch meeting with the Board. You know I'm on the Board of Directors at the bank."

"Well, I'll just call you later, okay?"

"Yeah. Just think about the hunting deal. I don't get many opportunities like this."

"All right, Joey. Talk later."

What I feared was that Joey might decide to come over anyway unannounced and Clayton and I would once again be putting on the gloves. I should have listened to Clayton when he told Adriana and me to call family and friends with a made up story about fumigating or something. She followed his instructions; I didn't. But, other than my brother, I can't remember the last time any of my friends just dropped by to hang out. Mainly because I don't have many friends.

* * * * *

Our B&B is only three miles from the county airport as the crow flies. Even though the flight pattern is not exactly over our house, every so often we'll see a light aircraft circling above us to do 'touches and goes.' At just before noon, however, we heard the beating blades of a large helicopter overhead. Both Adriana and I scurried to the veranda steps to see if it was by chance Marine One. Although it was too high up to see the markings without binoculars, I was convinced it was the President getting a crow's-eye view of our estate.

"Shall I wave?" I asked.

Agent Cabella, who were standing below us in the gravel driveway with Bacon, turned his head toward us and smiled.

"Don't embarrass us by acting like a hillbilly, Skippy." Skip is my nickname that goes way back to my childhood. Don't call me that unless you're my wife.

"But I *am* a hillbilly. Born and raised."

"You don't have to showcase it. Let's go back in."

Thirty minutes later, the Cadillac limo and Crown Vic cruised slowly into our parking lot. This time, *five* agents...Howard, Franks, Huynh, Bartow and Davis...piled out of the Crown Vic. With Heckler and Koch MP5s in a ready stance they exited, separated and took up positions around the Presidential vehicle facing outward covering a 360 degree span. Clayton, brandishing his MP5, exited the driver's seat of the Lincoln and opened the left rear door. Smithers did the same on her side. However, no one had given *her* an automatic weapon. Chauvinism again?

Cabella then gave Clayton the A OK sign and strolled off with his K9 to his SUV.

Adriana and I stood just outside the front door and watched as the President of the United States and First Lady stepped out of the Caddie, officially giving our quaint B&B, Wolf Laurel, a veritable spot in country inn history. Adriana squeezed my arm and giggled with delight. "They're actually here at our home, Skip. I can't believe it."

I smiled. "When this is over, my dear, you will be crowned by your friends as the Queen of Greenbrier County. And you're cutting off the circulation in my arm."

Clayton and Smithers led our guests up the steps and then stood aside to allow us to greet them. Clayton then did the honors, "Bruce and Adriana McGowan, I present the President of the United States of America and the First Lady."

With that introduction, I should have worn a tie. This was like being at some kind of State formal or dinner. However, the President had on jeans, a leather jacket and cowboy boots. Maybe it was *me* who was over-dressed in my Blazer and gray slacks.

"Hello, Mr. President and Ma'am," I greeted. He held out his hand and shook mine. Leaning over to me, he whispered, "Hello, Scorpion." My code name with Team Zulu.

Adriana then gave them both a slight bow and a smile. He took her hand and kissed it. Very genteel, sir.

Eagle One...*his* code name...had kind eyes and a genuine smile. I don't think I actually observed that when I sat opposite him in his Oval Office. Of course on that occasion he was wearing his serious face and trying his best not to have me investigated for murder. The First Lady, a lithe spirit with flawless skin and dancing eyes, appeared as everyone in America perceived her...warm and unpretentious. They looked perfect together and in this casual environment, *human* like the rest of us.

"I can't tell you how often we thought about getting away to your beautiful place," she said. "I showed my husband the photos on your website and actually got a smile out of him. We thought about coming in the spring when we would experience the lilacs and red bud like we saw in one of the photos. But once we vacate the White House next month, we'll be heading west to our ranch."

"And none too soon," added the President with a wink.

Adriana said, "If you'd like, I can show you now to your room. At your leisure, in our sitting room, we'd like to offer you some ginger and oatmeal cookies for something sweet. You may also have your choice of coffee, hot tea or hot cider. At four we have brie and crackers with a choice of White Zinfandel or a hearty red. Dinner is served at six in the dining room. Today we have pot roast with potatoes and sautéed carrots, our home-canned green beans and corn and yeast rolls. There is red velvet cake for dessert with French vanilla ice cream on the side."

"Well, that sure makes my stomach growl, Mrs. McGowan," the President said. "Can't wait."

The First lady added, "We actually didn't expect dinner here, you know. We thought we'd just be getting breakfast like with most B&Bs."

"Normally, yes. But when the First Family is staying with us, they become *our* family."

"That is beyond sweet, Adriana," she replied. "We are going to feel most comfortable here."

Adriana smiled. "Your room is this way, ma'am. Is there anything you and the President need?"

"Just to freshen up and relax for a few minutes is all. Thank you, dear. Oh, what a lovely tree," the First Lady remarked as she passed through the den toward the hallway. "I love the blue globes with the white lights. You know that's the color scheme I went with this year for the White House tree."

Adriana beamed about as bright as the light inside of the angel at the top. She smiled at the First Lady and performed a slight curtsey. I then spoke up to tell them about a Christmas tree my mom had one year back when I was a kid in the early sixties. "It was a silver artificial job that changed color and lit up while the wheel spun around. Wow! My brother and I sat for hours watching the thing turn red, green, blue..."

The First Lady looked at me like my head was on fire. Her eyes darted over to Adriana's. I then saw my sweet wife roll hers.

"Well, it *was* just that one year," I added.

The President tried to stifle a smile. I knew he wanted to bust out laughing. But before following his wife down the hallway, he cornered me and placed his hand firmly on my shoulder. In a low voice he said, "Before I forget it, Bruce, I want to say something. I never did get an opportunity to tell you personally, but you did this country a great service by takin' out that Viper. Then you stopped that terrorist bunch from carryin' out its plan to attack Washington. All with the help of that crack shot you had with you."

"Steed."

"Ah, yes, Atticus Steed. Interesting man."

"A very *appreciative* man for granting him that pardon."

"I don't mind tellin' you, Bruce, I had to think long and hard about that one. He had a history that was hard to swallow, considerin' he took down a lot of people. I don't doubt their guilt, though, and somehow needed to be brought to justice. Just didn't like the way it was done."

"The Bureau, with Steed's help, also brought down the brains behind that Justice Club...two important Justice Department heads."

He placed his hands behind his back and nodded. "Yeah. Bastards."

Neither one of us said anything for a few moments, but then he added, "You know, I was hopin' you'd call me one day and tell me you decided to take the helm of the team. Nobody's more qualified to lead our counterterrorism division."

"My team was destroyed by a madman, sir. A man who could have ultimately had your office." I paused a few seconds. "I guess I just had no more heart to stay in the game."

"But someone got to him...*and* his henchmen."

"Yes, someone *did*, Mr. President."

I thought I detected a half smile.

"Maybe while I'm here relaxing with the Mrs at your lovely place, you and I can slip off somewhere and continue the conversation we had about that. More a matter of curiosity for me now, the 'lame duck' that I am. Any dialogue would be just between you and me. Nothing official. No repercussions."

I didn't respond.

"Yeah," he added. "We'll take that walk tomorrow. Anxious to take a stroll on your beautiful grounds. Thanks for havin' us here, Bruce. Thanks for openin' your doors to us." He then turned and strode down the hallway toward his room.

When I turned as well to go upstairs to our suite, I saw that Clayton had been standing behind us within proximity where he might actually have heard my conversation with the President. And I wondered if he *had*. His face was stoic; his eyes unwaveringly fixed on mine. We said nothing to one another when I passed by. But then he

nodded once, gave me a wry smile and said to me in almost a whisper, "Later, Mr. Bond."
He heard.

* * * * *

Just after one-thirty, the First Lady came out of their room and asked if she and her husband could enjoy the cookies and hot cider in their room. The President had stretched out on the bed watching a 24 hour news channel and was comfortable at the moment. Adriana told her she would be there momentarily with a tray.

We didn't hear a peep out of them for the next three hours and assumed both of them had sacked out. Considering the President's normal day was push-push, every moment something going on in the country that may require his attention, such an afternoon of relaxation was just what the doctor would order. They missed the wine hour, so all the more grape to be carried over into dinner.

Adriana suspected that the President would be dressing up a little for dinner, so she told me to put on a tie with my blazer. She and I fight nearly every Sunday about my wearing a tie and most of time she wins. But because we were having America's royalty at our dinner table, I didn't put up a fuss. There is one tie, however, she gets tired of me wearing. Having a Scottish heritage, 'tis my plaid Tartan tie of blue and green. She says the people in the church house "must think it's the only one" I have. But I tell her it goes so nicely with my blazer. She retorts, "And that blazer is another thing. You have so many nice-looking other jackets. Anyway, your blazer is getting too small for you." Another way of saying, "push back from the table a little sooner."

At five-ten when everyone was seated except for our hostess, it was nearly dark outside. The dining room light had been dimmed and I had just finished setting fire to the two large candles on the table. As our 1890 English Regency dining room table barely seats six, it still had to accommodate seven...two couples and three agents. The chairs on one side of the table were nearly touching, which meant so were the buns of the three agents occupying them. The Head of the Country sat at the head of the table on one end with the First Lady at his right. The head of the house, me, sat at the opposite end. Clayton had offered to have his dinner at the small kitchen table so that everyone would be seated more comfortably, but Adriana would not hear of it. She was also concerned about the four agents standing their posts outside. *They* needed to eat as well. Clayton told her as per usual in scenarios like this his team of agents would switch off. Howard and Smithers would first relieve two of the ground agents and then stay in place until the cycle was complete with the remaining two. No one was going hungry. The entire changing of the guard process would be complete by seven.

My quintessential social butterfly flit about between the kitchen and dining room filling the water and wine glasses. After yet another trip to the kitchen Adriana then brought out a large dinner tray containing everyone's salad. Once satisfied and all was set to her liking, she finally sat down in the chair beside the First Lady. Her eyes searched nervously around the table making sure she had arranged all of the details of the dinner and the seating to perfection, that we were after all observing proper etiquette in view of our honored guests. Taking account of her anxiety, I whispered to her that Emily Post was not dining with us. And anyway, I was sure the President was long tired of everyone around him at the White House insisting on all that phony felicitous protocol which always occurred at State dinners and such. She shushed me.

"Is everyone good with me saying a blessing?" she asked.

"We were hoping there would be one," the First Lady said.

And then she began, "Father in Heaven, we praise you..."

Her voice, soft, sweet and earnest, made me smile. Even though a blessing is not often said aloud over our food when it's just her and me, she has never failed to drop her head before a meal and whisper a few words. A heart so pure...makes me wonder what she ever saw in the likes of this sinner. Her prayer asked not only for blessings over our meal, but for the President and First Lady, for their goodness and example, for their health and safety, and for many days of happiness as they continue through life. Her mini-sermon lasted about a minute and then came the rounds of amens. Jeff Howard, obviously a Catholic, crossed himself. I think I even heard Mr. Clayton's amen.

As we picked through our salads, the small table talk began. Mrs. President apparently knew a good bit about the agents and engaged them regularly in conversation whenever the opportunity arose. Jeff Howard had a lovely wife and two young daughters, which she asked about by first names. She called Joanie Smithers 'Sweetpea' which I'm not sure Smithers liked, but I could see the two of them had a special relationship. Bill Clayton, whom the President referred to as Billy, was not married...not surprising...and smiled a lot as he conversed with his boss. They also seemed unusually close, Clayton appearing as much a friend and confidant as the President's number one security man.

But our royal guests made sure *we* were part of the conversation. The First Lady wanted to know Adriana's entire history, where she grew up and especially how she came to be the Mistress of Wolf Laurel. And did everyone know there was a resort area in North Carolina called Wolf Laurel? Then she wanted to know more about me. Besides my being retired FBI, she knew I was doing some important work for her husband and had been recognized for it. She remembered that day when Adriana and I came by the White House. But she wasn't sure what the scope of my real job was with the government back then. That's when Agent Clayton turned his face toward me and waited. I thought I detected a half smile...or was that a smirk? The President and I darted eyes back and forth. He already knew everything about me and knew as well my history wasn't open for table talk. He changed the subject. "Well, I think I'm now ready for some of that pot roast down there on your end of the table, Jefferson. Can you send it this way?"

"You got it, Mr. President."

After that, the conversations faded as everyone started digging in. Adriana was back up with a second bottle of Bordeaux, assuring that the wine glasses were not empty. Compliments continued throughout the dinner. The beef was moist and succulent. The vegetables, tender and wonderfully seasoned. The hospitality, warm and inviting.

"And here we were thinking we would likely be dining at The Greenbrier at least one of the nights here," the First Lady remarked. "My husband knows the owner there and has a standing invitation."

"Yeah, too bad it's winter," the President added. "One of the best golf courses in the country is there. I've played it a couple of times. Walked the same greens as Ike, Slammin' Sammie and a bunch of other notables."

"Then you'll have to come back in the spring," I said. "Maybe I can knock the cobwebs off my own weapons of self-destruction and join you."

He laughed. "We'll make that happen."

Dinner ended and no one seemed to want dessert right away, so the President and wife excused themselves to their room. "Just let me know when you're ready and I'll break it out before you all retire," Adriana said.

Clayton then sent Howard and Smithers out to relieve Huynh and Davis. "They shouldn't take longer than 30 minutes to finish up. Stay put until Franks and Bartow are in and out. The entire rotation should not take more than an hour. Before you go out, let me make contact." He pressed a button on the radio attached to his jacket and touched his ear bud to see that it was fully in. "Radio check. How do you hear me?" Pause. All agents apparently responded. "Good. Okay, Howard and Smithers are on the way out."

Once the dinner rotation was complete, Smithers and Howard returned at 2020. Even in their military grade parkas and toboggans with the word POLICE across the brow they were both rubbing the circulation back into their faces.

I saw that Smithers was shivering. She said, "It wouldn't be so bad if it weren't for the wind chill."

The agents then went directly into the den where I had earlier lit a fire in the stone fireplace. It reminded me to throw on another log, so I did. Clayton was sitting in an arm chair nearby talking on his cell phone, providing a rundown of the day's activities to someone I took it to be his boss at the Secret Service in Washington. While the agents were shedding their outer wear and warming their hands, the President then entered the room behind them. Placing both hands on their shoulders, he said, "I'm proud of you folks, you know. You've heard me say that from time to time, but it's cold nights like this I really appreciate-cha."

"Thank you, Mr. President," replied Jeff Howard. "I don't mind telling you, I've never enjoyed working for any other president like I have you. You and the First Lady go all out to treat us with respect."

"You earn that respect, Jefferson. We've always felt safe with you fellas. And now you too, Joanie." He then smiled. "I won't embarrass you by calling you Sweetpea. But, I've seen you at work these last couple of years and you're gonna be a good'n."

She gave him a head bow and smiled in return.

When I had finished stoking the fire and setting the screen back in place, I announced that "Adriana's in the kitchen now preparing you all that dessert. How about it?"

"My Mrs and I will take you up on that. I'll go get her."

Both Howard and Smithers nodded to the affirmative. Clayton, still engaged on his phone call, shook his head. A dichotic listener I presumed.

We tested both the social skills and knee balance prowess of our guests by serving their cake and ice cream in the den by the fire. As I was still stuffed from the dinner, I declined dessert and asked instead to be excused to the upstairs to change into my jeans.

"Yeah, get comfortable, Bruce...you too, Adriana," said the President. "We'd like to just sit a spell after this delicious dessert and get even better acquainted with one another. This is a refreshin' change from a lot of my evenings which are normally very often consumed with meetings and other interruptions. I've had a lot of fifteen hour days, especially lately. Sometimes they won't let me even go to the bathroom for my daily constitutional."

The First Lady then fired from her eyes a missile of reprimand in his direction. TMI, Mr. President. I waited until I reached the landing at the top of the stairs before chuckling.

As the dessert went down rather quickly, Adriana asked if they would like seconds. No takers. Would they like coffee? Yes, thank you. Smithers then helped her collect the dishes and silverware to dump into the dishwasher. Once that was accomplished she said to Adriana, "I guess my chauvinist partners think I'm doing this because that's what a woman would do. But I'm just helping you because I want to."

"And for no other reason but to be courteous. I'm with you on that. When it comes to kitchen chores, my husband understands that it's not a 'women's role' thing. On many occasions he's right beside me helping."

"The kind of man I will be seeking out when I'm ready to settle down. I like him, Mrs. McGowan. He's charismatic, funny and a darn good looking guy."

"And *mine*. Don't get any ideas, Sweetpea." And then she laughed. I wish I had been there to hear them make over me like that. I couldn't believe Adriana told me later they had had the conversation.

Chapter Five

Adriana would not have been happy with me had I changed into what I usually walk around in at home...my Special Forces or Ranger tee and my frayed, faded jeans with all the holes. So, I decided on dressy casual with my Greg Norman wool pullover and new unfaded Wranglers. Then moments later she joined me upstairs to go casual as well while the President, First Lady and agents continued to talk and relax by the warm hearth. Obviously, a bond had been established among them all, regardless of their differences in status. On a daily basis, whether at the Big House, on Air Force One or in a foreign country's hotel, they spent more time communing with one another than most family members. Clayton was finally off the phone and I actually heard him laugh about something. Of course when the President is telling a joke, funny or not, one laughs. It's not only understood, but commanded.

"Going well so far," I said to Adriana. "Don't you think?"

"They almost make you forget who they are. It's like I've been lulled by them into believing they're actually friends of ours. I know I didn't expect them to be haughty and to come across as arrogantly superior, but I also didn't expect they'd be this down to earth. They..."

I then held up my index finger to stop her. My ear had suddenly picked up the drone of motors from possibly two vehicles that seemed to be quickly decelerating on the roadway and turning into our driveway. And then just as suddenly, the laughter downstairs ceased at the sound of the vehicles sliding to a stop on the gravel near our steps. Upon hearing the scurrying down below in the den, I ran to the landing just in time to see Clayton starting for the center hallway and front door. *"Code Red!"* he yelled. However, before he was halfway there, the front door was flung open with such force, it crashed soundly against the wall. Charging into the room from the foyer were two figures dressed in black, faces covered by ski masks and MP5 assault weapons in their hands. But they didn't fire. Clayton's Sig Sauer was already in his hand.

Over the back of the sofa he fired the first of three rounds, one of which slammed into the throat of the gunman on the right. Just as he went down, the second man fired two quick bursts, which thumped into the thick cushions, and he then ducked back into the foyer behind the wall. *"Cover the President!"* Clayton yelled to Howard.

Agent Howard immediately wrapped his arms around the President and half carried him to the hallway while Smithers pulled the First lady from her chair and dragged her through the dining room into the kitchen. I then hustled to my bedroom to snatch up my XDM. Just as I was on the move while throwing a clip into the .45, automatic weapons fire began down below. I heard Clayton's gun answering. I reached the upper landing just in time to see two more figures charging into the room, the first gunman spraying walls, lamps and the glassware in Adriana's curio. The second man with a shotgun caught sight of Howard and the President still retreating toward the main hallway. From the balcony, I fired two well-placed rounds, one each into the skulls of the gunmen. Blood splattered out the opposite sides of their heads. Unfortunately, the second man's shotgun went off as he fell, its pellets striking both Agent Howard and the President. Both men lay crumpled against the hall wall. Howard wasn't moving and his body nearly completely engulfed the President.

I then yelled back over my shoulder while scrambling down the staircase, *"Stay put, Adriana!"* I was apparently just a little too quick for the remaining gunman who had now turned his MP5 on me. Already at the bottom landing, I began firing off a series of rounds in his direction. The gunner then sprayed the sheetrock behind me while retreating back into the foyer. It was momentarily quiet. I could almost hear him thinking. He knew that when they exploded into the room at least one of the agents would be shielding the First Family and not trade fire. That would take one gun out. The gunmen would then expect the resistance to be limited. However, our defense had not only stopped their assault, but we were also keeping them at bay. Three of their men were quickly dead. And the other two now knew they had *me* to reckon with...whoever the hell I was. But I was also thinking. Where were the ground agents? And the cavalry?

Clayton shoved in another clip and continued pumping out bullets toward the foyer. I was then able to make it quickly over to the President, the last few feet diving and sliding on the slick wooden floor. After I pulled Agent Howard off him, I saw that the President's shoulder was bleeding. He was conscious but in a lot of pain. But then when I looked at Agent Howard, I saw that much of his face had disappeared, obviously taking the brunt of the blast. I felt for a pulse and found none. Turning back to the President, I said, "Let me help you..." But he cut me off.

"No. Go to Clayton. I'm okay. *Go!*"

I then saw what the President wanted me to see. Clayton had been wounded as well. Blood was spurting from a severed artery in his thigh near the groin. I half ran half crawled over to him, reached in and pulled off his belt, then used it to create a tourniquet.

Clayton shouted, "The President, is he hit?"

"Yeah. Took some pellets in the shoulder. Not bad."

Suddenly, the automatic fire started up again. The MP5 was working us over at a cyclic rate, bullets impacting and ricocheting along the wood floor and into the fireplace. We were lying prone behind the protection of the seat bottom and cushions, but rounds were zipping through the seat back as though it were made of paper. Both of us responded with another volley of rounds into the corners of the wall. The machine gun barrage then ceased as suddenly as it had begun.

Clayton touched the button on his radio while simultaneously pulling out his cell phone. "Bartow. Franks. Come in. Come in. Davis. Come in." He looked at me. His face, grimaced and wanly, he said, "They're not answering." Turning his attention to his cell, he touched its face with his left thumb. "Tyson. Come on, dammit, pick up." There was a short pause and I guessed the guy on the other end finally answered.

Clayton yelled into the phone, "The Eagle is down. I say again, the Eagle is down. We have a breach. Code Red. Deploy Archangel. This location. Engage locals."

I didn't know what all that meant. But it seemed that he had ordered some kind of attack team in and also requested the State Police who were in ready status. But where would the feds be coming from and how long would it take them to get here? I looked around the room. Three bad guys dead. Clayton nailed one...I nailed two. But although there were two more positioned not twenty feet away strategizing how to break through our resistance, I guessed they were waiting for others for an all out assault. Where the hell *were* the perimeter agents?

As the shooting had stopped, Smithers yelled out from the kitchen, *"Clayton, Howard. What's going on? Is the President all right?"*

I answered for Clayton. "Just stay there, Agent Smithers! Stay ready and protect that kitchen door." There was also a third outer door to the house at the end of the main hallway. If they had decided to envelop us, with Howard dead and Clayton down, we were in deep shit. Then suddenly another spray of automatic fire from around the corners of the foyer began chewing up walls and furniture. I rolled back over to shield the President at the same time firing a half dozen shots in the direction of the muzzle flashes. Nonetheless, one of the attackers running at a crouch finally made it into the den unscathed behind the sofa chair, thanks to the second man who was in the foyer laying down a base of automatic fire. From his MP5 a hail of bullets again saturated the room, a few of which zipped under the couch. I saw Clayton's body jerk. The President saw it as well and grimaced.

As he and I were still lying low on the hallway floor behind a wall corner out of the line of fire, I began assessing the situation. It was interesting to me that there had not been an all-out onslaught by all the bad guys at once. A flood of attackers would have taken us all out in a matter of seconds. Perhaps somehow they knew there were only three Secret Service agents in the house and considering the agents' first concern would be shielding the President and First Lady, there would not be much resistance in the form of return fire. But maybe they didn't intend to attack in the first place. They hadn't come in firing. It was Clayton who initiated the gunfire. Maybe they just wanted to take the President. More automatic weapons fire from the lone gunman.

I had been in dire positions before where bullets were searching out my name, but not like this. I'm not a pessimist by nature, but the current situation appeared hopeless. We were pinned down with only handguns and the President was at risk. I knew there were other bad guys out there somewhere besides the bastards shooting across the room. Smithers and the First Lady were trapped and vulnerable. It was now down to only my gun to protect the President. To further complicate matters, blood was beginning to trickle down my forehead.

"Bruce, you're hit," the President said. Unbeknownst to me, one of the enemy rounds had apparently ricocheted and grazed the top of my head.

"I'm alright, sir. But I have to find a way to take these assholes out."

With the weapon I had elected to snatch from the upstairs, my XDM, the gun with the .45 caliber ACP metal piercing ammunition, I reached around the corner and quickly fired a three round shot group through the foyer wall. Immediately, I heard the man scream out; however, I couldn't tell how badly he was hit. I waited another fifteen or twenty seconds to listen. I then heard the latch on the front door along with his groans. Like a roach, he had crawled off. I assumed in hearing the sounds, he had retreated through the doorway. Of course, the closing of the door could have been a ruse. And if so, I knew I had to nail him before he worked his way around the other side of the wall toward the kitchen. Smithers would have her .357 ready, but I couldn't bank on that. I was now more concerned with the gunman behind the chair across the room. Only twenty feet, the hallway wall and that overstuffed chair separated us.

Not only was the blood now running into my eyes where I had trouble seeing, with my limited vision of the room from the hallway, I had no line of sight to the sofa chair. I knew I couldn't just lie there beside the President and wait for the prick to make his move, so I threw another clip into my pistol and began firing toward the chair to suppress any further fire, at the same time galloping across the room. If he unloaded on me I would be a moving target and there would be a chance he'd nail me. Maybe better than 50-50. But as I was on the move, suddenly the gunman raised up and fired a full automatic burst. Our Christmas tree which had temporarily concealed my movement unfortunately became a casualty and fell hard to the wooden floor. I actually felt one of the rounds whiz by my head and take a chunk out of the stone fireplace. However, one of *my* two rounds struck the man solidly in the mouth, proving I can still run and shoot straight at the same time. He dropped like a sack of cement.

Quickly, I ran toward the wall I had earlier plugged and peeked around it into the foyer. The last gunman was gone. Then upon hearing the sound of a car engine cranking up, by the time I made it to the door, the vehicle was already spinning out on the gravel driveway. I fired two rounds through its back glass, but the car continued on out the lane.

After running back inside, I then turned my attention to the President. The blood had seeped through his jean shirt and was now saturating his entire left sleeve. He was not as 'okay' as he had said. As we were not far from that same hall closet that Bacon had sniffed out, I pulled from the upper shelf box one of the pillow cases and applied pressure to the President's wound. He winced from the pain.

"Sir," I said. "Take your right hand and continue pressure on the wound. With the shot still in there, it'll hurt. But bleeding has to be stopped. I need to go back and check on Clayton."

When I got to Clayton, I found blood pooling in his mouth. I ran my hand over his torso to a point where his protective vest ended and touched warm liquid oozing around a large hole. He had been hit in the abdomen just below the vest. That was not good. He then pointed to one of the dead attackers lying no more than an arm's length away. "Pull...pull off the mask." As he spoke, the blood now gushed from his lips.

When I yanked the ski mask off the attacker and saw the face, a shot of fiery adrenaline ran through my arteries. Joachim Nazer. As it turned out, the bastard agent hadn't been a victim of the flu after all. But he was damn sure a victim of Clayton's Sig .357. I began thinking. None of the exterior agents had answered Clayton's call. Was this an assassination attempt by select agents of the Secret Service or was it only Nazer who had conspired with the terrorist group? And just what *was* the ethnic origin of the name *Nazer*?

Clayton clamped onto my arm. "I...recognized his eyes." I knew he was dying. And he was desperately trying to spit out a few final words.

"Shhh, don't try to talk," I said softly.

He then motioned for me to come closer. His words were nearly unintelligible now. Large blood bubbles formed between his lips. "Bruce...get the Eagle out of here...*now*. Trust...no one. *No one*. There'll be...others. Hide him." He tried in vain to say something else, but the words would no longer come out. He then laid his bloodied cell phone in my hand and clutched my fingers around it. In it were the numbers I would need. After taking in one final, raspy breath of air, he then spewed it out and laid his head back onto the floor. For some odd reason, it was a deja vu moment. The last man to die in my arms was my friend, Lionel Byrd. I didn't know Clayton, but for some reason as I stared into his open eyes, still open in death, the memories of the bloody day I found my boss and my team murdered came roaring back.

As it was now eerily quiet in the house, the only sound heard was the beginning of the rain on our tin roof. But then Smithers called out again from the kitchen. *"What's going on out there? Is it clear?"*

Chapter Six

I yelled back to her. *"Bring the First Lady...now! We need to get out of here!"*

Immediately their two forms appeared from the kitchen in the dim light, one cradling the other. They joined the President and me in the hallway.

"Stay here and watch the front and side doors, Smithers. I'm going up for Adriana."

Taking three steps at a time, I bounded up our staircase, simultaneously yelling for Adriana. She was already at the landing, my Glock .45 caliber in her hand. Bless her vigilant little heart. She froze when she saw the blood on my face.

"Skip, you've been shot!"

I shrugged her off. "Come on, Babe. We gotta vacate. Get your purse and keys. And get my keys from the dresser, quickly. This isn't over."

She didn't press the issue. After disappearing for no more than twenty seconds while I went back downstairs to corral the President and his Mrs, she surfaced with the items.

I then pulled from my belt my cellphone and ran my finger quickly down the contact list until I reached his number. Captain Harlan Williams, Commander of the local detachment. I got his voice mail. "Harlan. Bruce. Big problems here at Wolf Laurel. Need you and a platoon of your troopers ASAP. And I mean *now*. As I'm not reaching you, I'll call 911 and get patched through to your people. Call me!"

I immediately hung up and dialed 911. A woman answered. "911 Operator."

"Ma'am, my name is Bruce McGowan and I need to be sent to the Greenbrier detachment of the State Police."

"Please tell me the nature of your problem."

Well, let's see. The President and First Lady are staying with us and someone came here to kill them. It would be nice if you would accommodate us.

"I can't explain what's going on here. Just either get me through to the State Police or send several units out to the Wolf Laurel B&B off Seven Bridges Road."

"You're going to have to be more specific than that. What is the nature of..."

It appeared as she was going to continue with her game of Ring Around the Rosie. I needed to say something drastic to get her attention. "I've killed a lot of people tonight. Should I come for you? Now get the police to my location." That should do it. Of course now they'll be coming for *me*...locked and loaded.

As soon as I hung up the phone, it rang. Maybe it was Harlan.

"Hello," I answered.

For a long moment there was no response. Then a voice I didn't recognize.

"McGowan."

"Who is this?!" I yelled.

There was a pause. And then, "We didn't intend on any gunplay. We just want the President."

"To do what...hold him for ransom?"

"Until demands are met."

"What demands?"

"Never mind. There are more of us on the way. Surrender him peacefully and we will let you and your wife live. And we know the President is wounded. I have people who can treat him."

"No surrender, prick. And you will not get to the President. I'll personally see to that."

The President called to me from the hallway, "Bruce, who is that?"

I didn't answer him.

The man on the other end continued. "Put Clayton on."

I didn't want to let out that Clayton was dead. The terrorist or whoever he was had to believe that there were still three agents and enough guns to hold him and his cronies off until the locals arrived.

"The police are on the way," I said.

 "And they will find my people waiting. *Now put Clayton on!*"

"No. This is my home and I *will* defend it. Clayton has no say here and no responsibility except to protect the President and First Lady. He will not give the President up."

"Then you will all die. *Everyone.*" The phone went silent.

I didn't know whether the man on the phone was the surviving gunman who had de-assed or somebody higher up pulling all the strings. I suspected the latter. That survivor had likely notified his higher that the raid had not come off as planned... the President had not been taken and bodies were strewn all over the place.

I looked at Adriana who in turn was looking at the dead, especially Agent Howard who was missing half his head. She was pale and I thought she might be sick. "Agent Smithers," I said, "move the President and ladies to the center of the room where you can see the side and kitchen doors. I'm going out the front to see what the hell happened to Clayton's men."

"The terrorists may be waiting out there, Bruce," said the President. "Don't know that I'd do that."

"I've got no choice, sir. We have to abandon the place. The man on the phone, whoever the hell he is, said the intent was for you to be taken hostage."

"For what purpose?"

"He wouldn't say what his demands were, just that more of his troops were on the way. That may have been just a bunch of bullshit, but we can't take that chance. And by the way, Mr. President, apparently that last gunman who crawled out of here knew you had been wounded. The voice on the phone said so. The voice also mentioned Clayton by name. These people are well inside your system, sir."

The President then shook his head. "Damn."

I looked at Smithers and nodded without word. She picked up one of the MP5s and shoved in a fresh clip, then nodded back. Joanie Smithers, like the rest of us, knew that as the only remaining agent now in charge of the First Family, she would be calling the shots. But maybe because the scenario was well beyond her pay grade or perhaps out of respect for my experience, she wasn't quibbling about *me* taking charge.

Quickly, I moved through the open front door and crouched behind the right side banister. No bullets coming my way. The remaining terrorist vehicle, a black late model BMW with blacked-out windows, sat in front of the steps beside the President's limo. All four of the limo's tires were flat from bullet wounds. While stooping down, my hand touched something wet on the veranda floor. The dim rays cast from the street light out on the roadway picked up its shine. Blood. I knew I had nailed the bastard and that's probably the main reason he took off. He would either bleed to death at Wolf Laurel or get the treatment that would save his life.

I then spotted something shiny back in the trees at the entrance to my driveway where it intersected with the roadway. It appeared to be one of the agents' cars. Like a flash I jumped off the veranda over the steps and into the yard, running like a gazelle toward the car, the muzzle of my .45 leading the way. Considering an unmasked secret service bad guy was lying dead in my house, I was just as much concerned about taking fire from the car as I was from someone hiding among the trees. I had no idea at this point if there were others involved.

I have a sixth sense about some things. One of them is that I can sniff out a death scene without even seeing it. It didn't take me long to find that this natural gift of mine hadn't betrayed me. When I was within fifteen feet of the vehicle, I saw that the passenger side window was down and that a human arm hung motionless from the door side. Both driver and passenger were dead...ambushed, shot in the head. Huynh and Davis. So where were Bartow and Franks?

After racing back to the the front door I paused and yelled inside, "It's me."

"Okay," replied Smithers.

"What did you find out there, Bruce?" the President asked.

"Your agents Huynh and Davis are dead inside their car. No sign of the other two."

"My God!" he replied, placing his arm around the First Lady. "You're right...we need to get everyone out of here."

But before leading them out I quickly began pulling masks off the rest of the attackers.

The President looked puzzled. "What are you doing, Bruce?"

"Checking for other Secret Service faces besides Nazer's."

When I had gotten around to all of the bodies and not recognizing anyone else, I asked Smithers, "Anybody look familiar?"

She nodded and pointed to the last gunman I had nailed. "He's another agent. I think his name's Curlick or something like that."

"*Michael* Curlick," affirmed the First Lady. "I spoke with him at a state function in the East Room. I thought he was a good man when we talked."

"Good and *dead* now," I remarked. "This thing is deep into the Service, Mr. President. And I suspect there might even be other agencies involved. What their agenda is, obviously remains in question. Clayton told me to trust *no one* and that's how we have to handle this, sir."

"And your plan?"

"First, get the hell out of here. I'll explain things on the way to the airport. I'll drive you in my vehicle and Adriana will take the First Lady and Agent Smithers with her in her van."

"Why not all in one vehicle?" asked Smithers.

"We need to separate and I'll tell you why later."

The President commented, "You said that Mr. Clayton told you not to trust anyone; could the Marine detachment also be involved in this?"

"A chance we'll have to take, sir. Now, gotta go." I then began leading the four of them to the front door.

I didn't bother to lock the door. I knew the police, the FBI and the medical examiner had to get in there to investigate and retrieve the bodies. Anyway, Adriana's jewelry and all my firearms except one were hidden away in a wardrobe. If looters happened in there before the locals and feds secured the place, so be it. I had insurance.

It had been about ten minutes since I heard the warning from the mysterious voice and then made my phone call to Harlan Williams. If there were other bad guys waiting in the wings, were they poised close by for a second attempt to get to the President? And then how long would it take for the State Police to arrive and take charge of the scene? We couldn't wait around to find out. If I could get hold of Williams, a man who I could trust, we could get the President and First Lady into protective custody before getting him back to Washington.

When I was reasonably sure there was no further immediate threat on our grounds, Smithers and I very vigilantly walked ahead of the others down the front steps with the bad guys' MP5s in our hands scanning the area. Then when I was sure Adriana was behind the wheel of her van with Smithers beside her and First Lady in the rear, the President and I climbed into my Suburban. I shoved the MP5 into his hands and cradled my XDM while pulling away from Wolf Laurel. Once I was sure Adriana was on the highway close behind me, we picked up speed and set out in the direction of the airport.

"Okay, Bruce. What's the deal? Why are we in separate cars?"

"As a check valve, sir, if we find the Marine element to be compromised or in on the plot, Adriana will immediately take the First Lady and Agent Smithers to my family's fish camp that no one really knows about while I get you into the hands of the local State Police Captain. The bad guys, whoever they are, I suspect will eventually be on the road hunting for us and we need to make contact with Williams ASAP. We don't know who in the federal government is involved in this plot, so we're not turning you over to the FBI. If all else fails and if I have to, I'll drive you directly to the White House gate."

"I can't imagine this runs so deep that there are people even in the FBI involved, Bruce."

"Could you ever have imagined your own Secret Service would be? Somebody up the ladder is pulling the strings, sir. And if not, it's for sure that some high-up chieftan in one the terrorist groups, foreign or domestic, is ramrodding the plot."

"You got any ideas who?"

"Take your pick, Mr. President...al-qa'ida, and all its factions, Hezbollah, Boko Haram, the Islamic State of Iraq or *any* of the radical Jihadist groups. Also, on the domestic side, remember not long ago when we stopped the resurgence of the Weathermen. There's the Earth Liberation Front, which I understand is foremost on the FBI's own terrorist list, and how about Alpha 66?"

"You've obviously stayed abreast of all the threats out there, Bruce. You sure you don't want back in the chase?"

I smiled. "Not in the least, sir. I've now been fully domesticated...by the woman who's following us."

The President didn't return the smile. Instead, he glanced in his side mirror at the vehicle carrying his wife. "Nevertheless, you've found yourself back in the action business anyway, thanks to me."

My cell phone went off again. The mystery voice or Adriana? Neither. It was the call I was wanting.

"Bruce, Harlan. What the hell's going on at Wolf Laurel? You sounded frantic. And then I got wind of the call you made to the 911 operator. *That* wasn't nice."

"Big problems, Harlan. Our inn came under attack by a terrorist squad. A bunch of them and two Secret Service agents are dead."

"Come on, Bruce, are you actually being serious or is this some kind of sick joke?"

"You know I wouldn't give you a report like this if it wasn't happening."

"Why is the Secret Service there?"

"I can't go into it. Are your troopers on the way to my place?"

"Yes, they should be there by now. But..."

"No 'buts', Harlan. This is a Code Zero deal. Tell your officers to watch out for a second wave of bad guys which are also possibly on the way to Wolf Laurel. But I want *you* to meet me out at the Greenbrier Airport soon as you can. Better bring some troopers with you."

I heard him sigh in resignation. "All right, but I have to turn around. I was on the way out to your place. Two men are with me."

"Good. I'll be at the airport in zero-five. When you get there, pull around back to the tarmac. That's where I'll be."

When I flipped my phone closed, the President placed the hand attached to his good arm on my shoulder. "Sorry about all this, Bruce. I'm sure when you woke up this morning you didn't envision your place gettin' all shot up and dead people lyin' all over."

"Hell of a thing, isn't it, sir?"

With the aid of my instrument panel lights I could see the bleeding had started again between his shoulder and bicep. Blood was seeping through the makeshift bandage.

"We have to get you to the hospital, Mr. President."

"Don't know about that, Bruce. If they know I'm hit, could be somebody waitin' there we don't want to see."

"Good point, sir. There should be a medic on board Marine One to treat your wound until you get checked in at Walter Reed."

The President was silent a moment, but then said, "I can't figure this, Bruce. What's this about? Who are they and what do they want?"

A lot of questions. I wish I had the answers. I was sure somehow we'd find out soon.

A couple minutes later we pulled into the airport parking lot and whipped around to the tarmac entrance. While waiting for Harlan Williams, we watched what might have been the last jet of the night taxi down the runway, turn 180 and then take off. Marine One was positioned off to our right about 300 yards away still covered with a camo tarp. I called Williams's cell.

"Delayed for a few minutes, Bruce. Our vehicle came onto a pretty serious accident with injuries and since the bulk of my troop is pullin' into your place, we're compelled to at least administer help until county and the EMS get here."

"All right. When you get here, go ahead and pull around back toward a hanger that has a large helicopter sitting by it. That's where I'll be."

"Can't wait to get this story, Bruce. It had better be some kind of national emergency."

"You might be surprised, Harlan. Okay, I'm out." I then flipped my phone shut.

Immediately, I began driving toward the chopper and Adriana followed in the van. But when I was within about 200 feet, the President grabbed my forearm and yelled "Stop! Stop now."

I jammed on the brakes which nearly caused Adriana to rearend us. "What is it, sir?"

"It's not right. There should be at least one guard outside, and seeing us approach, at least one more would exit the bird and put a light on us."

I hadn't thought of that. He was right. Reaching down behind my seat, I pulled out my NVD (night vision device) and began scanning the tarmac. No Marines visible, but neither were any bad guys. Just as there might have been gunmen waiting for us at the hospital, it was possible they could also be waiting on or near the tarmac, knowing I would take the President and his wife to Marine One.

"I don't see any good *or* bad guys, sir."

I picked up my cell and called Adriana. "Hey. Stay put here and don't follow us in toward the helicopter. I'm going to make a sweep around the chopper first."

"You're scaring me, Skip. What's happening?"

"Nothing right now. Just tell Smithers to stay ready."

"Now you're really scaring..."

I quickly shut down our conversation.

I looked over at the President. "Sir, can you switch guns with me?"

He nodded and handed me the MP5. I placed my XDM in his hand. "It's ready to fire. Just pull the trigger."

"You forget I'm an old cowboy, Bruce. I can handle the thing. What are we doin'?"

"You're not doing anything, Mr. President, except joining the ladies in the van. What I have planned does not need to expose you to any terrorists that may be waiting for us."

He didn't argue. I backed the Suburban to where we were side by side. He then jumped out and into the van. As I had my window glass down, I yelled to the inside of the van, "Be ready, Agent Smithers. Take care of our precious cargo."

I then gunned the old beast laying rubber more than a dozen feet and charged toward the chopper. When I was within 50 feet, I swerved to the right of the aircraft and made a sweep around to the reverse side. What I found there was no surprise. But it was definitely something that *shouldn't* have been there.

Chapter Seven

Obviously the terrorist element inside the black Mercedes intended for the helicopter to block the view of their car to anyone approaching the chopper. And obviously the men inside that car didn't count on me being so aggressive as to swing around to the rear and open fire on them from my dropped window. I didn't know how many were inside, but I know I bagged the driver. Unfortunately, someone from the back seat answered by unloading on the old Suburban, adding yet more battle wounds to its carcass. But *fortunately* for yours truly, I didn't suffer a scratch.

After making that pass, I jammed on my brakes, violently turned the steering wheel all the way to the left and spun back around in the direction of the Mercedes. After dropping the passenger side glass, I sprayed MP5 rounds from one end of the sedan to the other. This time there was no answer. I can also *drive* and shoot at the same time.

After screeching to a stop, I jumped out and attacked the dead Mercedes once more, sending into its insides a hail of automatic fire. Allowing the muzzle to lead me forward, I peered into the car. Three bodies. Two in the front and one in the rear seat. I took out my mini-light and shined it on each of their faces. No masks over the faces this time; just a slew of bullet holes. All appeared Middle Eastern. So, I deduced, at least two members of the Secret Service, Nazer and the agent identified by the First Lady as Curlick, were definitely in cahoots with Jihadists. But, I knew there was at least one more agent involved as well...the man on the phone.

Before I decided to pull the bodies out to check for IDs, papers, propaganda and etc, I knew I needed to get inside of Marine One. Again, that sixth sense, which is like having another appendage, started up again. I was sure that I would be both incensed and sickened at what I would find. It was inconceivable that these Marines would have for some reason abandoned their post or worse, been a part of the conspiracy to take down the President.

My cell began ringing and when I saw that it was Adriana, to quell her fears, I just answered and said, "I'm all right. Now entering the chopper," then hung up.

No sooner had I dropped the door to Marine One and shined my mini-light into its dark interior, I spotted the blood. Lots of it. Searching through the chopper's compartments, I found them all. Nearly every wall had been bullet riddled along with the bodies of the Marines. The terrorists must have taken out the posted guard and worked their way inside. I couldn't imagine how they would have gotten the drop on them, but I knew that *these* terrorists were professional. Cunning, calculating and determined. I wouldn't say the Marines were easy targets, but they certainly wouldn't have expected an attack on their chopper. And I couldn't rule out the fact that perhaps one of the bad guy Secret Service agents went aboard and set them up. The bodies were piling up and if I didn't go hide the President somewhere, he might soon be one of them.

Seeing death doesn't ordinarily bother me, but when the dead are fellow soldiers, agents and team members such as from my previous life and present day honorable young men in uniform like these polished Marines, I just don't have the stomach for it. I was almost physically sick when I took that last step off Marine One.

After sliding back into the Suburban, I saw that Harlan Williams had just pulled onto the tarmac and was parked beside Adriana's van. By the time I drove back to the edge of the runway he was out of his unit, butt leaning against the fender and arms folded. His troopers stood at the rear of the car.

"All right, Bruce McGowan, start talking."

"Okay, this has to be quick. I..."

At that moment a call came in on his radio. "Yeah, Williams here. What do you have?"

His face was suddenly grimaced. "How many?"

He then took a deep breath and let it out slowly as he listened. "Holy shit."

Another pause. "Okay, get the coroner in there and keep the place secured. Search the grounds. I'll be there sometime later." Looking at me, he added to his trooper, "I've got something to take care of out here at the airport. I'm out."

Harlan then outstretched his arms to invite my explanation about what was going down. "I'm listening."

"See that helicopter over there, Harlan? It's Marine One. Five dead inside. Good guys. Behind the chopper is a shot up Mercedes with three more dead. Bad guys. Now then, stick your head inside the van there. It's belongs to Adriana. What you find in there will go a long way to explain everything you're witnessing."

Harlan shook his head, and without word, walked slowly to the van. He opened the driver's door and saw Adriana behind the wheel as well as a young woman in the passenger seat cradling an MP5. Turning to me, he said, "Okay two very lovely women...one of them being Annie Oakley."

"Check out the back seat."
He sighed and then opened the left side sliding door. After he had stood in position a long moment, I thought he had suddenly spiraled into a catatonic state. He didn't move or say anything.

Finally, "Uh...Mr. President?"

"He and the First Lady were our guests today," I explained. "Most of the bodies at Wolf Laurel are terrorists who raided our place and tried to take him hostage. But he's been wounded, Harlan, and we need to get him treated, then back to Washington."

The President then said, "The bleeding's stopped, Bruce. My concern right now is those Marines. Are they okay?"

"No, sir. They were all murdered. Their killers were laying for us."

He buried his head in his hands. "Those kids. God, that's...I just don't have the words."

"But I just took care of their killers, Mr. President."

"You got them?"

"Big time."

"Mr. President, I'll go ahead and call the EMTs to get you to the hospital," Harlan said.

"Thanks, but I'd rather just have Mr. McGowan take me. It'll be quicker. Understand we need to keep the process discreet. No press. No attention. However, before we do anything I need to get my Chief of Staff and FBI Director on the phone and clue them in on things. They need to send down a bird to get me back to Washington. You still have Mr. Clayton's phone on you?"

"Yes, sir."

"Clayton's boss is number one on the quick dial and my Chief of Staff is number two. Would you be so kind to contact the chief?"

"Mr. Kessler."

"Yes. *He* will notify the Directors of Secret Service and the FBI."

I took from my jacket pocket Clayton's bloodied phone and touched the Number 2 as instructed. After hearing three rings, Kessler answered, "Yes, Agent Clayton."

"Mr. Kessler, it's Bruce McGowan."

"McGowan, yes. You obviously have Agent Clayton's phone. Is everything okay with Eagle One?"

"Sir, I have no other way to send you this information except in the clear."

For the next few minutes I gave him the details of the attack, the attempted taking of the President, the known involved agents and finally the current status. "Two agents, Franks and Bartow are missing. Four agents including Clayton are dead. Agent Smithers is fine. Marine One has been compromised and its occupants killed by the terrorists. The President and First Lady are safe with me...and the West Virginia State Police."

"Good God! This can't be happening. A freaking damn nightmare. Is the President close by? If so, please put him on."

"Will do." I handed the phone off. "Mr. President...your chief."

Somberly, he opened the conversation. "Arnie. Yeah. We have a serious breach. Like Mr. McGowan told you, hostiles have infiltrated the Service. Any ideas about this? Who these people are and what their agenda is?"

I wasn't hearing what Kessler was saying. The President was apparently listening to his chief explain what would happen from there as well as his extraction plan.

"All right, then. To be sure I understand, you will send local feds to meet me at the medical center in Ronceverte."

He turned to me and whispered, "You know where that is, right?"

I nodded.

"We'll have a State Police escort there. Once I'm treated, your people will return me here to the airport, whatever time that is." He paused to listen. "That's fine, Arnie. Suggest dispatching a C-130 to pick up all of the bodies. The Bureau and Secret Service will know how to handle that. Besides the bodies, they'll do a thorough search of the terrorist vehicle and secure any cell phones they find for information retrieval. Also include a replacement crew for the Whitehawk. Assume the Nighthawk is ready in its place." Another long pause. "Yeah, I agree. Heart wrenching to say the least. Thanks, Arnie, See you later tonight in the Oval Office." He then handed Clayton's phone back to me.

"Are you ready to go, sir," I asked him. "About a fifteen minute ride to the medical center."

"Give me a few minutes. I'd like you to take me over to the Whitehawk. I want to see what these bastards did to my boys."

"Mr. President, with all due respect. You don't want to go there."

"Take me there, Bruce."

"It's grisly."

"I'm sure."

"We need to get you to the medical center."

"In time."

"All right, sir. Will do." I then turned to Williams. "Harlan, this all may not be over. We don't know how many bad people are left. We've seen the numbers *already* involved. Suggest you get more uniforms out here. A couple cars for escort and troopers on site to secure Marine One."

"We'll make it happen." Harlan then motioned me off to the side and we strolled to the rear of his unit. In a low voice he said, "Damn, Bruce, I know I was briefed a few days ago that some Washington VIPs were coming into the county, but the President of the United States? This blows me away."

"Yeah. Let's just be sure we're not *literally* blown away. Get the additional troopers in here as well as the FBI. After the President and I leave Marine One, we need to roll out. Can you alert the ER? We whisk him in without fanfare. He's treated and then swept out of there as soon as it's medically safe to do so."

After walking back to the Suburban, I then opened the passenger door for the President to enter. I definitely did not want him to get inside the chopper. It was a gruesome scene even for a hard case like me. The most important man in the world didn't need this visual invading his dreams. But then again, maybe it *would* serve to further deepen his resolve in his war on terrorism.

I could tell from his face that his very soul was smarting from having seen the mutilated bodies of his Marines. He hardly said a word all the way down U.S. 219. And I had no words for *him*. The Suburban and Toyota van were sandwiched in between now two trooper units which were proceeding Code Two. No lights. No sirens. The caravan would attract no attention. No one on the highway would be the wiser as to who was being escorted through the dark countryside.

But as we approached Fairlea, the venue for the West Virginia State Fair, I started keeping my eye on the headlights of a vehicle positioned approximately fifty yards behind the trailing State Police unit containing Harlan Williams and his two troopers. Ordinarily, I wouldn't have had any concerns or even be watching a car behind me. But this vehicle had kept perfect distance all through Lewisburg and southward along 219, not even varying the distance when we slowed for traffic lights. I popped open my cell and touched Williams's name.

"Watch the vehicle behind you. It may be nothing, but looks like a tail. If so, I don't know how they got onto us unless they were watching from the airport. Tell your lead driver to make a right just after the high school up ahead."

"Roger."

We went another quarter mile when the lead trooper vehicle made that right turn and I followed suit. Adriana hadn't expected the turn and almost tapped me in the rear. However, she stayed behind me through the turn with Harlan close behind her. My apprehension finally eased a bit when I saw through my rear view mirror the sedan pass on by the side street. In the street light it looked like a light colored Chrysler 300, but I couldn't be sure.

Back on my phone, I said "False alarm. Sorry."

"Can't be too careful," Williams replied.

Back on the road, we were now within a mile from Ronceverte and the medical center. We had actually gone into a left hand curve a little too fast, but of course I was merely making every move at the same speed as the trooper to our front. When I looked back to see if Adriana had negotiated the curve as well, I suddenly saw spinning lights behind her. Harlan Williams's unit was out of control and leaving the roadway. Another car which appeared to have the same headlight configuration as the vehicle which I thought had been tailing us had apparently pulled the same type of PIT maneuver used by the police on Harlan's car. Now the subject vehicle had zeroed in on Adriana's van.

Upon hearing the skidding tires of Harlan's cruiser and watching the Chrysler 300 move in on the van, I was temporarily at a loss as to what I should do. While I was yelling out "*You asshole son of a bitch,*" which the President must have thought referred to him, I made sure Adriana was not right upon me. I then spun the Suburban in the middle of the road until we were in the opposite lane facing the other direction. Adriana had now come to a complete stop. My headlights reflected the astonishment in her face. Wasting no time, I gunned the old beast by her and slammed the left front end of my bumper into the driver's side door of the silver Chrysler. Both vehicles now at a dead stop, perpendicular to one another, I saw the driver's and passenger's windows slide down.

"*Get down!*", I bellowed. He did. I did the same, just in time before a spray of bullets took out my windshield clean through to the back glass. As my bumper was still jammed in against the side of the Chrysler, I accelerated, keeping the pedal on the floor. The Suburban began pushing the car off the road until its right side wheels crossed over the shoulder which then caused the entire vehicle to slide over the sharp embankment and turn over what looked like three or four times. I jumped out to assess my handiwork and saw that the car had come to rest against some pretty good sized boulders down the grassy hill about 40 feet away. If the car's passengers were wearing their seat belts, probably just bumps and bruises. If not, maybe some broken heads and necks. Or could we be that fortunate?

I then ran to see if Adriana and her passengers were okay. They were...just frightened half to death. Finally, I started running back about five hundred feet to where Harlan's unit had left the roadway. The car had spun into a tree, but all three of the occupants were now out of the car looking up the road in our direction.

"Nice going, Bruce," Harlan said. "I guess your instincts were correct about that car. He was smart enough to go by us when we turned off back in Fairlea and then stopped off somewhere to wait till we moved back onto 219."

It was at that moment something must have imploded in my brain. Maybe it was a temporary spark of insanity. Maybe I had just freaking had enough. I then turned without word and strode back to the Adriana's van. Sticking my head through the open driver's door, I said, "I want you to listen carefully, sweetheart. Go now to the fish camp. Don't stop for anything. Joanie, you see to her and the First Lady's safety. There's plenty of food in the freezer and an arsenal of hardware. Adriana knows where the guns are. No one knows about the place and you'll be safe there."

"What are you going to do?" she asked me.

"I'm getting the President some medical help and then going to get him to safe grounds somewhere. I don't know at this point if even Washington is safe."

Smithers shook her head. "No, Mr. McGowan, there's a helicopter coming in that will take him to Andrews tonight."

"Not going to happen, Joanie." I then gave Adriana a quick kiss on the lips. She registered her protest as well.

"Listen to her, Skip. She's responsible for both of their safety. She..."

"No. We're leaving. You know the drill. We talked about a day like this. You know what to do. Keep your cell charged and call me when you get to the camp. Now go! Don't stop for anyone or any*thing*."

I turned quickly and charged back to the Suburban. After jumping in, I threw the car into reverse, reset myself in the road and headed back in the opposite direction.

"Are you all right, Mr. President? I hope you didn't get banged up."

"I'm fine, Bruce. What are you doing?"

I looked over at him and then turned my attention back to the road. "Change of plans. It's not going to be safe at the hospital. I'm taking you somewhere else."

As we passed by Harlan Williams and his wrecked cruiser, he yelled. "Bruce, where are you going...?" His voice trailed off as I picked up speed. I didn't even make eye contact with him as we passed. Yeah. I think the screws finally came loose. There would be a hell of a lot more people now looking for us.

Chapter Eight

In my rearview mirror I saw that Adriana had pulled away as well leaving Harlan Williams and the troopers from his detachment to deal with whoever was in the banged up Chrysler. So why did I take off? That's what the President was asking me.

I responded, "You and I both have huge bulls eyes painted on us, sir. First and foremost, I don't want our ladies to be anywhere around us. They'll be safe at the McGowan fish cabin. It also appears that even with a State Police escort, whoever this relentless terrorist element is, they're not bashful about trying to get to you. And as for who you can trust, well it's surely not the people assigned to protect you. You can only trust one person, Mr. President, and you're looking at him."

"My Chief of Staff has set up trustworthy people to extract the Mrs and me out of here tonight, Bruce. I think you're bein' a bit too paranoid here. I have confidence that Mr. Kessler and the Bureau will come through and send the people that will make that happen."

For a long moment, I didn't say anything to rebut his plea. Maybe I *was* being somewhat a renegade, but having your home shot up and then being pursued by anarchists at every turn can make one paranoid. And whether I liked it or not, the responsibility for the biggest fish in America's pond had been thrust squarely on my shoulders. If I in any way facilitated turning him over to *bad* feds, that's something that would haunt me the rest of my days.

"Mr. President, does it not seem just a little coincidental that thirty minutes after speaking on the phone with your Chief of Staff, a car full of goons made a play for you as we were on the way to the medical center?"

"You're thinkin' that the very man I've known for more than twenty years and has even stayed a number of times at my ranch is either in cahoots with terrorists or may even be drivin' the train?"

"I don't know what to think at this point. This terrorist element is obviously pretty damn wide-spread and may have even infiltrated other federal departments. Believe me when I say that this was one elaborate plan that has involved a lot of people. You've seen the evidence that there are radicals out there who are not afraid to attack any law enforcement we have engaged for protection. So, who else can we turn to? There's only one other person I can trust implicitly. I've known him since he was a baby. He can also take a look at your wounds."

"Who's that?"

I looked over at him and smiled. "My brother."

McGowan and Sons Funeral Home is about a half mile off 219. What bothered me about landing there is that both the good *and* bad feds might have known that the business was in my family and had already staked it out. But my primary concern was to first get the President patched up before more bleeding began and infection set in. Besides being a mortician, my brother was both a medical doctor and the county's assistant coroner. The back room in the large funeral parlor also had a half dozen body drawers called cold chambers. So when the M.E., who was likely still at

Wolf Laurel examining all of the bodies was done with his work, he might temporarily put them on ice with Joey.

"You're taking me where? I only have some buckshot in my shoulder, Bruce; I don't plan on takin' a dirt nap."

I think I *needed* something right at that moment to make me chuckle. "We'll make sure he won't keep you, sir."

Just before turning onto Crater Road, my cell phone went off. Harlan Williams. I wondered if I should even bother answering the call. However, Harlan had been a good friend and I owed him the courtesy.

"Okay, I know what you're going to say."

"I'm sure you do. Get your ass back here. I don't know what's in your head, but in running out on your security, you're putting the President in a hell of a lot of danger."

"Like he hasn't been in any danger all night?"

"You need me and my officers for protection, Bruce. You can't be a lone wolf out there."

"The more police and police units there are, the more attention that attracts. You guys would be magnets and the terrorists have shown they're not afraid to take you out if necessary."

"If the governor has to activate the Guard to provide the necessary security for the President, I'll get him on the phone right now. You get on back here."

"Did you get the bastards in the Chrysler?"

"Don't try to change the subject, Bruce. But yeah, one of them is dead and the other unconscious and looking *near* dead. Now turn yourself around and bring the President to me. I got a bunch more troopers on the way."

"Can't do that, Harlan. At least not just yet. Be back in touch." I then flipped my phone shut.

I noticed that smoke or steam or something was now spewing from under the hood of the old Suburban. Could be from one of the bullets that penetrated its armor back at the airport or maybe when I smashed into the Chrysler back near Ronceverte, the radiator got itself punctured. I was close to the funeral home anyway, so I pulled off onto the edge of the street under some hickory trees and sat for a few minutes to where I could see the entrance to McGowan and Sons. The *'Sons'* was now just Joey. Dad left the business to both us boys in his will. Years ago I had some financial interest in the place, but as my *personal* interest dwindled, I turned over my half to my brother. So would he still be there this late at night? Before I went up and tried the door, I needed to call him.

He answered. "Brewster."

"Are you still working?"

"Aren't I always? Preacher Wilkins died early this afternoon and I just finished draining his blood."

"Vampire."

"What have you been doing today?" he asked.

"Oh, not much. Entertaining the President and First lady, killing bad guys, you know, the usual stuff."

"Funny. How about some fishing tomorrow?"

"No. Hey, man, I got a bit of a problem right now. I'm sitting just outside and need to come in."

"Well, what's stopping you? You have a key."

"Are you alone?"

"Does Preacher Wilkins count? What's going on, Bruce. You sound strange."

"Has anyone come by tonight or have you seen anybody in the parking lot?"

"No, Brucie. Look, just get your butt in here. Geez."

"I'm pulling around back by the hearse garage as we speak. I'll come in the rear door."

"Why so secretive?"

"See you in a couple."

Before I moved out, with the aid of my night vision scope I canvassed the street and funeral home parking lot for vehicles that looked like they might be driven by terrorists. At least what they *usually* drive...large, high dollar sedans or SUVs with blacked-out windows. But, no vehicles at all in the parking lot or on the perimeter of the funeral home. A ten year old Dodge Ram sat in front of a nearby house on the side of the street and on down was a Honda Civic with a different color right fender in an adjacent driveway. Satisfied with my findings, I then moved out.

I parked my spewing albatross beside the Lincoln family car which Joey uses as his personal ride most days. He didn't know it, but I was going to have to borrow it. We exited and I shoved the MP5 into the President's hands while I hung my XDM down by my side. I hoped my key to the back door that led directly into the morgue area still worked. It did. We then entered and closed the door behind us.

"Joey!" I called. "We're in."

His voice bellowed from the embalming room, "We? Is Adriana with you?" He then began walking down the hallway in our direction. "I thought she told me she'd never come back here..." He stopped when he saw our two forms, noting that the *second* one was not Adriana. "Uh, hello."

"Hello, Joey," the President greeted.

When the light hit our faces, I thought Joey would drop his eye teeth. "Are you...who I think you are?"

"Who do you *think* I am?"

"You're either the President or somebody has cloned him."

"Well, no one has cloned me that I know of."

"Holy crap, Bruce. You weren't kidding. Uh...hello, Mr. President."

Joey peeled off his right glove and held out his hand. The President switched the MP5 to his left hand and they shook.

A frown came over Joey's face. "You're bleeding, sir."

"That's one reason we're here," I said. "I also wasn't kidding when I said I had taken down some bad guys...terrorists to be exact. The President and his wife decided to stay a couple of days with us and tonight several gunman raided Wolf Laurel. The President took some pellets from a shot gun."

"You didn't take him to the hospital?"

"Long story, Joey. We don't have much time. Can you remove the shot and patch him up? We have to make tracks."

"You bet. Mr. President, please follow me. Unfortunately, I'll have to put you on one of the metal slabs."

"Just don't get carried away and embalm me." And then he laughed.

Joey chuckled nervously as well. I didn't know if it was because he was anxious about actually meeting the President or operating on him. Maybe he feared something might go wrong with the surgery. MRSA infection, pulmonary embolism, sepsis. Of course if there *was* a problem, he could plead *not guilty on grounds of being an undertaker.*

"And by the way, can you also patch up my head?" I asked him.

He as much brushed me off. "I'll get to you later. You're not that bad."

Joey then placed a sheet and blanket on the slab. "Please lie back, sir, while I grab some instruments. I hope Preacher Wilkins under that sheet on the table next to you doesn't freak you out."

"It's not the *dead* that troubles me tonight, Joey."

While my brother was collecting the instruments he needed, I helped the President off with his blood-crusted shirt, which caused him a bit of discomfort. Joey is not a practical joker like me. If *I* was the one rounding up the surgical tools, instead of a scalpel, forceps and surgical stapler, I'd have returned with my handsaw, hammer and chisel just to get a rise out of the patient. But maybe not with *this* patient, the man who was America's equivalent to a king.

Joey then began assessing the wound. "Hmm, not too bad. I don't think the shot went too deep and appears there are no bones broken. Assume you want to stay awake while I do this. I can give you a local and you won't feel anything but a little pressure."

"Correct. No knockout drug," he responded.

I watched as Joey cleansed the damaged area with a surgical disinfectant he referred to as Certol. The President winced a couple of times and I think I felt his pain as well. Then out came the needle. Joey tenderly placed four or five shots into the flesh and as I don't like needles, it was *me* that winced this time.

As the shoulder was in the process of turning numb, I got Joey off to the side and filled him in on all that had occurred this long, long day. I also warned him that sooner or later, somebody, maybe feds, maybe terrorist types, may even come by the mortuary looking for the President and me, them thinking we might consider the place a safe haven. I also suggested after he was done with the President he swing by his house and take the wife to a motel for a couple of days. He could let his co-director handle the business. And sorry that all this likely exposed he and Cora to danger. But, such are the perils and pitfalls of being my brother. Something that Adriana had long since begun to understand as my wife.

My brother attended to the President's wounds as skillfully as any of the ER surgeons over at the medical center. One by one, after being dug out by forceps, I heard eight pellets clang into his metal pan. "Appears the impact to the shoulder was more of a glancing blow. Considering this is triple-aught buck, a direct hit closer in would have absolutely shattered your shoulder, sir."

"Unfortunately, the remainder of the shot struck one of my best agents in the head. He died instantly."

Joey shook his head. "That's tough."

In less than a half hour the surgery was over. Although Joey didn't have an x-ray machine to assure all the .36 shot was removed, he was satisfied he had gotten everything. Taking a few seconds to cauterize the area, he then began the stapling process. The wound was disinfected again and bandaged.

"Well, Mr. President, not quite as good as new, but this should hold you until you're seen at a hospital. In about an hour you'll feel some pain. I have some pain capsules to give you."

"I guess you don't find much use for the pills considering the kind of customers you have."

I actually thought that was funny and laughed.

"I'm glad to hear you laugh, Bruce," the President remarked. "Not much chance to do that these last couple of hours, eh?"

I was just about to add some of my own wit, when we heard a buzzer go off.

"Someone's ringing the door bell out front. I'll see who it is," Joey said.

I grabbed his arm. "You expecting anyone?"

"No, but maybe a member of Mr. Wilkins' family has stopped by."

"Don't assume that, Joey. Could be people we don't want to see."

He held up one finger. "Let me check it out. I have a security camera mounted above the door out there. I can see who it is on the monitor." While the most important man in the world lay recuperating on the slab, Joey went to his office. I followed.

As we both studied the monitor, in the dim light we could make out two figures. One was a large-frame clean-shaven male wearing a ball cap and parka and the other a medium-sized skinhead fellow sporting a goatee. Neither looked like feds and I couldn't pick up any letters on their outer wear that read FBI or POLICE. But what shouted *bad guys* to me was the Uzi the smaller man had hanging off his shoulder.

"Do you see it?" I pointed to the weapon clearly visible on the screen.

"Yeah."

"Obviously, you don't want to answer the door. So let's see what they do."

We watched as both men stood for a full minute ringing the doorbell every fifteen seconds. Finally, the larger one looked up and saw the camera. From a shoulder holster beneath his coat he pulled out a semi-automatic pistol, lifted it high above his head and smashed the camera's lens. The monitor then went blank.

"Come on. Let's get back to the President," I said.

Once back in the embalming room, we found him just a little out of it, but eyes still open. Then suddenly we heard the perps smashing through the front door of the building. I thought about taking the MP5 down the hallway and spraying the front door, but for two reasons I didn't. First, the door was made of steel and the bullets would ricochet back. Secondly, there could also be others busting through the back door and I didn't want to be that far away from the President. "You need to hide us somewhere, Joey, and then get the hell out of here."

Joey said, "I got an idea. Mr. President, it's too soon to move you. You could go into shock. I'm just going to throw this sheet over you, but you have to make sure you lie here without moving...play like Preacher Wilkins there. Bruce, I'm shoving you in one of the cold chambers."

"What?"

He pointed to the wall of silver drawers where bodies were stored either waiting to be embalmed or to be dressed out for show.

"You know I'm claustrophobic."

"Either that or one of the coffins. I got no place else to stuff you where you can't be found. Now get in."

Oh boy.

We suddenly heard the sound of wood splintering around the metal door. "Sir, it won't be long till they break through. Please lie very still."

"I will."

To make it look as though the embalming process was set to begin, Joey shoved the line to the aspirator up under the President's sheet and then placed the embalming tank next to the slab. While Joey made sure his 'body' was completely covered, I then took some of the President's blood from the surgical tray and splattered it on the sheet at the drain line. Perfect staging of a corpse being prepped for an embalming.

I also turned off the cell phones...mine and Clayton's. They didn't need to give us away.

"I'm staying here in the room, Bruce. I'll go over and uncover Wilkins to start sewing his eyes closed. If and when they charge in here, they'll see what I'm doing. Maybe it'll gross them out. If they act interested in the other body, I'll just tell them what's going on under the sheet will give them nightmares. Now, go jump in the drawer. They must've gotten in. No more banging going on."

Joey was clever, all right. And why not? He's a McGowan.

I climbed into one of the floor level cold chambers and laid on my belly facing the room. I left the door to the drawer partially open, about four inches, so that I could peer out to see if the intruders would be curious as to what was under the sheet. Curiosity would then kill both those cats.

Hearing their voices in the hallway, I positioned myself in the chamber on my elbows with the muzzle of my .45 trained on their avenue of approach. I noticed that the drawer was hard under my right elbow, but mushy under the left one. I shuddered to think what it was that Joey could have left in the drawer, but upon closer examination was relieved to see it was only a ham and cheese sandwich. Joey and his damned habit of placing food in the cold chambers. Obviously too cheap to buy a fridge.

The intruders seemed to be taking their time and I suspected they were searching the main portion of the building...both of the viewing parlors, the family visitation room, the casket room, lifting the lids on the coffins, and finally into Joey's office before working their way back to where we were. Sporadically, I kept hearing their voices, saying things like "nothing in here." But as the voices became louder I saw at last their shadows moving further down the hall toward our location.

When the two men entered the room, the larger one yelled to Joey, *"You! Freeze what you're doing!"*

But Joey yelled back, *"What are you people doing in here and what do you want!"*

"Is anybody else in here with you?"

"Just the two corpses lying there. I'll say it again, what do you want?"

Through the small crack made by the open door I was getting a better look at the two men. They were *definitely* not feds. Both were caucasian and the big man appearing in control had either a Boston or upper New York brogue.

I then thought the bald goatee man was acting a little too interested in the body under the sheet and that he might be thinking about pulling it off for a look. That would be *his* mistake. But then he turned his face toward Joey. "Where is your brother!" he barked.

"My brother? Hey, I'm not my brother's keeper."

"You're some kind of smart ass, aren't you?"

"Why are you asking about him?"

"He has something we want."

"Well, I haven't seen him. And you people need to leave."

I wondered in retrospect if the goons had done a thorough recon of the outside and recognized my Suburban out back. But then again, maybe they hadn't been briefed on what I was driving. My hope was that they were so hurriedly focused on finding us, they had gone directly to the front door

As the bigger man started walking toward Joey, my stupid brother decided to pick up a scalpel. The man then stopped, pulled his pistol and aimed it at Joey's head. I started to plug the varmint right there, but as I knew they merely wanted information out of him, they weren't going to kill him. Right now, anyway. And I also wanted to see and hear more to determine if I could *learn* more. By the way, Joey, not good to bring a scalpel to a gunfight. Joey then smartly laid the blade down on the sheet where the President lay and the man who was now within an arm's reach snatched Joey up by his shirt.

"What's your name?"

"I think you know it or you wouldn't be here looking for my brother."

"Now you look, undertaker, if you don't want to be laying on one of them slabs a cold stiff yourself, tell me where that goddam brother of yours is."

Before Joey could answer, goatee man who I saw had been eyeing my chamber said, "Why is that door partly open?"

This attracted big man's attention and he released his grip on Joey. Joey quickly replied, "I just didn't completely shut it a while ago."

"You store stiffs in there, don't you? I'd think you'd want it closed to keep it cool inside. Alright, get down on the floor on your belly, hands on top of your head where I can see them."

Slowly, Joey did as instructed.

Both of the men then brought their weapons up as though they were going to unload on the chamber. I knew in less than two seconds, I could split both of their skulls wide open. But they didn't fire. I also knew it was too dark inside the chamber drawer for them to see anything, but as they continued walking cautiously toward me they tried their best. If they looked hard enough they would have been able to see the very big muzzle of my XDM out of which some very big bullets would make some very big holes in their heads.

Skinhead man then slung his Uzi around his shoulder and began walking toward the chamber while big man moved up and locked in a bead on my position with his pistol. When the smaller man placed his hand on the handle and then quickly threw open the door, he got the surprise of his life. Something that actually surprised him to *death*. As I was firing the round that smacked him between the eyes, the larger man's eyes suddenly rolled back. Gradually, he then sank to his knees and fell face first onto the floor. Quickly, I threw open the chamber door and saw the President standing over him with Joey's bloody scalpel in his hand. Not only had he slipped off the slab, but he had slipped the blade into the man's cerebellum.

I climbed back out of the drawer, wiped the mayonnaise off my elbow and shook the President's hand...which was already shaking. He dropped the scalpel and looked down at the man whose life he had just ended. "I...I've never killed..."

"I know, Mr. President. The first time you take a life, it hits your insides like a ton of bricks. I hope you'll never have to do it again. Unfortunately, it only gets easier when you have to do it again." Actually, the saying goes something like this: 'After the first time you've tasted blood, each kill gets a hell of a lot easier.' But I wasn't going to phrase it like that.

Joey then returned to his feet just as the President suddenly seemed to lose his balance. He quickly grabbed him by the shoulders. "Sir, are you doing all right?"

"Yeah, I'm fine. Just a little woozy." He looked again at the two dead goons. "Looks like we took care of business, Bruce."

"Believe me, this won't be the last of them."

"And the bodies keep pilin' up. I know these are bad people who are either wantin' to take me prisoner or kill me, but don't you think it's time to try endin' this? You took charge after my agents lost their lives and got us out of some pretty hairy situations, but there *are* agency people I know we can trust. I gotta get the Mrs and meet the Nighthawk at the airport."

"I agree there are people out there who aren't connected to whatever terrorist faction this is, but can you be sure who they are? And then we don't know whether there are any terrorists lying in wait for us at the airport. The State Police and FBI I hope have secured the site, but this is a determined, highly motivated terrorist organization and they will *not* give up their mission."

"Then get Mr. Kessler back on the phone and see what protective measures he's implementin' before we leave. Like I said, I trust the man. I appointed him to his job. He wouldn't betray me and he *will* see to my safe delivery back to Washington."

"I hope you're right. But please understand, I cannot and *will* not give you up. If I get the slightest whiff of somebody or some*thing* rotten waiting on us, you and I will suddenly disappear from everybody. Bad guys *and* good guys. I have keen instincts, Mr. President, and they never let me down."

"Fair enough, Bruce. Now call my Chief of Staff."

Chapter Nine

"Mr. President. If I might beg your indulgence, I'd like to make another call first. To my wife."

"Yeah, please do."

I turned both cell phones back on and then hit the number *one* on mine. Adriana answered after the third ring.

"What's going on, Skip?"

"Just staying low. Are you there yet?"

"Almost. Turning down the road now. I was going to call you when we got there."

"How's the First Lady?"

The President picked up his ears.

"Confused. She's not sure you're doing the right thing. Neither am I, Skip."

"It's temporary, Adriana. I had to get him some treatment. You *know* what happened on the way to the medical center. We couldn't continue there."

"Did you go somewhere else?"

"Joey fixed him up."

"You took him to the funeral home? Oh, wait a minute." I could then hear her talking to someone in the background. "The First Lady wants to speak to her husband."

"Hold on." I handed the phone off to the President. "The First Lady, sir."

"Sweetheart?" he said.

He listened.

"Yeah, I'm fine." A pause. "You heard what? Oh, yeah, the funeral home. Bruce brought me here to his brother Joey's place of business. He's also a physician...and don't worry, I'm still alive and kickin.' Got as good care here as I could have at Walter Reed." More listening. "Okay, I know. We'll get through this. Bruce has taken care of things to this point. It'll be over soon. We'll be on that bird back to Washington shortly. You know I love you, Pet. Don't worry about me. I'll be all right." He then handed the phone back to me. "Your Mrs."

"Skip?"

"I'll keep you informed," I said to her. "Stay ready. I don't know if it'll be tonight. Prepare to stay there at least until morning. I have to be convinced about the people we hand him off to. It's still dangerous around here. Bad guys busted in here at Joey's."

"What happened?" she asked me.

"Not to worry. They were neutralized."

"I'm scared, sweetheart. Give this up and let's get back to our life."

"We'll see. But gotta go, Adriana. Love you." I ended the call quickly. Any further discussion of the matter was going to be futile. I didn't need to listen to any dissuading dialogue. From *anyone*. I just needed some time to think...and strategize.

"Now the call to Kessler?" the President urged.

I switched cells and touched the number on Clayton's phone.

"Mr. McGowan, I was just going to call you. Did you get the President to the medical center?"

"What do *you* think, Mr. Kessler?" I was testing him.

"I don't understand. Did you or did you not?"

"It wasn't ten minutes after your call we were attacked on the way there. A bit of a coincidence, don't you think?"

The President raised his eyebrows.

"What are you insinuating, Mr. McGowan?" Kessler asked. I guess I had struck a nerve.

"Just speculating, Mr. Kessler."

"If you think I or the people I contacted to make ready the President's admission at that medical center have had anything to do with the attempt on his life, you're depraved, McGowan. I resent any implication and furthermore demand you..." He broke off his sentence." Is the President right there with you?"

"Yes. And he will *continue* to be until I can get him into the right hands."

"Put him on the line, McGowan."

For the second time in a matter of minutes, I handed off a call to the President.

"Hello, Arnie. Uh, yes, I know. He did not intend to suggest..." He paused to listen. "I understand, Arnie, but he's a good man. Mr. McGowan has faithfully demonstrated his ability to keep me out of harm's way." Again listening. "If I heard you right, the bird will be on the tarmac at 2330. It's what now..." He looked at his watch. "...2145. We'll be there." Listening. "Who?" Long pause. "All right, got it. Sounds good. I'll tell him. Thanks, Arnie."

When the phone was back in my hands, the President filled me in on his conversation.

"Bruce, Mr. Kessler who is my gatekeeper in times of peril, is already pulling together the Crisis Cabinet in the White House Situation Room. The Vice President is prepared to assume the presidential role should something go south with me. Secret Service Director Tom Campanello, Secretary of State Mahoney and the Pentagon have already conferenced and two companies of Marines on C130s have been deployed. They're slated to arrive at the airport by 23:30 at which time Nighthawk will land. We are to be there ten minutes after that. This gives us a little more than an hour and a half. You and I are to meet Campanello's Senior Agent in Charge, Curt Tyson, who's somewhere here in the county, at 22:45 at a location already secured, and he along with three of his people will take us in to the airport."

"That's the SAC that Clayton was trying to get hold of back at Wolf Laurel just before he died. And Tyson has other agents with him?"

"There's always a back-up team."

"Then why didn't Tyson respond and have his people ready to roll when the action started?" I asked. "Neither was he at the airport when we got there."

"I can't answer that, Bruce. All I know at this point is that plans are in place to get the Mrs and me out of here. You will need to tell Adriana to meet us at that rendezvous point."

"Which is where?"

"A school here in the county. Jackson Elementary. Do you know where that is?"

"I do, sir. It's located near Sam Black Church, as inconveniently remote as you can get. Why way out there? Why not closer in to the airport?"

"I don't have the answer, Bruce. I..."

Now *my* cell suddenly rang. I looked at the dial. Restricted, it read.

"McGowan," I answered.

"We spoke earlier. You're a very troublesome prick."

"I do my best. What do you want?"

"Save yourself and your family some grief and place your cargo in my hands. All you have to do is drop him off to where I tell you and drive away. Your wife continues to live and you go back to your golf game at the country club."

I'm not a fan of people threatening my family.

"I met the goons you sent a while ago. They tried to rough up my brother. But then they met my .45 and now they're shaking hands with the devil. Don't mention my wife again or I'll hunt you down and stop your heart."

"It just goes to show you; I can get to *anyone*, eventually."

"And I can *easily* get to assholes like you. So, what's your agenda? What do you want?"

That's when the President's antenna went up. He whispered, "Who is that, Bruce?"

I mouthed, "Terrorist bastard."

"My demands right now are that you surrender the President or it will result in an extremely horrific scenario."

I then touched the *speaker* icon on the phone so that the President could listen. "Go on. What's the scenario?"

"Just do what I tell you."

"No. The ball's still in your court. You made a threat. I'm supposed to deliver to you the President or else *what*?"

There was a pause. The voice knew he was not getting anywhere with me. "I can hear that you put your cell on speaker, McGowan. So, Mr. President, here's the ultimatum...if McGowan does not surrender you to me, our people are prepared to detonate an RDD (a dirty bomb) in a small city, which I will not name, that will release enough radioactive material throughout to cause sickness and ultimate death to everyone living there. And that's only for starters. Every day you stay on the run, one goes off in another city."

The President clenched his fists. "All right, yeah I'm listenin'. Who are you with and what're you about?"

"Who we are doesn't matter right now. You just need to give it up. Once you're in our hands, then we have big enough bait to land our objective."

"Which is?"

"You will soon find out."

"So, am I talkin' to somebody in charge or are you just a piss ant pawn?"

"You're speaking with someone who can not only save the life of your wife and children... and be assured we do have long enough arms to get to them...but thousands of innocent U.S. citizens."

"You should know that the United States does not give in to terrorists' demands."

"You have your warning. And you hear this as well, McGowan. If you do not surrender to our representatives by eleven o'clock tonight, that's 2300, we will detonate the bomb on a city of sleeping people. Think of all of the children and babies who will die slow, horrible deaths."

The President's face became pale and his lips trembled. "I will tell you this. If you follow through with your threat, there will be no place on God's green earth that you will be able to hide. I will engage every resource I have at my fingertips to find you and bring you and your terrorist regime to justice. Then I will issue an executive order to have your ass prosecuted and executed promptly, without appeal, before a firing squad. And I will personally be there behind that big caliber gun that will place the first bullet through your heart."

I wondered if somehow the President was actually my fraternal twin and had become separated from my family at birth. I reminded myself to check out his birth date. He sounded like *me* talking the game. But then, after the President had finished with his little soliloquy, it was *me* that took over the conversation. I didn't want him to burst a vessel just having come out of surgery.

And then the light bulb went on in my head. "You know what, maggot? I'm very good at remembering voices. It sometimes might take me a few minutes, but considering I have meticulously keen hearing and can distinguish voice tenor and intonation very readily, I now know who you are...*Agent Franks*."

The President mouthed in amazement, "*That's Steffen Franks?*"

There was no response on the other end.

"I take it from your silence that I guessed correctly," I added. "So, is Agent Bartow also with you?"

Finally, he spoke. "Someone will find Agent Bartow's body in the woods near your house where I left him. He turned his back to light up a cigarette. I always told him that smoking could be hazardous to his health."

"So, it was you, Curlick and Nazer, huh Steffen? How many more in the agency?"

"I misjudged you back there at your house, McGowan. Sitting around the dinner table listening to you, I took you for a soft bellied innkeeper capable of nothing more than killing a large pizza and a six pack of Bud."

"You have no earthly idea what I'm capable of, asshole. But as God is my witness, you're soon to find out."

He laughed. "Here's the deal, hero. You cart the President west on Route 60 where you'll enter some very attractive farmland. Take a right onto County Road 30 and drop him a quarter mile down at a lean-to on the right. It's a school bus stop. Then you drive away. Once you're out of there, we'll pick him up."

The President jumped in. "That's not going to happen and you know it, Franks, you treasonous bastard."

"Tsk, tsk, Mr. President. Temper now. You know what needs to be done. Only you can save all those people including the innocent little kids. 2300, gentlemen." Those were his last words.

I flipped my phone closed and locked eyes with the President. "Two scenarios given us, sir. One, per Kessler, you are to be delivered to an agent named Tyson, who your dying man Bill Clayton couldn't seem to get on his phone during the attack, or two, you agree to be dropped in the hands of a *rogue* agent, who is a terrorist, or a bomb goes off."

"Is that a question or are you telling me this is a choice?"

"You know we're not delivering you into terrorist hands, but how do we know we're not doing the same thing when we meet up with Tyson? Why does he want to meet well west of the area in a schoolyard out in the country?"

"You're talking like you're not planning for us to meet up with him."

"I haven't decided yet, sir."

His eyes narrowed and I could tell he was getting steamed. "Bruce, do I need to give you a direct order?"

"I'll do what you tell me to do, Mr. President, but you just need to look at the situation through the same lens I am. Maybe I'm just a little too cautious..."

He smiled. "I'd say *anal*."

I nodded and returned the smile. "Yeah, anal. But let's do *this*. I don't want Adriana, Agent Smithers and the First Lady to be exposed any more than they need to be out there. We meet with Tyson and his people, and if all's well, I will call Adriana and she'll bring your wife to meet us at a designated area on 219 near the airport."

"With a battalion of Marines and the FBI sittin' out there at the airport, I'd say it would be safe for them to just drive on in there to meet us."

"If that's the case, sir, we could then be driving to the airport ourselves. So why do we need to meet Special Agent Tyson fifteen miles way out in the country in order to get there?"

"I see your point. I don't know, Bruce."

"I have an idea. It'll involve some Sneaky Pete work, though. Joey, I need to borrow your car."

"The Lincoln?"

"Yeah."

"What's wrong with the Suburban?"

"It's been shot up, chewed up and banged up. I think the radiator is punctured."

"So, you'd like to expose Mary to the same detriments."

"Mary?"

"The Lincoln, Bruce. That's what we're talking about, isn't it?"

"I get it. Mary...Lincoln. Corny, brother."

"Bring it back with no bullet holes."

"If it gets chewed up, the President will send you one of his. One that's bulletproof. Right, sir?"

He grinned. "Absolutely."

Before we left, I rifled the two gunmen's clothing for IDs or any items that might give us clues as to what organization they were a part of, who dispatched them and what the group's agenda was. They were clean. Not even one slip of paper. This of course was SOP for terrorists. If they happened to be killed or captured they would not have any items on them that would tie them to anyone or any group.

"Go ahead and stick these stiffs in cold storage. They'll be sorted out along with the other bodies lying all over the county." I then handed Joey my .45. "Keep it handy just in case anybody else decides to come looking for us. But get the hell out of here as soon as you can."

I doubted that any other goons had been dispatched to McGowan and Sons to look for the President and me. However, I was sure their people were everywhere else canvassing the county stretching from the medical center to the airport to the Greenbrier resort. Still, when we exited the funeral home out the back door to where the beast was parked, I scanned not only the rear lot, but backyards of adjacent houses and a nearby tree line with my pocket night vision device to discount the probability of anybody of the terrorist persuasion lurking about in the night. Satisfied, I took out Joey's key bob, hit the remote to unlock the door to the Lincoln and asked the President to hop in.

While he was getting situated in the front seat, I entered the Suburban, first securing my commo pack and then grabbing up my .308 sniper rifle from the concealed floorboard, plus my other handgun, my Glock .40 cal, and abundant ammo for both. Joey would hang onto my XDM.

Before I left, I told Joey to "Go home to pick up your wife and make yourself scarce. Don't go to the fishing camp, though. You might be followed and that will expose the First Lady. In the meantime, I'll be busy keeping the hounds of hell from getting to the President."

"Gotcha, big brother. Hey, wait a minute. I didn't fix your head."

In all of the excitement, I had forgotten about my ouchie. I then checked myself out in the lighted visor mirror. I guessed the wound had clotted on its own to a point where the blood was no longer running down my face. Blood had crusted along my forehead and eyelids. "Oh, well. I've got so many scars already from bullets whacking my body, what's one more? My hair will grow back and cover this one up anyway." One more look in the mirror at the dried blood and I added, "I ain't pretty, but I ain't dead either."

It was just after ten fifteen when we pulled out of the lot. After chugging around in my ten year old Suburban, I was in high cotton behind the wheel of the Lincoln. I was still apprehensive to say the least about heading all the way out the interstate to Western Greenbrier County to place the President in the hands of one Special Agent Tyson, someone I didn't have a good feeling about. And if it was Kessler who made the arrangements, maybe I didn't have such a good feeling about *him* either.

I had an idea. I not only owed Harlan Williams an explanation for my actions but some professional courtesy as an officer of the law. I got him on his cell as we pulled back onto Highway 219.

"I wondered when you were going to resurface. Whether you know it or not, you're in deep shit with the feds."

"How's that?"

"They think you're a renegade who's now kidnapped the President. If you wanted to kidnap somebody, couldn't it have been someone a little less important...like the Secretary of Arts and Basket Weaving?"

"Funny, Harlan. Hey, I need your help."

"Me help *you*? I'd be helping myself right into a jail cell."

"What's happening with you right now?"

"I'm out at the medical center waiting on one of these yay-hoos from that Chrysler 300 to come out of his coma so we can get information out of him."

"You got officers there with you?"

"I got officers all over the place watching for bad guys we don't even know who they are. Did you get the President treated for his wounds?"

"Joey operated on him."

"Your undertaker brother. That must have been fun to watch. He didn't embalm him afterwards, did he?" And then he chuckled.

"Good one, Harlan. Did you find any cell phones on those bozos in the Chrysler?"

""We secured one and will turn it over to the FBI."

"Good. Maybe we'll be able to retrieve information about their hierarchy and who dispatched them. All right, I got something else. I need you to break loose and meet me at the Chevy dealership on 219 near the interstate. The President and I are arranging for his and the First Lady's extraction. We have a rendezvous with the Secret Service at the elementary school parking lot in Sam Black Church to hand him over and I need you to escort us."

"You're meeting way out there? Why?"

"My question exactly."

"What time are you meeting them?"

"10:45. Once the handoff is complete, we're back at the airport just after 11:30."

"So you want me to do what?"

"We'll meet up at the dealership. You'll follow behind us on the interstate west to Exit 156. We'll pull off at the gas station there. One thing, Harlan. From now until the handoff, no radio traffic."

"Understood. We get to the gas station, then what?"

"You get to be my emissary."

Chapter Ten

I personally felt a lot safer riding along in the shiny black Lincoln, a vehicle that no one should suspect was containing the President and me. And it didn't hurt to have the unmarked state car that was following me, Harlan and two of his uniformed troopers. Of course in our last mini caravan out on 219 that didn't matter to the baddies in the silver Chrysler who ended up ramming and totaling his patrol unit. I didn't ask Harlan, but I assumed he had *appropriated* his replacement vehicle, the spiffy gray Dodge Charger, from a couple of his men at the medical center.

We hadn't been on the road fifteen minutes when my cell phone rang. Joey.

"Did I forget something?"

"Yeah. *Me*. The feds are here and they're looking for you. They say if I don't tell them where you are, they will hold me for conspiracy and accessory to kidnapping the President."

"How did they know to go there?"

"Well, the bad guys found you here, didn't they? A rookie cop could find out you're my brother and easily connect you to the funeral home."

"Did you ask for IDs? They could be fake agents."

"They showed me badges and I checked their IDs. They're real."

"Are they listening to you making this call?"

"No, they're checking out the bodies you left here. And their car out front. They found their bodies without any trouble where I stuffed them in the cold chambers. I excused myself to the toilet."

"Scared the crap out of you, did they?"

"Funny, bro. Thanks for getting me in this mess. They want to know how these guys got dead."

"Tell them they broke in, you shot one of them and stuck a scalpel in the other. Being my brother, you're naturally a force to be reckoned with. Remember, I left you with my .45, so that would support your story. And no, you haven't seen me."

"All right, I'll make it work. If not, come see me in Sing."

"I'll call you later to let you know what's going on. Get the hell out of there after they leave."

"Unless they ask me to leave with *them*...in handcuffs."

After pulling off the exit and into the Chevron station we parked side by side. Harlan quickly exited and came around to my window. Looking past me toward my passenger, he grinned excitedly like a starry-eyed groupie in line for an autograph from a rock idol. "Are you doing all right, Mr. President? This guy been taking care of you?"

I wanted to jump in and say "Forget it, Harlan. He's not going to offer you the Homeland Security Director's job."

But I let him continue making a salivating ninny out of himself.

"Okay, down big fella. Here's the deal. I'm not absolutely convinced that the people waiting for the President down at that school are good guy agents. Two turncoat agents died in the firefight earlier tonight at my house and then just a while ago I got off the phone with another agent turned terrorist who currently seems to be the big dog running the show. Since terrorists have already infiltrated the President's protection detail and are this widely spread throughout the county, maybe they're also imbedded in this little reception team. And then we've unwittingly delivered him into their hands."

"What do you want me to do, Bruce?"

"If you're good with this, Mr. President, I'd like Captain Williams to first drive in there to meet with Agent Tyson and feel out the situation. If everything looks good for us to come in, he'll call me and we'll go. If not, Harlan, just cautiously exit out of there, but still lie to them that we're on the way."

Harlan nodded. "Okay. I consider myself pretty intuitive as a cop, but is there anything in particular I should be zeroing in on?"

"Tyson should readily identify himself. He's likely going to be pissed it's just you and your troopers showing up. He'll want to know where the President is. Just tell him the President and I are close by in another car. Standing by with him should be several members of his team. There might be others taking up defense positions on the perimeter. You and your troopers need to do a visual on these people. I'm sure you know this, but because this would be considered a national crisis, everybody you see should be members of the Secret Service Evidence Response Team or ERT wearing SWAT gear or something similar. And have badges. They'll also be armed with P90 submachine guns and Glock side arms. If any of them aren't, ask for their IDs. Tyson would expect you to do that. So how about it, Harlan? You still okay with this? It might be a bad deal and things could go south in a hurry."

"What do *you* think, Bruce? *You* know me. Any way I can assist in protecting my President, I'm ready to roll. And by the way, sir, I voted for you. Twice."

The President grinned. "Twice, huh? I hope not on the same day."

Good one, sir.

"Er, uh, just once each term, Mr. President."

I smiled. I had an open shot at some smart-ass quip, but Harlan was doing us a huge service, so I played Mr. Nice. We'd save the juvenile potshots and comebacks for the golf course.

After stepping out of the Lincoln, I then pulled from my commo pouch a pair of GXT 1000 radios complete with wrist mics and ear buds. Even though the President and I would be in a hidden position just under a mile away from the school grounds, the range of the radio was 35 miles, give or take. I handed one of them to Harlan. "We'll use these to keep in touch. This is a wireless unit you can stick in your pocket. And here're your wrist mic and ear bob. Go to Channel 13. I'll walk to the other side of the station and do a radio check."

Harlan grinned at the President. "Like a boy scout, he is. Always ready for whatever. He has more gee whiz toys and weapons than my entire section."

Once I had stepped off enough yards, I brought up my wrist mic. "How do you hear me?"

I heard him reply, "Lima Charlie (Loud and Clear).

I then walked back to the cars. "I'd like you to leave the mic in the *on* position when you approach Tyson so I can hear your conversation. I might not be able to hear *him*, but you can keep me apprised. He'll of course ask you why *you're* there and the President and I are *not*. Just tell him the truth...the State Police, as a local law enforcement asset, is collaborating to help assure the President's security."

"Okay then." He checked his watch. "It's 10:40, we'll move on in."

"Thanks, Harlan. There's a campground on the right on the way to the school. You'll see it about three-quarters of a mile before you get there. That's where we'll be back off the road. I'll be listening. Just tell me to come on in if in your judgment there are no red flags."

We shook hands and he popped a hand salute to the President. Then he and his troopers lit out.

After returning to my seat behind the wheel, I looked over at Eagle One. "And so we wait, sir."

"I've been watching your work with a great deal of admiration, Bruce. Mr. Byrd, God rest his soul, was pretty darn high on you. Said you were the best in the counterterrorism business. The perfect agent. Those were his very words. Of course with all the skills you brought into the job,...Army Ranger, Green Beret, Silver Star in combat, 20 years with the Bureau and decorated with the Shield of Bravery...I'd say you were indeed the perfect agent."

"Mr. President, you are too kind to say so, but I was far from that. How do you know these things about me?"

"I had to do my homework on you before engaging you in those special missions. After the terrorist incidents, one of which actually took place there at Wolf Laurel, I got to know a little something about you. That's why you were chosen to investigate the matter of the village massacre over there in Vietnam and get the goods on the man who did it. I don't get personally involved in much; but on that deal I was compelled to act." He then looked at me with laser beam eyes and asked the very question I dreaded I would one day hear and which would finally put me on the hot seat. "Straight up, Bruce, was it you that killed that congressman?"

I actually didn't know how I was going to answer that. I knew he wouldn't have me prosecuted if I said *yes*. Maybe the worst that happened is that his impression of me would be tainted. I could live with that. Prison, I couldn't. But just at the time something was going to come out of my mouth, I heard Harlan Williams' voice.

"Bruce, we're pulling up now."

I looked at the President and tapped my ear, signaling something was about to happen. He nodded once.

"All right, there are three vehicles...two SUVs and a sedan. I see three people standing by one of the SUVs. One of them is moving toward us. He *is* in SWAT gear and cradling what could be the P90 you mentioned. The others I can't tell. It's pretty dark even though there's a street light on opposite ends of the school ground near the building. Both troopers and I are getting out now. My men are remaining beside the cruiser, but I'm now walking up to meet the man. He has on a toboggan cap and I see his badge. So far so good."

I turned up the volume on the radio so that the President could hear as well. Harlan's footsteps in the gravel were audible.

"Are you Agent Tyson?" I heard him ask.

Faintly, I could hear the response. "Yes."

"I'm State Police Captain Williams. I have two troopers with me."

"What's your purpose here, Captain?"

Harlan must have gotten closer as the voice was now louder and more succinct.

"We understand you're looking to receive a VIP."

"Do you have him with you?"

"No, but he's in position to come in."

"This was not what we were expecting to happen, Captain. Is there a man named McGowan with him?"

"There is."

"Then why aren't both here? My higher had that set up."

"How many men do you have here with you?"

Harlan was handling the dialogue well. Both men were displaying caution.

"Why does that matter?"

"Before the VIP comes on site, they all need to present themselves."

"I have two men behind me."

"That's all?"

"That's all."

"I see three vehicles. Are you saying each of you is driving one? Is that not a waste of resources? I'd think you would have a team of more than three meeting up with the VIP to escort him out to the airport considering the apparent widespread terrorist activity. That being said, I'm sure you were clued in on what went down at McGowan's B&B, at the airport and on the road to the medical center. Yet just the three of you in three separate vehicles sitting way out here fifteen miles from the airport."

I looked over and nodded to the President. Harlan was definitely pressing Tyson's buttons.

"What are you insinuating, Captain?"

"Can you have your two men back there approach?"

"And your reason?"

"If I'm going to give Mr. McGowan and his VIP the green light to come in and meet up with you, I want to see everyone involved here."

There was a long moment no words were exchanged.

"What's happening, Harlan?" I asked.

Under his breath he whispered, "Tyson signaled them to walk forward."

Tyson then said, "All right, satisfied? Now make this happen."

"I would have expected your men to also be wearing tactical gear, Agent Tyson. One has on a parka and the other a leather coat. Neither are identified as law enforcement nor are they wearing badges. Your..." Suddenly I heard a *thwap* and then a choking noise from Harlan's throat. His breathing was now raspy and in just a matter of five seconds there was no sound at all.

"Harlan!" I yelled. *"What's going on?"*

All I could hear from there on was a shuffling of feet in the gravel and someone away from the mic screaming out as if in pain.

"Harlan!"

I waited and listened for his response. For *any* sounds. A few seconds later I then heard men's voices in the background, but nothing more from Harlan Williams. I didn't need that intuitive sixth sense of mine to tell me what just occurred.

"Damn!" I exclaimed.

"What?" asked the President.

"My worst fear realized."

Suddenly I heard clatter on the mic as though someone was handling it. "McGowan," a voice said, "I know you're on the other end of this. You're out there somewhere close by with the President. You had your opportunity to deliver him to us and then your responsibility was over. You could have just done your duty and driven away unscathed. Now there won't be a rock you can crawl under. We will from this moment on pull out all stops to find you."

"You treasonous bastard, what did you do to Captain Williams?"

"He got a little too inquisitive and ate a bullet. Same with his backup."

The words struck me in the chest like a bolt of lightning. The President placed his hand over his mouth and shook his head.

"You will die a horrible death when I come for you, Tyson."

"*You* know where I am. Come on. And by the way, before you try, there are not just three of us as your man assumed."

He was baiting me...counting on my anger to force me out in the open. I had to take a deep breath before my very heart imploded.

"What's your answer, McGowan? You can't win this. You can make it easy on yourself by just dropping your baggage and going back to your safe and uncomplicated life of retirement."

Out of frustration, I dropped my window glass and threw the small hand radio into a nearby tree trunk, smashing it into several pieces. There was no need for further dialogue. He would now personally be on my kill list. Whether or not I was successful in getting Eagle One handed off to someone we could trust, even if I had to drive the President to the guard gate at the White House, I would see that Tyson paid with his life for killing my friend.

"I didn't hear any shooting, Bruce," the President said. "Are you sure it happened? Maybe they just overpowered and clubbed the officers."

"No, they killed them. Used silencers. I heard the sound of the bullet hit Harlan somewhere in the head or throat."

"God."

"Yeah. God. Where is He tonight?"

"What now?"

Actually, I was out of answers. Even though the Lincoln was sitting far enough back in the trees in the roadside park that it couldn't readily be detected, I could see the road. I figured they would be scrambling out of there and heading along that road back toward the interstate. And as much as I wanted to be waiting somewhere alongside the road in ambush, I knew that even in pumping out a clip load of automatic fire from the MP5, I might nail only a couple. But the others would swarm from their vehicles like ants and I'd be mincemeat. Anyway, one or all three of the vehicles might be bulletproof.

I did, however, snatch up my .308 with the night vision scope and just momentarily leaving the President in the Lincoln by himself, positioned myself behind a huge oak a few feet from the road. I at least wanted to get a look at the bastards. The scope was amazing...the latest in gee whiz technology. All it needed was the slightest bit of light to perform its magic. That light would come from the vehicles' instrument panels, enough to make their faces and bodies visible.

I watched as a number of cars and trucks passed by, none of which were sedans and SUVs traveling in a caravan of three. I knew they'd have to scram out of the school lot in a matter of minutes so they wouldn't be found with three dead state police officers by the cops I'd be sending out. I hadn't been in position more than five minutes when I saw what I thought to be them approaching.

In the first vehicle, a black Ford Expedition, the driver was a hispanic man with a mustache and wearing the parka and toboggan as described by Harlan. The front seat passenger was the guy with the leather coat. His hair was jet black and long, tied off and draping onto the seat back. Definitely not Secret Service. Two men whose faces I could not plainly see sat in the second row of seats. Neither was wearing anything resembling SWAT gear.

In the second vehicle, a black Crown Vic, was the man I thought might be Tyson. He was forty-ish, clean shaven and I could clearly see that he had on tactical gear. His badge glinted in the dim light. He also had three passengers, one of which in the back seat also had a badge. Perhaps a second agent involved? I brought the crosshairs back to the front seat and put a bead on the driver's forehead. It took every ounce of willpower for me to refrain from cracking it open with a 7.62 round. I did, however, let it go by and focused on the third vehicle, another SUV.

Alarmingly, the driver was female, Black, maybe thirty, stocky body, which told me she was not an agent of any kind, and wearing a ball cap out of which a heavy head of hair sprung. She had a front seat male passenger and one other person in the rear seat whose face was hidden under a ski mask for some reason. Interesting. Combination of government agents, foreign and ethnic minorities, females and jihadists. A terrorist organization with diversity. Whatever they were calling themselves and whatever agenda they had, it was unlike any subversive element I had run up against. Mainly because I had never encountered a terrorist element that had designs on taking down the President.

So, I let them all go by and retraced my path back into the woods to the Lincoln, thankful that the President hadn't run off. I couldn't imagine what was going on in his mind now. He not only had to be confused but apprehensive about his situation. I'm sure he now was beginning to realize the reason I had to basically disappear with him. It was not safe out there anywhere...except hopefully where his wife was being hidden. Which reminded me to make another call.

"I wanted to call you," Adriana said, "but I didn't know what was happening. What *is* going on?"

"The White House Chief of Staff arranged to have the President handed off to the Senior Secret Service agent in Charge, a man named Tyson. Tyson was supposedly waiting off site earlier tonight with a backup team in support of the First Family's presidential detail. So, sometime within the last hour the chief apparently called Tyson to meet up with me to take the President off my hands. He would then see that the President and the First Lady were transported back to Washington."

"And?"

"We found out the hard way that Tyson is yet another agent anarchist involved in this conspiracy."

"What do you mean 'the hard way'?"

"I engaged Harlan Williams to first meet up with him and his team to feel things out. We just didn't want to rush in there blindly. He reported back that things did not add up and so when he confronted Tyson, it went sour in a hurry. Adriana, they...they killed Harlan and the two troopers that were with him."

"My God, Skip. Has the world gone crazy? I can't believe this is all happening. It's like a nightmare that I can't seem to wake up from." I could then hear her sobbing.

"We'll all get through this. How're the First Lady and Agent Smithers doing?"

"Let me get off to myself for a moment." I could hear her walking away, but then a half minute later she was talking again. "Joanie has done a check of the surrounding area and is very vigilant. She's bent on making it safe for us out here. The First Lady is calm outwardly, but I can tell she's nervous inside...very worried about the President. I'm a little concerned about her."

"If I had been able to hand off the President to reliable people, I was going to call you to have you all meet us somewhere near the airport so that both of them would be in position to get on the bird. Looks like you'll be staying put for a while. Are you settled in?"

"Pretty much. I broke out some red wine a while ago to try taking the edge off. Joanie wanted to keep her faculties sharp, though, and the First Lady merely declined."

"Can you put Agent Smithers on the phone?"

"I'll get her. Hold on." I heard Adrian's footsteps moving across the squeaky porch and then the next voice I heard *was* Smithers'.

"Mr. McGowan."

"Bruce, remember?"

"Okay, Bruce, everything is quiet here. Just the babble of the river and an owl."

"My favorite place to relax. Lay back and enjoy it while you can."

"I will probably not get any sleep. Need to keep my guard up. I've actually put out some makeshift early warning devices...cans with metal shot in them strung on some cord I found. I keep the MP5 at bay along with my sidearm. I also found a 12 gauge in one of the bedrooms."

"Very resourceful. I think you all will be safe there, Joanie. No friends or neighbors know we have the place and a person would have to go to the courthouse to see if I own any other property. On paper I don't. The camp is still in my father's name. I won't tell you any more in case the Bureau or Homeland Security is listening in. Which reminds me I need to keep the conversation short to avoid cell tower triangulation. Can you put Adriana back on?"

"I will, but you need to fill me in on what's happening on your end. Have you set up the plans for the First Family to fly out? Is Nighthawk on the way?"

"Joanie, got to get off here. Adriana will fill you in on the details. Go ahead and put her back on."

A few seconds later. "Okay then, Skip. You'll let us know when we'll need to move out somewhere."

"I will. Somehow I've got to get them back to Washington and in safe arms as soon as I can. But, I'm running out of options."

I then turned to the President. "Sir, do you want to say anything to your wife before I hang up?"

"Just tell her not to worry and give her my love."

I nodded. "Adriana, the President says to tell the First Lady not to worry and he loves her."

"I'll relay that, Skip. Just please, please be careful and end this thing when you can."

"I will. Love ya. See you soon as I can. Bye."

The President then shifted in his seat. "All right, Bruce, what goes from here?"

"First, I need to go by that schoolyard to where they ended Harlan and his troopers' lives. I just want to see how they died."

"I know you were close to him but do you really need to see that?"

"I do. I just don't want to drive off without viewing the bodies. I want that mental picture of what we find embedded in my mind right up to the moment I put a bullet in Tyson's brain. It might not be tonight, but I *will* hunt down that bastard and leave his head in about six pieces."

"All right, do what you need to do, but we're in dire need of a game plan right about now."

I looked over at him and replied, "Right about now it's time we took matters into our *own* hands, Mr. President. We're cutting off all contact with your feds."

Chapter Eleven

I knew it was going to be a bad scene. As many times as I've come upon aftermaths of murders, gun battles and terrorist attacks, it's never bothered me to look down at the bodies of low-life vermin who deserved to die. Many of them at my hand. But just as I saw a couple hours before on the Whitehawk (Marine One), I've never been fully prepared to see the riddled bodies of friends and brothers-in-arms. I saw enough of that in combat forty years ago with two tours in Vietnam. And then there was that horrific day when I returned to Washington from that last mission to find Team Zulu wiped out at our headquarters. I know I seem like a broken record. I've mentioned it more times than I'd like? But the fact that my boss and mentor, Lionel Byrd, choked to death on his own blood in my arms still haunts me to this day.

At such time we would depart the murder scene, I would be making the call to the state police, anonymously of course, and probably from Clayton's phone. I'd make the call to assure Harlan's and the troopers' bodies wouldn't be lying out there all night. I doubted that Tyson would be leaving a couple of men back to see if I'd be foolish enough to go in there, but we proceeded to the site with caution anyway.

Harlan's cruiser was sitting about ten feet beyond the point of entry and to the left of the last parking space near the school building on the gravel driveway. Slowly, I pulled in beside the car. The area wasn't well lighted so I couldn't readily see evidence of bodies lying near the car. From the rear seat I snatched up my .308 and stepped out of the Lincoln. Using the night vision scope, I scanned the grounds around the building 180 degrees all the way up to the tree line in the distance looking for human forms, alive or dead. At first sight nothing was readily visible. But then only forty feet away partially hidden by a cluster of bushes, I spotted three clumps on the ground. I couldn't fully make out what they were, but the toes of their shoes sticking up told me they were bodies.

"I have them, sir. I'm walking over there to check them out. You have the Glock. If any goons happen to approach the car before I return, empty the clip on them."

"Do you want me to go with you?" the President asked.

"I'd rather you not be exposed outside of the car, sir. Even though there should be no bad guys left out here, I still might be walking into a spray of gunfire."

I found them lying all in a row on their backs as though they had been posed, hands folded neatly on their abdomens. Was this some kind of statement? I didn't touch the bodies. I didn't want the state's CSI team to pick up my DNA.

Since the troopers were wearing flak jackets, the terrorists had made sure to shoot them in the head so that immediate death would be certain. High powered rifles fired at a distance. With my LED pin light I began inspecting Harlan's body, the result of which promptly brought me to tears. He was struck in the throat by what appeared to be a bullet from a .45 or .357 at close range. As we hadn't heard any gunshots while sitting at the roadside park less than a mile away, Tyson and his snipers likely used affixed suppressors.

I took a long, deep breath and let it out slowly. The pain in my heart was so intense it felt like cardiac arrest. "I am so sorry, Harlan. It's my fault. I asked you to do this and can't tell you how much I regret it. It should be me lying here." The man who had sat with me on the banks of the Greenbrier on many occasions swapping lies and downing Rolling Rocks, his favorite, died because of me. Something else that will haunt me until the end of my days. "I swear on my mother's grave that I will make that bastard pay, Harlan. Rest in peace, my friend."

I stood, wiped my eyes with my sleeve and turned back toward the Lincoln. When I slid in under the wheel, I saw and heard the President on a cell phone...Clayton's cell. He was deeply engaged in an intense conversation with someone. I think I knew who.

"Look, Arnie. All I know is that you set up this Agent Tyson to rendezvous with McGowan and me and it was nothing but an ambush. I'm not saying you were behind it, but your man on ground, Tyson, is a terrorist. Three fine state police officers were murdered and you set it up. We could have walked right into it. Mr. McGowan has had the right instincts about everything. He has kept the First Lady and me protected where your federal officers can't." A pause. "Yes, he's right here." Another short pause. "All right, I'll hand the phone over."

I was already hightailing it out of the parking area just in case the terrorist element came back for some reason or a nosy county cop stopped to see what we were doing on a Friday night at an elementary school. Once back out on the road, I took the phone and put it on *speaker*.

"Mr. Kessler."

"Mr. McGowan, I can't tell you how..."

"Save it. I don't need your sympathy. I've lost a very good friend tonight and you set up his murder. Let me make this very clear. I am now in total control of the President's security. We will meet up with no one else you arrange for a handoff. I don't care if it's the Director of the FBI himself. We've been burned twice tonight and you arranged both scenarios. No more. And understand this...I will also not risk taking the President to the airport to get on the Marine chopper."

"Wait a minute, McGowan, you're not calling the shots here. This is an executive matter of the highest degree...a Code Red situation. And I'm very aware you know what *that* is from your previous job with the government. My office in conjunction with the Secret Service and Homeland Security is..."

"Is incompetent, if not malfeasant. Unless you want to talk again to the President..." he shook his head..."you will not hear from me again. I personally will assure that somehow he and the First Lady make it home. Goodbye."

"McGowan..." I could still hear his protests as I clicked him off.

The President seemed to be a little uneasy with what I told Kessler and narrowed his eyes. "Bruce, I can understand your reluctance to meet up with people you don't know and trust, but we have to find a way to get us on my helicopter."

"Sir, I have a bad feeling about *any* arrangement involving the airport. You realize what happened there earlier. The only way out of this, short of me driving you directly to Washington, is that when the Marines land, they'll not only need to be posted at the entrance to bring us in, but will have cordoned off the airport's perimeter."

"And we would need a Marine contact for that to be arranged. I could get hold of the Pentagon or even the Secretary of Defense. Just one problem."

"What's that, Mr. President?"

"The Chief of Staff generally takes care of all the contacting. But, I just hacked him off and you just *cut* him off. I haven't had a need for a personal cell phone, so I can't even contact the Vice President. The First Lady does have one, however, but she doesn't have in her address book the numbers of anyone official. I guess in some ways I'm still livin' back in the 20th Century."

"Don't you keep on your person a little black book with phone numbers of all the important people who can respond in case of national emergency, nuclear war or if you want to call up an old girlfriend?"

He smiled. "That's what I like about you, Bruce...you can put a little levity into any dire situation. No, I don't. At the White House I rely on the Chief of Staff to make the contacts. Or I just pick up the phone on my desk and hit a button. I can have the Secretary of Defense on the line in a matter of seconds."

"And how does it work when you're away from the White House like this?"

"I had Special Agent Clayton for that."

"Umm."

As we were back near the interstate, I pulled off at the same filling station as before and put the Lincoln in *park*. "Time for me to make that call to the state, sir." I then used Clayton's phone to dial 911.

"911 Operator. Do you have an emergency?"

"Listen carefully. You need to send the cops out to Jackson Elementary School off Route 60 down from the Sam Black Church exit off I-64. Some people have been shot."

"What is your name, sir?"

"Never mind. Just get the message out." I then pressed *end call*.

"Now that that's done, I feel relieved that their bodies will soon be discovered." I settled back in my cushy driver's seat and closed my eyes for a moment. "But it doesn't make me feel any better."

The President then said, "Now I need to figure out who to contact about the Marines and how to do it?"

For a moment I just sat resting my arms on the steering wheel and looking through the windshield at the beginning of a hard rain. Large drops pelted the roof and hood, pinging the metal at the cyclic rate of a machine gun. Then suddenly the light bulb went on. Reaching into the open compartment in the console I again retrieved Clayton's phone and held it up. "Voila!"

"Good thinkin', Bruce. But I don't know who all's in there."

I flipped open the phone again. "Maybe we can figure it out. However, the phone is flashing that we're low on juice and I don't think my charging cord will fit this; so we need to extract the information quickly." I then pulled from my jacket pocket a pen and pad. Scrolling through his address book, I started reading off names. "Abbott." He shook his head. "Alford." No. "Allen." Again no. I got down to the C's and Campanello, the Secret Service Director. It was me who said *no* to that one. As far as i was concerned, he might just be the kingpin in this whole deal, given tonight's experience with the Service.

I continued reading and the President either shook his head or said *no* to every name. "See if Foxworth is listed."

I continued scrolling. "Yes."

"Marine commandant. He'll make things happen out there at the airport. Go ahead and touch the number."

I did as instructed, but then we both heard the disappointing message. "This phone is no longer in service. To have your service restored..."

"Damn!" I exclaimed. "Service cancelled. Could that have been Kessler? If so, he got it cancelled quickly."

"He could have ordered it when he realized we were no longer involving him. That could also mean he's possibly a party to this conspiracy. And that would shatter all my good history with him."

"Would anyone else have known I had Clayton's phone?"

"I don't see how, Bruce."

"Well, I can still access the address list in the phone...hmm, no I can't. It's totally dead now."

"And we're back to square one," he lamented. "I'm cut off from everyone. What are our options at this point?"

I sat for a few moments stroking my forehead with my fingers. "Do I eat my words and take you to the airport anyway? Big risk there. But maybe the Marines will just go ahead and set up a perimeter as part of their mission SOP. We can drive to a point outside the airport where we have good observation and just sit and watch. We see uniforms and activity, we go in."

"And getting my Mrs there?"

"Adriana can bring her and Agent Smithers to a designated area somewhere nearby. I'll set up the location when we get there."

"Fine. Not sure how you feel about it, but I favor taking the risk, Bruce."

"I'm still 50-50 on the idea."

"I don't think at this point we have a choice."

"Another thought," I added. "We can go by and pick up the ladies. Adriana stays at the camp. I drive you, the First Lady and Smithers to Washington in the Lincoln. Nobody out there should know it's us in this car. Four hour trip."

"Don't know I like that option, Bruce. That has a certain amount of risk as well. I wouldn't be good with exposing my wife to imminent danger like that. The night has not been kind to us out here on the road."

"Maybe we could just join the ladies at the camp and stay there for a while where it's safe. You get to continue your mini vacation."

He chuckled. "Now that doesn't sound like a bad deal."

"Complete with all the perks...a freezer full of steaks, a couple cases of beer and half dozen bottles of wine. A little fishing. And oh yes, warm, good-natured people to hang out with."

He laughed again but then just as quickly put on his serious face. "I guess we'll have to make that happen in better times."

"And then there's that other matter on your plate, sir. Franks and his ultimatum. He gave you till 11:00 to surrender or the dirty bomb supposedly gets detonated."

"Which may be just an idle threat...a bluff. But whether it is or not, I suspect in using me as his pawn, Franks and whoever is driving this train are wantin' somethin' big. What do you think? A billion dollars? Maybe a capacitor of uranium 235 they can sell to North Korea? They've gone to great lengths to plan out and pull off this deal. And to infiltrate the Secret Service like they did, causin' some of our agents to become turncoats, it's all been well thought-out." He glanced at the time on the dash. "Yeah, eleven o'clock is ten minutes away. And I'm not in the situation room with my crisis team dealin' with it."

"If you don't surrender, which you wouldn't of course, do they make their demand to the Vice President who then becomes the Commander-in-Chief in your absence?"

"Who knows what they'll do. The fact that I'm missin' in action will make a lot of people in Washington nervous. They won't know if I've been captured or killed. I can't imagine that the Vice President and a crisis team would give in to any demands. Remember, our country doesn't make deals with terrorists even if its president is in danger of losing' his life."

We waited the ten minutes watching the digital time change on the instrument panel, minute by minute, with hardly a word between us. Eleven o'clock finally came and went. We waited some more. At nine minutes past the hour my cell phone rang. I knew who it was. I put the call on *speaker* again. The all too familiar voice then came on the line.

"Are you having a good evening, McGowan?"

"I've had better ones."

"So, you and your President have decided to ignore my instructions."

"You knew I was not going to be surrender him."

"Then 50,000 people will pay with their lives."

"Why are you trying to take the President? And just what the hell *is it* you people want?"

"I assume you're listening on the speaker as well, Mr. Big Man. We were planning to use your arrogant ass as collateral to have our demands met. But since you've obviously chosen to run and hide with McGowan like the sniveling coward you are, we're going to have a little change of strategy. It's now open season on you. That's right. We've got a bullet with your name on it. And you're out there where even an asshole like McGowan can't protect you. Maybe now we'll get the attention of all you important bastards in Washington. And oh, by the way, just as I promised to show you we mean business, in less than ten seconds that innocent little sleeping city in Maryland will have a rude awakening."

I answered for the President with the flavor of words that are probably nowhere in his vocabulary. "You're not just an asshole traitor, Franks; you're a goddam piece of shit."

"Sticks and stones, McGowan. But the countdown continues...four, three, two, one. *Boom!* Too bad. Too late. Now you can turn on your radio and listen for all those special reports. And you were asking about who we are and our demands? Catch CNN around the midnight hour for the communique we sent them. From this moment on, your night has just taken a turn for the worse, Eagle One." And then he was gone.

I could see the horror in the President's face. "Would these people really set off a radiation bomb?" he asked. "It would be unprecedented in this country."

"You'll recall that the kind of terror attack on 9-11 was *also* unprecedented."

He leaned his head back against the seat. "If they did detonate a dirty bomb that would rain radiation down on a hell of a lot of people, God help them. Go ahead and turn on the radio, Bruce. Maybe find a live, late night talk show."

I pressed the radio's *on* button and music from Joey's favorite country station blasted our ears. I wondered if my brother had become deaf. I then turned it down and touched *scan* which sequentially provided five second samples of each station. Out of Washington I found talk show host Ben Stoner's *Night Train.* I listen to him on occasion. He professes to be fair and balanced like Fox News, but when I hear his dialogue with call-ins, I think he leans mostly left. At the moment he was deeply engaged with a woman who was a decibel or two shy of screaming at Stoner for registering his opinion about the President's foreign policy. Stoner was heard on most nights taking a shot or two at the President, at the same time massaging his own ego by intentionally pissing people off.

"I can choose something else if you want, sir."

"No. Every once in a while I listen to *Night Train...*when I need a good laugh." I caught just the slightest of smiles.

As we were still sitting at the Chevron, I noticed that it was going on 11:15. Whether or not we would retrace our route back past Lewisburg and settle into a spot where I could observe the goings-on inside airport grounds, we still had to go *somewhere*. As it would take about fifteen minutes anyway to reach the exit leading to the airport, we should be in proximity about the same time the Marines arrived on the C130s. The problem was, we had to drive through the entrance and weave our way again to the tarmac in order to get to them. I knew that Harlan had left troopers to secure Marine One until the FBI arrived to take over. And I was sure that we would be okay at such time we were able to marry up with the Marine battalion. I was *not* sure we'd make it in unless we saw Marines setting up at the entrance and positioned throughout the parking lot. Even though the terrorist element might not know it was us in the Lincoln, anywhere on the road or in the airport parking lot there could be people with even more advanced night vision equipment than I had, strategically situated to look inside our car and see every whisker on our faces. They may not necessarily recognize *me*, but they definitely would the President. And Joey's family car was not bulletproof.

We were about halfway along I-64 when Ben Stoner stopped his conversation with a male caller from Buffalo to provide a news flash: "Uh, ladies and gentlemen, apparently there's been some kind of major explosion in Carthage, Maryland, about twenty minutes from our station here in D.C. I'm going to Kay Bradley, at our news desk, for the story."

"Yes, Ben. At approximately ten minutes past eleven, an apparent bomb went off in the downtown area of Carthage reportedly damaging buildings and vehicles over two city blocks. Thought at first to be some kind of gas line explosion, the police and fire department assessed the damage and said it was likely a car bomb. Why Carthage and why this time of night is anyone's guess. At the moment there is no information on casualties, but most people with the exception of party goers would have been off the street and home in bed on this Friday night. There *are* a couple of night spots in the area and it is feared there will most certainly be people who were seriously injured or killed in this devastating explosion. No one has immediately come forward to claim responsibility. No comment as yet from Maryland's governor or the White House. We'll keep you updated; for now back to you, Ben."

I looked at the President who was shaking his head. "Damnation.They really did it," he said.

"This is obviously a much more extensive terror network than I gave them credit for," I said. "True to their threat, we can now realistically expect more bombing. I didn't hear the reporter say anything about radiation though. But maybe it was simply a very large vehicle-borne IED. Usually an RDD device doesn't have the explosive power to take out two city blocks. However, I'm not up on all the bombs out there anymore. Either it isn't a dirty bomb or the city's hazmat team hasn't arrived to check for radiation. But maybe they have and they're not letting their findings out as yet to avoid mass hysteria. I'd say they chose Carthage because of its proximity to D.C. to make a statement. The next bomb might very well *be* set off in Washington."

The President nodded. "Why is it that this is the first time we've heard from this organization, whatever it is? Al-qa'ida, Boko Haram, Hamas and other terrorist groups, principally made up of radical Islamists, may also tack on a few converts here and there. But it seems most all the bad guys you've knocked down have been Americans with the exception of a couple of Middle Easterners."

"Four of which we find are members of your own protection team."

"Regrettably."

It was dead on 11:30 when I spotted the road off U.S. 60 which would take us up to higher ground that overlooked the county airport. From a pull-off area that provided unobstructed visibility, we could clearly see the entrance, the parking lot and much of the runway to the south of the terminal. I couldn't see Marine One which was behind the adjacent hangar, but through my night field glasses I was able to make out two vehicles in the vicinity, one marked and one unmarked state cruiser. Harlan had called them in to secure the chopper until the FBI arrived, keeping the massacre of the on-board Marines on the Q.T. for the time being.

I could also see that the C130s and Nighthawk had yet to arrive. If everything went to plan, the two birds with the small battalion of Marines and the substitute presidential chopper would touch down on the airstrip at any time. Again, once that occurred and I was able to determine that the entire perimeter was secured, to include the entrance, I would call Adriana to load up and drive the eight miles from the camp to meet us. We'd be escorted by the Marine guard to the tarmac where the President, First Lady and Agent Smithers would soon be on their way to Andrews. It would all go down like clockwork.

Having gotten this close to getting out of town, the President now appeared a little more at ease. "Thanks, Bruce," he said. "Thanks for protectin' me and for keepin' the hounds of hell at bay. I hate that so many people have died tonight; but some of them *deserved* to die. You've risked your life for me and I appreciate it. I appreciate your loyalty."

I nodded.

He continued. "It's my fault all those good people died tonight...all because the Mrs and I wanted a little R & R."

"Sir, you can't blame yourself. However..." I stopped short of finishing my thought.

"I'm listenin.'"

"I don't mean to be critical, but why weren't there more agents assigned on your protection detail and a company of Marines securing the grounds around Wolf Laurel? That's what happens at Camp David."

"Truth be told, Bruce, it was what I insisted on. I wanted our stay at the B&B to be as covert as possible. No parade of limos and police motorcycles. No military presence. No press. Just our agents and the small detail at the airport. Nobody would know except a handful on my staff. Clayton tried like hell to talk me out of it. But, because I broke protocol, he and some very fine agents paid for my mistake with their lives. You're right to criticize, Bruce. And don't worry, I appreciate your candor."

I didn't respond. I knew he was beating himself up with remorse. But then I heard the drone of large propeller aircraft in the distance. I pointed to our ten o'clock where the lights of the first C130 appeared about a quarter mile away on the horizon, followed by the Marine One clone.

"Ten minutes late boys," I said. I then looked at the President and smiled. "I'm a stickler for punctuality you know."

It was like in slow motion although in reality it wasn't. Like something out of a movie. Unreal. From a position above us the sky suddenly lit up. A simultaneous streak of light and whooshing sound overhead.

Chapter Twelve

There was nothing we could do. We watched helplessly as the warhead's flaming tail became smaller and smaller until it impacted with the descending C130. The huge bird instantaneously exploded into a ball of fire causing its fuselage to separate from its wings and its blazing remains to skid more than three hundred feet along the runway to a stop.

"God in Heaven," the President said in almost a whisper.

As large pieces of the C130 sat burning at the end of the runway, the Marine chopper immediately veered off to the south. The trailing C130 which had also been on approach promptly increased its altitude and then quickly disappeared into the low ceiling.

"We're getting out of here, sir. Not just off this hill, but completely out of the area."

"Agreed. Go," he replied.

The President's transportation back to Washington had just been cancelled. As our eyes remained transfixed on the burning corpse of the C130, I began retracing our course down the winding hillside road to Highway 219. After entering the highway, I pointed the Lincoln back toward the interstate. Where to go now? Greenbrier County had officially become a war zone.

"We have no recourse now, Mr. President. It's either my fishing camp or I drive you from here to D.C."

"We're now in an all-out war with this terror outfit, Bruce. I need to be sittin' down at this moment with my crisis team. Take me on to the White House. The ladies will be all right until it's safe to extract them outta there. In a couple of days, I'll send Marine One down to pick up my Mrs and Agent Smithers."

"Good call, sir. We'll be in Virginia in about ten minutes."

As we zipped along I-64 in the rain, I turned the radio down while the President used my phone to call the First Lady. As she would likely hear about the bombing in Maryland and downed C130 at Greenbrier Valley on our radio there at the camp, he filled her in on the details as delicately as he could. He said he had given me the green light to strike out for Washington since it was obvious that we were facing certain danger where we were. It also appeared there were few people both locally and back in D.C. that he could now trust. And he wasn't sure who they were. This conspiracy thing was so widespread even people on his staff and in his administration may very well be involved.

At five minutes past twelve when we were about halfway to Lexington, on the same D.C. station, there was both a new report about the fiery crash of the C130 at the Greenbrier Valley Airport, where it was feared more than 70 Marines had lost their lives, and an update on the bombing in Maryland. Nine were reported dead in Carthage and in excess of forty injured, three critically. Were the incidents occurring only a half hour apart connected? The blast had already been determined to be from a car bomb. And then down in West Virginia there were more than a half dozen reports from observers seeing some kind of missile streaking across the sky just before the military craft went down. A series of terrorist attacks?

I then began scanning more stations and found considerable dialogue already about America being under attack by some terrorist element. But as of yet no one had claimed responsibility. Still, no statement issued by the White House or State Department.

Moments later, my cell phone which had been hot all evening rang once again. It was Franks.

"Do we now have your attention?"

"Terrorist Special Agent Franks. You are indeed a murderous bastard."

"I'm not out to win your praise, if that's what you want."

"What I want is what I'll be getting sooner or later...a bead on your forehead with my .308."

"Keep dreaming, McGowan. You're living in a fantasy world. But, as I promised, we've got something else coming your way. Something all of America will hear which will put a little pressure on the big man you're trying to shield. So tune in and be enlightened." Without further word he again ended the conversation, giving me no chance to call him a few more colorful names.

I then asked the President, "What do you know about Franks?"

"I know that Bill Clayton liked him and chose him from a pretty good list of agents for the presidential detail. Intelligent, speaks well as you hear. Kind of reminded me of a young professor type with the glasses and studious look about him. I don't think he's married. As I remember he works out a lot and is a runner. Used to run some with Joanie Smithers."

"That being the case, is there any chance she's tied in with him?"

"I can't imagine it. Knowing that she's with my wife, don't be scaring me like that, Bruce."

"I'm sure you're right about her, sir. Forget the supposition."
On Joey's Sirius radio, I found the CNN broadcast channel. A panel in process of discussing the night's events was abruptly interrupted by breaking news.

"From the CNN news desk, I'm John Drinkwater. We've been following the stories out of Carthage, Maryland and Greenbrier County, West Virginia where there have been two horrific incidents we can now confirm as related terrorist attacks. CNN has received exclusively from a group calling themselves the Stealth Jihad of America something they call a manifesto claiming responsibility for the incidents. It reads as follows:

> *"You have been warned tonight, America. You now bear witness to our far-reaching capability. We have the weapons, we have the personnel and we have the propensity to tear the very heart out of America. This is only the beginning. September 11, a singular event, will pale in comparison to the sustained onslaught we have now commenced. We are the Stealth Jihad of America and this is our declaration. The United States of America has been many times appropriately labeled by the Nation of Islam and its subsidiary factions as the Great Satan. In its unholy alliance with the State of Israel, which*

illegally occupies the land of Palestine, the Great Satan continues its attacks on and imprisonment of our Muslim brothers who bear witness to the world that Allah is the one true God and that Sharia Law is the only true law. As it is commanded in the Quran that all believers of Islam, the one true religion, must rid the world of all infidels, we take it upon ourselves to begin with the Great Deceiver himself, the President of the United States. From this manifesto, we issue the warrant for his execution. We also demand that twenty-four of our brothers whose names accompany this communique and who are illegally incarcerated in the military prison at Guantanamo Bay be released within three days. Each day thereafter they are not released, an American city will see many dead lying in its streets. The bombs will be bigger and more deadly each time, causing an ever escalating number of American infidels to die. You have seen our might and our mettle. If you value the lives of your loved ones, America, you will demand the execution of your morally reprehensible president, who remains in hiding, and that the evil, despicable government in Washington release our innocent brothers. The clock is ticking."

Janell Trudeau, the moderator of the special panel, responded to the reporter, "John, this has always been our worst fear, that the major terrorist acts occurring throughout the world such as in London, Paris and Hong Kong may now become numerous here in the United States. What do we know about this group?"

"Well, Janell, from what we've learned..."

The President had his own commentary. I turned down the radio to listen. "This group has been on the terror watch by the FBI and Homeland Security ever since they surfaced about a year and a half ago. The CIA had also uncovered information that recruiting was high and a large number of non-Middle Easterners and Islamic sympathizers were jumpin' on their band wagon. My administration for years has received threats from several radical Islamic organizations that if certain terrorist captives were not released, there would be attacks on American soil. We've mostly been able to thwart the intentions of these groups by goin' after their leadership and stoppin' 'em before they happen. A few of them are now actually prisoners down in Gitmo. This Stealth Jihad is a branch of al-qa'ida and claim to be its American equivalent. It's not that we haven't taken them serious, there just haven't been to this point any threats carried out."

I added, "And as they had recruited and infiltrated even the Secret Service, I wonder what other federal law enforcement agencies they've wormed their way into?"

Flipping back and forth between the radio broadcasts of CNN and Fox News, I found the commentary from all networks to be one of outrage versus peppered with partisan political blame. In scenarios such as this, the focus is always on people coming together to express their shock, anger and sympathy for the families of the those losing their lives at the hands of terrorists. However, one reporter asked, "The declaration asserts that the President is in hiding. So, just where *is* he? We have tried contacting the White House Press Secretary's office but received no response."

"Hand me your phone, Bruce. Since I've found myself 'communication handicapped,' all I can do at this point is call the White House operator and try to get through to someone on my staff."

I handed off my cell and he dialed 911. The phone was still on *speaker*. "911 operator. What's your emergency?"

"Please connect me to the White House, Washington, D.C," he said.

"Again, what is your emergency?"

"Ma'am, this is a matter of national security and I know you're not going to believe this, but this is the President of the United States. I need you to get hold of the White House operator."

"You're the...President," replied the voice, a voice heavily laced with sarcasm.

"That's right, I am. I know it sounds dubious, but I am in a dire situation where I neither have the resources nor personnel to assist me at this time. Just put me through to the operator there."

"One moment."

More than one moment later, a male voice came on the line. "Sir, this is the 911 supervisor. I must warn you that providing false information on this emergency line and especially pretending to be the President in order to gain telephone access to White House personnel is a criminal offense and punishable under federal law."

"I'm familiar with the law...what is your name?"

"Jim. I..."

"Look, Jim, I was an advocate in getting that law passed. Now understand that this *is* the President and I need to speak with the White House operator."

"If this is the President, then where are you located?" We could hear laughter in the background.

"On the road. I can't tell you exactly where."

"Don't you have people in your entourage, like the Secret Service, to get you through to where you need?"

"I can't go into my situation with you, but I need you to help me out here. Don't you recognize my voice?"

"I've heard a lot of impersonators and they were quite good. In my book, you're not a very good one."

The President and I looked at one another. I wanted to laugh. I think he wanted to scream bloody murder.

"Okay, Jim. I know any average American citizen can call the White House and at least talk to the operator there, regardless of whether one gets sent any further."

"Then they need to use the public telephone service to do that, not this emergency line."

"I guess I'm not going to convince you that I *am* the President, huh Jim?"

"Good try, *Mr. President*. But, no. You need to end your call now. Understand that we will report this call and the authorities may be following up."

"I hope so, Jim. I'll be sure to get through to the White House then. Goodbye." The President then sighed and said to me, "I guess I need to dial 411 and become an average American citizen."

"Go for it, sir."

"Operator," she answered. "May I help you place your call?"

"Yes, please. The White House operator in Washington, D.C."

"The White House?"

"Yes, ma'am."

"Please hold a moment and I'll look up that number." After that moment, she said "I've tried the number but get a message that 'all lines are busy.' Do you want me to keep trying?"

"Please."

Another moment.

"Sir, all lines are still busy."

"Can you break into a call and tell them its an emergency?"

"I can't do that, sir; if you have an emergency, perhaps you can dial 911."

The President allowed his head to roll back into the seat rest. "Un-be-lievable."

It was like listening to an old radio comedy routine...*the Great Gildersleeve* or *Life of Riley*. Again, I wanted to laugh, but it was not a laughing matter. Actually, it *was* unbelievable. The President of the United States stranded without his protection detail or a cell phone of his own or a book of important numbers on his person. And he didn't have programmed in his brain a single phone number for significant notables in the government or friends.

"Maybe the First Lady has some numbers she can call even if its only wives of your staff and cabinet members."

"You know what, Bruce? By the time we get through to somebody, we'll be halfway to Washington. Let's just drive on." He then turned the radio volume up.

We had been handed a hell of a lot of surprises already and it all began just after seven nearly six hours before. What more were in store for us? We found out as we were passing Lexington deep in the Shenandoah Valley. It was not only implausible, but downright stupefying that the President of the United States was resigned to getting his informational reports from radio media.

> "From the CNN news desk, this is Sandra Lombardi. An official statement from the White House has finally been put out to the press. And this potentially tragic matter is a first in the history of the United States. Press Secretary Linda Eichelberger reports that...and I quote..."*yesterday afternoon The President and First Lady had slipped quietly out of town to enjoy some weekend rest and relaxation at a B&B in Greenbrier County, West Virginia. While staying last night at the small country inn called Wolf Laurel, the First Family was suddenly and viciously attacked by an apparent terrorist faction allegedly associated with the Stealth Jihad group claiming responsibility for both the bombing in Carthage, Maryland, and the downing of the Marine C130 at the airport only five miles from the B&B. Federal agents at the scene provide that five Secret Service agents were killed*

in a raid on the premises as well as the crew of Marines posted at the county airport on Marine One. We regretfully report that the President and First Lady are missing. It is suspected that they have been abducted at gunpoint from the inn by the owner of Wolf Laurel, Bruce McGowan, who is also alleged to be connected to the terrorist group. We believe McGowan to now be on the run with accomplices and forcibly holding the President. McGowan is ex-Special Forces and a retired FBI Special Agent who also worked for the Department of State in an international role. His official photo is shown here. We have engaged all federal and state resources to look for McGowan. If you see this suspect, do not approach as he has allegedly killed at least a dozen people just last evening. He is considered armed and extremely dangerous. There is also evidence that the President was seriously wounded in the attack at the inn. This is all we have at this time."

Lombardi continued. "As there was a battery of follow-up questions to Ms. Eichelberger, she left the podium without responding. And as I said before, this is absolutely unprecedented, a horrific series of events, and we all now fear for the President. Calls are coming in to the station by the hundreds expressing shock and sadness. Some even calling for this Bruce McGowan not to be taken prisoner but to be shot on sight. He allegedly not only had a hand in the attack on the President at his own B&B but also allegedly fired the missile that brought down the C130 loaded with Marines."

I turned down the volume and looked over at the astonished President. "Funny, but I don't remember it happening like that. I guess this means my membership at the country club will now be cancelled."

The President looked at me and frowned. "Here you sit, making jokes after hearing these asinine reports," he said. "I would be livid at hearing something like that. Who the hell authorized Linda to put that report out?"

"Probably the man I pissed off, your Chief of Staff. He didn't like what I said and did, so he falsified an official report to the American people and added me to the America's Most Wanted List, in the number one position. Sounds a bit like defamation, don't you think?"

"It's irresponsible if not criminal."

"Thank you, sir. Makes me feel better. I was just beginning to wonder about myself."

He shook his head again, his non-verbal telling me to stop with the quips and get serious. "So, do you think this fatwa was Franks' product or did this come from whatever radical Islamic kingpin is running the show?"

"Franks, like Tyson and the others, I believe are just paid monkeys. And being in the federal system within an arm's reach of you, they've been instrumental in getting the Jihadists the opportunities they wouldn't normally have. I'm sure Franks is smart enough to write up the communique and send it to the media, but I'm convinced he's just one of that organization's lieutenants."

"Looks like Homeland Security will have to do some real house cleaning with the Service. Who knows how many more cockroaches are imbedded in there."

"And in *other* agencies. Maybe the Bureau."

Suddenly my phone rang. Adriana. She must have had the radio on.

I beat her to the punch. "Hello, Bonnie. Clyde speaking."

"Skip, don't joke about something like this."

"Hey, that's what the President just said."

"I...I can't believe somebody did this to us. When I heard the Press Secretary's press release, I was beyond stunned. So is the First Lady."

"I know, sweetheart. Just relax and let the President and I take care of this. It'll all be recanted once we get to Washington. You'll see. Some heads will roll up there and there will be a corrected press release."

"But in the meantime, somebody might get trigger happy if they spot you."

"I have Joey's Lincoln and so far no one knows we're traveling in it. Don't worry. A couple more hours and we'll be there. I'll be careful."

"All right, Skip. Call me when you arrive."

While I was talking with her, I think I may have received a half dozen missed calls. Kept hearing beep after beep. I'm sure it was some of my golf or fishing buddies wondering why I'd do such a thing...and while I'm at it to say *hi* to the President for them. There was also a 212 call which was Washington, so I decided to check *that* message. Maybe it was the FBI telling me to give up. Mmmm, *no*. But, I thought maybe I *should* hand the phone off to the President to follow up. Even if it wasn't the Bureau, the caller might be someone who could get us the ear of the White House.

But then I had an epiphany. There *was* someone in Washington after all that I could call Somebody I actually had in my phone address book. And he would be just the man to assure we were brought in safely...the President's man. The man who hired me not long ago to take down the Viper.

"Preston Johns," I said out loud.

"Yes, absolutely. Definitely a body you can trust. You have his number?"

"I do."

Preston, a well-educated African American, was hired into the Bureau about the same time I was. For a while our careers tracked along together. We actually served in the same field office together on two occasions; but then as our assignments and locations changed, we lost touch. However, while I was still out there bagging bad boys, one of which I had suddenly become, *his* career took off like a rocket. The next thing I know, a bunch of years later, he's the National Security Advisor.

I touched the number, making sure we were still on *speaker*. We heard three rings. "Hello."

"Preston."

"Yes. Who is this?"

"Apparently a brand new fugitive who's supposed to have turned terrorist and kidnapped the President."

"Bruce."

"That would be me."

"Let's see, you're in cahoots with a terrorist group that wants a bunch of other terrorists released from Gitmo or else you continue bombing cities and knocking military aircraft out of the sky, leaving all of America in a frenzy of fear."

"You know *me*. Always looking for excitement."

"I know you haven't turned terrorist, but how the hell did you get yourself into this mess? And just where *is* the President?"

"The President's riding beside me. We're on our way back to Washington. Here, I'll let him tell you all about it. I'm driving and need to concentrate on what I'm doing."

"Hello, Preston. A hell of a thing, isn't it? Let me lay it all out for you." The President started at the beginning when he and the First Lady decided to have their little weekend get-away at our place. He then gave Johns in minute detail a summary of the events occurring over the past few hours. Meanwhile, I kept zipping along on I-81, at that point with the city of Harrisonburg in my rearview mirror.

"So, you're saying that at least four Secret Service agents are parties to this conspiracy, Mr. President. These are supposed to be the most carefully screened and scrutinized people in federal service. How did these bastards finagle their way in?"

I jumped in on that one. "My thoughts are that these rogues didn't come in to the Secret Service as terrorists. Some of them might not even be sympathetic to the extremists' ideals or purpose. Maybe one or two agents were approached with some big money and suddenly all sense of duty and devotion went out the window. Then they could've talked to a couple others whose $80,000 to

$100,000 salary just weren't getting it and suddenly you've got a seedbed of disloyal agents who aren't letting patriotism stand in their way of making some big bucks. And that's just the Service. I'm thinking if they got to them, they might have gotten to Bureau agents as well."

"Maybe so, but we won't know for sure until a few of these defectors are reined in. Anyhow, sounds like you need some help from my end, Mr. President."

"We haven't had any good luck getting out of here otherwise. Unfortunately, twice we ran into hornets nests right after my own Chief of Staff arranged set ups...once when I was bein' taken to the hospital and then when we were slated to meet the Secret Service SAC who'd get me to the airport. We were *set up* all right. Seems like the only opportunity we've had for safe passage is what Bruce is doing right now."

"I was going to ask you about that. The press release also said you were wounded. How bad? You *sound* okay."

"Slight shoulder wound, but we found somebody to patch me up."

"Good. Where are you on the road at this time?"

"I-81 about 45 minutes from our turn at I-66," I answered.

"I'll get the Director on the phone and have a satellite office in the upper Shenandoah, perhaps Winchester, marry up with you and bring you on in. I know you're not trusting people from *any* of the agencies right now, but I'd say the chances this terrorist organization did recruit agents from the Bureau in a greater number of field offices is nil. We'll get someone in Winchester dispatched. Once he's been noticed, I'll make sure the SAC in Richmond contacts you for the rendezvous point."

I wasn't going to say so, but this was like deja vu all over again, except the last arrangement was made with the Secret Service SAC. I had absolute trust and confidence in Preston Johns. However, if we happened to land on the acerbic end of *this* hook-up, something probably went sour somewhere down the chain.

"All right, Preston," the President replied. "We'll wait for the call. You need to contact that Press Secretary of mine and tell her the information she received was complete bogus and to quit referring to Bruce as a terrorist. Also, do you have Arnold Kessler's cell number?"

"Yes, sir. Let me get it for you."

Preston took a few seconds to apparently look it up in his rolodex. The number was on his cell, but as he was *talking* on his cell, he couldn't get to it. But then he found it and rattled it off.

"Good. Thanks. What's the status at the White House?"

"The Vice President is in the Situation Room with the Director of Homeland Security and your chief. I'm headed there now. By the way, we have officially gone from Defcon 3 to Defcon 2."

"Tell the VP I'll be there soon and not to make any rash decisions. What's going on in Carthage?"

"Sir, the Maryland National Guard is deployed and patrolling the streets in Stryker personnel carriers wearing protective gear. We also are protecting the government buildings and streets here in Washington."

"Like Bruce said, we're now living in a war zone. Okay, be seeing you, Preston. See you in a few."

"Be safe, Mr. President. We'll get you in."

As soon as the call had ended, the President tapped in the numbers to his Chief and then hit *call*.

"Kessler," was the answer.

"Arnie, this is the President."

"Mr. President, are you all right? Where are you?"

"Not dead. Does that surprise you?"

"Uh...no sir. Why would you ask that?"

"Seems a lot of information coming out the White House is inaccurate if not irresponsible."

"You mean Linda's press release."

"Precisely. Did she get that information from you?"

"I uh...well, not in so many words."

"Then what words *were* they, Arnie? And who came up with the crap about Mr. McGowan bein' part of the terrorist group...and that he abducted me?"

"Sir, in that last conversation I had with McGowan, I didn't know *what* was going on with him. From his reluctance to cooperate with me and the fact that he not only failed to meet with the SAC and further refused to facilitate getting you to the airport, can only mean one thing to me...he's connected with them. And although you might *think* he's protecting you, he's the same as holding you hostage...only you just don't realize it."

The President took the phone away from his face and looked over at me. In almost a whisper he said, "My Chief of Staff has somehow turned into a moron."

I merely smiled and turned my eyes back to the road.

"Look, Arnie, you and I are going to have a serious conversation when I get back there. And for your information, the SAC, Agent Tyson, is the one who's tied into that terrorist bunch. Mr. McGowan had the foresight and savvy to send the State Police to meet with Tyson before we drove in to his location to assure things were on the up and up. But Tyson and his henchmen murdered them. Three of West Virginia's finest are now dead. A second agent, one of the very ones assigned to protect me, is who's ramrodding this terrorist operation. He's the one who demanded my surrender and then sent warnings that he'd bomb that city. And then you know what happened from there."

"I'm sorry, Mr. President. Where are you now, sir?"

"Driving back to Washington."

I clenched my teeth. Under my breath I said, "Shouldn't have told him that, Mr. President."

"I can get Andrews to scramble some F-16s and a couple of choppers to provide you cover and dispatch a team of agents to meet up with you."

I shook my head *no*.

"Don't worry about it. We'll make it there just fine."

"But, sir. If you'll only tell me where you are..."

"Just be in the Oval Office when I get there. We'll talk then." He then flipped the phone closed.

I wasn't sure if that conversation was long enough for Kessler to have the federal location-based server pinpoint our exact milepost, but I was sure he would try. I just didn't trust the man. However, I do have a highly suspicious nature. Had he already set us up twice to be captured or killed or was I being a little too paranoid about him? Adriana keeps telling me that I should be more trusting with people and give them the benefit of the doubt. Maybe she's right.

The I-66 turnoff loomed ahead.

Chapter Thirteen

I had been keeping the Lincoln at a constant speed of 65 along that 81 corridor to make sure that I wasn't breaking the law. Being a fugitive from justice like I was, I didn't need to attract any state or local cowboys who would stop me and make things difficult for the both of us. Not only would my ass be jerked out of the car, but I'd be thrown across the hood as though I were the biggest piece of game ever bagged in the State of Virginia. The President would then be placed in the hands of feds, likely the Secret Service, with whom we didn't exactly have a good history the past few hours. But, if all went well, in less than two hours we would be entering the gate at 1600 Pennsylvania Avenue. Preston Johns was making sure the Winchester satellite office was alerted and the Richmond SAC would be contacting me on my cell within the next few minutes.

We had just passed milepost 283 at Woodstock when I spotted in the median three unmarked sedans parked side by side by side. When I pointed my finger in their direction the President nodded that he had seen them as well. Gliding on by them, I felt comfortable that they would have no reason to stop me. However, in my rearview mirror I suddenly saw their headlights come on.

"Hmm, all three of them just pulled out and are now behind us."

He turned to look back. "Wonder why? You weren't speeding."

"But I also see they're keeping a distance and haven't turned on their blue lights."

Over the next mile the three vehicles made no moves on us. I started thinking maybe they had just been sitting off the road talking through their downed windows to one another where they might go to get their early morning donut...Krispy Kreme, Dunkin' Donuts, Starbucks...and it was time. But then that busy brain of mine began pondering some things. Maybe they weren't unmarked smokies after all. In our last conversation with Kessler, the President had, to my dismay, informed him that we were on the move back to Washington. I-81 to I-66 was the quickest and most direct route. And the feds that had visited McGowan and Sons after the President and I left, if they *were* feds, likely found my Suburban sitting out back of the funeral home and subsequently ran a DMV check on all of Joey's vehicles. It wouldn't take a rocket scientist to then guess what vehicle we were in. And considering that most law enforcement units were now equipped with tag recognition devices...well there you go.

As my brain was deep down in all that deducing, the sudden ringing of my cell phone startled me. A number I didn't recognize. 540 area code. Winchester.

"Yes?"

"Is this McGowan?"

"Who wants to know?"

"I'm Senior Resident Agent Roy Delaney, Winchester FBI satellite office. We received a call directly from National Security Advisor Johns to contact you."

"Finally, a friendly voice."

"He didn't explain much, except that you are *not* to be considered a fugitive and that you have a VIP with you."

"That's correct."

"You're located where?"

"About five miles from the I-66 exit. But, I've noted there are three unmarked units on my tail. Yours or the State's?"

"We have communicated to *all* law enforcement that no one approaches your vehicle. You are in the Lincoln, West Virginia tag number 867-DEF, aren't you?"

"You did your homework."

"Doesn't take us long. As soon as you make that turnoff on I-66, take that first exit, 1a. We will meet you at the BP. We'll be the black GMC Envoy and will escort you on in."

"Great. The VIP and I need a cup of coffee."

"Will have some for you."

"Thanks. See you in a few."

Well, I think the President and I both were feeling a bit more relaxed knowing that in a mere five minutes we would be in good hands. I supposed that the unmarked units behind us were State and had been alerted as to what the plans were. So, things were finally going to go our way after a harrowing damn night. The rain, however, had picked back up with a passion and I actually thought I saw some sleet on the windshield. No matter.

After another mile, I noticed a kind of drone noise overhead and after opening the headliner unit to expose the moonroof, I looked up and saw a small helicopter keeping pace with us. As the I-66 exit loomed ahead only a half mile, suddenly all three vehicles behind us converged on the Lincoln. One of them sped up to pull even with me in the passing lane while another came up on the right and rode the shoulder within inches of the President's door. The third unit closed in tightly on my rear bumper. By the time we reached the exit to I-66, a fourth vehicle, an SUV that had been sitting off on the right of the interstate, pulled out into my lane ahead of me and slowed. All four vehicles kept me from getting off.

"What the hell?" I knew within seconds of seeing the first of the vehicles bearing down on us that these were neither Virginia State unmarked units *or* FBI. Seemed like everyone these days had official-looking black sedans or SUVs, even bad guys.

"Sir, get to the floor." Fully expecting the windows in the vehicles on the left and right to drop down and spurts of automatic fire to begin, I knew I had to make some kind of decision...and quickly. So I jammed hard on my brakes causing the car behind to rearend us, then jerked the steering wheel abruptly to tag the right rear of the vehicle on our left in a PIT maneuver. The nudge then caused it to spin on the wet road and subsequently fly into the median. Stomping the accelerator I swerved into the passing lane and didn't let off until I reached speeds in excess of 120. The maneuver apparently caught all of the vehicle drivers off guard and as I had gotten a jump on them, the nearest one was more than a hundred yards back. I didn't know if any of their cars had intercepter engines, but I was going to bury the speedometer needle on that Lincoln until the pistons and rods blew through the hood, if that's what it took.

I figured eventually one or more of them would catch us and we couldn't stay on the interstate much longer. There were also low spots on the road that contained standing water, and at my speed, chances were that I'd be hydroplaning. As we had already sailed by the I-66 turnoff and a couple exits thereafter, we still needed to duck off where we'd be in the midst of businesses and activity, even if it *was* almost two o'clock in the morning. The helicopter had stayed on us and was now beaming its searchlight directly down onto the Lincoln. It would be difficult for us to find cover out of its line of vision unless I somehow got creative.

About the time I was decreasing my speed to turn off onto the Winchester exit 313, my cell phone lit up.

"Could you get that for me, sir? I'm rather busy at the moment."

When the President said 'hello,' I heard, "McGowan?"

"This is McGowan," I answered. "I'm on speaker. Delaney?"

"Yes. I thought you'd be here by now."

"We were accosted by several vehicles that surrounded us in a hurry at the I-66 turnoff. We weren't able to get off."

"They still on you?"

"I did some fancy driving and got away; but, they're still behind us. Also there's a chopper buzzing over us. Right now I'm getting off on 313. Is the bird yours?"

"There's nothing federal out there at this moment, but I have one on the way. Again, everyone was told to stay away from you. I don't even know how anyone would have gotten onto you. I'll come your way. I'll also recheck with the State in case the order didn't get down to everyone."

"How many agents do you have with you."

"Two."

"That's not going to do it. If these guys are bad, which I believe they are, they're ruthless and don't care who they shoot up. You'd better engage the State or get more of your buds to join you."

"Roger. I'm coming your way. When you land somewhere safe, let me know where you are."

"Will do."

As soon as I zipped off the exit, I ran the red light at the end of the ramp and turned left toward Winchester. As expected, few people were out on that early Saturday morning. Two or three chain restaurants still showed signs of life, but there were only a couple of cars in their parking lots which likely belonged to restaurant personnel cleaning up.

About the same time we were speeding down Millwood, I figured the vehicles chasing us were just now getting off at the exit. However, it didn't matter how far back they were, the chopper was still dead on us and would serve as their eyes. What we needed right about then, even more than that promised cup of coffee, was a hiding place. I had to find a spot where I could make the Lincoln disappear from that chopper. Even though a few of the streets were treelined, all the leaves were gone and would not offer concealment

Winchester is a beautiful, revitalized small city with a quaint Old Town atmosphere. Having worked a case there in the 80s back when I was a Bureau agent, I returned after I retired on a couple of occasions just to take in some of its history, culture and of course its good southern cuisine. One of those times was just a couple of years ago. Adriana shopped one antique store after another most of the day in the pedestrian mall area. Of course I spent the better part of the afternoon myself in one of the more popular pubs sampling a variety of English ales, stouts and lagers. *She* drove us home.

When the President and I were finally deep into the Old Town village, I turned down a side street that dumped into the pedestrian mall. I did find a parking garage to zip into, but all they're good for when people are giving chase is trapping you inside. How many movies have I seen where people are doing nothing but climbing levels, round and round, until they've run out of territory. So obviously I didn't elect the garage. What I did see was a pitch black alley on my left sandwiched tightly between two buildings. At a point where the helicopter was circling around adjacent rooftops and momentarily out of sight, I turned off my lights and ducked in.

I called Delaney back. "We're in an alley off the village. The chopper is buzzing close overhead. It's location will give you an idea where we are."

"I see it," he said. "We're close."

After a few moments, I eased out from behind the wheel of the Lincoln and got out to peek around the corner. The bird in the air finally did move on, focusing its penetrating beam on a vehicle similar to mine parked a street over. I watched for a couple of long minutes while one of the vehicles that had been on our tail converged on the car. But because in no time at all I was soaked and shivering from the bitter cold rain, I jumped back into the car.

Pulling out slowly, I kept the headlights off and made a right turn onto Loudoun. I had no idea where we'd go from there, but now we needed to get out of town somewhere out in the wooded countryside. However, we had not covered more than two blocks when suddenly on our left approaching from a side street a black Expedition came barreling down on us. Immediately, I knew these people were not feds. What gave me a clue was the man I spotted on the passenger side of the vehicle pointing a shoulder-fired RPG out the window directly at the Lincoln. Sphincter pucker time.

It was one of those split second moments when at the exact same time you're fully expecting to die, from out of nowhere comes your savior. As though it had somehow materialized from thin air, a GMC Envoy equipped with a push bar slammed at high speed head-on into the gunner's door causing the rocket launcher to fall harmlessly to the asphalt. As the impact had to have killed the would-be assassin, the driver had to be seriously banged up as well. Immediately, three men in dark suits with badges hanging from their breast pockets and sporting MP5s poured out of the ramming vehicle and converged on the heavily damaged Expedition.

The President and I looked at one another and grinned. I thought about offering up a high five, but in order to salvage my dignity somehow managed to curb my elation. I then pulled off to the side of the street and parked within about thirty feet of the two vehicles.

These new guys, these daring dealers of doom, were our cavalry arriving in that proverbial nick of time. One of the heroes rounded the Expedition to the driver's side, first smashing the door glass with the butt of his machine gun and then pointing the muzzle inside. Apparently, the driver was either knocked out or dead since he was not immediately yanked from the vehicle.

"Mr. President, would you remain here in the car while I go talk with these agents?"

He nodded. He was still cradling the MP5.

Even though our previous experience with people wearing badges that night had not been exactly hunky-dory, these guys I knew we could trust. If they *weren't* the good guys, then why would they be wiping out their own? However, as I trekked toward the wreck, Glock hanging down at my side, one of the suits suddenly turned and pointed his weapon. directly at my torso. Was I wrong about them? Had I misread the situation. But considering what had just gone down, I couldn't have. They had seen we were under attack and without hesitation made that split second decision to take the bad guys out. Nonetheless, I quickly holstered my Glock and lifted my hands. The rain beat cold against my face.

"McGowan?"

"You must be Delaney."

He nodded. "The President with you?"

"He's there in the Lincoln and appreciative as hell that you arrived on the scene when you did. How did you know where to find us?"

He pointed up. I thought he was going to say it was divine insight. "Like you suggested, I just followed that chopper, which now seems to have de-assed the area. I guess they saw what happened down here. You can put your hands down now."

Before we could continue our chat, two Winchester Police units and a local wrecker swept in from different directions. Both officers quickly exited and walked toward Delaney who held up his badge and ID. He promptly announced that he was "FBI." While they talked, I joined the agent who was still looking into the driver's side of the Expedition.

"Thanks for getting here when you did. A couple more seconds, we'd have been vaporized."

"Don't we know it. Life is all a matter of timing."

"And *death*. My guess is that the gunner in the passenger seat bought the farm. What about this one?"

"Dead as well. Nasty head wound. Looks like the airbag didn't do its job."

"Too bad. One of these two might have sung a song for us."

Agent Delaney broke away from the cops and joined me while I was checking out the bodies. "I told the City to have these people put on ice until I can get our Evidence Response Team to check them out. Looks like they're both Middle Eastern," he said.

"I doubt you'll find any papers or IDs on them or in the vehicle, but maybe they slipped up. You should find at least one cell phone, however, since that would be the only way to communicate with one another."

"Looks like Agent Harrison just came up with one. We'll have it gone through."

"Where are the rest of your people?"

"You're looking at us."

"You mean you were still only prepared to escort us to Washington with two other agents and one vehicle?"

"There'll be a Bureau AH-64 Apache in the air covering us."

"As I told you on the road, there are other extremist vehicles out there, that seem to have now disappeared, and none of these people have been hesitant to attack anybody in their way." I took a moment to give him a description of the units and then continued with my lecture. "Bird or not, you're going to need a hell of a lot more people and guns protecting the President the remaining distance to Washington. These people want to make the biggest statement they can. They plan to do that by taking him down. And I'm talking nothing short of assassination here. So get more bodies, Agent Delaney."

I got the impression from the expression on his face he actually resented my pushy attitude, my being only a civilian nobody these days. But to his credit, he didn't get his bowels in an uproar. "Understood. Given what's happened with you and the President tonight, you're right. But until our other agents make the scene, I'll contact the State to send us a squad of troopers."

"The sooner the better. We're vulnerable as hell right now. The people in these other vehicles could be reconsolidating for an assault as we speak. That being said, I'm going back to the President."

"Okay, when my other agents get here we'll form a makeshift perimeter around the car. I understand a couple more City officers are on the way as well."

While Delaney was returning to his unit to make the call to the State Police, I started back toward the Lincoln. There we stood with only the three feds and me protecting Eagle One on that downtown street. I actually *did* feel vulnerable. The reinforcements couldn't get there fast enough for my liking.

Almost as quickly as Delaney had made mention of the Apache, it appeared seemingly from nowhere above the town's buildings, its raucous vortex beating the air and whipping the pouring rain around in every direction. I saw that Delaney had apparently completed his call to the State as he then brought his wrist up to his mouth and looked up toward the chopper. "Predator, this is Delaney. We're good here. Push off and wait for further. I'll let you know when we're ready to move out."

 A couple seconds later it banked away.

"Two units of troopers will be here in zero five. I have six agents in three vehicles on the way as well. The state and locals will be canvassing for the subversive vehicles you described."

As the city cops were attending to the accident scene, which really wasn't an *accident* at all, Delaney and his two agents converged on the Lincoln. Giving the President a quick two finger salute from his eyebrow, the senior agent then took his position alongside the right front door.

"By the way, McGowan, while we were waiting back at the BP station, I spoke again more at length with the National Security Advisor. He filled me in on what you and the President experienced tonight. Damn harrowing to say the least. But he also says the Greenbrier airport has now been secured. Deputy FBI Director Graywall put two Apaches in the air to patrol the hills around the airport. Once satisfied there no longer appeared to be an imminent terrorist threat, they allowed the trailing Marine C130 to land. Our Charleston field office also inserted a tactical response squad in there. It serves to reason that since the extremists knew you and the President had set out on the road, they were no longer interested in the airport. It should now be safe for the First Lady to fly out of there."

"Good. Agent Smithers has been keeping her and my wife under wraps at my camp. We'll call her to arrange a hand-off with the team. Just keep the Secret Service out of the deal."

"It'll be an exclusive Bureau operation."

Less than ten minutes later, two State Police units were on the scene. I watched as the lead officer, Sergeant J. F. Thomas, spoke briefly with Delaney, both pointing and gesturing, but the conversation was cut short when the agent placed his wrist mic near his mouth and said, "Yes, I see you. Park behind the Lincoln on the side of the street." A gray Charger and black special edition van then pulled in. Two agents wearing dark jackets with the letters FBI printed across their front exited the car and Delaney struck up a conversation with them. He then turned his attention to the occupants of the van, who had stayed inside. When the driver's window dropped, I could see he was part of an FBI SWAT element. Finally, Delaney walked up to where I was leaning against the front fender of the Lincoln.

"We can take the President on from here, McGowan. You're free to drive on back..."

"Agent Delaney, I've seen the President through a tough damn night to this point and I want to see him all the way through the White House gate."

"I don't know, McGowan. You don't actually have an official capacity and although your service to the President has been nothing less than heroic, it's time to end it. I'd think you would want to get back to your wife."

The voice from inside the Lincoln then said, "If Mr. McGowan wants to continue on to see that I get home, I can understand that. It's been a hell of a night and no sense of him driving all the way back down there. Our ladies are probably sleeping soundly anyway. I can put him up for the night and he can get a fresh start in the morning'. I'll still ride with him if that's all right with you."

"Whatever you say, Mr. President," replied Delaney. "Your Lincoln will be sandwiched in between our units. One of the trooper's cars will lead, I'll follow, and after your vehicle, the Charger and SWAT van in that order. Predator, our eye in the sky will watch for bandits. Let's prepare to move out."

I commented, "The front of your SUV looks a little banged up, Agent Delaney. You don't want it to break down on the road."

"The wrecker driver, who's a mechanic, checked it over and said it's all cosmetic. The radiator's not hurt, but I do have a headlight out."

"Then I'm ready if you are. Let's get the show on the road."

Chapter Fourteen

The rain had finally subsided and by the time we reached the exit that led to Manassas, fog had begun to set in. We hadn't talked much along the way, mainly because in glancing over at the President, I noted that he was bailing on me. His head would nod slowly and then he'd catch himself in a sudden jerk. After about three of these attempts to go unconscious on me, he reached over and turned on the radio.

"As much as I don't want to listen to these media fat heads providing their takes on tonight's terrorist incidents, I guess I need to catch up on things. Nobody *reports* the news anymore; they only spew out their stupid speculations and opinions, level inaccurate accusations and take malicious pot shots at people when most don't know what the heck they're talking about."

I grinned. "Don't beat around the bush, Mr. President; tell me how you *really* feel about the press."

We listened. Reporters were still slamming me. I was suddenly Public Enemy Number One...a conspirator, a terrorist, mass murderer. The President was still missing and I was either holding him coercively to get the Gitmo twenty four released or he was dead. There was specifically more commentary about the Carthage bombing and the downing of the C130, but I was at the core of it all. Couldn't my friend, the National Security Advisor, who was to have contacted the Press Secretary, Director of the FBI and the rest of the free world to tell them the President was safe and that I had saved him from hounds of hell, have done so by now? I would be sure to place my hands around Arnie Kessler's throat if I ever saw him.

As to the bombing, it had now been determined that the device was indeed a large radiological dispersive device or RDD and that a high degree of widespread radioactive material was being detected. Its residual effect could potentially be more catastrophic than the attack on the World Trade Center in 2001. Homeland Security and both state and federal law enforcement resources were on site to investigate. The Maryland National Guard had been activated to handle looting, out-of-control panic and evacuation and relocation of the populace. The EPA's Radiological Emergency Response Team was mobilized to assess the amount of radiation that may have been released throughout the city and its suburbs. Finally, local and adjacently supporting resources from EMT services and fire departments were on the scene to provide casualty assessment, emergent first aid and transport to medical centers. Those American citizens who heard about the terrorist outbreak and the taking of the President when first broadcast would be too panic stricken to sleep the rest of the night. Those who had already retired before the reports hit the airwaves would be rising from their beds in a few hours stunned.

For a few moments the President sat listening to the commentary looking reflectively out his side door glass without saying a word. I could imagine what was going through his mind. So many brave and true had died in that fiery C130 crash. Innocent citizens in southern Maryland would soon be dying. The rest of America would be in a state of panic, wondering if their city was next. His wife, the First Lady of the United States, still had to be retrieved from that danger zone where the terrorist mission began. Even considering Greenbrier County was now saturated with feds and military, would her extraction come off safely? And all this was happening on his watch with only a month left in office. Not the best of ways to go out.

"Mr. President, anything more you can think to tell me about Franks?"

"I only know that he was pushed onto Bill Clayton's protection detail by one of the Secret Service Assistant Directors. Don't know the name, though. He supposedly told Agent Clayton he was very high on Franks, that he'd been in the system maybe ten years and was a seasoned agent. I think I remember Bill makin' some comments such as that Franks was quiet and very smart, but only marginally communicative. My question would be how people like him get into important federal service positions this close to the presidency in the first place. I know they go through a battery of psychological tests to determine if there are any deviancies or abnormalities. But four agents goin' sour on us?"

"Like I said, sir, this was all set up somewhere at the federal hierarchy. Somebody near the top is in league with the jihadists, and I guarantee that he and these bastard agents stand to make a lot of money. I doubt that most of them give a crap one way or another about extremist goals and vision *or* getting the Gitmo prisoners released."

"And I will not rest until we weed out every last one of them."

We entered the city without incident. Delaney's SUV had held together and no jihadists attempted any aggressive moves. Knowing that the Apache with its 30 mm cannons and Hellfire missiles would have blown them into oblivion, the extremists had obviously decided to use discretionary judgment. Apparently Delaney had communicated ahead of our arrival with White House Security. His vehicle was met without any fuss from the guards. We were all motioned on through. I had hoped that if there were any other Secret Service agents who had chosen the more, shall I say iniquitous path, they were not serving on the White House staff.

When we pulled up to a stop, one of Delaney's men immediately jumped out and hustled to open the door for the President. I was left to open my own damn door.

"Come on in, Bruce. We'll get you a place to sleep tonight. I know you want to get back at the earliest opportunity, so I won't let anyone try to keep you for interrogation. I can tell them anything they need to know."

"And you'll have somebody not only call off the dogs, but order a new press release so that I won't get shot on sight on my way back."

"As soon as we get upstairs."

"Should I leave my weapons in the car?"

"I think the Secret Service would appreciate that, Bruce. Don't worry, nobody has ever stolen anything on White House grounds since I've been in office. I'll have the Lincoln parked with the official vehicles."

"Mr. President," began Delaney. "I have had further conversation with the National Security Advisor and he has ordered Bureau agents to temporarily replace all Secret Service here in the White House. I don't think you'll see any familiar faces around here tonight."

"Good move. What's been *done* with the usual agents?"

"He has further ordered all White House Secret Service to be assembled in the briefing room. Homeland Security Inspector General personnel along with CID have been summoned and will be there to begin interrogating everyone at 0500."

"Looks like you're on top of things, Agent Delaney. Up through your channels I want you to notice the director, Tom Campanello, to also be there. Are you stickin' around tonight? Given the late hour, we can bunk you here."

"No sir, I'm going to go on back. I have a meeting with my agents at 0900."

The President shook his hand. "Then thank you, Roy. You got us out of a very big scrape tonight. I'll be sure to brag on you with the director when I see him." He then turned to one of his personal staff, Walt Taylor, who was waiting to escort him in. "Walt, is the Chief of Staff close by?"

"He left, Mr. President. Left about an hour ago."

"Knowing that I was on the way? Why?"

Walt shrugged. "He didn't say, sir. He just left."

My suspicions about Kessler had just been heightened a hundred percent.

"Is his deputy, Ms. Holland, here tonight?"

"She is, Mr. President."

"Then send her a message to assemble the National Security Council in the Situation Room...and the press secretary. Who all on the team are here tonight, Walt?"

"The Vice President, sir. Also Secretary of State, the National Security Adviser, Mr. Johns, Chief Counterterrorism Adviser Macy and of course Ms. Holland."

"Good. But get the rest of the council in here as well. Bruce, while I spend the night with the council, you go get some sleep. Walt, show him up to Mr. Lincoln's bedroom."

I'm sure my eyes ballooned to the size of ping pong balls. "Sir, I couldn't. From what I've learned, that's reserved for royalty and special guests."

"They don't get any more special than you, my friend. Now go have a good night's sleep." He then turned to me and said in a low voice, "You know that sense of intuition you have about people, Bruce? Mine is off the chart right now about Mr. Kessler."

I was basking in euphoria. I had become a 'special friend' of the President of the United States and I was sleeping in the 16th president's bed. My only regret was that Adriana was not there with me to share in some frisky nocturnal delights...and on Abe Lincoln's bed of all places. Of course she would have no part of my intentions, claiming it was not only an impure notion on my part but to defile that bed would be downright indecent.

In spite of my monstrous headache where the bullet had bounced off my head, I was tired. So tired I knew I wouldn't stay awake long enough to appreciate the room's ambiance. I did take a washcloth to my head and face to erase the dried blood. Unfortunately, I couldn't get the blood to rinse out of the cloth, so I wrang the red water out the best I could. Hopefully, it would dry enough overnight so that it wouldn't leave a wet spot in my jeans when I stuck it in my pocket later in the morning. Better for housekeeping to find that I had stolen the washcloth than for me to leave its bloody carcass on the sink for them to find.

I hit the sheets, said a quick prayer for the wife, the President, the country...and that was it. The next thing I knew, I turned over in the cushy bed and the red numbers on the digital clock on the nightstand met my eyes. Six-twenty. I hopped up, emptied my aging bladder and threw water on my face. Considering I would still have on the same clothes as last night, I didn't bother to shower. I did find an unused toothbrush, some mouthwash and a complimentary tube of toothpaste on the bathroom sink. My mouth would be clean whether the rest of me was or not. The headache? Still there. I also noticed a new part in my hair.

After snapping a photo of the Lincoln bedroom with my cell phone, I closed the door behind me only to find a stern-looking White House security guard standing outside the room along the wall. Without word, he held out his hand. I didn't know if he was looking for a tip or wanted me to shake it.

"Your phone, Mr. McGowan."

"You...want my phone?"

"I want your phone."

So I handed it to him. He then touched its face, found *photos*, located the picture I just took and hit *delete*.

"Not authorized, sir." he handed it back to me. "The President will see you in the dining room. It's down on the first level. Take the stairs, turn right and its the second room on the right. Have a nice day, sir."

"Uh, right. You too."

So now I couldn't prove to Adriana that I had actually slept in the Lincoln bedroom. Maybe my new special friend would convince her...if she ever had the occasion to see him again. And just how did the security guy know I took photos with my cell? Were there cameras in the bedroom?

When I entered the dining room, the President was seated at the head of the table with a woman in a gray suit and blonde hair sitting to his left and a white-haired, distinguished looking man in his mid sixties on his right.

"Come in, Bruce. Been expectin' you for about a half hour. You sleep well?"

"Fine, Mr. President. Did you not sleep at all?"

He shook his head. "I did shower and put on clean clothes, however. How about some breakfast."

"Just some coffee, sir. I'm not much for putting on the feedbag this early in the morning."

"Okay, then. I'd like you to meet our Chief Counterterrorism Adviser Howard Macy and the Deputy Chief of Staff Diana Holland." They stood and held out their hands. I shook them.

The President continued. "I want us to talk about getting the First Lady and Agent Smithers on that bird down in Greenbrier County. Bruce, I assume that our ladies are up by now and thought we'd go ahead and make the call. We've decided that it might be better to have the Marine helicopter go in to your fishing camp and pick them up rather than to have Adriana drive them to the airport. There still might be a degree risk if they did. Is that feasible? Is there an open field close by where the chopper can land?"

"Not really, sir. Adriana could take them along the road that parallels the river to a clearing about a mile away."

"Or if you tell us where the camp is, we can send a couple units of FBI in there to take 'em to the airport. Either way."

"Either way, sir. I can give you the coordinates of the camp."

"Give them to the Bureau Chief, Mr. Jenkins. He's still here from last night. He'll coordinate with his team down in West Virginia and make it happen."

"What did the Secret Service director have to say in last night's meeting about his four turncoats, two which of course are dead?" I asked.

"What *could* he say? He was stunned. Said because they were all on the First Family protection team, he was personally familiar with them. He's none too happy, however, about the temporary suspension of his White House detail. But, he is personally committed to working with the Inspector General's office to investigate these traitors and determine if there are even more scabs internally in the Service."

"Although we don't have any reason to think so, I would be very distressed to find out that Agent Smithers was one of them."

"As the wife has gotten to know her very well over the past couple of years, I can't imagine it. That bein' said, I guess it's time to see how the ladies are doing. Shall I call my Mrs. or would you like to make the contact with Adriana?"

"I'm sure the First Lady would like to hear your voice this morning, Mr. President."

"That she would." He dialed the call on the table top conference phone so that everyone could hear.

We heard the phone ring two, three, four times.

"Hello," she answered.

"Good morning, my dear. I trust you had a good night there. We finally made it to the White House, thanks to Mr. McGowan."

She didn't immediately respond.

"Are you there, sweetheart?"

Still silence. For some reason my chest slowly began to seize with angst. Something didn't feel right. And then, to our horror, it was a male voice that responded. "Your sweetheart is still here, Mr. President. And so am I."

The President jumped up from his chair as though he had been shot. My heart suddenly leapt into my mouth.

"I guess you didn't think we'd find this place, did you McGowan? Oh, I know you're there close by. As you've figured out by now, we have eyes everywhere."

The President mouthed silently to me, "Franks?"

I shook my head *no*.

"As I told your cohort in crime, I don't forget a voice, Tyson...especially one belonging to a murderous prick."

"You have a perceptive ear. And I have to give it to you, McGowan. You're good. But, not quite good enough. Remember, you got your State Police captain killed. He started getting too smart for his own good. How does it feel to know that you sent him to his death?"

"How does it feel to know you're going to die only seconds after I find you?"

"Again, you don't have to *find* me, McGowan. You know where I am. I'm looking at three very lovely ladies, one of which is your very own wife. Don't worry. They're fine...for now."

I glanced at the President. His eyes seethed with anger, but the rest of him appeared absolutely petrified.

"They'd better be, maggot," I replied.

He then put the First Lady's phone on *speaker*. A second male voice came on the line. "Since you're into voice recognition, McGowan, I guess you'll now recognize *mine*. You had to know I wouldn't be far."

Franks.

He continued. "Nice little camp you have here on the river. In better times, I could have enjoyed a little time out here. Maybe I'll have the lovely Adriana whip me up some steak and eggs for breakfast."

"Snide and contemptible as usual, Franks. You have to resort to taking women hostage to get what you want. So, what *is* it you want?"

"We *have* what we want. The First Lady. At least what will *get* us what we want. So, Mr. President, if you want her back, you get the Gitmo prisoners released. You don't? She'll be carved up into bait and fed to these magnificent rainbow trout out here in the Greenbrier. Hungry little bastards, I bet."

The President grit his teeth and raised his fist above the conference phone as though he were ready to smash it to pieces. But then he took a deep breath and sat back down. For a long moment, with his elbow resting on the table, he massaged his forehead.

"Are you still there, Eagle One? What's your answer?"

"I...need some time to consider my options here."

"There *are* no options," Franks replied. "But I'll give you one hour. After you confer with all the government *big* heads up there, be ready with your answer. You *will* call your wife's cell phone again at 0745. And Mr. President, don't even think about sending your heroes down here to rescue the wife. I have people all over this place. We hear or catch sight of any choppers...even one would-be liberator...everybody dies. Am I clear?"

Neither the President nor I responded.

"I'm going to assume from your silence you understand. One hour!" He then ended the call.

The President pointed to his Deputy Chief. "Diana, get Bureau Director Jenkins in here. We don't have much time. I'm goin' after those bastards."

"But sir, you heard what this Franks said. The lives of the First Lady and other women are at stake here. There has to be another solution."

"Then my ears are open. Talk to me, people."

Holland again. "What if you offer to release just *some* of the prisoners, maybe those that don't pose an immediate threat when they get back out in the street. Put some kind of location device on them and when they're released, pick them back up."

"Gentlemen? Your thoughts."

"Got a question," Macy said. "Which of these rogue agents do you think is driving this train?"

I answered that. "Tyson may have been the SAC among the agents, but most of my contact tonight has been with Franks. I think he's the one actually in charge and could even be one of the key principals in this Stealth Jihad organization. But there's somebody else on the inside as well. Maybe a mole right here in the White House. *You* heard him. He knew I was actually sitting here this morning."

Holland and Macy quickly glanced at each other.

The President asked, "By the way, has anyone heard from Arnie Kessler?"

They both shook their heads. His question insinuated one of the key players might be his own Chief of Staff. "When you get hold of the director, Diana, tell him to send a couple people by the chief's residence and pick his ass up."

I was glad he was finally coming around on that bastard. I hadn't trusted Kessler from the get-go.

"But gettin' back to your comment, Diana, these jihadists are not going to accept anything less than having the entire twenty four released. However, I do like your idea about putting some kind of tracking device on them so that we could later go after them. Howard, would that work?"

"Possibly. But let me insert a comment, sir. I hate to say it this way, and I know it's the First Lady we're talking about here, but the policy of the U.S. government is that we neither negotiate with nor allow ourselves to be coerced by terrorists. We've seen hostages taken before by such extremists and we haven't bent to their demands."

"And the hostages usually end up dead," Holland added.

"My wife is out there facing certain death as well, folks," I remarked. "I'm not saying you need to cave and meet their demands to save our ladies, but if some kind of a decision is not made in an hour, I have no doubt they will follow through with their threats."

"You're right, Bruce. We've personally seen evidence of what they're capable of. So, let's talk about makin' somethin' happen without doin' damage to our national security."

"We might have a workable solution, Mr. President," I replied. "Why don't you go ahead and commit to having the Gitmo twenty four released, but tell these bastards it can't happen overnight...maybe not for a few days until all the red tape is dispensed. That will buy some time for you to put an FBI Hostage Rescue Team in there."

Holland shook her head. "You heard them, sir. At the first sound of aircraft or sight of ground forces out in those woods, they kill the hostages. I vote *no* on the HRT."

"If I may, Mr. President," said Macy. "I *like* McGowan's idea. Our people are pros and specifically trained for this kind of mission. I'm convinced the HRT does guerrilla tactics just as well as the Army's Special Forces. Remember they train with Delta Force. They'll make it work with a great degree of stealth."

"I wish I could be sure about that."

"Even though I'm with McGowan on this, and I hate to say it this way, but who knows what these renegades will do *anyway*, They may just go ahead and...well, you know."

"Yeah." The President looked away and shuffled in his chair. He was in the unenviable position of having to think like the President of the United States *and* as a husband. All I knew was, I wanted my wife back in one piece.

"Whatever you decide to do, sir, I'm going down there to get my wife out of the clutches of these mad men...even if I have to do it by myself. I know that area around the camp like the back of my hand. Be assured...they'll never see me coming."

"And I know *you*, Bruce. You and I not only have a history together, but I saw you in action last night. If we do send a team in there, I want you with it. You would be their eyes and ears anyway."

Macy shook his head. "But Mr. President, McGowan is a civilian and would be unauthorized to accompany an HRT. They have their tactics and he might be in the way."

"Mr. McGowan has the best skills of any covert operator in the business. If we hatch this plan, he *will* go in with them. You and Barry Jenkins put something together. In the meantime, I need to strategize as to how I'll communicate back with these terrorists."

"Is that your final decision, sir?" asked Macy. "You will agree to the release, but before it would ever happen, we send in the HRT?"

"My final decision. I want you, the Secretary of State and Director Jenkins to have an attack plan ready to go in the Situation Room by noon. Mr. McGowan will sit down with you and give you the layout of his camp. Call down to Quantico and get an HRT element ready ASAP. The commander of that team needs to be in your strategy session as well. Get it done, folks. The sooner we go, the better. Everybody good?"

Everyone nodded and replied, "Yes, Mr. President."

After Macy and Holland left the dining room, I remained seated with the President. I would join them momentarily, but I stayed behind on purpose to speak privately with him.

"Sir, I am so sorry about this."

"About what, Bruce?"

"It was my suggestion to send our ladies out to the camp. But I don't understand how these people could have found out about it. It's a place that not even my golf and hunting buddies know about. A place that only my family uses. Could Smithers have brought them in?"

"Now I'm not so sure, Bruce. But don't beat yourself up. In retrospect, our wives *couldn't* have remained with us, considering what we went through. They had already seen enough carnage at Wolf Laurel and bein' with us at your brother's place and what we encountered on the road, they would have been even *more* traumatized. And how did these agents find out about your place? Don't forget that these two traitors have had a great deal of investigative experience and are experts at gatherin' Intel."

"Nevertheless, I still feel responsible our ladies are in this mare's nest."

He placed his hand on my shoulder. "In a few minutes I have to talk with some very unpleasant people. I'd like you to be close by to listen. After that, go make plans with the others to get our ladies back."

Chapter Fifteen

My watch read 0739 when the President touched the numbers on the conference phone to ring the First Lady's cell. After the third ring it was Franks who answered. He was short and to the point. "Six minutes to spare. What's your decision?"

"Before we get down to business, I want to talk with the First Lady." The President was just as abrupt.

"I'll give you thirty seconds."

A moment later, she was on the line. "Hi, sweetheart." Her voice sounded cracked, obviously from signs of fear and stress.

"Hello, Pet. Are you okay?"

"I'm okay. I hope you are."

"I am. They haven't hurt you, have they?"

"No. They charged in here..."

"That's enough!" Franks spouted.

"How about Mrs. McGowan and Agent Smithers?"

"You're wasting my time, Mr. President! Now let's get to it!"

"No! Put my wife back on the phone. Before any conversation happens on the Gitmo deal, we *will* talk with our wives. Now put her phone on *speaker*. No time constraints this time."

We then heard him let out a puff of air.

After a moment, the First Lady continued. "I'm fine. They didn't hurt Adriana *or* me."

"How about Joanie?"

There was a pause. Then Franks jumped in on the conversation. "Sweetpea tried to play the hero. Unfortunately she was roughed up a bit."

"What's her status?"

"She caught a butt stroke and is lying over there against the wall with one hell of a headache," he said.

"But she's conscious," added the First Lady. And then suddenly she raised her voice. "*Just don't give these people what they want...*" There was a sudden noise I couldn't identify and she let out a scream.

The President winced and shouted, *"Franks, you son of a bitch, you'd better not have hurt her!"*

He laughed sarcastically. "She's all right. I just had to sit her down...with a bit of force, I might add. Now can we do this?"

The President tightened his fists.

"This is McGowan, Franks. I know you're a homicidal sociopath, but how about having a little respect for the

First Lady of the United States? Just keep your hands off her. And as for Smithers, do you enjoy beating up on women? Now if you don't mind, let me talk with *my* wife."

"Shit fire, what is it with you bleeding heart assholes and your women?" He then let out a long sigh. "All right, make it quick."

After a moment, Adriana was on the line. "Bruce, don't worry about the First Lady and me. We're not hurt. I think Joanie needs a doctor, though."

She called me *Bruce*. Never does that. She was trying to tell me something.

"You're sure you're all right, Adriana?"

"Yes. But I'm not sure our camp and roads in here are. I've noted problems from the bad weather everywhere. There are wash outs in several places...three major issues on Sydenstricker, a couple on Elderberry and this morning I counted four leaks here inside the cabin."

"What the hell *is* this?" Franks yelled. "Cut the chit-chat. This is not the goddam HGTV channel. You women get over there and sit the hell down. Okay, Mr. Big, your turn. Tell me what I need to hear. And I'd better hear the right words."

"All right, Franks. I've conferred with my staff. Reluctantly, we will cut the twenty four loose. But I need some time to put together the arrangements. We can't just set them outside of the facility and tell them to go home. I'm sure you realize they need to be handed off to their governments...Yemen, Egypt, Iran, Saudi Arabia."

"I see a stall game here. But, how much time are you talking about If we agree to it?"

"Two, maybe three days. This is Saturday and in most cases the world is not open for business."

"You have twenty four hours to get twenty four people released. Eight o'clock tomorrow we'd better see the prisoners gone. We don't, people start dying. And don't forget that another even larger city will go up in flames on Monday night. Bigger bomb, bigger city. After that, bombs go off during business hours and you can only imagine the numbers that'll be lying dead in the streets."

I wanted to jump through that phone line and rip the bastard's heart out. All the while I was wondering how these men who were so carefully screened and selected for such trusting positions as government agents could dishonor and betray their country by falling in with America's enemies.

"That is not gonna give me enough time to..."

"Tick tock, Mr. President. This is my last conversation with you until I find out the prisoners are actually released. And don't bother trying to reach your wife on her cell. After this conversation, I am smashing all of the women's cell phones. Tick tock."

When the line then went dead, the President leaned back in his chair and expelled a long breath of air. "Bastard. I want his head on a stake. When do you think is the best time to go in, Bruce?"

"During the hours of darkness. I'd say not later than 2100 tonight."

"Do you think the task force can be put together and the mission executed that soon?"

"Yes, I do. And I'll help make that happen."

"By the way, why was Adriana goin' on about pot holes and leaks?"

"She never calls me *Bruce*. But when she did, I figured she would be trying to tell me something in metaphoric terms. So she encoded her message. The bad weather is the bad guys. The pot holes are the outside guards and three of them are positioned in and around Sydenstricker Road. Two more are at its intersection with Elderberry that leads into our fish camp. There are four bad guys in the cabin with our women, two of which are of course Franks and Tyson. How she knew about the positions of the perimeter guards, I don't know. Maybe she overheard them being briefed about where they were to be placed. There may be more gunmen on site, but we now know there are at least nine."

He smiled. "I guess she learned stuff like that bein' married to you."

"She's learned a *lot* of stuff being married to me. Some things I wish she hadn't."

He looked at his watch. "They should all be assembled by now, Bruce. Go work with these people." He then smiled. "But watch out; there might be an ego or two in the room."

And I knew that the plan had to be finalized and in the President's hands in less than four hours. We were under the gun and needed to execute the attack before the sun came up on Sunday. A lot of coordination had to be done and if I was to be a part of the mission, I'd have to fly down to Quantico and on to Greenbrier County with the HRT within minutes after our strategy session broke up in the Situation Room. I was also hoping the HRT commander would suit me up in some SWAT wear after we landed in Quantico. Somehow it just wouldn't feel right me hitting the woods in my North Face parka, Greg Norman pullover and nice new Wrangler jeans.

* * * * *

0835. White House Situation Room, West Wing basement. A lot of history made there. Convening for the second time in less than seven hours were select members of the National Security Council. Present were the Deputy Chief of Staff Holland, National Security Advisor Johns, Counterterrorism Chief Macy, Homeland Security Director Bob Shanahan, FBI Director Jeremiah Jenkins, the White House scribe and yours truly. The HRT commander was on his way by helicopter from Quantico and would be arriving in a matter of minutes. Absent was the Vice President who was attending a prayer breakfast on the other side of the city.

Sitting in one of the heavily-padded conference chairs behind the long, mahogany conference table with all of the important heads in the intelligence and law enforcement community around me, I actually felt like *somebody*. However, given that everyone was dressed in suits, the men in ties, and I was in a long sleeve gray pullover with everyone's blood splattered on it including that of the President and Agent Clayton, not to mention mine, I also felt like a pair of beat-up tennis shoes in a community of wingtips.

On one end of the Situation Room was a set of wood panels that opened up into screens, monitors and other high tech audio-visual systems that offered real time network coverage of events happening around the world...the National Intel Daily, Pentagon briefs on friendly and not-so-friendly military movements and intra-agency videoconferencing. The big nerve center of the White House. Yeah, I *was* somebody.

It was good seeing my friend, Preston Johns, again. We shook hands and he introduced me to both the FBI's and Homeland Security's directors. Glad-handing all around. Two gentlemen dressed all in white brought in trays that contained water and glasses and wide-mouth mugs for the coffee that sat on an adjacent table.

"Bruce, you look beat up, my friend," Johns said. "All that blood yours?"

"I think most of it belongs to the Commander-in-Chief. Royal blood. I may not ever have the shirt laundered."

That brought a few smiles and helped start things off.

Diana Holland began her briefing almost immediately. "Gentlemen, if you will kindly take your seats, we will begin. I am the White House Deputy Chief of Staff Holland and in Mr. Kessler's absence, I'll assume control of the meeting. As you are aware, the country is now in crisis if not at war with this terrorist organization that calls itself the Stealth Jihad of America. We are very fortunate to have our President back, who with the help of Mr. McGowan seated here, escaped certain capture or death last evening down in Greenbrier County, West Virginia, at Mr. McGowan's residence where the First Family was enjoying a short retreat. *Unfortunately*, we now know that two of the President's own agents from his protection detail have allied themselves with the extremists and have taken the First Lady, another Secret Service agent and Mr. McGowan's wife hostage. To coerce the release of twenty four Gitmo captives, these jihadists have already detonated a dirty bomb over in Carthage, Maryland. Reports have been coming in of wide-spread radiation. As an added arm-twist, they now threaten to terminate the lives of their hostages if the President does not actually release the Gitmo jihadists by 0800 tomorrow. We are in uncharted territory here, folks. A new and different kind of terrorist act has gone down...the kind of act we always feared would some day occur. Per the President, job one is to go after these people with no holds barred.

"The President has made the proactive decision to deploy an HRT element into the location where the First Lady is being held and to rescue the hostages. The HRT commander should be here shortly to advise when and how this mission can be accomplished. The President has asked Mr. McGowan, who is a former counterterrorist operative himself, to not only be a part of this team, but to also brief you and the HRT as to the location, topography, avenues of approach and other specifics about his camp."

Holland continued her briefing with more detail about the Carthage bombing and its residual radiation effect. She provided as well a historical assessment of the jihadist group, what was previously known about them and their association with both al-qa'ida and the American based organization, Jamaat ul Fuqra...about which I had acquired a considerable amount of knowledge. My sniper friend, Mr. Steed and I, put a huge dent in that group of extremists by taking out not only an entire training camp of those bastards, but by separating the head of the most dangerous terrorist in the world from the rest of his body.

At 0910 HRT commander, Special Agent in Charge Chase Rogers, a six-four hulk of a chap with the BMI of 3 and looking every bit the GI Joe in his SWAT gear, was ushered in by security. Ms. Holland sat him down next to me which didn't do me any favors image wise. Compared to him I probably resembled somebody on the order of Barney Fife. And I was already looking wrung out. Anyway, I shook hands with him. He nodded and smiled. Seemed like a nice enough guy.

Holland continued. "Now that we're all here, Mr. McGowan, I will pull up the satellite view of Greenbrier County taken at first light this morning and as I begin to zoom in, I'll ask you to pinpoint the location of your fishing camp."

"How about if I give you the coordinates?"

"Great. Is that map coordinates or GPS?"

"I have both. I'll give you the GPS." I then pulled from my wallet a folded piece of paper containing the coordinates of my camp, Wolf Laurel and my favorite watering hole. You can find me at one of these locations most any time.

She posted a smile. "Are you always prepared with information such as this?"

"I try to be always prepared about everything. Goes all the way back to my Boy Scouts days. Okay, here we go. 37.7864981 N by 080.389189 W."

When Holland typed in the coordinates, the map automatically zoomed in until we could all see in living color the entire property and the road in. "Looks like two, no three vehicles sitting there. As you can see one is approximately a half kilometer from the other two. I don't see the house though..."

"My shack is covered by those trees there." I pointed out a grove close to the river bank. "The one vehicle there..." I again pointed... "is my wife's Toyota van."

"There don't seem to be any images of human forms around the vehicles or anywhere along the river," she remarked. "Mr. McGowan, can you describe the layout of your camp to include all trails and approaches? Anything specifically Commander Rogers needs to know?"

His name and title nearly caused me to chuckle out loud. I hoped I wouldn't slip up and call him Buck.

"Shall I come up to the screen?"

"Please."

She handed me the pointer, but instead of taking it, I pulled from my pocket my pen...the one with the red laser at the tip.

I looked over the group, a group of very bright people, very important people, feeling like a fish out of water. Maybe I didn't fit with them or even fit in the room, but I knew I had to[give them the best information I could. However, I did identify with the HRT commander, this tough guy who would, like me, give up his life for his country and his president.

"Before I begin, I want you to know something. There's a woman right there..." I pointed. "...somewhere under those trees in that little house you can't see, a woman who means everything in the world to me and who's at this very moment experiencing a morning of terror. And she's enduring that horror with two other women, one that you and the President want out really bad as well. There's nothing else nagging at my mind right now except how we have to pull out all stops to get them out. In my years of government service, I've been on a hell of a lot of missions. A lot of bad people died at my hand, unfortunately a few innocents along with them. Collateral damage, it's called. But let me tell you something; I intend that this will go down as clean and predictable as can be done *without* any collateral damage. Our offense going in there will have to be swift, imperceptible and clever. Commander Rogers, you have the professionals, the guns and the devices to do that. But I know the camp like no other person on this earth. Yeah, I know you'll be the one in command of your team, but you *will* follow my lead. We're going to do two things, sir: we're going to bring those hostages out alive and kill every son-of-a-bitch with a gun in his hand. But there are two of those bastards I want alive. They are, as of last night, *former* Secret Service agents Franks and Tyson. Traitors to our flag. However, if they have to die because they won't give it up, so be it. Now here's the picture..."

Rogers then raised his hand.

"Mr. McGowan, I wasn't here for the first part of this meeting, but you're saying you are going in *with* us? I thought you were just the camp's owner and were providing us some Intel about the terrain, the roads in and layout of the building. You say you worked for the government, but what qualifies you to join in with the CIRG?"

From the other end of the room a new voice spoke up. "I can answer that." The new voice that had slipped in caused everyone to turn their heads in the opposite direction and then jump up to attention.

The President continued. "There is no one else I know of with the skills and abilities that Bruce McGowan brings with him to this operation. This highly capable man knows how to get things done and I've seen him do them with nothin' short of swift and violent execution. I know you're good at what you do, Commander Rogers, but whatever he comes up with here, listen to him. I guess I can now let this out, now that things are de-classified as far as he's concerned, but Bruce is a former counterterrorist operative who was part of an elite, covert agency that maybe only two people know about...and I'm one of them. So follow his lead. And after you come up with your best and worst case scenarios, lay them on me." He then paused. "But, sorry I interrupted here, folks. I just wanted to see how things were goin,' I'll let you now get back to work and catch up to you at noon."

He then left the room as silently as he had entered and closed the door behind him. So, now who I used to be and what I did for the government would no longer be a secret.

"Okay, so you're the *man*," quipped Rogers. "I'm all ears."

"A couple of questions, Commander, how many agents do you plan on fielding on this mission and are they ready for deployment?"

"Eighteen...nineteen including me. And yes they are preparing for mobilization at this very moment."

"I assume that you'll be leaving from here and flying back to Quantico to move out from there. That being the case, I'll need a ride down with you."

"Fine. I'm sure there's an extra seat."

"Good. My suggestion then is that we fly in just before the hours of darkness. I think it would now be safe to fly into the airport since it's still heavily occupied by feds, NTSB and state law enforcement. If the airport *is* being watched, the bad guys won't know that we're any different from other federal elements that have been flying in there over the past 12 hours. Mr. Jenkins, can you have vehicles ready for us to deploy out of there after we arrive?"

"We can have as many as you need for this mission."

"We need to stagger the vehicles...leaving one vehicle at a time around 1545, maybe two minutes apart, so as not to give the impression that a task force is on the move."

Rogers nodded. "Good thinking."

"I also suggest they not be the typical long, black government-looking SUVs. Maybe one such unit might not attract attention, but if someone positioned in the general area watching for government vehicles sees them going into the AO even one by one, might raise an eyebrow or two. There's a place locally called Marvin's Rent-a-Wreck that besides three to four year old sedans, offers crew-cab pickups, Jeep Cherokees and the like. And they're not really wrecks; they're actually late model, dependable vehicles."

"I think we can have someone who's already there on the ground arrange that."

"We keep at least a half mile between vehicles and each takes this secondary road off U.S. 60 near Caldwell. If you took this primary road..." I again pin-pointed with the laser. "...the terrorists will consider it a predictable route and may have an OP set up. This road I'm suggesting takes you to the opposite side of the Greenbrier River, ultimately ending at an old fish hatchery, but crosses a small bridge here and winds up near a friend's hunting camp. Don't be concerned about any hunters; they may base out of the camp, but hunt further to the east over in here (I pointed again). Only a half klick away is a small clearing here where we can consolidate and leave the vehicles. You're still two klicks north of my camp at that point and on foot we have to negotiate some fairly thick bush from there on in, staying off the trails. I would imagine they'll position listening posts at these points which are trail intersections." I pointed out several locations that enveloped the camp on all sides.

I continued by asking Rogers, "I assume each of your commandos have the latest in night vision devices."

"All have generation 2 PVS-7 night vision mono-goggles."

"And their weapons?"

"Some are equipped with HK 416s with suppressors, NATO ammo, but two carry larger HK 417s that fire 7.62. We have two carrying Remington shotguns for close combat, two snipers with HK PSG-1s and four bearing MP5 506s."

Any other time I might have growled that guttural sound Tim Allen makes on his *Home Improvement* show, but decided to keep it serious. "My wife had sent me by cell phone a quasi-encrypted message indicating there were as many as nine bad dudes on site, four in the shack and guards located here, here and here. Now that's all she knew about. I suspect there're more. Do you still think you have the right amount of people going in?"

"I believe so, given the element of surprise, our night vision capability and our armament. Our guys have gone into venues with less against more and taken them down. We've had only four casualties since we've been in business."

"Remember that some of the hostiles will *also* have NVD and might be looking back at us. They're pros at the insurgency game as well. We know at least two of them are well-trained Secret Service agents...should I now say *former* agents?"

"Yeah. Hard to believe. The President's own protection detail. Anyway, let's talk timeline and considerations when we blitz the building."

I continued. "If you're good with it, suggest we arrive at that clearing on the other side of the hunting camp at 1600. We then move out to a staging area and wait for dark. By around 1700 it'll be nearly fully dark and our purple vision should have set in. And you know that because it's December, EENT will come early. I suggest you split your team into twos, having them move out simultaneously to neutralize any targets located at these anticipated locations. As you can see, the targeted areas are on all sides of the camp." I again pointed them out on the large map. "This tactic would in essence envelop the house synchronically as each sub-element moves in on it."

Rogers smiled and looked at the other faces at the table. "And I'm needed why?"

I gave him a half-smile in return. "My suggestions only. As you're the commander, I welcome your comments and edits as we go along."

"Appears you've thought this out very well."

"Well, as you know, situations change. Considering any detection of our movement and possible resistance, battle plans may need to be altered."

"I know all too well," he remarked.

Homeland Chief Shanahan. "Take us inside your place. Describe the building, the layout, rooms and et cetera."

"The house was built back in the 1920s. A rickety old wood frame structure about 1200 square feet, sags in a couple of places and might just wash down the river if there's a monsoon in its future. There are two entrances, the main off the front porch and a rear door off a small deck that enters the kitchen. The living room is fourteen by seventeen and there are two bedrooms on the right side of the house joined by a jack and jill bathroom. At the back of the house is the kitchen, small but functional. Finally, off that kitchen is a pantry room with a large freezer and shelves of canned goods. Basic old fish shack."

Preston Johns raised a finger. "Bruce, did you install any security cameras in or outside the house?"

"No, sir. As the place is kind of off the beaten track, few people know it's even there. No one except members of our family knows it's McGowan property. My family figured if someone would happen to stumble onto it, there's nothing valuable inside to steal. Maybe a couple of nice fishing rods. They might also raid the freezer or grab a case of Rolling Rocks. But I do keep a few weapons there which might be readily located. However, it's basically a fishing camp and a place to get away to relax."

Rogers again. "How about outside lighting? Any dusk to dawn lights?"

"We have two spot lights, one on either end of the house. They're manually operated by an inside switch."

"I have a question," began Director Jenkins. "Do you think that the extremists might move the hostages before EENT this evening, thinking an HRT element may in fact try to rescue them? Understanding the enemy is an important facet of counterintelligence. Staying too long in one position increases vulnerability."

"Good point, Mr. Director," remarked Rogers. "If I'm thinking like a terrorist, I'd be puling everyone out."

"So then what real time Intel do you suggest and should we get a recon team in there or in proximity?" Jenkins asked.

I answered that. "Putting anything in the air close enough to observe activity in the camp is going to alert them that they're under surveillance. They'll surely believe something's coming and that will put the hostages in even greater danger. We can't risk that. Perhaps placing some of your Bureau types wearing hunter's attire in pickups and other vehicles that don't look federal at the far ends of every road and firebreak leaving out of the camp might alert us whether they're moving out."

"I like it," Johns remarked. "Can you get on that, Jerry?" he said to the Bureau Director.

"Can do. As we expect the terrorists are likely driving dark SUVs and sedans with blacked-out windows, they should be easy to spot."

"The very reason I'm suggesting alternate vehicles for movement of the HRT," I remarked.

For the remainder of the morning, we all sat around with freshly distributed 12,000 to 1 maps of Eastern Greenbrier County, protractors, notebooks, pads and pens, and coffee that kept coming. I did ask for a donut. The dialogue continued back and forth, each of us coming up with opinions, ideas, suppositions, schemes, alternative courses of action and recommendations for assuring a successful mission. Holland was in and out of the room, mostly out, dealing with other White House matters...and the disappearance of Arnold Kessler.

The President came in at five minutes till twelve to listen to Commander Buck Rogers' verbal operations order. It all reminded me of my military days when in planning a combat operation the commander and his staff utilized all those strategic terms found in OPORDs and the decision-making process like 'key terrain, avenues of approach, control measures, scheme of maneuver, analysis of courses of action, coordinating instructions and command and signal.' Much of the terminology, plans and tactics performed by law enforcement agencies have increasingly been borrowed from the military anyway. Even though I had been away from it for quite a while, it was amazing how I could recall all those acronyms and terminology like it was yesterday.

Chapter Sixteen

The President listened intently as Commander Rogers and I provided a comprehensive briefing on the hostage rescue plan, covering in detail the situation, expected weather, maneuver plan and anticipated result. I could see the look of worry in his eyes, especially at the point where we discussed moving in on the terrorists who would be holding our precious women at gunpoint inside the house. In the attack, would an errant round find one of our ladies? Or at the first inkling that commandos are outside ready to rush the house, would the terrorists then go ahead and end the lives of their captives? Although my brain was focused on mission success, my heart and stomach were basket cases, scared to death to face the reality that I may not ever see my beautiful wife again.

"Okay, gentlemen and Ms. Holland, looks like a plan," the President commented. "Let's make this go down as clean as possible. I know with you two fellas leadin' the charge..." he pointed to Rogers and me. "...it'll be successful."

I asked him, "Did your Chief of Staff ever materialize?"

"No one at his house. Not even his wife. Got me concerned. At this point, we don't know what to make of it."

My suspicions and doubts about the President's man were now even more solidified. In some way, shape or form, he was definitely involved.

Before I departed the White House, the President had a few words for me. "As I promised, I had the press secretary recant the statement about you becomin' the number one domestic terrorist in America, that you actually saved my life doin' battle with the extremists. I hate that you have been placed in this predicament, Bruce. You've been a loyal patriot and friend and I will not be forgettin' that you risked your life to save mine."

I nodded once in thanks. "I see a new bandage on your shoulder, Mr. President. Apparently, you've received treatment."

"The White House physician fixed me up. Gave me a tetanus shot and an antibiotic. It'll do till I get checked out at Walter Reed. But I got other things on my mind today. Some *other* time."
"Sir, I'll be going down to Quantico with Commander Rogers in a few minutes. Could you have something taken care of for me?"

"Sure...anything."

"Could you see that the Lincoln gets back to my brother at the funeral home?"

"I'll have someone drive it down as soon as possible. But Bruce, you know you can just drive it back yourself and let the HRT..."

"I'm going *in* with the HRT, sir. It's something I have to do. And I know you want me there."

He then wrapped his fingers around my elbow and smiled. "All right, Bruce, go. Go get our women back." He then handed me a small scrap of paper. "My direct number. You call me when the mission is done. I'll be waitin'."

I noted that my cell phone which was on *vibrate* had buzzed on my belt several times especially that first hour and a half while I was standing at the map giving my pitch to the big cheese in the room. While Rogers was engaged in conversation with Jenkins and Macy about the meticulous details of the mission, I pulled the phone off to review my missed calls. More unknowns, likely calls from curious golf or hunting buddies, and two others to which I did need to respond.

I dialed the first. After one ring, *"Dad! What's going on with you?"* Her voice was in near panic.

"Hi, Caroline. Guess you heard about me on the news, huh?"

"I couldn't believe what I heard. Why are they calling you a fugitive...and you supposedly kidnapped the President?"

I then gave her a Reader's Digest version of the previous night's events and the current situation...of course leaving out the mission plan which would be classified Top Secret.

"And Adriana's being held by terrorists? What's the government going to do to get her and the First Lady back?"

"In case my call is somehow being monitored, I can't go into that. People are working on it is all I'm at liberty to say."

"Do I need to take off and come be with you?"

"No. Don't do that. Things should be worked out by tomorrow. I'll let you know. How're things with the Bureau out in Denver?"

"My SAC approached me yesterday and asked how I'd like to transfer to Quantico to teach at the FBI Academy...teaching foreign counterterrorist tactics to SAs and linguistics to LAs in the Language Services Section since I'm fluent in Spanish. I'm seriously thinking about it. Would be closer to you. That is unless they send you to Leavenworth. Then I'll just stay here so I can visit you." I think she wanted to laugh at her quip, but kept the chuckle under her breath.

"That would be great, Caroline. I..." Rogers was signaling me by pumping his fist twice over his head. Time to go. "Hey, Sweetie, I have to go. I'll call you sometime tomorrow."

"Okay, Dad. I hope people work things out to get them released. Will say a prayer."

"Thanks. Bye for now. Love ya."

I then walked down the corridor to the White House security office and retrieved my weapons, in the process getting the evil eye from the custodian. He warned me to, "Be sure not to lock and load until you're off White House grounds, Mr. McGowan."

"Absolutely," I replied.

While catching up to Rogers on his way out to the helipad, I saw there was another call on the cell from Joey. He of course knew the truth about me and was probably just checking to see if I had made it safely back to Washington with the President. I would probably still need to call him at some point. If he wasn't able to contact me and then an agent drove the Lincoln back to him without me, he would be thrown into a state of hysteria. And I don't mean the laughing kind of hysteria.

On the short flight down to Quantico, Rogers and I had a few minutes to get better acquainted.

"So, you're retired FBI, Bruce."

"Twenty plus years."

"And the President mentioned you were some kind of covert counterterrorist operative."

"Yeah, that too."

He then glanced down at my Remington 700 I was cradling. "You always carry that .308?"

"On special occasions."

I know he was getting tired of hearing my bullet responses, but I don't communicate all that well when stuff's rubbing on my mind. Right about then I was deeply focused on two things: us pulling off a successful mission and in doing so, Adriana making it through the raid unscathed.

But I did finally come around with a couple of questions for him. "What's our transportation from Quantico on in to West Virginia?"

"My HRT is already standing by with another Blackhawk. As it is specially armed, it will also be used in support of the rescue mission as necessary; however, it will only be on station at the airport and not used in the raid. Like you said earlier, we don't need any sight or sound of a bird in the air, letting the terrorists know something's coming."

"Got one other question. As I can't hit the woods in what I'm wearing, you got an extra SWAT uniform on hand?"

"I think that can be arranged. You're about my size I guess...maybe a little shorter. I'll call ahead. How about weapons? You comfortable with the .308 and the Glock you have holstered there or do you need something else like an Uzi or M4?"

"I'm good. I could use some extra 7.62 ammo, though. I do have a couple clips of .40 cal on my belt. Can't imagine needing any more than that. If I do, we might be in deep ca-ca."

"We've got about anything you need."

Having a remarkable resemblance to Superman in SWAT gear, or to yours truly twenty years ago, Chase Rogers was an affable enough chap. Nothing pretentious or flamboyant, he seemed to be a fairly down-to-earth guy. It was obvious to me he was one of the best America had in federal law enforcement, but his ego didn't broadcast it. And to my appreciation, he had without question afforded *me* not only the respect for my years in government service but for my special skills. Although he knew nothing specific about those skills, he realized from the President's introduction in the Situation Room that he needed to give me a lot of latitude on the mission. In terms of mutual respect, I also wanted him to lead his team into the rescue zone without a lot of hoo-ha from me.

I had been on similar but different types of raids with considerably less operatives, as my Zulu organizational structure was generally simpler and lighter. Team Zulu didn't venture on lengthy operations requiring tons of SWAT gear that bogged us down or on many missions that accomplished anything less than total annihilation of the enemy. Occasionally for Intel and interrogation purposes we may allow someone to live so he would spill his guts. If he didn't tell us all, *we* would then spill *his* guts. Often, you might find just one of us operating on his own, reducing the risk of detection. The downside was, if we ran into some shit, we'd be outgunned. On the upside, a lone wolf like me could more easily achieve the element of surprise, bringing my own recipe of swift and deadly punishment, taking out every human obstacle in my way with a 7.62 round from my suppressed sniper rifle before ultimately reaching my target.

As we neared the FBI helipad at Quantico, Rogers lifted his headset and said, "I can't imagine what's going through your mind at this time, Bruce. Although I wouldn't be placed in that situation since I'm not married, if I were somehow set up to participate in a mission to rescue *my* wife from terrorists, I'd be an emotional wreck."

"You have no idea, Chase. What I'm feeling right about now is nothing short of terror. And that's not me. I don't have any trepidation about dying. I passed that fear eons ago in my combat days. But the only thing since then that I've ever been afraid of is losing my wife or daughter."

"What's your wife's name, Bruce?"

"Adriana."

He then crossed himself and brought his clasped hands up to his mouth. "A prayer for Adriana."

I smiled and placed my hand on his shoulder. "Thanks, Chase. Means a lot."

And I knew from that moment on, he and his team would do everything in their power to assure that Adriana, the First Lady and Agent Smithers would make it out without a scratch.

At 1425 when the skids touched down, we were immediately engulfed by eighteen combat-ready members of the CIRG's HRT. As we set foot off the Blackhawk, the senior agent popped a salute and Commander Rogers returned it. His team had just practiced a run-through at the Shoot House, the urban practice facility there at Quantico, anticipating all possible scenarios. Immediately, we all then range-walked to a nearby hangar and one by one piled into a military style conference room. For a couple of moments there was a little glad-handing and then Rogers went to the front of the room to tape up a gigantic map of the AO that covered three kilometers in every direction, the center most point being my fishing camp.

He took less than twenty minutes to set out the entire mission plan from where we would enter the dirt road leading to Junior Brooks' hunting camp, dismount and consolidate in the staging area, commence the foot maneuver, take down any sighted perimeter guards by suppressed sniper fire, begin the envelopment action, and finally culminate at the point where the cabin is rushed and captors neutralized. Rogers flashed official government photos of both Franks and Tyson, telling his men if at all possible, they would not be killed. However, if the hostages' lives were in danger, *all* bad people die.

Rogers reminded his team that they had successfully conducted more than thirty HRT missions throughout the world without losing a hostage. "And I don't have to remind you that this is *the most important* rescue mission you will ever undertake...for obvious reasons." He then glanced at me and nodded. Of course the seventeen men and one woman assumed he was referring to the rescue of the First Lady of the United States.

* * * * *

Flights in or out of the small West Virginia airport had been suspended with the exception of federal aircraft, specifically FBI and National Guard Blackhawks. So far there had been no follow-up attacks on government aircraft, but as a light observation helicopter and an AH-64 Apache had been sweeping the surrounding hills in search for terrorist emplacements periodically during the day, it appeared the missile gunner that brought down the C-130 had long since vamoosed. Anyway, both of the UH-60 Blackhawks flying in with our split team of twenty combat-ready warriors in full tactical gear, were equipped with two each M-60 GP machine guns, two Hellfire missiles, radar warning receivers and one each AN/ALQ 144 infrared countermeasure system. I felt pretty damn secure going in there. During the rescue mission, one of the birds would remain flight ready to provide air support only if called in where needed.

At 1615, as the red sun was setting over the mountains to the west, the airport came into view...and so did the slightly smoldering remains of the Marine C-130 at the end of the runway where it was determined that 72 of America's finest had lost their lives. That brought the total, including the Marine One crew, to 77. As the NTSB was still deep into their investigation and bodies were still being accounted for by personnel from the State and Federal governments, we landed at the opposite end of the airport among a gaggle of privately-owned Cessnas and corporate Leers. In case someone was observing us through heavy lenses, we didn't storm out of the choppers as though we were ready to hit the ground running. Even though we *looked* like we were going to war, we simply casually walked away from the birds until we disappeared into a small hangar where standing ready were the Rent-a-Wrecks...a gray Jeep Cherokee, two crew cab GMC extra-duty pickups, one red, one white, and a black Suburban similar to mine, except in a hell of a lot better shape.

As we were in the process of doing commo, equipment and weapons checks, Rogers tapped me on the shoulder while receiving a message on his cell. Once he finished listening, he said, "*More* interesting news, Bruce. They found Kessler dead...bullet through the head and floating face down in the Potomac."

I shook my head. "*Nothing* surprises me considering everything that's happened in the last twenty hours. How about his wife?"

"Missing."

The news immediately caused a score of questions to zip through my brain like: was he actually involved with or even heading up the American facet of this jihadist group or had I read him wrong? If he *wasn't* somehow connected, why did he end up dead? Was he killed because he was about to turn himself in and spill a mess of information? Or was he demanding an even bigger cut for his role in the deal...instead getting *himself* 'cut' down? And then, if he did betray his boss *and* his country, did a guilty conscience drive him to suicide?

But I then changed subject. "Are there any reports from your 'hunters'?" I was asking about the agents in hunter's attire and pickups who had been placed in position to monitor traffic leaving the camp roads.

"Just one negative report about ten minutes ago. No vehicles spotted. It's a minor surprise to me that they're not moving the hostages out of there. They have to be thinking somebody's coming after them."

"Maybe they're also thinking that as we *would* have them under surveillance, both by air and on the ground, they risk being spotted moving the hostages."

"No matter what the scenario, as long as they have control of the hostages, they control the situation."

Rogers then held up his right hand and whipped his index finger twice in a circle. "All right, team, let's saddle up. Time to move. I'll be in the first vehicle, the Cherokee, with Mr. McGowan. The rest of you squeeze into the other vehicles and leave out from the airport every two minutes. Remove your kevlars and hunker down so that your uniforms won't be spotted on the road. The last unit should arrive at the clearing by 1700. Any questions?"

They all shook their heads.

"Good. As each vehicle leaves, the lead agent signals me by radio with one single word..."Out." Otherwise, maintain radio silence. Let's go make this thing happen."

Each vehicle carted five of us humans. Rogers was driving our Cherokee. However, considering we all added inches with our flak jackets and the ton of crap hanging off our web gear, the back seat passengers were jammed in together like sardines. Each agent was compelled to hold his (or her) weapon straight up and down between the legs. It didn't much matter smell wise; by now I was sure they were used to each other's breath and B.O. Except, someone in our vehicle had recently been gnawing on a clove of garlic. Good that I was in the front passenger seat with the air vent blowing in my face.

After making a left turn onto 219, we drove under the interstate bridge and entered town. Turning left again on Washington at the light, we began climbing the long hill to the east, in the process passing a score of the town's stately historic homes. Finally, upon leveling off at the hill crest, we then started our long curvy downward grade toward the Greenbrier River. Everyone was quiet and reflective...even

Rogers. And me? I was looking out the passenger's side window nervously chewing on my thumb nail. The nervous part had to do with Adriana. If any harm came to her, the combination of guilt and grief would devastate me. Of course I would then have *zero* guilt about carving every one of those goddam terrorist bastards into infinitesimal pieces. I placed my fingers on my razor-sharp Ranger knife hanging from my belt as if to reinforce that thought. It's not that I enjoy killing people...well, hell yes I do, when the lives of my loved ones are at stake. And then I told God I was sorry about the taking of His name in vain when I closed my eyes to say a prayer for the protection of all the ladies.

"You asleep, Bruce?"

I opened my peepers and flashed Rogers a half-smile. "Just a little prayer, Chase."

He nodded. "Make it a good one."

Not far from where we would turn off the road was the start of the Greenbrier River Trail, a seventy eight mile crushed rock recreational byway, frequented by hikers, bikers and campers, that winds along the river through Seneca Forest. There was a segment of it we had to cross, but in my experience, in wintertime along the trail just a couple weeks before Christmas, we would expect few if any adventurers taking advantage of the nature scene, especially on a frigid Saturday night. And once we divagated off the trail deep into the woods to Junior Brooks' hunting cabin, we should run into nothing but forest critters.

And little did I know that my prediction on that proved to be literal. Just past the river bridge, we had turned left onto a rough asphalt road known as Fish Hatchery Way, named for a now defunct aquaculture hatchery further down on the Greenbrier. It was not yet fully dark. In military operational terms it is the time of day called Ending Evening Nautical Twilight. It was still light enough, however, where the twisting narrow road could be negotiated without the need of headlights. And it was the time of year the deer were running...running not only from their natural predators but from the human kind who want to put their heads on walls. And when a deer jumps, it has no air brakes. We nailed a doe dead center in the grill which tossed the animal back into our windshield. Good news for Bambi. She was only a little bruised up and bounded off into the woods like nothing ever happened. Bad news for Rogers and me. We could no longer see out of the shattered windshield and both of us had to stick our heads out of our windows to assure we were staying on the road. And because a front had come through the night before and radiational cooling had set in, it was colder than a witch's...well, you get the picture. Frost was forming in my nasal passages. However, we only had another quarter mile before reaching the dirt road leading to Big Junior's cabin and the adjacent clearing.

According to Rogers, who remained in contact with his drivers, all vehicles had now entered Fish Hatchery and were gradually closing up their distance. The deeper into the woods we drove, the quicker we found ourselves on the dusk side of twilight. Considering also the damage to our windshield, which resembled a kind of crystal mosaic, our visibility was even more demanding. As we drew near the entrance to the Brooks camp, I pulled my head back inside the Jeep and put up my window...not because of the cold, but because of what my instincts picked up.

"Chase, as soon as you pass this dirt road, continue on slowly and then pull off to the left into the woods before you get to the clearing. Tell all vehicle drivers to stop where they are and pull off the road whenever they can as well."

"What is it, Bruce?"

"I don't know. Maybe nothing; but something back there is not right."

Chapter Seventeen

Rogers went ahead and radioed his team to cease progress, pull off and wait for further instructions. After we were well past the lane's entrance, he then found a wide spot between two poplars to pull into.

"Okay, Bruce, what gives?"

"Junior Brooks, a large bubba with a full beard and a hunting friend of Joey's, spends nearly every day of hunting season in the woods. Although I'm not much of a hunter myself, I've spent some evenings attending meetings at his cabin which served as the headquarters for the local Rod and Gun Club. It's not only a place for Junior and his hunting buds to land after a long day in the field, but a place to kick back, throw a burger on the grill and down a few brewskis. I know the place and know Junior's rules and routine. Everybody that frequents the camp knows the gate leading in there stays closed. You drive through, you park on the other side, get out and close it. When we went by it, it was wide open."

"Maybe someone forgot."

"That someone would then face the ire of Junior Brooks...a six-five, three hundred pound former WWE wrestler."

"Okay, so you're thinking somebody else might be using the place...like the kind of people we're looking to take down."

"Maybe. But I need to check it out. First, I need to call my brother."

"You're taking time out to talk to your brother?"

"It's not a social call. Before I go in there, I've got to find out a couple things. This is a Rod and Gun club and he's a member."

I pressed his number on my cell. He answered, promptly recognizing my number on his caller ID.

"Damn, Bruce, where you been...and what's this thing about you..."

"No time for chit chat, Joey. I'm here in Greenbrier County and down at Junior's camp."

"What the hell you doin'..."

"Listen, Joey, I need to know something. Do you happen to know if Junior and his buds are out hunting today?"

"I...think so. It's Saturday and it's huntin' season. Unless he's on his death bed, he's out there. But why..."

"I want you to give him a call now and then call me back. I know he and that cell phone are inseparable. He keeps it in his shirt pocket and on *vibrate*, remember? He'll answer."

"All right, but..."

"Just do it, okay?"

"I'll call you right back."

Rogers then asked me, "What should I do with the team while we're waiting?"

"Have them all dismount and take up a defensive perimeter on the edge of the woods."

He brought his wrist up to his mouth. "This is Bullitt. Your location?"

He listened.

"All right. Dismount and defend. Out."

A guy as cool as Commander Buck Rogers damn sure *should* have a cool call sign like Bullitt. Actually, I think he did kind of resemble McQueen in the face.

The five of us stepped out of the Cherokee and took up makeshift positions back in the trees. We then waited nearly five minutes. A veil of darkness seemed to have almost suddenly set in and it was difficult to make out each other's faces. My phone then vibrated.

"Joey," I whispered.

"Yeah, Bruce. I tried three separate times. He doesn't answer. Either he's stalkin' a deer or he's out of juice."

"All right, Joey, thanks."

"Okay, Bruce, come clean. What gives?"

"Talk later, Joey."

I flipped my phone shut. "Something's amiss, Bullitt. A man who's always accessible *isn't*."

"You're talking about this Junior guy?"

"Yes. I'd like just you and I to move straight in. Have your three agents here fan out and take scout positions on our flank. The rest of your team flanks the road where they are and stays ready to move on command."

"Sounds like a plan. All right, gentlemen, you heard him. Ready, Bruce?"

"If the bad guys are anywhere out here, somebody will be positioned near the open gate. We move through the woods until I signal halt. We then use night vision to scan. Are we good?" Everyone nodded.

The four of them adjusted their Gen 2 night vision monoculars to their left eyes and gave me a thumbs up. I preferred my Armasight Orion scope versus some bulky eyepiece that messes up my vision. But, whatever, it was a perfect night for use of our NVD. There was a half moon and the Evening Star was sparkling brightly on the horizon through the naked branches. A beautiful night for fun in the woods.

I thrust my fingers forward and we moved out. By instinct one of Rogers' men stayed on the west side of the road. He would pull up and stop well back in the tree line just opposite the entrance to the camp. Rogers and I moved with extreme stealth through the brush approximately ten yards to the east side. His other two men spread out to our left, one at our ten o'clock and the second one trailing at our eight.

When we were within fifty meters of the gate, Rogers tapped me on the arm and pointed. I then brought my .308 up and peered through my scope. A lone figure stood just inside the open gate smoking a cigarette. Every fifteen seconds or so, the glow would brighten when he took a drag. Was he a hunter or a bad guy? He wasn't wearing orange, which in Junior's club, he insisted on. And a seasoned hunter wouldn't be standing at the gate like a guard at a listening post. I did make out the semblance of a rifle being cradled in his left arm, but couldn't tell much more about him. Now we knew, or at least were pretty damn sure, that Franks and/or Tyson had taken over Junior Brooks' hunting camp. But for what reason? And where was Junior?

I whispered into my mic, "You want to take him or shall I?"

"Been wondering about you, Beau," he whispered back. "I'd like to see you in action."

"Then prepare to be amazed. If he hears me coming and draws down on me, put a bullet in his head."

"Be glad to."

Fortunately, with the rain we had the night before, the brush was still moist. No snap, crackle or pop as I moved steadily forward in small, carefully-placed steps in the direction of the guard. At the point where I was only a half dozen yards from the dirt road where he was standing, *un*fortunately, a branch *did* snap beneath my boot. As he turned and brought up his gun, I ducked behind the trunk of a large oak. I waited for the whiz of Rogers' bullet that would zip by my ear and tear into the man's head; but it didn't happen. Apparently, Rogers saw that the man didn't advance further toward me. The guard merely stood in one place, craning his head and neck to listen for more sounds from the woods that didn't come. Finally, he turned back around and took another drag of his cigarette. He definitely wasn't a pro. Likely just a hired goon.

After a few seconds I stepped back around the tree. Then on a dead run, I closed in on the guard, at the same time swinging my rifle around sideways at laser speed, applying to the man's head a classic horizontal butt stroke. He dropped like a rock. But no sooner had he hit the gravel, I was startled by a voice from further down the driveway.

"Hey, what the hell?" the voice yelled.

I turned, finding another figure standing in the center of the road about twenty feet away with his MP5 aimed in my direction. Before I could swing my .308 around, I heard a *thwack* sound as I watched the gunman's body jerk violently backward. I turned my head again and looked back toward Rogers who was standing at the side of the road, pointing to one of his agent snipers who still had a bead planted on the man's body.

The man I had cracked on the head lay groaning at my feet. As hard as I hit him, I thought his head must have been made of granite. I then reached down, grabbed him by his coat and flipped him over. Another Arab. Or at least he *looked* Middle Eastern in the dim moonlight. I pulled my Ranger knife from its holster and placed the blade across his throat. Rogers and his sniper then walked up beside us.

"Okay, Mohammed, you speak English?" I asked the guard.

"A...a little," he replied in a thick accent.

"Then start talking. How many are there of you here?"

He didn't respond.

I slapped him across the bridge of his nose with the back of my hand. *"How many!"*

"I think five."

"Five? I know there are more."

"Five here."

"Where are they?"

"Two more guarding outside. Two in the house."

"Is that one of them over there?" I grabbed a handful of hair and shoved his face around to where he could see the dead guard lying behind him.

"Yes."

"One other here in the woods?"

"Yes."

I turned to Rogers. "Chase, have your men search in there."

He nodded and brought his wrist to his mouth.

"The two in the house...are they guarding a hostage?"

He stared at me for a moment and then turned his head away.

"Answer the question!"

He shook his head.

I then stuck the tip of my blade into his flesh near the Adam's apple. Blood began oozing. "Get the point?"

"Okay. One woman."

"One? Who?"

"I do not know. A blonde woman."

The blonde would of course be Smithers.

"No other women?"

"No."

"I know there are two more. Where are they?"

"In another place."

"What place?"

"Another house...across the river."

"Do you know the American men named Franks and Tyson?"

"Yes."

"Is Tyson in the cabin here?"

"He is not."

"Where is he?"

Again the man decided to clam up. Not a good decision. I flung my knife into the ground only a inch from his left ear. His eyes enlarged. But then I shut them with a straight punch. Blood began gushing from his nose.

"Maybe you didn't understand the question. *Where is he?*"

"In...the other house."

"The cabin across the river."

"Yes."

"And the man named Franks?"

"I think so."

"Are the other women hostages also there?"

He again hesitated.

I cocked my fist again and he held up his hand. I guess he wanted no more pain.

"Yes...yes."

"How many of your people are there with them?"

"I do not know."

"Yes you do."

"I must think. Maybe eight. I...I cannot be sure."

"Are you lying to me?"

"I am not lying. I think eight."

"How many outside and how many in the house."

"When I left there, maybe five outside."

"How many are American and how many are Muslim pricks like you?"

"They are all American...they look like you."

I then looked up at Rogers. "Anything you want to ask him?"

He shook his head.

"One last question. The two women...have they been harmed?"

"No harm has come to them. They are only tied up."

I stared for a few moments into his eyes. They glistened with tears like two shiny black marbles, primarily from the break at the bridge of his nose.

"Last night was a long night for everybody. Did you get any sleep?"

He gave me a puzzled look that asked why I would be concerned. "No. None."

"Well, you will tonight." I then drew my Glock and clocked him on the top of his head at the cerebral cortex. It's the part of the brain that controls sleep.

I then pulled Sleeping Man off the road and laid him in the bushes. We'd collect him later for more interrogation. Rogers and his sniper agent dragged the dead man into the woods as well. Only he wasn't going to tell us anything.

We reconsolidated just off the gravel road as Rogers radioed the rest of his team to double-time up to our location. We would take Junior's cabin and then move up to the clearing, cross the bridge and converge on *my* cabin. It could be another long night. But hopefully, we could avoid another night of gunplay with the element of surprise.

As the two agents Rogers sent out to look for the third guard were still sweeping, he and I talked in a low voice. "Does it make sense?" he asked me. "Splitting up the hostages and adding a second hideout? I'd think that tactic would tend to weaken their disposition."

"Hard to figure," I said.

Rogers then touched his ear bud. "Okay, 360 sweep," he commanded. "Once accomplished, hold in place till further orders. Out."

"Are they close behind us?"

"They are. Beginning their envelopment now. When they've worked their way in and have the cabin surrounded, they'll wait for my command to move in."

I nodded. The Rod and Gun cabin sat approximately five hundred feet down the gravel road and back in the woods. Adjacent to the cabin was a small storage shack and then a third building to its right was a place where meetings were held. As I remember, on its walls were animal heads...bucks, does, wild boars and one very large black bear. I would like to see a couple of other heads on those walls. Of the human persuasion.

"What?" Rogers was listening to a radio transmission from one of his men. "Okay, approaching now."

He turned to me. "One of the two I sent on ahead found a body."

A shard of adrenaline surged through my chest. "Male or female?"

"Male. Appears to be one of the insurgents." He motioned for me to follow.

In less than two minutes we located Rogers' agent. He shined his flashlight with the red lens on the man's face and said, "A white male as you can see in a camo field jacket and toboggan. Knife wound on his throat appears to be the cause of death. No weapon on him."

"Doesn't make sense," I remarked. "How did this guy end up dead...and why?"

"Unless he wanted out and walked away. Somebody followed and whacked him."

We moved on but then began spreading out. The cabin and its companion buildings then came into view. I was now at a loss as to what I should be thinking. Our carefully laid plans had been interrupted. It goes like that sometimes. And that caused a sudden deja vu feeling to come over me. Forty plus years ago in Southeast Asia I was on a patrol in triple canopy jungle with a Ruff Puff unit moving in to raid a hostile village. The plan was to surround the village and kill or capture any and all resistors. But, they were ready for us. An ambush cut down more than a dozen of our forty man team. They hit us with everything from AK rounds to arrows. We did manage to beat them back, however. After the firefight, other than a few enemy dead left behind, the hostiles had vanished. It was as though they had dissipated into thin air like a band of ghosts. When we swept the village, we found no one. Nothing. Not women, children, chickens or water buffalo. Nothing. When it was all over and I briefed my commanding officer, referring to the mission as...the Ghost Raid. Just why I was remembering something like that, I hadn't the foggiest. Maybe it was because I was once again in the eerie woods on a raid with what sounded in my head night spirits swirling through the tree branches and a thousand voices talking at my brain, warning me, taunting me, laughing...

I knew what was happening to me. It had happened before...several times. It was a war that could rage in my head at any given moment when triggered by some catalyst. And it could be sparked by anything of hostile nature going on at the time or when I'm mad as hell out hunting down terrorist pricks. Fortunately, I had long since trained my mind to snap out of those classic PTSD moments. But the fact I was having them at all made me think maybe I should no longer be running around out in the woods with a gun in my hand.

Suddenly, someone slammed into me, knocking me down. And then a shoe caught me on the jaw, spinning me further around. When I tried to get up, another punch and a kick dazed me. However, somehow I managed to sweep my leg under my attacker and spill the bastard onto the ground, whereupon I jumped squarely onto his gut, pulled my Glock and stuck the muzzle between his eyes. He was surprisingly small and not that strong and I was able to wrestle the knife from his right hand without too much trouble. And then I realized something. My attacker wasn't a 'he.' It was a woman. Her shoulder-length, light-colored hair was faintly visible in the moonlit forest.

"Joanie?"

"Appreciate it if you'd take your gun off my forehead, Bruce."

I pulled her to her feet and she then threw her arms around me. "I knew you all would come."

"How did you..."

"They moved me from your cabin this afternoon. Five of them. Threw me into that house back there and tied me up. They left two guards inside with me...an Arab prick and an African American woman. That was *their* mistake. The ropes weren't all that tight and I was able to work free. When the Arab guy went to the kitchen to look for something to eat, I jumped the woman and whacked her in the head. She went down as easy as swatting a gnat. When the man came out, I busted his head as well. Anyway, sorry I hit you. When I saw you, I thought you were one of the guards."

Rogers and his three agents then converged on us. "Uh, Bruce, who's this?"

"Gentlemen, meet Special Agent Joanie Smithers, Secret Service."

They each nodded a greeting.

Rogers said, "Agent Smithers, we found a dead guy back there a few feet away with his throat cut. Was that you?"

"Yeah. He had a bit of an accident. The knife I took off the woman got in the way of his throat."

Man, did I like this girl.

"I gotta ask you, Joanie..."

"You want to know about Adriana. They still have her at your cabin along with the First Lady."

"Why did they split you up?"

"I gave them a hell of a lot of trouble over there. So much in fact I don't know why they didn't just go ahead and kill me. They figured you'd be coming for the First Lady. And if you did, they thought I'd be a pain in their ass. Anyway, I didn't matter all that much as a bargaining chip. The First Lady, however, is another story. And maybe Adriana."

"How did they know about *this* cabin?"

"Like I said, Franks figured it was a matter of time a CIRG team would hit your place. There's another Secret Service agent, who is or should I say *was* our SAC, named Tyson..."

"Yeah, I know about him."

"Well, anyway, I overheard them talking out on your porch. They were dispatching a recon element to go find another cabin that wasn't in use to move us to. So they found this place. They're still looking for another place to hide out as well from what I gathered. If they can stay on the move they won't be sitting targets."

Rogers then interrupted. "Bruce, one of my men found something else. Two men tied to trees up near the cabin. Both shot through the head. They appear to be hunters. One of them he described as small and thin. The other, a very large-set man having a full beard. Had a cell phone in his shirt pocket."

"*Damn,*" I exclaimed. "The big man you're talking about I'm sure is the cabin's owner."

And that meant Junior Brooks would not be going home tomorrow to his wife and three kids. I then dropped my head, crossed my arms and kicked at a rock with the toe of my boot.

Smithers placed her hand on my arm. "Bruce, when they brought me here around three o'clock, there wasn't anyone in the cabin. I guess the owner was out hunting. But the bastards then heard a truck pull up and charged outside. I heard some yelling, but since I was tied up, I didn't know what happened from there. I guess now we know."

Both she and Rogers saw that the news had shaken me. Junior was the gentle giant around there that everybody loved. Another good man dead at the hands of these butchers. And another good reason I would eventually personally end the lives of two former Secret Service assholes. I knew one thing: when I killed them, I would make sure they did not die quickly.

"Chase, can you have two of your people take Agent Smithers out of here in one of the vehicles?"

"I think we can do that. Since four of these goons have been taken out of action, reducing the total number of tangoes (terrorists), the remainder of my team can handle things across the river."

"No, Bruce," said Smithers. "I'm staying. I want to be a part of the HRT when it goes after Franks. The First Lady is my responsibility and..."

Rogers shook his head. "I can't let you do that, Agent Smithers. I know how you feel, but you're not trained to operate with this team. Every member of this HRT has an assigned, well-rehearsed role and function. You need to go back with my agents as Mr. McGowan suggested."

Smithers glared at him for a moment and then picked up the MP5 still lying on the gravel drive. She then dropped the clip into her hand, checked its contents and slammed it back into the weapon. "I don't want to argue with you,

Agent Rogers. When you move out, I'll be on the move with you."

I looked at Rogers and nodded. He in turn took in a deep breath of cold air and expelled it in a puff. After a long moment, he finally replied in resignation, "Tag along if you wish. Just stay the hell out of our way. If any one of my people gives you an order, you'd better damn well follow it. Am I clear?"

"You are."

"All right, let's go see what you left for us inside that cabin."

Chapter Eighteen

Just off the gravel road leading to the cabin we met up with the agent who had found the bodies of Junior Brooks and Dave Holt. Their arms and hands were tied behind them and around tree trunks. Both of their heads lay down on their chests. It wasn't enough that the terrorist bastards had strapped them to the trees; they had to put bullets in their brains. I cut the ropes and then laid their bodies side by side at the edge of the road. They would be collected along with the bodies of the two dead terrorists as well as the ones still alive that I *felt* like killing.

When the HRT had finally completed their sweep and had cordoned things off, we moved forward to Junior's cabin. His truck sat in the driveway in front of the house, doors still open apparently where the insurgents had rushed them. Rogers then led Smithers and me onto the porch and after turning the doorknob, he kicked the door open. We didn't expect that anything had changed since Joanie performed her handiwork, but we were ready to spray the cabin with pointy bits of metal anyway, just in case. They laid together against one another where Joanie had conked them, looking as though they had fallen asleep. But then I checked their pulses. Apparently, she had struck them a little *too* hard. They were both dead.

The male was an Arab with a short cropped beard. A skull cap lay beside him. Obviously an al-Qa'ida wannabe. I also noted that he had pissed himself. I guess a hundred ten pound case of dynamite like Joanie Smithers can easily cause that to happen. The woman lying against him had the same face I had seen the evening before through my night vision scope...part of Tyson's element.

I examined the bodies. "Both their skulls are crushed, Joanie. What did you hit them with?"

"Like I said, I worked myself loose and jumped the woman. While the Arab guy was out of the room, I grabbed a fireplace poker. When he returned, I hit him...maybe a little too hard. The woman then got to her feet and came at me. I whacked her as well. I guess my adrenaline surged so much, I...I didn't realize my own strength. I thought they were just unconscious. That's why I tied them up."

"It would have been good if *one* of them had lived. We might have learned more about what's on the other side of the river. But, sometimes when you're defending yourself, you can get carried away. I understand that."

I was happy that at least Smithers had made it out from under her captors; however, it made me feel that much more fearful for Adriana's safety. As the First Lady was the terrorists' remaining big prize, they could just as easily have moved my wife to Junior's cabin as well. *She* wouldn't have added that much to their equation.

"Nothing more here, Bruce," Rogers said. "I'll be radioing for the cleaners to remove the bodies after we perform the strike on your cabin. Might be more casualties to come."

And I prayed that Adriana and the First Lady wouldn't be among them.

"Are you then ready to roll out?" I asked him. It was obvious I was anxious to go rescue Adriana.

Rogers nodded and brought his wrist mic up to his mouth. "Saddle up, people. Move in twos to the staging area. Radio silence from here on."

The clearing where we initially intended to launch our assault was only a half kilometer away, so we decided to leave the vehicles where they were. On Rogers' signal we moved out in a formation on both sides of the road that in tac military terms is called 'squad column with fire teams in column.' We would continue that alignment until we reached the staging area.

At 1853 we reached the clearing and Rogers sent two of his agents forward to scout the bridge that crossed the Greenbrier at the River Trail. We waited approximately fifteen minutes until they returned with a thumbs up. That meant no bad guys or civilians had been spotted. At 1910 Rogers then pumped his fist in the air twice which was the green light to commence the operation. Each HRT agent had been well briefed on his or her facet of the mission, specifically where each would come to a halt just before road intersections to scan the woods with use of NVD and then when the envelopment of the cabin was achieved, wait for further from the commander. Take down any insurgents spotted with suppressed fire. Take no prisoners.

Upon crossing the pedestrian bridge at a run, two at a time, we then set out into the woods. We'd stay off the roads and trails and move as quickly as we could, stopping only to set up briefly to observe and assess the immediate area. One squelch of the radio meant hold in place as insurgents had been spotted. Two squelches meant all clear and continue on.

Rogers, Smithers and I patrolling together had ventured nearly a klick into the forest, keeping the river about thirty yards off to our left, when we caught the first whiff. The smell of smoke...not the smell of a campfire or a wildfire. The smoke contained the stench of burning electrical wiring, cloth and plastic. As the breeze shifted up-river, the smoke billowed thicker toward our direction. And then through the forest up ahead we saw the flickering glow filtering its light through the trees.

"It's my cabin!" I exclaimed.

Charging out ahead of the other two, I tore through the trees and brush at a dead run. I could hear Rogers calling after me, "Bruce, wait! It could be a trap!"

I didn't care. My wife could be inside.

Rogers then broke radio silence. "Everyone. Target is ablaze. Continue moving in with caution." He then started catching up to me with Smithers on his heels.

As the flames finally came into full view, I could see that the cabin was already half gone. Old wood burns like tinder. When I was within a hundred feet of the place, I tossed my Remington to the ground, drew my Glock and headed for the front porch. The fire was burning profusely on the right side of the cabin in the kitchen and in the spare bedroom. As the flames were not yet licking in the area of the front door, I blasted through it with my shoulder. Once inside I shined my flashlight into the gray-black choking smoke to begin searching for anyone who may have been inside. Although I found myself coughing violently and gasping for air, I wasn't giving up.

As the fire was quickly catching the remainder of the cabin and moving into me, I called out, *"Anybody in here?"* After going through every room and finding no one on the floor or tied up, I lumbered back through the front door, teary-eyed and practically blind from the suffocating smoke. Rogers grabbed me as I stumbled off the porch and laid me in the grass.

While lying there, my burning eyes also caught sight of another object on fire off to the right side of the cabin. As our focus had been on the dwelling, I almost missed the fact that Adriana's van had been torched as well. Considering that an accelerant had also been used to advance the flames, it had gone up quickly.

Suddenly, there was a *whoosh* sound accompanied by a calamitous flash of intense heat. The entire cabin was now totally engulfed in flames. The fire had obviously reached the gas lines. I had made it out just in the nick of time. I shuddered to think that my wife and the First Lady might have been left tied up in the areas of the cabin that had already been consumed by the fire before I went in.

There was nothing we could do to fight the fire. Dragging tubs of water up from the river would have been futile. All we could do was wait it out and pray there had been no precious cargo inside. Obviously, the terrorist element had set the blaze and departed most likely out the road on that side of river leading to Highway 60.

Rogers switched channels and contacted each of his fake hunters sitting out at those intersections of the side roads with the main highway. "This is Bullitt. Any traffic out?" He paused to listen. "All right, stay put then."

He shook his head. "They've seen no vehicles coming out onto the highway. These people are still somewhere in these woods. Where do the roads Elderberry and Sydenstricker come out on the other end?"

I finally got my breath back and replied, "Elderberry dead ends about a mile to the north. Sydenstricker continues parallel for a couple miles with the river and then veers off to the left. It ultimately intersects several miles to the northwest with 219.”

“How long would you think the cabin has been burning, Bruce?”

“Maybe ten to fifteen minutes before we got here. It wouldn’t have taken long to erupt in flames considering how old it is. I’d say they helped it along with fuel oil. I smelled it in the smoke.”

Rogers then turned to yet another frequency. “Base, this is Bullitt. Put the bird in the air. They’ll see a cabin on fire off the west bank of the Greenbrier. Work the area north of that and if no apparent tango vehicles, concentrate on Highway 219 between Lewisburg and Pocahontas County. Watch for several sets of headlights in caravan. Do not engage. I say again, do not engage.”

As I sat in the grass watching the walls of the McGowan fish cabin cave in, it was as though all my hope was also crashing down into the flames. I didn’t care about the place and I couldn’t care less that Wolf Laurel had been shot to pieces either. It was all board and batten. Material property. I just prayed to God that when we finally sifted through the embers and ashes of the old cabin, we wouldn’t find bodies. I had to take it on good faith that when the terrorists left the cabin they took their two hostages with them. It would make no sense if they didn’t. One of them especially was a valuable pawn. Of course that made me worry all the more. Adriana wasn’t all that valuable to them. In fact, I wouldn’t put it past either Franks or Tyson to have left her in the rubble just to cause me to have an aneurysm. They had already pissed me off by burning down my cabin.

Rogers' team reconsolidated in my front yard, the area between the cabin and the river. The licking flames, now gradually dying down, still cast an eerie orange hue onto all that remained of my camp which was the dock and my tied-off rowboat that I had intended to bring up on the bank over a month ago. All that anyone could do at this point was to patiently watch the cabin burn to the ground and wait to sift through the ashes. It would be no use to go hunting for the bastards. We were a band of twenty or so and the forest was massive. They could be anywhere, but more likely *nowhere* any longer in the county. They had disappeared like that ghost enemy had done more than forty years ago, the memory of which just a couple hours before decided to re-visit me. But as we stood there watching, it was obvious that the air had gone out of our balloon. We all had such high hopes that the mission would be a success. That the President's lady would be rescued. That my lovely wife would go home with me that very night. And that the two traitors who appeared to be ramrodding this heinous act of terror would be taken prisoner. However, if I got to them first, they would not make it beyond my crosshairs.

Joanie Smithers excused herself to the woods for a few minutes. She then turned to flash a quick grin as she walked off. "Call of nature. I haven't been all afternoon."

"Watch out for the poison ivy," Rogers quipped.

Maybe we *needed* a little levity right about then.

We soon had to send the bad news to the President. However, *my* message to Eagle One would be to not give up hope. We *would* run down these terrorist pricks. But above all, we would do everything in our power to assure that no harm came to his wife.

Rogers listened again to a transmission and pointed up. "The bird is in the air. Will be over us in zero-two."

One of his men then came up to me with an axe in his hand. My axe. "Sir, we found this and a couple of shovels in your woodshed out back. Once this fire burns down, we'll start working through the rubble. If there *are* any remains in there, you shouldn't be the one to find them."

I nodded and gave the agent a smile. "Thanks."

A half hour later, after the Blackhawk had long since passed overhead and the fire was nothing but embers, three of the HRT agents began sweeping the foundation with their flashlights. While they worked, I walked down to my dock and sat with my feet dangling off its end. Many an evening I had done that...sometimes with a glass of Shiraz or Merlot in one hand and the sweet hand of my wife in the other. Maybe a night where the full moon was rising in all its glory over the trees, casting its radiant beam onto the waters of the Greenbrier. On a number of occasions, when the night was warm and the river placid, I took her hand and helped her down into our small boat, then shoved us off. One night we just drifted for a while without use of the oars to see how far the river would take us. She laid back against me and I buried my face in her wonderfully perfumed hair.

I couldn't help thinking how much her malady was my fault. She had a nice, comfortable life as the hostess of Wolf Laurel before I came along. Over the past seven or eight years I had given her much cause to worry. I might strike out on a mission, unable to tell her what it was about, where I was going or when I was coming back. And when I did return, I might come home with bullet holes in me. Then because of an incident way back in my past, a mad domestic terrorist had come to our home in revenge to kill me and she was the one who ended up taking the bullet. This time, she had been taken captive by a jihadist element, her life again hanging in the balance. It was because of one of those missions that I had become acquainted with the President and that brought he and the First Lady to our B&B. You see how my mind works? I was the bad link in this long chain of events. Whether directly or inadvertently, I had been poison for her. And I was now wallowing in self-blame.

I found my eyes suddenly wet, but not from the smoke. Some very dangerous people had her. At least I hoped they still did. I glanced back up the hill to where the agents were combing through the ashes. The fire had burned itself out and all I could now see was the smoky beams of their flashlights. And then I saw a large figure coming toward me. Chase Rogers' boots clomped heavily along the dock until he was within a few feet of where I was sitting. He leaned against one of the vertical supports and folded his arms.

"It was a nice place, Bruce. I could just see myself out here on the river pulling in a nice-sized trout, then later slapping it on the grill while frying up some sliced potatoes and onions..."

"I just remembered...I didn't even have lunch," I interrupted. "Thanks a lot for reminding my stomach."

He laughed. "I've got a protein bar in my ruck."

"No, thanks anyway. I'd probably gag on anything right now."

He leaned down and placed his huge paw on my shoulder. "It'll be fine, Bruce. We'll get her back. We'll get both of them back."

But then at that moment, one of the agents that had been searching the cabin's remains lumbered down the hill to where we sat. A sudden chill went through my neck and back in anticipation of what he would tell us.

"Commander, Mr. McGowan, we turned over every piece of debris in that rubble. No evidence of human remains."

"You're positive," said Rogers.

"We are."

Rogers reached down and offered me his hand. I grasped onto it and pulled myself up. He then crossed himself. "I said another prayer for the ladies a while ago, Bruce. We are never without hope when it comes to our Maker." Chase Rogers was the kind of friend I needed in my life. The complete man. Good Christian man, but a man who could also bring on hellfire when necessary.

It was as though the weight of a millstone had been lifted off my chest. My worst fear had been relieved. At least for now. Franks could have easily left Adriana in the ashes. Maybe there *was* an ounce of compassion left in him after all. And maybe I wouldn't make him suffer all that long before I ended his life.

Smithers then came up to me and gave me a hug. "The agents up there just told me, Bruce. I'm so happy for you...and personally relieved."

I smiled back at her. "Which gives me hope they still haven't been harmed." I then grabbed her shoulders with both hands. "Joanie, they didn't hurt them at any point when you were with them, did they?"

"I'll give them *that*. All Franks did was have them tied up. Neither the First Lady nor Adriana were knocked around. Me? That's another story. A couple of times I got my back up and paid for it. That's why they wanted me out of the way."

"Does Franks appear to be the big man in charge? I know that Tyson was the SAC for your people, yet one of your fellow agents seems to be calling the shots."

"Agency relationships don't mean squat in the terrorist game. I know Franks to be a very influential character. He was apparently approached by someone in the jihad game that offered big money and then somehow convinced Tyson to sign on. Money talks."

Suddenly my cell phone started vibrating on my belt. I pulled it, looked at its lighted face and read the word *restricted*. The only restricted calls I had been getting was from the person I was now hoping *would* call me.

I answered, "Franks."

"Obviously, you were expecting me."

I wanted to reach into the airwaves and strangle the bastard. I signaled Rogers.

"You have something that belongs to me," I said. "And I want her back."

"Won't happen until the Big Man comes through. I told you that this morning."

"Our ladies, are they safe?"

He ignored my question. "The bonfire was a warning, McGowan. Yeah, I knew the President would try something, even at the risk of losing his wife. How does it feel standing there watching your nice little retreat go up in flames?"

"Answer my question, Franks. Are my wife and the First Lady with you all right?"

"They're both right here with me and I haven't harmed a hair. *Yet.*"

I couldn't figure it. It was as though he were somewhere in that ghost world watching us at that very moment. But the immediate area had been thoroughly swept by the HRT and there were no signs of people *or* vehicles. And how the hell did he know we were standing at the remains of my cabin?

"Okay, maggot, what happens from here?"

"You get on the phone to Eagle One and tell him to get the ball rolling on the prisoner release. He will never again see the First Lady's face until that happens. He will also not be able to stop what goes off Monday evening. And I promise you that something big *will* go off. Oh, and you might as well give up the chase, McGowan. You'll never find us."

"How about just you and I having a meeting, Franks? Nobody else...just us."

"You'd like that, wouldn't you. That would of course serve no purpose. One of us would be dead and then so would your wife."

"I hope the money you're getting from these radical jihadists is worth your head, Franks, because I'm coming to separate it from your shoulders. Treason doesn't come cheap."

"The President is running out of time, McGowan. Make the call." I then heard the line go dead. I could tell my comment pissed him off.

Once again, I was feeling very helpless. We were outfoxed by an American jihadist and were no further on his trail than we were twelve hours before. But I did have to make the call. The man who told me I was his new best friend, or something to that effect, may not *want* me to be after I gave him the bad news.

I decided to walk away from everyone to make that call. I don't know why, but maybe the President and I had struck a chord with one another, considering what we had been through, and my conversation with him didn't need to include inquisitive ears.

I left Rogers and Smithers on the dock talking and walked back up the small hill past the ruins that used to be my cabin. Flipping open my cell, I pulled from my ammo pouch the small piece of paper that contained Eagle One's direct number.

"Hello," he answered. I guess since several of his confidants had the number, he didn't know who was calling.

"Mr. President, Bruce McGowan."

"Bruce. Do you bring me good news?" he asked in an up-beat but hopeful tone.

"Not so much, sir. As we were cordoning off the camp, we found my cabin on fire and the terrorist element gone.

They took the First Lady and Adriana with them and are now on the run."

"That's disappointing, Bruce. I don't mean that to reflect you boys didn't do the job. I'm sure you executed the mission flawlessly."

"They surmised we would be coming, according to Smithers."

"Yeah, Smithers. I wondered about her when you said the terrorists took our wives."

"They separated her from your wife and Adriana and stuffed her in the cabin of a hunting camp across the river. She sprang herself loose and terminated her captors."

"She's a pistol all right. I'm glad she escaped."

"I'm sorry this didn't turn out better, sir. But we're not giving up. We *will* find them and we *will* bring our wives home."

"I'll be prayin' that happens, Bruce. And I will pour out every Intel and manpower resource for you and Commander Rogers to utilize. Just let me know what you need."

"Sir, I hope I'm not out of line in asking, but what do you intend to do about the prisoner release? It's not only about our wives, but another device will be set off. You *know* they will do it."

"All I can tell you, Bruce, is that it is this administration's policy to never capitulate to terrorist demands. The American people may even demand it so they can feel safe. We yield this time and mark my word, there will be other times. I have directed all federal, state and local law enforcement agencies to put every officer on the street to keep eyes on every vehicle, backpack and suspicious-lookin' character out there, even if it means profilin' people. The National Guard has been activated in every state to support 'em. And to hell with the ACLU and PC police if they start squawkin' about it."

"I think the American people will be behind you, Mr. President."

"What are your plans from here, Bruce?"

"I'll be getting with Rogers on that. I imagine we'll continue looking for clues and redeploy to where the trail leads. I know that sounds generic, but we don't have much to go on. But in the meantime, perhaps you can get someone to gather some specific information for me personally."

"I'll do my best. What would that be?"

"I want every stitch of information on these two Secret Service rats, Franks and Tyson. I want to know everything about everybody in their families, who their friends are, their service history, where they went to school and have ever lived and what they eat for breakfast. No stones unturned. I'm thinking we'll be returning to our local base at the airport and if someone could deliver that to me there as soon as possible, I'll start to work on it."

"I'll make that happen. Whatever you do with the information, you have my blessing to go to any lengths necessary to find these terrorist bastards. You and I both have a lot personally at stake and I know you'll do your best."

"Thank you, Mr. President. Will talk again soon. Goodbye, sir."

I then flipped the phone closed and walked out of the tree line back toward the others, running almost immediately into Joanie Smithers.

"I was concerned about you, Bruce. Are you all right?"

"Yeah. Just took a little break to get away from the smoke."

"Commander Rogers is ready to pull his team out and wanted to see you."

"I'll be there in a moment."

She nodded, turned and began walking back toward the dock where several of the HRT had now congregated. I then took from my web gear my flashlight and made my way to what was left of the McGowan fishing cabin. Stepping over its foundation blocks, I walked onto the still smoldering flooring of our bedroom. The floor itself had maintained its material firmness as everything else had burned down around it. The rubble was difficult to navigate through, but the beam of my light did pick up a few items of nostalgia that had not totally burned or melted...my father's First Place trophy from the 1961 Greenbrier River Bass Tournament, of which he was most proud; my first rod and reel which was hanging over the fireplace, the reel being the only piece of it left; and Adriana's huge, ancient Bible that sat open on a table top, which belonged to her grandfather in the early 1900s. But upon sifting through the ash, I found one other item that troubled me: what was left of her heavy parka, the coat she was wearing when I last saw her. That meant she was out there somewhere in the cold without an outer garment.

Surely, even Franks would see that she wasn't placed in a situation where she would freeze to death.

And although the agents had combed the debris very carefully, I reconfirmed there wasn't any sign of lost life in the rubble. As embers were still burning and smoke billowing in several places, I then skirted around those areas to return to the camp's foreground where Rogers stood waiting.

"Bruce, there's nothing more here. I suggest we return to the base camp back at the airport. We've been given a small hangar to operate from."

"Are you planning for the HRT to return to Quantico tonight?"

"No. We'll debrief with the SIRG Agent-in-Charge who just flew in and determine what goes from there. We're waiting on further orders from the Director. The cleanup crew which will meet us back at the other cabin will begin bagging and tagging the bodies."

"Fine. I'm ready."

It took us about an hour to retrace our steps back through the woods and across the bridge to the Brooks cabin. The clean-up team in two SUVs was there waiting. A couple of Rogers' men pointed out the bodies along with that of the still unconscious guard. As we had parked our Jeep in proximity to the cabin, we waited until the remainder of Rogers team trudged further down the camp road to where they had left their vehicles. Once they had mounted up, one of Rogers' male agents jumped into the cargo area of the Cherokee so that Smithers could ride in the back seat. It was a disconcerting trip back to the airport, everyone solemnly realizing the mission was hardly a success. And hardly a word was spoken.

We shared the small hangar with a short body Beechcraft Baron that was under repair. It's left engine lay in several pieces under its wing. Still there was adequate room for the HRT to sack out for the night in sleeping bags. A small office was located off the right side of the bay and a unisex toilet room was in the rear. The men allowed its lone female member and Agent Smithers to go first and then a line formed containing those who hadn't previously hit the woods back at my camp.

Rogers and I remained outside the hangar door in the cold talking over what if anything we would do now. I was out of answers. Together we had laid out a very smart plan back in the Situation Room and were prepared for nothing but success. But as he was an Iraq war vet and I a veteran of a war fought decades before that, we both knew that the best laid plans of mice and men oft go awry. My apologies to Steinbeck. The battle seldom goes like clockwork.

"At this point unless we receive further orders from the Director, there's nothing we can accomplish here," he said. "If the Blackhawk spots Franks and his bunch somewhere on a main or backroad, we can move to intercept. But if they remain elusive, we'll have to abandon ship and pull out in the morning."

"I hate to admit it, but there seems to be no alternative."

"What do you plan to do?" he asked me.

"My place is here. The last conversation I had with Franks, I got the impression he was still in the county. That means my wife and the First Lady are somewhere in the area as well. That will change, however, if they leave the state.

Then, I don't know what. I told the President I would not give up the fight. I asked him to have someone deliver me a complete profile and history on these renegades. Maybe I can piece together something that will help me determine what their next move will be. And that's where I'll be."

As we were talking, I heard another voice. A woman's voice around the corner of the building. Being naturally curious, I walked around to see who it was. Chase Rogers followed. Agent Smithers was talking to someone in a low voice on a cell phone. As I continued walking toward her, she took the phone away from her ear. We stood looking at one another without word for a few seconds and then I pulled out my Glock.

Chapter Nineteen

"How much are they paying you, Joanie?"

She flipped her phone closed and then dropped her hand down by her side. She appeared as stone frozen as a terra cotta warrior.

"It's not like that, Bruce."

"Then how *is* it?"

She didn't answer.

"Commander Rogers, please take Agent Smithers into custody."

Rogers then walked up to her, spun her around and cuffed her hands behind her back.

She finally spoke. "How did you know?"

"I didn't until now. Franks told me this morning on the phone when I was at the White House that he was smashing everyone's cell phone. Yet you still have yours. And I kept wondering how the terrorists knew we were standing in my camp watching the place burn down. Now when I think about it, you slipped away on two occasions feigning that you had a 'call of nature.' I know now it was a call all right...a to call to Franks to report what we were doing so he could stay ahead of us."

"Bruce, I..."
 "You and your friends were scouting out a place for Franks to move the hostages. You came across the hunting cabin. But here's the thing...you didn't expect the HRT would choose the approach route that took us by that cabin. I found the night vision device you hurriedly left on the front porch banister. You were watching as the HRT moved in, weren't you. You knew we'd capture the place and it wouldn't take long for us to find out you were involved. You bashed the heads of your two unsuspecting friends inside the cabin and started working your way into the woods. Why not then kill the other guards? If we captured rather than killed them, they might incriminate you. You took out one of the guards and would have *done in* the others had we not moved in so quickly. It was a nice little touch to attack me, wanting us to believe you thought I was one of the guards. Do I have all that right?"

"I'm not a traitor, Bruce."

"Don't personalize my name like you're my friend. You are *not* my friend, Agent Smithers. And you *are* a traitor."

I then approached her and stopped at a point to where my face was within a foot of hers. I wanted to smack that face with the back of my hand. She had not only betrayed her charge, the First Lady, but pretended to befriend Adriana. All the while she was Franks' eyes and ears. Also a nice touch to fake being knocked around while the President and I were talking to our wives earlier in the morning.

"All right, you say you're no traitor. Then talk. Convince me otherwise."

Tears formed in her eyes. "They have my daughter."

"What do you mean they have your daughter? In all of our nice little conversations we had the past couple of days, you never mentioned a daughter."

"Can we go some place and sit down? I think my sugar has dropped."

"Commander, give her one of your protein bars. She's about to be grilled and I don't want her passing out on me."

After he had shoved the honey and nut bar into her coat pocket, I took her by the arm and escorted her inside to the hangar office. Rogers took off her shackles and we sat her down. She then unwrapped the bar and began hungrily devouring it. I poured her a cup of water from the Aramark dispenser that sat in the corner.

"If you're now comfy, let's have it. What *about* your daughter?"

"I live in Alexandria in a town house. I'm a single mom and my daughter, Cathy, is ten. When I am away on assignment, my mother, who lives nearby, keeps her. Last night around two in the morning, Steffen Franks called me on my cell. This what he said or words to that effect:

"We have your daughter, Smithers. Our people took her tonight. Don't worry, she's safe and will continue to be unless you fail to cooperate."

"I didn't believe him, so then I called my mother right away. She was screaming at the top of her lungs. She said some Middle-Eastern looking men broke in and took Cathy. However, they didn't hurt Mother *or* her. Then Franks called me back and coerced me into telling him where we were. I didn't have a choice. They came in on us at your cabin a couple hours later. This morning I asked him if it was his people who put the bomb in that Maryland city and he said yes. Then he started telling me more. I couldn't believe all he said they planned to do. He said he and the other agents involved were going to make a shit load of money by taking the President hostage. He had made some kind of agreement with a Saudi based jihadist group who would demand a number of Gitmo prisoners be released. I was not just panicky about my daughter, but livid that he and other of the President's detail would sell their souls and their allegiance for mere money. I did hear him and our SAC talking about the place they would end up, somewhere in Mauritania I think they said, living like kings on the money." She then suddenly broke down and sobbed bitterly.

Neither Rogers nor I said a word or changed our expressions. We just let her sit there and cry. But then I started wondering why Franks was so liberally telling her about their plans. Was it because dead hostages tell no tales? I was getting that pain in my chest again.

She wiped her eyes with her sleeve and continued. "I am so, so sorry. I did make sure Adriana and the First Lady were not harmed in any way, not that I think Franks would do that. But, yes, I did feed his information by phone tonight when I could. I can't help what I did. My little girl is being kept somewhere in the D.C. area. I know that much. But I don't know who has her or if they will hurt her. I have seen how some of these Islamic radicals that Franks is running with do business. That's why I fear for my daughter. If Franks hadn't intervened a couple of times, maybe Adriana would have gotten hurt. She was pretty feisty this morning and one of the towel-head bastards even spit on her. That was when she told them that if and when you caught up to them, you would cut out their hearts and feed them to the crows."

I almost smiled. I think Adriana might have heard me make that very statement the day I left to go after the domestic terrorist who kidnapped Caroline some time back. It's obvious I have not been a good influence on my wife. But God bless her for not taking any crap off the Islamobastards. I just hoped she didn't push the envelope and piss them off to a point where they might even end her life. Under their Sharia Law, taking the life of a woman, especially an infidel woman who would disrespect a man, would be no greater sin than stomping on a bug.

"All well and good, Smithers," I said, "but you're going to sit here even if it takes all night and tell me every fricking detail from the time you arrived at my cabin until we found you on the other side of the river. I want to know about every player in that subversive bunch and their descriptions. You will tell me anything you've overheard that they're planning to do. And as to phone calls, any conversation between you and Franks, I want to hear. I will tell you what to say when you give him your SITREP. Furthermore, if I have the slightest inkling you're lying about somebody having your daughter and you've made all this up just to save your neck, I will not hesitate to *break* that neck. Am I clear?"

"Yes. What I told you is the God's truth. And I *will* help you. I'll help you find them. I'll do anything you ask if you can help me get my daughter back. I know she's scared...and so am I. I don't care what happens to me. You can later have me prosecuted and throw me in prison. I just want Cathy unharmed and out of the hands of these people. So, tell me what you want to know."

"All right, was Franks on the phone at any time talking with someone else...like someone he may be taking orders from?"

She nodded. "A couple of times I saw and heard him saying stuff like. 'Okay, okay, I'll do what you say.' And then he was giving statuses to somebody about what was going on there. One time he said something about money and that it didn't matter whether or not everything went to plan. The First Lady was just as good, maybe better. He expected the same payoff, nothing less."

"Sounds like someone higher up that's pulling the strings was going to slice his payoff because they didn't end up with the President," commented Rogers.

"Where is Franks now?"

"That I can't truthfully answer. He had ordered some of his people to go scout out another site for everyone to move to. He told them to take me with them. They found the hunting cabin and then Franks was to make the decision to move. But you're right. He ordered me to stand outside and help watch. First, the cabin owners returned in the afternoon. The guards took them before they could even get out of the truck. And then I was posted with that NVD on the front porch when it got dark to continue the watch. I caught sight of your men and knew immediately what was going on. I guess I panicked, all the while thinking about my daughter. I hit the *last call* feature on my phone and called Franks to tell him what was happening. I lied when I told you they had tied me up. But I did take the woman down and then slugged the male guard when he came back into the room. And yes, I meant to kill them and make it look like I was nothing but an unwilling hostage. I then took the male guard's knife, and on the way out to hook up with you all, I came across one of the guards who had also spotted you and had raised his weapon to fire. I slipped up behind him and sliced open his throat." She stopped to take a gulp of the water and again wiped her eyes.

"I then saw you all take out both of the terrorist guards there on the perimeter. Afterward, on the spur of the moment, again thinking about my daughter, I decided to take you down, wanting you to believe I mistook you for one of the terrorists. I lied to you about the reason I did that. Later, when you two stepped away to talk, I did call Franks to warn that you had moved in on that cabin and would soon be redeploying in his direction. And yes, just a few minutes ago, I told him where we now were and that you had given up on finding him. He told me to stick with you from here on to continue updating him on what you all were doing. He said the life of my daughter depended on that. He of course doesn't know you've now found out the truth about me."

I glanced at Rogers and he shook his head in astonishment. But then he said, "You know, this could be a *good* thing, Bruce. She could feed him bogus information about us, maybe tell him we've given up the mission entirely and are on our way back to Quantico. That may then cause him to put the brakes on and find a new place to settle. And maybe she could somehow get him to let slip where that might be."

"Yeah, could work. Something to think about."

I then noticed that Smithers was shaking. Could be because I had found her out or just that she was cold. But she looked rather pale.

I asked her if the protein bar had helped. She shook her head. "Not much. I do need something more to eat. I just can't shake the shakes."

Rogers rose from his chair and stepped out of the room to signal a member of his team. When the agent joined him, he said, "There's a restaurant here at the airport. I want you to go get a burger for Smithers and a soft drink. Nothing diet. She needs something with sugar." He turned to me. "Anything for you, Bruce?"

"Maybe a large coffee. It might be a long night of conversation. How about your people?"

"They've already popped open MREs."

"Wonderful." MREs. Meals Rejected by Ethiopians.

It was half past ten and Smithers, now refreshed and feeling stronger, talked openly about Franks and Tyson. "I never liked either of those guys. Tyson liked to play the role as our SAC. I never had much contact with him, but when I did, I found him boorish and condescending. Always full of himself and strutted around like a peacock. But Franks can be an enigma. He was a nice enough agent when I worked with him on various details, very bright and always reminded me of an accountant or a corporate lawyer in his glasses. I think I remember that he *was* a lawyer at one time. But then I saw earlier this morning that vicious jackal side of him where he can be barbaric, even ruthless. At one point when I gave him a little lip, he shoved me up against the wall and placed the tip of a knife within inches of my left eye, telling me if I crossed him, he would put both of my eyes out and I would literally never see my little girl again."

Rogers asked, "At any point, did he allude to any locations where he might ultimately take the hostages or where any other members of this Stealth Jihad group might be?"

"I think when I overheard them talking at one point, Franks said something about going to the Dar el...uh, I think the next word starts with an 'a.' And when this was all over they would commit Zabiha or something like that on the hostages."

I asked Rogers, "Do you know what those terms mean?"

He shook his head.

"Anything else? How many of them were there at my cabin after you and the others relocated?"

"I think maybe nine, including Franks and Tyson."

"How many were Middle Eastern?"

"Five. There were two other Americans that looked like mercenary types."

"Did the Arabs communicate well in English?"

"Not too much."

"How about Franks? How did he communicate with them?"

"That's what surprised me. He knew a lot of Arabic words. I didn't know that about him the times I worked with him."

Rogers and I exchanged glances.

I could see that Joanie Smithers was now drained. She had gotten no sleep the night before and her heavy eyelids reflected that.

"I think that's about all for right now. Commander, I'd like for your female HRT agent to take charge of Ms. Smithers and see that she's settled in for the night in one of the sleeping bags. We need to have her under guard in shifts to assure she doesn't run off."

Smithers quickly spouted, "I'm not going to do that, Mr. McGowan, I promise you. Guard me all you want, but I'll be right here when everyone opens their eyes in the morning."

I nodded and then motioned with my head for Rogers to take her on out.

I didn't know how much help her information was or whether she would be any help to us in picking up anything from Franks when they talked again. She would be the one initiating contact to alert him about anything significant the HRT was planning.

I'd be borrowing a sleeping bag as well and although I wasn't sure my brain would turn off at any point, my body was in fact wasted. But as I was still sitting in that office mulling over just when I *would* sign off for the night, a new face appeared at the door. Black suit, white shirt, modest tie and black wingtips. Nice looking young man every bit of thirty. Obviously from one of the Alphabet services and probably a whiz kid on an accelerated move up the food chain considering his age.

"Excuse me, but I'm looking for a Bruce McGowan."

"You got me. What can I do for you?"

He came inside the room and stuck out his hand which I shook. "Mr. McGowan, I'm FBI Special Agent Mark Purcell, a profiler for the Bureau's CIRG."

"Pleased to meet you. What can I do for you?"

"I flew down here tonight on special orders from the Director to hand off two Secret Service agent shields. I'm also to coordinate with you and the HRT commander as you continue some kind of operation I don't know anything about. Are you in a position to enlighten me?"

"May I see your ID? I'm not questioning your credibility, but it's just SOP with me."

"I understand completely." He pulled from his jacket pocket his badge and identification.

"Please have a seat. Let me get Commander Rogers."

I stepped out of the room briefly and signaled for Rogers to join us. He had been speaking with his female agent on Smithers' situation for the night. After he entered the room, I introduced him to Purcell and then we took some time to exchange pleasantries.

Purcell then opened up the dialogue on Franks and Tyson. "Gentlemen, you may look at anything in these shields, but I am to stay in the room with them at all times. I've studied them, but have not been apprised as to what I should be looking for. I think the Director wanted me to speak with you first so that I could remain objective and not have any pre-conceived notions about these two agents. Give me the entire story. Hopefully, I can then provide you with my insights."

I took no more than fifteen minutes to lay out a capsule of the events that had occurred the last two days, to include my phone conversations I had with the renegade agents. I also told Purcell what Smithers had said about Franks' and Tyson's personalities.

"That's the kind of information I need. I know you'll be dissecting these files to pick out what you perceive to be important information, but allow me to give you a condensed synopsis on what you'll find.

He opened one of the shields. "Let's take Curtis Tyson first. Forty-seven years old, born in Syracuse, New York, now lives in Falls Church, married, two teenage children, boy and girl. Bachelors degree from CCNY and Masters in Sports Psychology from Rutgers. Former Navy SEAL and has been with the Service for eleven years. He was promoted four years ago to Special Agent-in-Charge on the President's team. No decorations, but did receive a reprimand by the Assistant Director for having a beer while on duty. That was in his third year with the Service. Clean record since he's been on White House duty. Scored satisfactorily on the last MMPI, but a low score on the Pd measurement...conflict, anger, respect for societal rules...Pd being Psychopathic Deviate. After a personal interview and retest, he scored normally, possibly skewing the answers. On his last performance review he was assessed with having positive management skills, however, with a tendency to be over-bearing and denigrating."

I looked at Rogers. "Fits with what Smithers conveyed. Sorry to interrupt."

"I was done with his information. You can dig out more on your own that might be of interest to you. As to Steffen Franks, he's forty two, never married, born in Chicago to German immigrant parents who returned to Hamburg a year after their son graduated from high school. Educated at UC at Berkeley, Bachelors in Political Science and MBA from MIT. No military service. IQ suggested to be 148. Selected as Special Agent with FBI at age thirty, served three years and then transferred to the Secret Service. Been a Service agent for nine years including assignment two years in counterfeiting, a year in dignitary and cabinet protection, and the rest of his time on the First Family protection detail. He lives alone in a D.C. apartment. Scored satisfactorily as well on his MMPI, but also had a low score on SC, Schizophrenia, odd thinking and social alienation. And here's a kicker...Franks was recently considered for intra-agency transfer to the Company. He speaks fluent Arabic. He had spent eight months on a leave of absence in Saudi Arabia two years ago, in the same region, Al Madinah, that harbors this Stealth Jihad terrorist organization. Amazing that his visit to that region was not investigated and that he was allowed to remain on the President's detail.

"Today the Director secured both a search warrant on both agents' residences and a bench warrant for their arrest. This afternoon members of our CIRG team raided Franks' apartment and as of 1900 were still performing a complete shakedown, even ripping out upholstery, checking floorboards for hiding places and looking for false walls. No computers or other electronic devices were found and it appears every piece of paper except toilet tissue had been removed from the premises. Apparently knowing what was planned to go down, Franks cleaned everything out and left no incriminating evidence. Absolutely no evidence he had ever lived there. Neighbors in the apartment complex continue to be questioned.

"Tyson's wife was horrified when the Bureau came in. She claims she knows nothing about her husband's connection to all this and genuinely appeared shocked that he had been accused. Says he's been a good husband and father, but is away a lot because of his job. So far, nothing incriminating has been found tonight."

"Sounds to me that the Service needs a complete personnel overhaul beginning with their director," Rogers commented. "I understand Bureau agents have now temporarily taken over responsibilities of the Presidential and White House protection details."

"That's correct," I said. "That happened last night as soon as it was learned that agents in the Service were involved in the attack on our B&B and the attempted seizure of the President."

"What else do you need, gentlemen?" Purcell asked.

"Smithers mentioned to me that she overheard Franks talking with Tyson and one of the Arab terrorists. She heard them talk about people in the Dar al something or other."

"That would be a *Dar al-Amn* which is a house of safety where Muslims live in the Western World. Many of them are radicals suspected to be supporting American jihad efforts. The place in D.C. is called the Caliph House. An imam who is reported to be a descendent of and successor to Muhammed, controls all Muslim religious activity in the United States as regards Islamic theocracy. The place is protected under the doctrine of sovereign immunity and cannot be entered by law enforcement."

"Lovely," I said. "Maybe that Caliph House is the planning nucleus and location of their operation. Can we get a court order to have the place raided anyway?"

"Not likely. As you would expect, there has to be indisputable evidence and probable cause. Merely overhearing a conversation containing words that couldn't totally be discerned will not get it."

"Okay, Smithers also said the hostages would undergo *fabiha* when this was all over."

Purcell looked at me, frowning and with mouth agape. "Fabiha?"

"Yes. That was clear."

"Mr. McGowan, I hate to be graphic but the terrorists are planning to kill the First Lady and your wife by cutting their throats through to the windpipe. Fabiha is the slaughter of an animal with a knife."

Chapter Twenty

Upon hearing the words, I felt the blood drain from my face at the same time a fiery shot of adrenaline cut through my arteries like a shard of broken glass. "Then we have to be all the more hell-bent on finding these bastards."

"You said Agent Smithers would be back in contact with Franks to keep feeding him information. As Franks' calls come in as *restricted*, he probably has a burner phone. How is she calling him?

"She told us she's touching star 69," I replied.

"Mostly that doesn't work, but I guess it depends on the service and the phone. However, I've got an idea. I have a couple of gee whiz items with me that might help in pin-pointing his location."

My spirit suddenly perked up. "I'm listening."

"First, I have installed in my phone a roving bug feature which will allow me to then use a kind of spy listening device called ShotSpotter. With it, we all can hear both the caller's and receiver's conversation. If she's using her own phone and merely places it on *speaker*, Franks will hear that and wonder why she's doing it. The jig will then be up."

"But the feature is on *your* phone. They're contacting each other on hers."

"She can make a quick call to him on her phone and then tell him she's out of juice and has no way of recharging it. She'll tell him that she now has to borrow one of the agents' phones. She'll give him *my* number to continue the communication."

"Won't he get suspicious about that?"

"Maybe, but if he wants to continue using her as a spy, he'll have no choice."

"Okay, we'll be able to listen in, but how will that pinpoint his location?"

"Ah, good of you to ask. I also have installed in my phone a device called StingRay, the latest in cell phone software. As the conversation goes on, I can touch the feature and within a minute or so, depending on the distance, determine the other person's location and movement. Kind of like using GPS, but instead of determining your *own* real time location, it zeroes in on the receiving party. This eliminates having to depend on cell tower triangulation."

I looked at Rogers and grinned. "He's not just a Bureau profiler, we have our own James Bond gadget guy sitting here." I then turned back to Purcell. "And these devices are fail-proof?"

"They've been tested numerous times and there were no glitches. The CIA has used them with complete success."

"Then we have our first glimmer of hope. Chase, as to the location of this Islamic safe house that may have a connection to the Stealth Jihad, can you still contact the Director and try to get a warrant to raid the place?"

"I can do that, but whether he will be successful with our liberal federal court system that always seems to be protecting the rights of radical organizations, it's doubtful."

"That never stopped *me* from surging ahead when *I* was in the business."

"Yeah, but from what I think I might know about you, adherence to legal protocol is not necessarily in your playbook."

"Well, I've always done my best. Agent Purcell, can you at least have people gain Intel on that place and do so ASAP? We don't have much time until threats are carried out."

"I'll call the Director right away."

"Good. Tomorrow morning we will get Smithers to make the call and get the ball rolling here. If your phone can perform all that spook stuff, we have a good shot at finding Franks."

My earlier assumption that my brain would not allow me to get much much sleep that night turned out to be correct. After throwing my borrowed sleeping bag on the office floor around 2330 and shoving my body into it, I must have laid there nearly an hour wide awake until I finally got up and sat back down in the chair at the desk. My mind remained dichotically focused...on how we would finally nail Franks and his merry band and on what the love of my life might be going through at that very moment. Rogers was now out in the hangar bay with his men getting the shuteye they needed and Purcell had returned to his motel just off the interstate. Other elements of the FBI's CIRG that had responded over twenty-four hours ago to the terrorist downing of the C-130 were out on the airport grounds on 50% alert along with the Marines that remained on the perimeter. Occasionally, I heard a Blackhawk either coming in or taking off, but there was still a lockout of any commercial traffic.

I took from my pants pocket a notebook at one point and began writing a kind of script for Smithers' to regurgitate at such time she communicated with Franks. Not only did we want to gain from him on the sly what information we could, but to give us enough time to get a fix on his location. As Purcell suggested, she would call the mad man and tell him her battery was low. She was then borrowing someone's phone so they could continue their random contacts. Would he agree to it, that was the question.

I also couldn't stop thinking about the fabiha that was planned. Franks had said it would occur with the hostages when it was all over. When *what* was all over? The prisoner release, which was not going to happen, or at such time it was understood there would be no release? Franks not only needed to continue using the ladies as pawns, but to prove to the President and me they were still alive. I would have to wait for him to recontact me, if he ever did again, because my phone and service would not allow a callback on restricted numbers.

Sometime during the morning I was planning to take a few minutes to return to Wolf Laurel to assess the situation there. Rogers had told me some of the CIRG agents would be posted on site until further notice as it was a crime scene. The investigation would take several days. I was mainly concerned about my weapons that remained exposed there considering the curiosity seekers who now had knowledge of the tragic event at the B&B...or maybe perps that might decide to plunder the place. But, Rogers assured me the inn would be protected and that two agents were actually bunking there. My financially prudent wife would probably want to charge them for their stay.

Just after 0100, I walked through the nearly dark hangar bay to the rest room, careful not to step on any sleeping bags. Somebody might be curled up with his Glock and get excited.

I think I finally dozed off about 0400 lying on top of the sleeping bag. Because the office as well as the hangar itself was not heated, I was awake again around 0630 shivering. The temp outside had dropped well below freezing. When I sat up, I found Rogers at the desk going through the two agent's shields. Purcell must have changed his mind about releasing them to us. Rogers then glanced over at me and said, "Good afternoon." Of course, it was still dark outside the window which was my first clue he was just yanking my chain.

"How long have you been sitting there?" I asked him.

"About twenty minutes. What time did you turn in? You look like crap."

"Feel like it, too. I don't know...maybe a couple of hours ago."

"I was just reading something interesting in Franks' personnel file. Check this out. Steffan's father, Jurgen, came to the U.S. in 1945 with his parents, Hans and Margo. In 1967, the CIC for Nazi Crimes found that 62 year old Hans was a guard at the Auschwitz concentration camp and both he and his wife were subsequently deported along with Steffen's parents. That's why they left the United States. Steffen, however, was allowed to stay. That doesn't mean a whole lot, but if he grew up in a household of Nazis, maybe something deviant got programmed into his personality."

"Interesting," I said. But what was *more* interesting to me at the time was what Rogers was holding in his hand. "Where did you get the coffee?"

"It was brought in to us by a couple of members of the other CIRG element along with several boxes of Krispy Kreme donuts."

"Ahh, the *real* breakfast of champions," I said. "To hell with the Wheaties."

He said, "In about an hour, I'm thinking we need to bring in Smithers so she can call Franks. What'll we tell her to say?"

I pulled from my pocket the note sheet on which I had scribbled out some thoughts and showed it to him. He read it and nodded.

"So then, as we talked, she'll make the first call, then get him to call her back on Purcell's phone."

"That's the plan." I then stifled a yawned. I couldn't imagine why I woke up tired.

Rogers shook his head. "Man, go get yourself some coffee and wake the hell up."

First, I returned to the toilet room to splash some water on my face and then used the toothbrush and paste I took from the Lincoln bathroom the morning before, which seemed like a *week* before. On the way back to the hangar office, I snatched a couple donuts from a small table and poured myself a cup of hot coffee. All of the HRT was now up and moving around. Smithers was standing near the plane with the female HRT agent engaged in conversation. She *needed* a friendly face to commune with.

Purcell arrived at 0710 looking revitalized like he had enjoyed fresh bed sheets last night and a hot shower this morning. Maybe he even had a nice hot motel breakfast as well. My donuts were starting to turn over in my stomach.

"Good morning, everyone," he greeted.

I think I might have grunted something, but the ruff-n-ready HRT commander came to his feet with a smile and shook Purcell's hand. I hate bright, bubbly people this early in the morning. I've got to get through my two mile run and two cups of coffee just to get the corners of my mouth to turn up.

"Well, this is a new day, gentlemen," began Rogers. "A day we hope we can make things happen. Ready for Agent Smithers to come in?"

"I'm ready," I said. I then stood and walked to the door. As soon as my form appeared in the hangar bay, Smithers looked in my direction. I motioned to her and she nodded. When she entered the room, I shut the door behind her. Either she slept too hard or very little as evidenced by her puffy eyes. But maybe she had been crying through the night. If her story was true, she had every reason to cry. I felt for her. After all, the bad guys had someone *I* loved as well.

I pulled up a chair for her. "Did you get coffee and something to eat?"

"Yes, a half of a donut. Not usually the kind of stuff I eat in the mornings. Of course I didn't have my run either."

"Agent Smithers, this is Special Agent Purcell, a profiler from one of the CIRG teams. He's helping Commander Rogers and I with the profiles on Franks and Tyson. In a few minutes we want you to make contact with Franks. I've written out what I want you to tell him. You'll make one quick call and say you're just about out of battery juice. Tell him henceforth you will use one of the agents' phones. Give him the number of that phone and he can call you right back."

"Why do that? Why not maintain contact on my phone?"

"You'll be using Agent Purcell's phone. He has some software on it that will allow us to not only hear Franks' conversation with you, but can within a few minutes determine his location. Your dialogue with him has to be believable and convincing. If he has any impression that you're working with us and against him...well I hate to say it this way...but he has already threatened the life of your daughter."

Her eyes immediately watered up. "God forbid."

I then gave her a half-smile. "You were such a good actress with us yesterday evening, I know you can pull this off."

"I can do this and I *will* be convincing," she said.

"I've written down what I want you to say. Study the dialogue for a few minutes and tell me when you're ready make the call."

She moved her lips silently as she read it, moving her index finger around as though she were directing an orchestra. Then she looked up toward the ceiling, closed her eyes and rehearsed what she had read, this time talking to herself in a low voice. "Okay," she finally said. "I think I've got it."

"You ready?" I asked her.

She nodded and picked up her cell.

After taking a deep breath, she touched *last call.*

We sat silently, careful not to make a sound.

She sat listening. More than fifteen seconds passed and no pickup.

Finally, after about a dozen rings, she took the phone away from her ear and shook her head. "He's not answering." She then touched *end call.*

"Wonder *why* he didn't answer?" asked Rogers.

"Maybe where he is now is out of cell tower range." I replied.

"Wait a few minutes, then try again."

Less than a minute later, the phone rang.

"Hello," she answered. Then a pause to listen.

"Yeah...hey, I just needed to let you know, my cell phone is almost dead and I don't have a charger. I'm still here at the airport. What?" A pause. " My phone's now flashing and will go off in just a few seconds. I borrowed another phone from one of the agents here. If you want to know anything, you'll have to call me back on it. The number is..." She read it from the paper slowly. "Do you have it?"

Pause. "I can't help it, I..." And then she touched *end call*, giving the impression the phone in fact died.

I nodded slowly. "Good. Let's see what he does."

While we waited, Purcell picked up his ShotSpotter device and handed it to me. I stuck in the ear piece. "Is it on?" I asked him.

"It's ready."

Suddenly, Smithers' cell phone rang again. She jumped as though she had been hit with electric current.

"Don't answer it," I said. "He'll call back on Agent Purcell's phone eventually. He just wants to see if you were lying to him."

After the phone had rung a half dozen times, we then waited. More than five minutes passed. I was thinking that *he* was thinking. Would he trust her talking on another agent's phone? And I'm sure he wondered who *was* this agent? Did the phone have some kind of built-in tracking gizmo? Franks was a smart operator and just might be well up on all the latest phone tech.

Another ten minutes went by and no call. None of us said much and it was like waiting for the other shoe to drop.

But then finally at 0745 Purcell's phone went off. The ringtone was some kind of crazy Looney Tunes song. I was somewhere between laughter and 'are you kidding me?' Anyway, this was serious business and I had to concentrate on the upcoming phone conversation.

After the third ring, Smithers said, "Hello."

I then heard Franks say. "Smithers, what the hell is this cellular change? If you're trying to set me up..."

"No, Franks. You wanted me to continue contact with you to let you know what was happening with McGowan and the HRT. I'm doing that the best way I can. My cellphone is dead. I got this one from one of the agents."

"What agent?"

"Somebody left behind here at the airport with McGowan."

I was picking Franks' voice up like he was sitting there in the room. I love new age technology.

"What about the HRT?"

"Gone. They left for Quantico this morning."

"You had better not be shitting me, Smithers. I have eyes all around that airport. The life of your daughter is on your head."

She looked at me and then closed her eyes. "They're *gone*, Franks."

"And McGowan?"

"Pacing around the place like a wounded animal. He doesn't take defeat very well."

I made a face. That wasn't in the script, but a nice touch.

"What's his next move?"

"I don't know."

"Is he still planning to come after us?"

"How can he do that? He sure as hell doesn't know where you are. You could be in a whole nuther state."

"I'm closer than you think."

"As in where?"

He laughed. "No, no, Smithers. For all I know he could be standing there beside you listening."

"Do you think I'd risk my daughter's life allowing that to happen?"

"I don't know *what* to think. Remember, I only released you so that you could be my eyes and ears where he's concerned. He's dangerous. And as long as he's buying your story and you're feeding me what I need, he won't be a threat us."

"The HRT is gone. How can he any longer be a threat?"

"He single-handedly took out several of our men and successfully got the President back to Washington. I'd call *that* being a threat. I don't know who the hell he was, but he has the skills of a spook."

"He wasn't CIA. All I know is that he was former FBI."

"Well, I want you to stay with him at all costs. When my people get what they want out of the White House, you get your daughter back. I don't need to keep looking over my shoulder for somebody like McGowan."

I was glad she was furthering their conversation. The longer she kept him talking, the better chance Purcell's software could pin-point his location.

"Where is my daughter and what kind of people have her?"

"Your daughter is not a topic for discussion. All I can tell you is she hasn't been harmed...and *won't* be as long as you come through for me. Let's just say that the people who have her are highly proficient with the jambiyah and they don't care if their victim is an adult or a child. Do you hear me, Smithers?"

Her lips began trembling and tears formed in her eyes. "I'll do what you tell me, Franks, but if any harm whatsoever comes to her, if it takes the rest of my life, I will find you. Now do *you* hear *me*?""

He laughed again. "Call me when you find out McGowan's next move, Smithers. You and I are done here." He then ended the call.

Smithers laid the phone down on the desk and covered her face. Her sobs were loud and pitiful.

I pulled the plug from my ear and walked over to her. Squatting down beside her, I placed an arm around her shoulder. I didn't say anything. I just let her cry.

She then raised her head up and said, "I'm sorry, Mr. McGowan. I don't normally cry like this."

"You have every right to cry, Joanie. And you did well for us. You didn't follow my script, though. You were better than the script." I then smiled. "Like I said, you have a unique talent as an actress and should go into theater when this is over."

And that made *her* smile. It was as though the sun had come out on her face after the rain.

"Thanks, Mr. McGowan."

"I'm back to being Bruce, Joanie. I may still be a bit pissed at you because of what you did, but now that I've heard what I needed to hear out of that snake's mouth, I can understand your actions."

Purcell picked up his phone and touched the locater feature. "I have him, Mr. McGowan."

I hustled over to where he sat. "Where?"

He pointed to the face of his phone and the GPS image. "There."

Chapter Twenty-One

"Hmm. Looks like the location is out just off 219," I commented. "As we suspected, they went out the back end of Seneca. That's a pretty rugged dirt road and considering the mud after that hard rain we had Friday night, you'd just about need a four wheel drive."

"Where would they hole up in that area?" asked Rogers.

"Could be a house back off the road or a business. I'd have to look at a roadmap to accurately determine that."

"Whatever is out there, I'm sure they'll have mobile sentries posted. They'll quickly spot anyone driving around looking.

"Tell you what, Chase. I'd like to run over to our B&B and check things out. The CIRG is supposed to have agents still located there. You go along as well and I'll give you some hunting clothes to put on. Don't worry, most everything I have for the woods is generally big on me, so it all should fit you fairly well. Maybe that bunch won't get excited seeing two good ol' boys checking things out. If this place is where I think it is, there's plenty of woods back off the road there."

"Alright. Sounds like a plan. When do you want to head out?"

"As soon as you're ready. Agent Smithers, you'll need to go with us. And Agent Purcell, we'll need your phone."

 "It's the Bureau's phone anyway. I have a personal cellular. Do you want me to accompany you?"

"You're a profiler. Do you ever get out there and do business with your CIRG?"

"If you're asking if I gear up and do missions, well not usually. But, I'm one of the best shots on our team."

"Have you ever put a bead on somebody and pulled the trigger?"

"No, but I knock the bull out of the target every time."

Rogers gave me a quick glance and a half smile. "Purcell, I thought you were headed back to Washington," he said. "Anyway, you're in a suit and as you can see, the HRT is dressed for battle.

"But if I'm needed..."

"Tell you what. If you're not flying back, I'll need a good operative to remain here for communication purposes. My HRT will remain here as well for now."

"Okay, but I'm available if needed."

I know we were a bit condescending with young Mark Purcell, but if we somehow suddenly found ourselves in the heat of conflict while we were on recon, it was experience we needed. Smithers, however, who needed to stay with us, would ride along and remain hunkered down in the rear seat of the Jeep.

* * * * *

When Rogers wheeled the Cherokee onto the gravel driveway at Wolf Laurel, we were met immediately by a man in black pants, a black coat and a ball cap that read *FBI*. A yellow *Police Line Do Not Cross* tape was strung across the driveway halfway in. A white, unmarked Ford Explorer sat off to one side.

Rogers rolled down his window and flashed his ID and the agent dropped the tape to allow us to continue on in. The old place looked the same from the outside, but I remembered how we left the inside when we hurriedly left Friday night.

The blood from the fleeing terrorist still lay on the veranda, but had now turned dark. We found the door unlocked and once we stepped inside, one of two agents was taking photos and the other was writing something in a ten by thirteen notebook. The agent writing crap down quickly approached us, first noticing Rogers decked out in his SWAT gear, and then he turned his eyes onto Smithers and me. "I'm Special Agent Jim Welch." He held out his hand to Rogers.

"Chase Rogers. And this is the homeowner, Bruce McGowan."

I shook his hand and then he turned to Smithers. Today she didn't quite resemble that cute, perky blonde who showed up two days ago wearing a bright smile and carrying a Sig Sauer. Her eyes were still puffy and hair wild and matted. Rogers introduced her as well. "This is Secret Service agent Joan Smithers."

Welch narrowed his eyes. "I understand you were here on the Presidential detail, Agent Smithers."

"Yes."

"You know that one of the CIRG teams has now taken over Secret Service responsibilities in the White House."

"I heard that."

"And I understand several of your agents were involved in the attack on this place with the intent to kidnap the President."

"Sounds like you're up on everything," she replied, coming across just a little testy. I thought she might be thinking Welch was associating her with the terrorist agents because she was on the same detail with them.

I asked, "When were the bodies removed?"

"Yesterday afternoon. A lot of head shots on the subversives. Somebody did some fine shooting. Was that you, Agent Smithers?"

"I didn't fire a shot."

"Well, there were two Secret Service agents down and one never fired his pistol. The other, found lying over by that couch, had practically emptied his weapon. Was it him who knocked them off?"

Smithers looked to me for the answer.

"It was Agent Clayton and me," I replied.

"We collected several weapons, mostly MP5s belonging to the decedents. Are the other guns we found upstairs yours, Mr. McGowan?"

My eyes quickly darted to my arsenal which Welch had laid out on a blanket near the fireplace. That's what I get for not re-locking my shifferobe.

"Yes, and I would appreciate it if you'd put them back where you found them."

"I believe we'll need to be keeping them for evidence."

"I believe *not*!" I shot back. "You can see they weren't fired, so there's no reason you should confiscate them."

"Just who the hell do you think..."

That's when Rogers took Welch off to the side and explained the facts of life to him. After he was through, Welch then *knew* who the hell I was.

When *that* fire was put out, I then took account of how sad the place looked. Most of the Christmas gaiety Adriana had put into the inn had been destroyed. The walls were filled with bullet holes; porcelain angels and wooden soldiers that had sat on the beautifully decorated mantle lay in hundreds of shattered fragments; the handsome fireplace stonework had pieces shot away; and the sweet smelling Douglas fir that I had chopped down with my own hands lay on its side like a ten foot *unjolly* green giant, many of its pretty blue globes broken and scattered over the hardwood floor.

The aroma of Adriana's Christmas potpourri still permeated through the house, however, seemingly a paradox to all that been shot up and turned over, not to mention the dozen or so stains of blood that had already soaked into the pine floor. And to me, for some reason, the house *smelled* like death. I wondered...was the stench from the blood that was ingrained in the floor, in the curtains and in the walls? But maybe there wasn't any odor at all; it was just in my head...a psychosomatic smell that I might equate to when one is convinced in his mind there is pain in the body. But it's actually *phantom* pain. However, I knew I quickly had to get both the smell and that feeling of death out of my head as it was freaking me out.

Agent Welch and I had gotten our noses back in joint after our mini-spat and it all went quite cordial after that. I didn't hear Rogers' conversation with him, but he must have told Welch something scary about me that made the man do some thinking.

Just for his own edification and official report, Welch asked us nicely for a moment by moment capsule of what happened there on Friday night. I gave him five minutes and Smithers, three. I didn't have time to play twenty questions with him.

I then took Rogers to our upstairs suite for some different clothes. From my steamer trunk I pulled out my Army green cold weather coveralls, which I use when I'm out in the woods either hunting or chopping down Christmas trees, and gave it to Rogers. From my wardrobe I snatched up my bright orange and camo field coat for me to wear. Then I tossed him a brown wool hat with fold-down ear flaps.

"You obviously want me to go out looking like Elmer Fudd," he quipped. "I thought Halloween was a couple months ago."

I had to smile at that. My headgear was a camo ball cap that had a Red Man logo on it. Joey gave it to me the Christmas before as a gag gift, mainly because of my disdain for tobacco chewers who tend to run around with crusty juice stains in the corners of their mouths.

Smithers had earlier asked me if she could take a shower down in her room and put on some jeans. I told her she had ten minutes. No time for makeup.

Speaking of Joey, I happened to look out the upstairs window and saw him down below in the parking lot arguing with the same agent who stopped us. "Go ahead and change your clothes, Chase. I'll be right back."

When I got to the veranda, I yelled, "Joey, what the hell you doing here? I thought I told you to make yourself scarce." I did wave him forward, however, and the agent allowed him to approach.

He met me at the steps and then replied, "Man, I was worried. You never called me back and I had no idea what was happening to you. I also just wanted to be sure nobody was pillaging the old fort here."

"Joey, it's alright. I can't spend any time talking with you. The place is safe and will be locked up when the FBI leaves."

"Where's Adriana?"

"Still being held along with the First Lady. That's all I can tell you."

"Is it safe for Cora and me to go back home...and the office? The coroner also says he needs me to help with all the bodies that have piled up."

"Yes. The bad guys shouldn't be interested in you any longer. But keep the pistol handy that I left with you."

"Got it right here."

I gave him a man hug. "Okay then. Go away. I'll call you later."

"I've heard that before."

We both turned away at the same time and I ran back upstairs to change.

Rogers had already donned his Elmer Fudd costume and I quickly changed out of the borrowed SWAT uniform. I did slap my gun belt back on and popped two extra clips into the cartridge case. The orange Red Man hat that I stuck on my head was a nice touch.

Ready to roll out?" I asked him.

"Let's do it."

Once back downstairs, I yelled down the hall, *"Agent Smithers. Time!"*

"Good meeting you, Agent Welch," I said. "Take care of the place and lock up when you leave. Here's a key. Just stick it in the dirt of that flower pot on the front porch. Burglars always look under mats. And oh, be a pal and return my arsenal to my upstairs wardrobe where you found them."

He stared at me for a few seconds and then nodded. I took it he was no longer afraid of me.

Smithers finally came out of her room, looking refreshed in a tight, black sweater and jeans. Her hair was now pinned back up on her head. She stifled a smile after taking account of our head gear.

I then performed a weapons and ammo check. I still had my Remington and Glock and Rogers his MP5 and Sig 225. Even though Smithers was just along for the ride and a non-player, I pulled from my boot my Bond issue Walther PPK for her general protection.

I drove this time. While on the road making our way out to Hwy 219, I glanced at the clock on the dash. 09:46. I suddenly remembered that the President had until 0800 to start the ball rolling on the prisoner release. And as we talked yesterday, he would *not*. Rogers had been keeping up with media on his fancy cellphone and learned that someone, probably Franks, had just called a local station to have another statement sent to the parent network, this time NBC.

Rogers restated in his own words what was in the message. "It said apparently the President doesn't care anything about the good citizens of the United States. He has not responded to the demands of the Stealth Jihad of America. Therefore, since he hasn't met their deadline this morning, they have no recourse but to carry out the plan to detonate an even larger bomb on a larger American city. Looks like they've indicated a window for the attack which is tomorrow evening between five and seven. Of course, he also promised to start killing hostages if the prisoners weren't released by 0800."

"Don't remind me," I said. "But as to a bomb or bombs, people will be getting off from work and the streets, subways and buses will be jammed full. A hell of a lot of people are going to die if the terrorists follow through with the threat."

"You think they will really carry it out?" he asked.

"Yes I do. The hell of it is, we might nail Franks and the rest of his cowards here, but there are more bands out there actually carrying out these attacks. Franks is just another pawn in this jihad element. He and the other Secret Service agents primarily had the responsibility to set up the raid on my place, kidnap the President and First Lady and being the smart, articulate operator Franks is, send the communique to the press. However, he got a bunch of men killed or captured, lost the President and is now on the run from us. Do you think whoever is the big cheese in this escapade is happy with him? No wonder whoever he was talking with wanted to slice his payoff. So now, it's more about the bomb than it is the First Lady. He won't kill her, because she still has value. But I think these people *will* explode the device."

Rogers remarked, "I also read just now that the City of Carthage and the entire county have been evacuated. Now a total of eighteen dead from the blast and some people are already showing signs of radiation sickness."

"My God," uttered the small voice from the back seat. I turned slightly in my seat and saw that she had her hands over her face.

"If that spy feature on Agent Purcell's cell is in anyway accurate, I think I have them pin-pointed. No question in my mind, we have to take them down today and get these hostages back. Then at least half of the President's worries will then be over. I'm sure he will be able to focus a hell of a lot better having his wife back in the White House."

"So, you know where they are?" Rogers asked.

"If we continue up 219, in another mile mile or so, you'll see a Marathon station on the right. As soon as we pass it, the next turn off on the left is Harvest Road. And the way I have it spotted on the cell, they may have broken into a church situated about a half mile from that intersection. It kind of sits back off the road and the closest building to it is a house about a quarter mile further down."

"Wait a minute. This is Sunday. Won't they be having services there?"

"It's a Seventh Day Adventist church. Their service is on Saturday. If the terrorists *are* there, they probably moved in last night. That dirt road they took, Sydenstricker, came out right back there. I'd say they stopped somewhere off this road, maybe at that all-night minute saver coming up on our right. And so that they would avoid being spotted on this main highway, Franks probably diverted off onto Harvest. When he saw the Adventist church, the light bulb went on. No services on Sunday. He's bright enough to think of that. The church would be warm and they might even find some food and drink in its kitchen. If they didn't, somebody might have gone by the Marathon to buy a few groceries. So, first we'll pull off there. You'll see it after we round the next curve."

"And you believe that church is ground zero on Purcell's locator device?"

"If it isn't, it's within a few hundred feet. That's where I replotted it on my map. And here's the station."

I signaled and pulled slowly into the parking lot, finding a spot between two mud-caked vehicles, a jacked-up Dodge pickup on the left and a Chevy Tahoe on the right. Early-morning hunters, I suspected, who had probably been out for hours and stopped in for coffee and a breakfast biscuit.

"Why did we stop here?" Rogers asked me.

"There's a wealth of information in these back country stores besides a lot of local color. Maybe somebody in there behind the counter remembers a customer who might have stood out. Never know. Just stay put, Mr. Fudd." I then grinned as I stepped out of the Jeep.

"Funny, McGowan."

But as I glanced back at our vehicle, I noted that he did crane his neck to look at himself in the rear view mirror. And then the hat came off.

The clerk behind the counter was a young caucasian woman with a large marshmallow body. Surprisingly not Indian or Pakistani. There were four other customers in the market...two scruffy, bearded good ol' boys clad in brown and orange, ergo the hunters, a nicely dressed elderly woman who had stopped for some coffee on her way to church, and a dark-complected man about forty with coal black hair sticking out from under a blue baseball cap with a Yankees logo. Other than that, I didn't notice much about anyone. I waited for the lady to finish pouring her coffee into a tumbler that she had brought with her, after which she gave me a nice smile. I then picked up the glass pitcher and poured the remainder of the piping hot nectar into a foam cup. A second store clerk, seeing that the pitcher on the hot plate was now empty, hustled out to make another pot.

The two woodsmen left and I watched them through the plate glass window climb up what looked like six feet into their pickup. The sweet little lady was next in line and she exchanged some pleasantries with the girl. I took it she was a regular on Sunday mornings or perhaps they knew one another. "God bless ya, darlin," she said as she pulled away from the counter. Then the Yankees fan and I took two steps forward. I wanted to wait until he had departed and then chat with the girl before another customer came in.

I eyed the man in front of me who could pass for being Middle Eastern or maybe Hispanic. I don't try to profile people or speculate as to ethnicity. I knew there were several Mexican families living up toward Marlinton. But then when the man reached around to his hip pocket for his wallet, his coat rode up just enough for me to see the bottom of his holster. That's when my antenna went up. Was he one of Franks' men?

I then watched him transfer from his basket to countertop a package of ground coffee, a loaf of bread, lunch meat, several granola bars and some plastic bottles of Gatorade. As the clerk began ringing it all up, he said in his thick Arab brogue "A carton of Winstons if you do not mind."

Stepping up beside of him at the counter, I pretended to read the protein content on a package of beef jerky just to get a better look at him. While he was doing business with the girl, I snuck a couple of glances at him. He was about five-nine, medium build and had a short-cropped beard. But I then suddenly found his piercing black eyes bearing down on me. So that he would continue thinking me just another Mountaineer country boy, I asked the girl, "Say, honey, you got any of that there teriyaki jerky. All I see is smoked and it don't much agree with me."

"I think we may have some back there next to the nuts."

"Okay, thank ya, doll."

I think I saw the guy shake his head at the ignorant hillbilly and then he slapped his greenbacks down on the counter. While he was paying, I walked to the back of the store and pulled out my cellphone to make a call. In two rings, the recipient answered. "Hello."

"Chase," I whispered. "This is Bruce. I'm watching a suspect who's at the counter in here. He's the only customer besides me. Check him out when he leaves. Apparently he's driving the Tahoe. Snap a photo of him as he's walking by and of his license plate when he pulls out. Careful he doesn't catch you."

"Got it."

As I was paying for the coffee, I watched the man walk out and down the sidewalk the short distance to his SUV. As he appeared preoccupied with something on his cellphone, he paid no attention to the occupants of the Jeep. As soon as he slid into his seat and closed his door, I said "thanks" to the clerk and walked toward the front of the store. I stood there a while waiting for him to pull away, but he just sat there taking his good old time, probably still studying his cell. However, as the Tahoe had smoked glass, I couldn't actually tell what he was doing inside. Finally, he began backing out.

Once he was away, I went quickly to the Cherokee and jumped in. "Did you get the photos?"

"Several shots. Nice and clear."

Smithers then tapped me on the shoulder. "He's one of them, Bruce."

"How do you know? Did you recognize him?"

"I think so. He stayed mostly in the background and he was the man Franks was talking with in Arabic off to the side."

"Then we're on the right track and not chasing a wild goose."

I began backing out. When we had driven to the end of the parking lot, we saw the Tahoe's brake lights come on approximately five hundred feet further up the road. After a vehicle from the opposite direction passed by, our suspect turned left. Onto Harvest.

"So far so good," I said. I then began a careful pursuit. At the Harvest Road intersection I made that same left turn. As we were keeping back at a comfortable distance, about two football fields, his brake lights suddenly came on again and he turned into the churchyard.

I tapped Rogers on the shoulder. "Bingo."

Reducing my speed, I began cruising on by the church. Smithers had already ducked down in the rear seat. What we did not see were any vehicles in the lot, including the Tahoe. However, as the church driveway continued around to the rear of the building, it made sense for them to park well out of sight. A number of people living on that road passed by the church every day. A strange vehicle or vehicles sitting for any length of time might cause some consternation.

But as our attention had been focused on the church and its grounds, what I almost missed was what I caught just a glimpse of on the left side of the road. Back in the trees was a vehicle that looked very much out of place in Podunk USA. A shiny black Mercedes...maybe a high dollar S Class. No hunters I know of drive luxury cars. A few rich, Islamofascist terrorists do, however. Since I wasn't focused on that side of the road, I wasn't able to see if it was occupied. However, in my split-second glance I did notice its smoked or blacked-out glass.

"Okay, what from here?" Rogers asked.

I had to think about it for a moment. Should we continue the recon or go for the gold right then and there? There were perhaps five to six of them in that group according to both Smithers and the sentry that I knocked in the head at the hunting camp. Possibly three vehicles...the one that turned off, maybe another behind the church, and the third sitting back in the trees.

"I'm pulling off so we can talk this out."

A few hundred feet on the left, I spotted a turn-around and did a 180. Pulling off onto the wide shoulder, I made sure the Jeep was positioned back in the woods somewhat. No one was going to even take a second look at a hunter in a ball cap sitting half asleep in a late model silver Rent-a Wreck Cherokee.

"Did either of you see the Mercedes sitting across the road from the church back in the trees?"

"Well, *I* didn't," replied Smithers. "My head was down in the floor."

"And I must have missed it, Bruce, being on this side of the vehicle and looking to the right. A Mercedes?"

"Expensive one at that."

"Do people make a lot of money around here?"

"You *know* better. Not exactly a hunting vehicle."

"If someone's inside the car, we need to go ahead and take him down," he said.

"We do that and this is no longer a recon for the HRT. If he doesn't communicate with them every so often, they'll know we found them. And then they'll either skedaddle or shore up for battle. If we take *him*, we take them all."

"They're something less than ten and we're two...or three." He turned to look at Smithers.

"I don't like shooting up churches and if there's any way we can avoid that, let's do. I'm sure that they've posted sentries out in the woods around the church, maybe five or six, including Mercedes Man, which might leave three or four inside. Suggest bringing in a half dozen of your warriors in civilian camo looking like hunters with .308s. Hunters 'accidentally' coming across a guard shouldn't end up as targets. There might be some words exchanged, but I doubt a sentry would shoot first and ask questions later. Anyway, hunters have a right to be out there; terrorist pricks don't."

"That might work," commented Rogers. "What's the rescue plan? Even if the sentries are taken out, the church has wide open landscape on all sides. Somebody may also be keeping a lookout from somewhere in the church and then how do we get in?"

"There has to be more than one way into the church besides the front door. This afternoon, we're finding the parson and cluing him in on the situation. Hopefully, he'll be able to advise a way to get the rescue team inside."

"And what time should this go down?"

"Not in broad daylight for sure. I'd say somewhere in the twilight hours. Hunters are not only out there until dark, it's the time of evening when a field of observation is tricky. Not light enough for good visibility and not dark enough for night vision devices to work."

Rogers leaned his head back against the seat and darted his eyes this way and that in deep thought. The wheels in his brain were turning, considering every possibility for success or failure. Finally, he nodded slowly. "Okay, I'm good with it. According to the President, you're the boss."

"We're a team, Chase." I then turned my head toward the back seat. "And how about you, Joanie? Sound plausible?"

"It could work. Something has to go down; that's for sure. I'm thinking the longer Franks and his Arab accomplice are saddled with the hostages, and things aren't going to plan, he might suddenly boil over and...well, I don't want to say it."

I knew what it was she almost said.

Rogers then held up his cellphone. "When we were leaving the Marathon, I went ahead and sent the tag number and photo of your suspect to our Criminal Justice Information Services which ironically happens to be in them there hills not far from here in Bridgeport. I should get a hit in the next few minutes."

"Good. I'd like to have the tag number off that Mercedes as well. I guess that's all we can do here for now. I'm driving back to civilization. When I pass by the church again, focus on the Mercedes and see if you can pick up anybody in there."

"Roger."

I pulled back onto the hardtop and drove the half mile that took us by the church. While Rogers was trying to make out some kind of image through the windshield of the car in the woods, I looked over at the church again. No sign of activity on the outside, but there was no doubt in my mind they were holed up inside. In there as well was the woman I prayed to God had not been harmed in any way. It was now approaching midday of day two that she was being held under the gun. As I passed slowly by, my heart sank. My stomach was nauseous. She was only a scant hundred yards away and I couldn't do anything about it. So close, yet so unattainable. But tonight, by God, come hell or high water, I *would* get her back.

Rogers apparently took note of my melancholia. "I know this can't be easy for you, Bruce, knowing that these bastards have your wife. I can't imagine how you feel. If I were married, I'd be a basket case. But I do admire your ability to still concentrate on the particulars of the mission."

I glanced over at him a second and then turned my attention back to the road. "Let's just say I have a personal motivation for its success."

Chapter Twenty-Two

We turned back to the south on 219 and went about a mile until we pulled into a small, brick country restaurant known as Katy's Diner. Adriana and I had actually eaten there one evening on the way back from Hillsboro. Rogers said he was starved, so I suggested the place instead of going all the way back to Lewisburg. Anyway, we were in proximity to our objective and we needed to stay in the area to find the Adventist minister.

As the country diner was remarkably not all that crowded on a Sunday afternoon, I asked the hostess if we could be placed in a booth that was situated in the back corner away from the booths and tables in the main dining area. Even there, we would still need to keep the volume of our conversation at a low ebb.

The Sunday special was some good ol' fried chicken. When I was a kid, I don't think a Sunday went by that Mom didn't have fried chicken on *her* menu. With all the grease, mashed potatoes and gravy, hot buttered rolls and some kind of rich cream pie, she tried her best to give both of her boys heart attacks before we reached the age of fifteen.

Smithers, with her featherweight body and Rogers, whose diet consisted of nothing but lean meat and green vegetables, appeared grossed out with the crusted bird on my plate that glistened with Crisco and was swimming in a pool of milk gravy. After taking a couple of bites of everything and watching my table mates' darting their eyes between one another, I put my fork down and just continued sipping on my soft drink. You see, I thought I had balanced things out in having my Blue Plate Special along with a Diet Coke.

The waitress, whose name was Irma, was a bit large and obviously had enjoyed too much of the diner's fried chicken along with the grease and gravy. But she was cheerful and friendly to me in spite of my grungy appearance. I had a three day growth on my face, was dressed like Junior Samples and because I hadn't had a shower since Friday, probably smelled like Mr. Ed. I think as Smithers took account of my bedraggled appearance and woodsy aroma, she kept looking at me like I had just crawled out from under a rock. Maybe that got her to thinking how *she* looked, because she reached in and pulled her compact from her purse to check herself out in the mirror.

"I must look a fright," she remarked. "But I do feel better having had the shower." That comment had to be directed at me. She then continued. "I'm sure I look hideous without makeup."

Rogers smiled. "Well, in my opinion you have a natural beauty *without* the need for makeup."

Uh oh. I didn't see *that* coming. I didn't realize with all that was going on, he might have kind of developed the hots for her.

But then he let out a low whistle while reading something on his cellphone. "Hey, listen to this. Our people did a facial recognition search on the photo I sent up. It matches one Ameen al-Jawhara, the number two leader in the Pakistani terrorist group, Lashkar-e-Jhangvi...I think I'm saying that right. He was sighted in Washington last month. And get this, he not only operates a website that issues calls to arms to all Muslims to engage in a jihad against America and our government, but pushes his jihadist message on several social networks. How the hell is he allowed to do that and why haven't we been able to nail him?"

I shrugged. "With enough money and support from the Muslim community and his friends hiding and protecting him, he's like a long list of other subversives that continue to roam around the country without fear of being arrested. But this tells me something else."

"What?"

"We were assuming all along that Franks was driving this train. But as prominent in the terrorist community as this al-Jawhara is, it's clear to me *he's* the man in charge. I was standing only inches behind him in that store and didn't know it. It also says that Franks, Tyson and the other American maggots involved were merely instrumental in setting up the attempted taking of the President. And Franks was the man al-Jawhara knew could handle all of the post attack communication, such as sending the communiques to the press and the ultimatums to the President. Like I said before, Franks is a pawn, not the BMOC."

"Well, here's a couple dots to connect. One place that al-Jawhara was spotted twice was that Caliph House in Washington that Agent Purcell described...you know, the one that claims protection under Sovereign Immunity? The President has just ordered the Attorney General to obtain a search warrant to secure evidence from that "safe house.""

"Based solely on a photo you took?" I asked him. "Will that fly?"

"That, along with Agent Smithers' identification of the man back at the gas station. Plus, we watched him turn into a location that was pin-pointed via Purcell's device when Joanie had her last phone conversation with Franks."

"I'm just saying, I don't know if there would be enough probable cause for a warrant, stemming from a phone gadget that puts Franks' call in merely a general vicinity. And Joanie, you said you *thought* al-Jawhara was the man you saw at my cabin. So, no real tangible evidence. All that any judge would have to go on with this guy at this point is that he's suspected of putting subversive material on the internet, not kidnapping and murder."

"Maybe so, Bruce, but maybe the AG *will* find the right judge. And perhaps a phone call from the President to the judge might make it happen."

"I hope you're right, Chase." I then looked over at Smithers who was probably still all tingly inside from Rogers flirtatious comment. "Joanie, I see you picked up your iPad from the room. Check to see if the Seventh Day Adventist Church, Greenbrier County, has a website."

It took her no more than ten seconds to access the site after which she handed the device over to me. I wasn't very good at navigating through electronic gizmos, but I *had* played around with Adriana's tablet. Everything looked much the same. I touched the link and immediately the image of the same church we passed by an hour ago popped up. I scrolled down a bit until I found the name of its senior pastor, Ralph Hastings, as well as his home phone number. The phone number for the church was also listed which made me wonder if during the work days there was a church secretary or other staff member who would arrive sometime the next morning. Franks had to be considering that, which also told me the church was just a place to hide out for a day or so until they could come up with the next steps in their game. But even though he may have been sharp enough to assume the Adventist church would have no Sunday services, he had taken a big chance anyway that there wasn't some kind of meeting or a Bible study scheduled that day. I needed to get hold of that minister as soon as possible.

Going from there to People Search, I put in the name Ralph Hastings, Lewisburg, Dubya Vee and there he was. I then scratched his number and address down on a napkin and handed it to Rogers. Can you do a MapQuest search on this address for me?"

While he was accessing the site, Irma the waitress came with the bill. One bill for the three of us. I knew both of the agents were on government per diem, so I told her to break it out. Both agents looked at me like they thought I should be paying. Like you're our host and this is your home turf. They were pulling in more money than *I* was making, so my look back at them said 'dig out your own dough.'

"Got him, Bruce. As the crow flies, he's not far from here."

"Tell you what, Chase. Since I don't have official credentials or carry a badge, the preacher might balk at even talking to me, thinking I was some sort of scam artist or somebody up to no good...especially the way I look. But if you flashed your badge and sat down with him and told him what was happening at his church, he'd buy the story...incredible as it is."

"That'll work."

I then turned to Smithers. "How about you. Are you good with it?"

"I am."

I looked at her purse. "They didn't take your ID and badge, did they?"

"No, thank God."

"Then give the minister a call and set up a meeting. Tell him who you are and you would like to talk with him about a problem at his church. Tell him also that an FBI agent will be accompanying you."

She nodded. As she was getting him on the phone, Rogers stepped outside to call his second in command to explain the evening's mission as well as who he wanted on it and how the agents needed to prepare for it. He would also arrange for a time and location to meet.

As for me? The meal came with banana cream pie and I was taking my time to savor it.

"Alright, we're set," Smithers said. "He gave me the directions and is expecting us in the next half hour. As Chase said, he doesn't live far from here."

Chase, huh?

"Did he sound alarmed?" I asked.

"Very much. He kept throwing questions to me, but I told him I couldn't get into it over the phone."

"Good. Then let's go."

* * * * *

Ralph Hastings told Smithers on the phone that he was now just a part time farmer, but as a full time preacher, he devoted all his energy to his congregation. For the Secret Service and FBI to be talking with him about something going on at his church, that made him "very afraid." We could find him on his twelve acre farm just off Westminster Road four miles east of Katy's Diner. If we got lost, anybody within five miles could tell us how to get to his house.

But it wasn't hard to find. He told her to go a quarter mile east on Westminster and turn into the driveway where she would see the mailbox with the big, bold letters HASTINGS. The driveway itself was nicely paved and took us about 600 feet back where his modest board and batten house sat under three very handsome elms. The house *and* the trees looked to be 80 to 100 years old. A vintage windmill was not far off to the right of the house and a well-weathered ten thousand square foot red barn sat maybe 50 yards to the left rear the house. Parked beside it was a rusted heap of a John Deere tractor that appeared inoperable. A smattering of chickens pecked the ground around a newer John Deere sitting directly in front of the house. Maybe Preacher Farmer Hastings had left it there because the dinner bell had rung. Smithers said her phone call had caught him and his Mrs eating lunch.

No sooner than Smithers and Rogers stepped out of the Jeep, Hastings was on the front porch. As they walked toward him, I rolled out from under the steering wheel and stood by the driver's door with my arms folded.

"Afternoon, Mr. Hastings," greeted Smithers. "I'm the agent who called you, Joanie Smithers. This is Special Agent Chase Rogers, FBI."

"Hello, Ms. Smithers," he responded. "You all are not wearin' any kind of uniforms I see."

"No sir. We are working on a case and are undercover. " She showed him her badge and ID. Rogers took his out as well.

Hastings appeared maybe seventy-eight to eighty, thin physique and even thinner hair. They shook hands and I could see his were indeed farmer's hands.

"Excuse my appearance. Been changin' the oil in my tractor and winterizin' it." He then looked over at me. "Who's the feller over by the car?"

I walked forward to where they stood.

"My name's Bruce McGowan, Reverend Hastings. I'm former FBI and working as a guide for these agents. I live a little further out beyond Lewisburg."

"McGowan, you say. Any relation to the undertaker over there?"

"Joe McGowan is my brother, sir."

"Yep, I knew your dad. Fine feller. Ever once in a while he'd be officiatin' when somebody around here was bein' planted in the boneyard. So what's this thing all about with the church that brings the feds in?"

"Can we sit down on your porch, sir?" Smithers asked.

"Be my guest. Here, they's enough chairs to go around. Any coffee? I'll have Wilma serve you up some if..."

"No, Mr. Hastings. We all just had lunch. But let me tell you what's going on."

We all took a chair. Hastings took his rocker.

"This might sound hard to believe," she began, "but a bunch of criminals we have been looking for have broken into your church and are nesting there. They..."

"Why did they want to do that?"

"They were looking for a place to hide out. We think they just happened on the place and seeing that no one was there, either thought it was abandoned or realized the congregation met for service on Saturdays."

"What do they want?"

"We think they may just be there temporarily to use it as a hideout and then will move on to somewhere else. Do you have any church employees or members of your congregation planning to go there today?"

"No. Everybody knows it's locked up today and nothin' is planned for nobody. We have somebody who comes in to clean on Tuesdays."

"You don't have staff coming in tomorrow?"

"No. You see, we're a small church. Maybe 150 on the roll, but no more'n 85 attend regular. We're a country bunch. No real staff and nothin' fancy."

"You have an internet site," Smithers commented.

"Oh, *that* thing. My daughter is one of them computer whizzes. She put that together. Showed it to me and it looks nice, but I don't have nothin' to do with it."

I then stepped into the conversation. "Reverend Hastings, we need your help. The FBI is planning to move onto the church today and arrest the people in there. They have taken two hostages and we're concerned for their safety."

His eyes widened. "That means gunplay. That also means the church could get damaged."

"Yes sir it does," I said.

"Can't you just wait 'em out? They gotta come out sometime. You said it's temporary."

"That may be an option, sir. But the hostages' lives are in danger. We're thinking there might be other ways into the church and we could surprise them. If we do that, maybe nobody gets hurt and no bullets will damage anything inside."

"Well, I certainly have to think about that. It's God's house that might get the raw end of the deal. And we sure don't want nobody to die in there."

"Take your time, sir."

We all sat a moment while the preacher was reflecting. Rogers looked over at me and raised his eyebrows.

Finally, Hastings said, "If you feel you have to go in and weed 'em out, maybe I got a solution."

"We're listening," Rogers said.

"You know, many years ago I was an Army sergeant. Back in the sixties used to teach infantry tactics down at Fort Jackson. South Carolina it was. One thing tricky I remembered was somethin' called a ruse. You know what that is?"

We all nodded.

"Of course you do. I should know that. Anyway, if you gotta go in, I'll tell ya somethin' a lot of people in my congregation don't even know. In the back yard of the church they's a door that's ground level...mostly covered over by weeds. Somebody guessed not long ago it was a coverin' to a well. I didn't tell 'em nothin' different. That door leads to a storm shelter. You see, way back about the time that church was built in the early 1900s, people-built shelters leadin' from the house down to the basement and then you walk out to the shelter. I don't think nobody's been down there for years, When the church was built, nobody livin' today was livin' then. As far as I ever knew, that shelter never *got* used. I don't know what condition it's in now...may be all caved in for all I know. Sorry to go on like this, but my point is, the bunker leads into the basement and goes up some steps into the back of the church where you'll find a hallway and our classrooms."

"If no one has used the shelter or basement in a while, will that door into the church easily open?" I asked him.

"I imagine so, but it's locked."

"If it's locked then do we have to break it down? That'll bring the bad guys to that part of the church in a hurry."

"But you see, there's a key to that door."

"Okay. Is the key by chance inside the church?"

"Nope. Got it right there in the house. And I'll give it to ya...but only on one condition."

"And that would be what?"

"The ruse I was talkin' about. When you all get into that storm cellar and 'bout ready to spring in on 'em, I'll attract their attention by opening the front door to the church and walkin' right in."

I felt myself frown. "Reverend Hastings, we can't let you do that. You don't know what these people are capable of. They would just as soon put a bullet in you than look at you."

"You think I'm scared of that?" He then laughed. "Tell ya somethin', Bruce. I'm eighty one years old and am *right* with the Lord. He's been waitin' on me to give up the ghost for quite a few years. Have had a heart attack, cancer and dadgum gull stones. I've done cheated death more times than I'd like to think. My body's been wantin' to die, but my brain won't have nothin' to do with it. But if it comes to that, I'm ready. I got a mansion up there just waitin' for me."

I thought for sure he was fixin' to break out into one of the old time hymns.

"Mr...uh Reverend Hastings," began Rogers. "It's Bureau policy that we not engage or endanger the lives of civilians. As much as we appreciate your offer to help, it just can't happen."

Hastings then stood. "It's my church, folks. The people chose me to be their spiritual leader. I can walk in there anytime and Jesus walks with me."

I looked at Rogers and he jerked his head to his right, indicating he wanted to talk privately. "Give us a minute, Pastor."

We stepped down from the porch and took a spot a few feet away under one of the elms.

"What do you think, Bruce?"

"Like he said, it's his church. We *can* stop him, you know. A civilian interfering in a federal mission. If he does walk into that church, what do think they'll do to him?"

Rogers shifted a stone around with the toe of his boot. "Elderly man, harmless looking. He'll tell them right away he's the minister. I doubt they'd shoot him. Maybe hold him prisoner till they leave. But, he actually might *have* something with that plan. I kind of like it. But, I don't like the fact that he's in harm's way."

"Well, the President gave me the responsibility to lead this operation. It goes like this...I make the decision to engage a willing civilian. You leveled your protest, but I went ahead with it. You get none of the blame if he takes a bullet."

"That will fly about as long as the Spruce Goose did."

"You got a better plan, Chase?"

"Like I said...you're the boss."

"Let's go put this together with him."

We began walking back to the porch.

"By the way, my boys will be on the way to our rendezvous point in about an hour."

"Which is where?"

"A park called Beartown that they located on the map."

"I know it well. Between here and Hillsboro…just up the road. They ready to go hunting?"

"They're stopping by the Wal-Mart for some jeans, flannel jackets and head gear. As for rifles, all they could get their hands on were four M40a1s from the Marine battalion at the airport. They resemble the .308 from a distance."

"Sounds like they're ready for bear."

When we sat back down in the chairs, I said to Hastings, "All right, Pastor, you're back in the infantry; but you will have to do exactly what we tell you."

"I'm ready."

"That cup of coffee you offered still stand?"

"Sure does. I'll get Wilma to bring some out."

After we had laid out the plan to Preacher Hastings in detail, I slipped out of the house, taking a few minutes to make an important phone call. Back under the same elm as an hour before, I tapped in the number.

"Hello, Bruce. I recognized your number when it came up."

"Hello, Mr. President. I don't have a lot of time, but so that you wouldn't hear it through Bureau channels, I thought I'd tell you personally. We believe we have found the terrorist element that is holding our wives hostage."

"That is good news. Where are they?"

"Still in the same area, but a different part of Greenbrier County. We have to move now as it's probable they will pull out after today. We have a small, very specialized HRT element going in with me. Our focus of course is on bringing our wives out safely. We will realize sometime after 1800 whether we've been successful. I will call you with a status as soon as the mission is accomplished."

"I appreciate your call, Bruce. Tell those folks that are on the mission with you that I'm proud of 'em. I'll be waitin' for your call."

"We'll do our best to make this happen, sir. This time the bad guys don't escape."

"Thank you, Bruce. Godspeed."

Chapter Twenty-Three

The HRT warriors *looked* the hunter part, although their duds were brand new. However, if they were spotted, it would be from a distance in the waning light and no one would be the wiser. An equipment check was performed. Protective vests of course were SOP. Weapons were dry-fired and the HRT brought with them plenty of ammo. I didn't expect a firefight and an ensuing battle, but one has to prepare for anything. A commo check was done with the portable radios and everyone was Lima Charlie (loud and clear). I was fitted for one as well.

Although Rogers had given his team a full briefing of the scenario at the church as well as instructions when encountering hostiles in the surrounding woods, I also added a few pearls. I'm sure that standing in front of his six seasoned professionals, Rogers and I both looked like bozos in the hats I had selected for us.

"All I have to say is that you are the people the President is depending on for the rescue of his wife, the First Lady. It's in our hands. As it's not a situation where he would send in a significantly large battle force to rout these subversives, you are the small specialized team that can get the job done. This mission will work only if we use our heads and employ good tactics. The President says he is proud of you all and is sitting by his phone waiting for good news. Let's give it to him."

It had turned colder during day and the wind had picked up. The forecast was for light snow or sleet to begin by

1800. Rogers, Smithers and I in the Cherokee led the small caravan of four vehicles out of Beartown State Park at 1500 hours that Sunday afternoon. Six of Rogers' best, looking very much the woodsmen, brought up the rear in two crew cab pickup trucks. A dark red '98 Oldsmobile sedan sandwiched in between was immediately behind us. Its only occupant, Ralph Hastings, had been freshly schooled at the park on what would go down and when. It was important that he not put his key in the front door of the old church until we made contact with him on his cellphone which was the only real modern device that he was comfortably familiar with. So that Franks and al-Jawhara would have little doubt as to who the elderly man was, I asked him to look 'pastor-ly' by wearing a suit and carrying his Bible.

At Rogers' instructions, we were supposed to keep an appropriate distance between vehicles so as not to look like an HRT caravan; however, as Pastor Hastings either apparently wasn't paying attention in the briefing or he was so eager to return to his glory days of yesteryear as a soldier for God and country, he began hugging our rear bumper. But no one who might be watching through heavy lenses would get excited about two hunters in a Jeep closely followed by an old man in an Olds wearing a black suit.

As we drove on past the church, we noted as well that the Mercedes was still parked in the same spot across the road and back in the trees. That told me the subversives had not pulled out as yet in search for a new, more permanent location. What their ultimate plans were, we had no clue.

A quarter mile down Harvest, I spotted an intersecting firebreak in the woods. A perfect place to pull in that would leave us only a short distance from the church. I slowed to make the right turn, but even though I signaled and tapped my brakes to make that turn, the preacher almost busted the Cherokee in the rear. But he did pull into the firebreak after me and when I brought the Jeep to a stop about three hundred feet in, he pulled up behind me. That's what set me to wonder if we could actually depend on the old infantryman to not only carry out our instructions, but to do so on a timely basis in sync with our move on the church. Specifically, he was to wait in his car and give us time to get inside. We may have to take out a guard or two along the way. We'd scramble to the shelter opening and ultimately end up in the church basement. I'd then make contact with him on his cell, telling him to move out. He would pull from the firebreak, drive into the front parking lot of the church and call me before making his way to the front door. I'd tell him to go on in and we would wait about a minute until I was sure they were now having to contend with him before we entered the rear door to the church. It was simple to us, but would he somehow get confused and foul up the synchrony?

As the pickup drivers, especially the last one, may have been too far back to see us pull into the firebreak, Rogers brought his mic to his mouth and informed them where we were. One by one, about forty seconds apart, they caught up with us.

I went to Hastings' driver's side door and he rolled down his window. "You have it all locked in?" I asked him.

"I do, sir," he replied sharply like the old Army sergeant he was.

"Again, you'll stay here until I call you. I'll tell you when to move out. It might be an hour from now. When you park your car at the church, you give me a ring on my cell. I'll wait about a minute to be sure you have gone in and then we'll do our thing."

"Yep. Don't have to tell *me* twice."

I wondered. Maybe engaging him wasn't such a good idea. However, I was going to give him the benefit of the doubt.

Smithers, Rogers and his six agents and I assembled in what is called a hasty staging area. Two agents would circle through the woods around to the east or far side of the church and spread out. Three others would position themselves at the edge of the tree line in the woods back of the church, also spreading out, and provide fire support of our advance onto the backyard shelter. One agent would then stay back, cross Harvest and work his way down through the woods, smash the driver's door glass of the Mercedes and draw down on its passenger. Ordinarily, he would just shoot the occupant; however, we didn't know for sure what the car was doing there. Although I was pretty damn sure one of al-Jawhara's men was sitting guard, there could instead be a couple of lovers in there doing the trick. But all afternoon? Naw. Finally, Rogers and I would come in through the woods from the west with Smithers trailing fairly much out of sight. I had not intended for her to be a player in the mission. After all, we were supposed to be hunters. She didn't look like one. But she did have her sidearm, my Bond gun, with a suppressor attached for defense. *All* of our weapons contained suppressors. I wanted her along for no other reason but that she was still the Secret Service's advocate for the First Lady. She needed to be with the attack element to focus exclusively on the protection of her charge if the bullets started flying. It was her job.

So, we were ready. It was now 1530, move out time. Rogers' first two men then began their wide sweep toward the east of the church. It was planned that once they had negotiated the woods past the rear of the church, they would key their mics twice to make the squelch sound, keeping as much radio silence as possible. The three agents who would post at the edge of the tree line in the north woods planned to key their mics when they were in position as well. At that point, Rogers and I, the command element, would begin moving forward.

We waited fifteen minutes, knowing the agents who were making their way to opposite side would not be anywhere close to their objective. Thirty minutes. We were now entering the beginning of twilight. At 1602, we heard their double squelch. That meant the agents had successfully passed the point in their patrol where the second team would move out. Unless that second team encountered any sentries, I thought they might also reach their objective by about 1615. Another ten minutes passed and suddenly we thought we heard a noise somewhere in the direction of their advance. It sounded something like a thump. And then we heard it a second time.

"What do you think, Bruce?"

"Hard to tell from this distance, but to me it sounded like two suppressed rounds."

"My thoughts exactly," he said.

Rogers then decided to break radio silence. "What goes?" he said in almost a whisper.

A voice replied, "Double tap. One tango down. Moving on."

He gave me a half smile. Now we knew for sure. The subversives and their hostages *were* inside the church. *My wife* was in there.

It was now 1620. I decided to go check on Hastings in his car to see if he was still awake. I tapped on his window glass. He turned immediately toward me.

"How are you doing, Pastor?"

"I'm not asleep if that's what you're thinkin'"

"It shouldn't be long until the last of us moves out. Expect my call somewhere between a half hour and 45 minutes."

He nodded. "Just sittin' here listenin' to my old tape recorder. Got about twenty good ol' hymns on here."

"Good for you. I appreciate what you're doing for us, sir."

"Happy to oblige. Anyway, gotta go protect the Lord's house and help you get them hostages out of there."

I placed my hand on his shoulder and said, "You're doing your country proud, you know. I'll let you get back to your music."

He rolled his window up and then I saw him work his ear piece back in. I not only admired the man for his patriotism, but also his heart.

Finally, at 1625 we heard the double squelch from the second team and the three of us as if on automatic cue began making our way through the trees. Rogers was twenty feet away on my left and Smithers ten paces to my immediate rear. As it was still forty-five minutes or so from total darkness, considering there was a drab winter's sky, it was that time of day when hunters would be catching the last opportunity of the afternoon to snag a deer. Deer are crepuscular creatures, which means they're most active either in the dawn or dusk. If any sentry we came across was a good ol' boy American WASP, he would probably be somewhat knowledgeable of hunter protocol, but I wasn't so sure about Middle Easterners.

Moving methodically over that half mile of forest, I calculated while checking my watch that we were within about two hundred yards of the tree line on the northwest quadrant of the church grounds. Once we reached the open area, we would have about fifty yards of turf to cross before reaching the shelter door at the rear of the church. Our three agents on that second team were at this point already set up in the northern tree line to cover our advance.

But as Rogers and I continued trudging forward with our minds and motives focused on reaching that crossing, we were both startled by an all too familiar sound behind us. Turning our heads abruptly to the rear, we saw Smithers standing with both hands wrapped around the grip of her automatic in an Isosceles shooting stance. The muzzle from which a faint wisp of smoke was drifting was pointed in our direction. And I was just at the point that day to where my trust in her had been restored. However, although the noise we heard behind us was a suppressed gunshot, neither of us had been hit.

But then she released her left hand from the pistol and pointed beyond us. We then turned back to our front. She had seen him, but we hadn't. Only fifty feet ahead of us was the faint figure of a man clad in a traditional Kurta shirt and wearing a skull cap, slumped against a large oak where he had been felled by Smithers' bullet.

"He had a bead on you two and was ready to fire," she said. She then continued on past us to see whether he was alive or dead. Rogers and I followed after her and it didn't take us long to discern that it was the latter. Not many people survive a bullet between the eyes. Damn fine shot.

He was obviously one of al-Jawhara's comrades…Middle Eastern of course and dressed for the part. His body had become sandwiched between the oak and a smaller tree which gave the impression that he might have merely fallen asleep standing up. His AK-47 lay on the ground at his feet.

"Could be that he was on orders to just shoot anything that moved out here, hunter or not," remarked Rogers. "I'd say that's also what happened with my second team over on the tree line. They would have taken their target down peacefully as they were instructed."

Rogers then put his arm around Smithers' shoulder and playfully bumped his head into hers. "Great shot, Joanie."

Not a time or place for *that* kind of thing, kids. You can get a room later.

There were now two down and although Rogers hadn't heard from the agent stalking Mercedes Man, he assumed that threat was also neutralized by now. Could be that al-Jawhara and Franks had only posted three guards, two roaming and one surveilling. Still, there could be more out there in hiding preparing to open up on anyone approaching the church.

It was now almost fully dark. Gradually, our purple vision had set in and our eyes were slowly adjusting to the coming night. But then a sudden breeze began whipping through the trees and we could feel little pings of sleet against our flesh. Right at 1710 we reached the edge of the tree line and the church came into view. There were no lights visible on the inside which didn't surprise me. I surmised the people we were looking for were in an interior room where a light wouldn't be visible.

We would be hunters crossing the field through the churchyard. If we ran from the tree line to our objective, our actions would give us away. Hunters would have no reason to be running at a clip anywhere at that time of evening. Now that there was only a waning amount of daylight left, all anybody watching would see is three people walking casually around to the back of the church, probably on their way to the eastern woods to an area where they may have parked their vehicles for the day. But I had two concerns. Had Mercedes Man already been taken out by the HRT operative across the road? That should have happened by now. If not, he would definitely see us, and if he had a telescopic NVD in the car with him, he would readily see that the smaller of the three was a female with a side arm and no rifle. Secondly, once we made it to the ground-level door, would it open? Or would we have to spend an inordinate amount of time trying to *pry* it open? The more time we spent fumbling with the door, the greater the chance we'd be detected by either someone standing guard at the back door of the church or someone somewhere out in those woods sighting in on us with a sniper rifle.

I looked at Rogers and then Smithers. "Ready?" They nodded.

Looking like we were tired from a day of the hunt, not having bagged anything, weapons hanging down, we strolled leisurely across the clearing toward the back side of the church. When we were within thirty yards, I had a solid view of the church's back door. No one was standing or sitting on the steps that led up to it or on the small porch. The door was solid with no window. So far so good.

The preacher had told us where the door to the shelter was and I thought we may have been right on it. I didn't want to search for it with a flashlight, so I had Rogers and Smithers spread out a little to comb through the weeds. If we spent too much time spinning around looking for the door and someone *was* watching us, we were no longer returning hunters. Finally, it was Smithers who stepped on something wood. "Here it is," she said.

I don't know what I expected, but on close examination found it to be a five by five square piece of hardwood, partially-rotted out and half-buried in the ground, nearly invisible in the dark. It did have a handle on it allowing one to grasp hold and pull the door open. However, Murphy's Law had caught up with me again. Hastings forgot to tell us there was a padlock on it, probably to keep children from climbing down inside and getting trapped. More time wasted, more exposure.

But then Rogers lifted his coat and extracted from his pistol belt his billy club. Quickly he inserted the weapon through the handle and pulled upward with an immense degree of force. The handle gave way fairly easily from the rotted wood, but with it went our ability to get the door open.

"All right," I whispered. "All three of us need to dig out around the front side of the door with our fingers and when you get a good grip on the edge, on the count of three, pull up."

On our knees we worked our fingers diligently through the mud until Rogers said, "Okay." After a few more seconds I was there. Smithers couldn't quite manage to get to the edge of the lid right away so she continued digging frantically. Finally, she said, "Got it."

"On my count...one, two, *three*." With all the strength we could muster, we lifted simultaneously with such exertion that the door not only lifted up from the ground, but as the hinges on the back had completely rusted through, we ended up flinging the door about ten feet on the other side of the opening.

Wasting no time, I went in first, at the same time touching the switch on my flashlight. Because the five or six stairs were completely rotted out, my weight caused them to collapse, sending me sprawling hard to the concrete walkway below along with them. *"Damn!"* I exclaimed.

"Are you all right, Bruce?" Smithers called down to me in a low voice.

"i think I hurt something," I replied.

"What?"

"My pride."

"You'll get over it," she said.

"Okay, can you see down in here? You all need to now jump down, but watch out for all the broken wood."

Rogers then said, "You go ahead first, Joanie."

She lowered herself down with her hands and arms the best she could, then dropped to the pavement. Rogers then handed down our weapons and like the sprightly dude he was, deposited himself onto the shelter's walkway soft as a cat.

Hastings was correct. The storm cellar hadn't been used in decades. There was evidence of serious erosion and nearly half of the tunnel had partially caved in. Mud was caked on the concrete walkway probably from the recent rain. There were spider webs throughout the cavern and the beam of my flashlight fell on what looked like a three foot long copperhead slithering like a flash away from my boot. Smithers saw it, but it didn't seem to bother her. Me? Rats and snakes and I don't get along. There's this crawly feeling I get in my gut.

The walkway only lasted about fifteen feet and then dumped into a ten by fifteen room which contained a dozen or so stacked folding chairs, some shelves stocked with a dozen or so dusty jars of canned vegetables and fruits and a homemade bookcase stacked full of frayed, vintage hymnals. From there, the concrete walk carried us into the large basement. Shining my light onto the walls, I found two wall plates. When I flipped the switches, nothing came on. Then I whipped the beam of light onto the ceiling and saw the problem. No bulbs in the naked sockets. Probably not even any electricity. The basement had also not been utilized in years. A few cardboard boxes sat here and there and against one wall was an ancient piano, covered with an inch of dust and a smattering of cobwebs.

Straight ahead of us were the concrete stairs that led to the door I was looking for...the door leading to the inside. Being careful not to let my voice carry, I called Hastings' cell. After two rings, he answered.

"Pastor, it's time. Ring me once when you get to the parking lot and hang up. Remember, when you get to the front door of the church, just turn the key and open the door like you normally would. As there is a bright porch light on the stoop, someone might have already seen and heard you pull up. If they did, they shouldn't perceive you as a threat. It might be a good idea to rev your engine once before you turn it off and then slam the door when you get out. I just don't want you walking in the church and surprising them."

"Gotcha, son. I'll let 'em know I've arrived."

"I know you're probably a little nervous about this and you can back out right now if you choose. I wouldn't blame you if you did."

"I'm doin' fine, Bruce. Don't you worry about me."

"Alright, good luck, Reverend."

I knew one thing...if he walked into that church and they immediately opened up on him, his death would hang with me the rest of my life. In hindsight, I was kicking myself for placing him in harm's way.

I laid my .308 against the wall and drew my Glock. The sniper rifle would be awkward if close combat ensued.

It was time for me to try the door key. I don't think I had even seen a skeleton key in years, much less tried one in a door. Pastor Hastings told me that door led directly into a back hallway where both a storage and a choir room were situated. Further down were three Saturday School rooms, one each for children, adult couples and senior adults. The terrorists could be in any or all the rooms. I was taking a chance on them hearing even the click of the lock, but that was our way in and whatever was on the other side of the door we had to deal with.

Gingerly, I put the key in and slowly turned it. I first turned it to the left, but nothing happened. Then I turned it to the right. I could feel it tightening and engaging the tumbler. Finally, it clicked and loosened. Thankfully, it wasn't a loud click. I waited and listened. As I was sure the floor was made of wood on the inside, whether carpeted or not, it would creak under the weight of anyone approaching the door. There was no sound. Neither could I hear any voices nor other sounds inside.

I looked at my watch. Two minutes had passed since I gave Hastings the green light. I'd wait a couple more. Rogers and Smithers stood on the steps behind me, both checking out their weapons. The suppressors remained just in case we met someone in the hallway.

It was now approaching five minutes. I turned and nodded to my companions then began slowly turning the doorknob. I was hoping the hinges wouldn't creak. They didn't. No sooner than I had pushed the door open, we heard a commotion somewhere in the front of the church which I thought might be the sanctuary. Voices. Loud voices. That meant Hastings was likely inside. He didn't ring my cell when he parked his car, like I asked. However, no gunfire, thank God.

Once in the hallway, I looked left and right. No one there. I then motioned for Rogers and Smithers to follow. I signaled to Rogers to look into the room on the right while Smithers and I were checking out the two rooms on the left, weapons leading the way. We took one silent step at a time, listening all the while to the shouting. I did catch a couple of words such as "*What are* and *who.*"

I grabbed the knob of the first room on my left, glancing quickly back to see Rogers opening the door down the hall. When I pushed the door open, I found the room dark. However, the light from the hallway filtered into the room enough for me to see a series of maroon colored robes hanging on a long metal rack. Choir room. No one inside. When I stepped back out into the hall, I saw Rogers approaching. He shook his head. Both of us then signaled to each other "clear."

The door to the next room on the left was also closed. I thrust it open quickly, finding it dark as well. In the dim light, I could see a dozen or so chairs set up in rows of four. Likely one of the classrooms. I couldn't make out anything else since the rest of the room was dark. But just as I began slowly closing the door. I heard something that sounded like a small kitten. Pointing the Glock through the threshold, I thrust open the door again, careful not to let it hit the wall. I then reached along the wall and switched on the light. In a flash, both Smithers and I burst into the room and swept our guns from one side to the other.

The shock of what I saw nearly took my breath away.

Chapter Twenty-Four

Tied to either end of the room's radiator, were my sweet wife, Adriana and the First Lady. Adriana opened her mouth I'm sure to express her elation, but I put my index finger to my lips. I pulled my Ranger knife from my belt and gave it to Smithers, then whispered, "Joanie, go cut their ropes."

As I stood just inside the door watching Smithers work on the ropes, Adriana and I smiled at one another without word. Rogers stood in the hallway behind me ready to fire at any head rounding the corner. Once Smithers had the women untied and had helped them to their feet, I said, "Take them down to the basement...quickly."

The three of them walked expeditiously from the room and into the hallway. On their way to the basement door, Adriana took just a second to throw her arms around my neck and kiss me on the lips, then hustled after the other two women. After two long days, they were safe at last. Now we could concentrate on taking out Franks, al-Jawhara and whoever else they had with them. One problem though. Hastings was now their prisoner and in harm's way. In essence, he had traded himself for the women.

Once we knew Adriana, the First Lady and their protector, Joanie Smithers, were safely down the basement steps, Chase Rogers and I continued cautiously along the rest of the hallway. After we checked around the corner to the right, we found that the hallway carried forward into an adjoining corridor where both the men's and women's restrooms were located.

At the exact moment I passed by the men's room, the door opened. The patron, a heavy-set, Caucasian skinhead, looking down at his hands while zipping up his pants, almost bumped into me. Startled, he opened his mouth to yell out while simultaneously reaching for the .45 in his belt. However, I placed the suppressor of my Glock in that open mouth and shook my head.

"Back inside," I said in almost a whisper. "You yell out and I'll paint the walls red with your blood."

The man's eyes looked as though he just might have to take another ride on the porcelain pony. They were nearly as big as ping pong balls. Without a peep, he shuffled back through the restroom door. Once the three of us were inside, I removed the Glock from his mouth and placed the muzzle against his temple.

"Please don't kill me," he pleaded.

"I *should*, you know. It depends on what you tell me that will stop me."

"Wha...what do you want to know?"

"How many and where are they?"

"Uh...four inside."

"How about outside?"

"Three, I think."

"Give me names of the people inside the church and where they're located."

"An Arab guy, al-Jawra or something like that...he's the one in charge of things. He's up front in the place where the congregation sits..."

"The sanctuary."

"Yeah. Last time I was there, him and Mr. Franks was pushing some preacher around wanting to know what he's doing here."

"And others?"

"Another Arab, name's Jamaal. Last time I saw him, he was standing about midway back in the...uh sanctuary watching them grilling that old man."

"You said four. One more."

"Yeah. The guy I run with, Brad Jarrett, he went out the front door for a smoke. Said the church isn't no place for smoking."

"And that's all that's in there? If you're lying..."

"No, I swear. Just those four...and me."

"But *you,* Bubba, I don't have to worry about."

"You don't?"

"No. You'll be unconscious." I then spun him around and cracked him on the head at the base of the skull. He would be out for hours.

So, one of the two men I had vowed to kill on sight, as well as the number one international terrorist on the President's list, were maybe ninety feet away. But where was Tyson? I wouldn't think he'd be pulling sentry duty out in the woods, unless he was the man in the Mercedes...but I doubted it.

"Okay," I said to Rogers. "So there are five inside the church, one out cold in the crapper, three in the sanctuary with Hastings and one outside smoking. Two of the three in the woods...if there *are* just three...are down. I'm not sure if our friend in the rest room was counting anyone who might be in the Mercedes. Can you check to see if your man across the road found anyone in the car?"

Rogers held his mic up to his mouth. "Lambert, come in." He paused. "Your status." He listened. "Okay, wait for further. Out."

He then gave me a thumbs up. "Arab male sitting behind the wheel of the Mercedes took a butt stroke to the head. My agent is still at the car and says he sees the man outside the church on the porch smoking. He'll stay ready to engage him given the green light."

"Tell him to take the man down. We don't need him back inside with the others and definitely don't need his gun in the mix."

Rogers brought his wrist mic to his mouth. "Lambert. Take the shot." He waited and listened. After a moment he looked at me and nodded. "Done."

"I'm now bringing my guys closer in to secure the church grounds. If something goes haywire in here, al-Jawhara and company won't make it out alive." Bringing up his mic again, he said in a low voice. "This is Bullitt. Move in and surround the objective."

"All right, let's do this," I said.

Keeping as thin a profile as we could against the hallway wall, we edged our way forward toward the sanctuary. Rogers hugged his MP5 and I was ready with my Glock. It appeared the hall ended on the left side at an open doorway where the choir entered the stage. Quickly, I peeked around the door facing to catch a glimpse of the sanctuary. Someone had turned on the lights since we last saw the church from the clearing, and it was likely because Hastings had walked in on them. In that hurried look I caught sight of three men standing over a fourth man, Hastings I presumed, who was sitting toward the back of the church in a pew on the right side. I could still hear someone that sounded like Franks shooting questions at him. One of the questions was "What made you just decide to happen by here on a night when there's no service, all dressed up like you are?"

I heard Hastings' reply back to him, but couldn't make what he was saying. Then a voice having a thick Arabic brogue chimed in. Likely al-Jawhara. We could draw down on all three men, but if bullets started flying, Pastor Hastings might get caught up in the crossfire.

I whispered to Rogers. "Okay, Chase. As the back row of the choir loft is taller than we are, I can make it around the back of it undetected and then zip under the first row of pews on the left side. I'd like you to take up a position on the right rear of the loft and give me cover. If anybody sees me and draws down on me, take the head shot."

"After you make it to that pew, what's your plan?"

"I'll low crawl under the rows of pews until I get close and then spring up to get the drop on them."

Rogers nodded. "I like it." Then he grinned. "You can still low crawl after all these years?"

"Like a snake."

"Go for it. I've got your back."

After scampering across the back side of the choir bleachers, I looked around the left end and saw that the three perps were still hovering in the same position above Hastings with their backs to me. They were making him strip off his shirt to see if he was wearing a wire. That told me they may be suspecting their little hiding place had been found out. I knew Franks was smart enough to think of that.

No one's attention was on the front of the church...the front being if you were sitting in the sanctuary facing the pulpit. Running at a crouch that twenty feet to the first pew, I dove underneath it and began snaking my way bench by bench to the back of the sanctuary. Since it was a small church, I only had about fifteen pews to crawl under. By the tenth one, I was about wasted. It was a heck of a lot easier thirty years ago. The good thing was, I wasn't crawling under barbed wire and there weren't M60 machine gun rounds whizzing by two feet over my head.

Franks was sounding off again. I stopped crawling to listen. "You might be the preacher here, old man, but this story of yours as to why you're here tonight is a damn lie."

"Look, Mister," Hastings replied, "I told you I was supposed to meet some people here tonight and that's the truth."

And it *was* the truth. He was meeting Rogers and me.

"Then where the hell are they?"

That's when I rolled out from beneath a pew and stood, my Glock aimed at Franks' head. "Right here. Now step away from the preacher."

The Arab man a few feet back immediately brought up his AR; but before he could get off his shot, the side of his head came off, a plethora of blood splattering forward onto al-Jawhara's white kurta. The man then fell between pews. Rogers indeed had my back. As well as a good piece of the gunman's head.

But al-Jawhara then reached for his AK which was lying on a pew. I swung my Glock in his direction and said, "No no. I'd rather have you alive. Don't make me kill you."

Unfortunately, while I was dealing with the Arab, Franks pulled his pistol from its holster and placed it against Hastings' head. "You willing for this man to die, McGowan?"

"The same 10mm round that split the Arab guy's head open will find yours if you don't drop your gun, Franks."

He quickly pulled Hastings to his feet by the back of his neck and stood immediately behind him. "Then he'll be taking a piece of the preacher's head as well."

I did not lower the Glock. Al-Jawhara rose to his feet, but made no sudden move. He had seen what happened to his Muslim friend. "You are the man in the store today making like a stupid redneck. You were very convincing. If I had suspected you were McGowan, I would have gutted you like the pig you are."

I ignored him and kept both my gun and my focus trained on Franks. "You have your choice," I said to him. "You can turn over your gun and walk out of here in handcuffs or the cleaner team will cart your dead ass away in their meat wagon."

"Let me give *you* an ultimatum, McGowan. Either drop your weapon and have your sniper friend do the same or the preacher man dies."

"And you'll die along with him."

Hastings then looked over his shoulder at his captor. "Mr. Franks, I am an old man and not afraid to die. You have another option. As you'll either die or go to jail, either way, you have the opportunity right here and now to make your peace with God. You might have done some terrible things, but if you let Him, God will speak to your heart and save you from your sins. If you accept that His Son, Jesus, died for your..."

"Shut up, old man." Franks then snatched Hastings tighter by his shirt collar and pressed the muzzle of his automatic all the harder into his skull. "You can spit that God garbage out to your church goers all you want, but there's only one person I believe in and that's me."

"Better listen to him, Franks," I said "He's trying to save you from going to hell, where I'll be sending you if you don't give it up."

"And you shut *your* damn mouth, too, McGowan. We have men surrounding this building and another one is in a back room with a gun to your pretty wife's head." He then took away the pistol from Hastings' head and pointed it at me.

"You mean the big White guy back there, skin head, goatee? We met a while ago. Unfortunately, he's lying under a urinal in a puddle of piss with a goose egg size knot on his head. Also, my wife and the First Lady have left the building. I made sure of that. And oh, I forgot to mention, your sentries out there? All lying in the supine position."

Although Franks didn't change his stoic expression, I knew he was about to burst a blood vessel. He didn't respond.

I continued. "And if you think this Islamo-prick here, and his people, are going to pay you one red cent seeing as how you failed them, just ask him. *Zippo*. Right, al-Jawhara?"

"How do you know my name?"

"Well, let's see. My friend who has his weapon trained on your head took your picture at the gas station today, sent it to his FBI resource, as well as to Interpol and I'm sure a dozen other places, and well, to put it mildly, you're quite a celebrity in the terrorist arena. You must be proud. However, you look pretty damn small standing there with a dumb, confused look on your face. Your game is over, maggot. Your hostages are gone and you're no longer in a position to order the detonation of any more bombs. And by the way, if it hasn't already happened, your D.C. Caliph House along with your terrorist friends there are also going down. Huge dent in your organization, pal."

His black eyes seethed with hatred. If looks could kill...

I then re-concentrated on Franks. "So, what will it be, asshole? Live or die. The reverend is prepared to meet his maker if necessary. Are you? Al-Jawhara has 72 virgins waiting on him. What's waiting for *you*?"

Franks just stood there in a frozen stance, not moving, not even blinking for what seemed like an eternity. His eyes burned into mine like lasers. For a couple of seconds I actually thought he was going to fire. However, to both my surprise and elation, he then raised his hands in surrender.

Al-Jawhara gritted his teeth and grimaced. "Franks, why did you not kill him, you bastard. You are a coward."

I then walked over to Franks. "No, he's smart," I said taking the pistol from Franks' hand. "He knew a bullet from my partner's weapon was about to smack him in the head. I'm sure if the situation were reversed, you'd probably have pulled the trigger and *welcomed* death. But, if you still want that, I can make it happen. Just go for your weapon."

He said nothing in response, but turned his head from me and sat back down. He deserved to die, but not at my hand...and not in the church house.

I then placed Franks on the floor on his stomach and cuffed his hands behind his back. Rogers continued training his weapon on al-Jawhara as he walked down the aisle to where we were. Nudging the terrorist with the muzzle of the MP5, he said, "Get down on the floor...on your belly!"

Al-Jawhara glared at him a moment and then slowly sank to the carpet in the aisle.

I picked up Pastor Hastings' suit jacket which had been slung to the floor and held it for him while he placed his arms into the sleeves. I then shook his hand and gave him a smile. "You're a hero, Reverend. And a brave man. You put your life on the line and the President will be eternally grateful for it."

"I just hate the Arab man had to be killed. Somethin' I'll be thinkin' about every time I walk into the church."

"And I'm sorry it had to go down like that."

Rogers brought his mic up to his mouth. "Okay everybody, Code Green. Move inside. All clear and the drama is over."

When I pulled Franks up off the carpet to set him in one of the pews, his glasses fell off. I picked them up and placed them on his face. This was the man I had been aching to kill for two entire days. Now, watching him sit there, head down and looking defeated, I realized the rage that had been gnawing at me for hours on end had diminished. He would serve a ton of years. But he would be alive. I did want to know one thing, however, so I leaned on the arm of the pew where he was sitting. "Where is Tyson?" Him I *would* kill.

For a moment, he didn't even look at me. But as the fight was now out of him and his spirit deflated, he said in a subdued voice, "I don't know. He left this morning. He and al-Jawhara had words."

"What about?"

He shook his head. I guess he had said enough.

I'm sure those words were about money and the ever increasing futility of al-Jawhara's jihad plan. Tyson had given up a lot for that big payoff. And now he would be on the run...a traitor and a man without a country. Nonetheless, I had a score to settle with him.

I did ask Franks one more question. "Smithers' daughter. Where is she?"

He didn't readily answer. I sat down next to him and put my face close to his, but he wouldn't look at me. "Look, Steffen, you're going to be facing a lot of charges, conspiracy to abduct the President of the United States and several counts of murder, including a fellow agent. You will *never* get out of prison. But if there is a compassionate bone in your body and don't want to end up with that little girl's death on your conscience, tell me who has her and where she is."

For several moments, Franks just stared off in the distance without any response. But then he turned his face back to me. "Uncuff me and give me your cellphone."

"My cellphone?"

"If you want the girl back, do what I ask."

I spun him around and took the shackles off his wrists. To be sure that he wasn't asking to use my phone as an opportunity to get loose and try something, I pulled my Glock again and held it down at my side. I then turned my cell over to him.

He took a moment to get familiar with the features and then dialed a number. Apparently, someone answered promptly. "This is Franks. Release the girl." There was a pause. "Yeah, things are...finalized. Release her." A pause. "Yeah, everything's okay. Al-Jawhara said to let her go."

He handed the phone back to me. Whether the child would be released or not, we now knew how to find her. I had the kidnapper's number in my phone.

"Thank you," I simply said. "Now hold out your hands." This time I didn't cuff him behind his back.

Al-Jawhara lifted his head from the floor. His eyes bore down onto Franks like two laser beams. "I knew I should not have trusted you Americans. You did not deliver...on anything. You are a deceiver and a betrayer." He then looked up at me and shouted. "And you will go to hell, McGowan. Fi sabil Illah. Allahu Akbar! (I go in the path of God. Allah is great)."

I formed a smirk. "If that's the case, Al Jawhara, why do you find yourself lying on your belly like the emasculated and defeated snake that you are?"

He held his angry stare for a moment and spit in my direction. He missed. He then laid his forehead back down on the carpet.

After Rogers' six warriors appeared at the double doors, they moved in and took custody of Franks and al-Jawhara. The two big-cheese terrorists along with the also-rans, Bubba in the bathroom and Muhammed in the Mercedes, would be carted off to the airport and flown to Quantico for interrogation and ultimate prosecution.

I asked Pastor Hastings if he wanted to meet the women whose freedom he had facilitated. He said he'd be 'most honored.' And it was selfishly first on my priority list, even before calling the President.

"Chase, I'd like you and the reverend to stay up here while I go down to get the ladies."

He nodded.

On the way to the basement, I stopped by the men's latrine to assure Bubba was still in la la land. He was.

When I opened the basement door, the light from the hallway lit up just a fragment of the cavernous area, mostly around the bottom of the stairs. As I started down those stairs, I stopped to think...Smithers couldn't readily see who I was. For all she knew, the bad guys may have won. After all, there were obviously more of them than the two of us.

"Agent Smithers? It's McGowan!" I called, my voice reverberating throughout the dank cellar.

"Bruce?" a small voice answered from what sounded like fifty feet away. I shined my flashlight in the direction of the voice and its beam fell onto three huddled figures in a corner. The first thing I saw was the muzzle of my Remington I had left parked against the wall and it was aimed in my direction.

"Thank God," she said.

Slowly, they came to their feet and Smithers led them to the stairs. One by one I helped them up the steps and into the hallway. Once we were all inside and moving toward the sanctuary, I gave Smithers a nod and a smile. The First Lady then grabbed both of my hands and said "Thank you, Bruce. I knew you'd come for us. I can't tell you how happy I was to see your face a while ago."

"Yes, ma'am. And I yours. This is Commander Chase Rogers. He and his HRT guys paved the way for this operation."

She offered her hand. "And thank you, Commander." Her demeanor was graceful like always, her smile, captivating.

I then turned to Adriana. She had the same sweet smile on her face she had that magical day I saw her for the first time back at Wolf Laurel. I gathered her into me and we stood body against body for several moments without saying a word. Finally, she whispered "I love you, Skip." Her warm breath felt like a gentle tropical breeze in my ear.

"And I love you," I replied.

We then broke off our hug and I said, "Ladies, I'd like you to meet a genuine hero, Reverend Ralph Hastings. He sacrificed himself by performing something he came up with called a ruse. Exposing himself to danger, he walked fearlessly in the front door of his church and captured the full attention of the terrorists while we slipped in the rear to rescue you." I turned to Hastings. "And Preacher, this is the President's wife, the First Lady."

She thrust out her hand and as he took it, he dropped his head smartly and clicked his heels like the old soldier he was. "Ma'am, happy to make your acquaintance and pleased things worked out like they did. It's these three young heroes here that made it all happen. Enjoyed watchin' 'em work."

"I will be sure to tell my husband all about you, Reverend." She then turned to me. "Bruce, would you be so kind as to get my man on the phone?"

"Be happy to, ma'am."

As Chase Rogers kept his weapon trained on Franks and al-Jawhara, I sat the ladies down in one of the pews. I then pulled out my cellular and touched the President's number.

"Hello," he answered.

"Mr. President, Bruce McGowan."

"Yes, Bruce. What's happening at this point."

"At this point, sir, I'm going to turn over my phone to someone else."

I handed the phone off.

"It's me, sweetheart. Bruce and the HRT got us away from them." She smiled as she listened to his excited response. I could hear his elated voice almost as clearly as if the phone had been on *speaker*. "Yes, he and his magnificent team swept in here so heroically and rescued us." She listened. "I'm fine and so is Adriana. They pushed us around a little, but didn't hurt us. My wrists are just a little sore where they kept us tied up." More listening. "The terrorists? I don't know. You'll need to talk to Bruce about that. I'll turn you back over to him now. I love you too, darling. See you very soon." She handed the phone back to me.

"Yes, Mr. President."

"Did you get 'em, Bruce?"

As I walked out of earshot of the others, I replied, "We did. We took them all down. We took down who we think is the kingpin of the entire jihad element, one Ameen al-Jawhara. If he *is* their mastermind, and I use that term loosely, he won't be in any position to order any more bombings. Both he and former agent Franks were taken alive. Franks may do some singing since he's not getting a big payoff like he expected. Maybe we'll learn the identities and locations of *all* the jihadists to ward off all further attacks. Al-Jawhara? I'd be surprised the interrogators will get a word out of him. But, as he was so interested in the Gitmo 24...he'll get to know them all intimately."

"I can't tell you what euphoria I'm feelin' right now, Bruce. I owe you big. You saved the life of my precious wife and saw to it that her captors are gettin' what's comin' to 'em. Any casualties?"

"No friendlies. Four subversives dead. Two more have busted heads. They were just hired guns and probably won't know squat."

"Would you kindly have Commander Rogers put the First Lady on a bird out of there tonight? I'd be most grateful."

"Will do, sir."

"And you?"

I looked at Adriana and smiled. "We'll be going home, Mr. President, to get a shower and a good night's sleep. Tomorrow, we start patching up holes."

"Well, I know you haven't had a great deal of sleep over the last 48 hours. Sleep in, my friend."

"One other thing, sir. There's still at least one renegade left out there...maybe more."

"Who's that, Bruce."

"Another former Secret Service agent. The special agent-in-charge of your presidential detail...Tyson. The bastard who murdered my friend and three other state troopers. He may have two or three hired guns with him."

"We'll get him, Bruce."

"One day soon, *I'll* get him, sir."

He didn't respond to that. "Rest well, Bruce. I'm beholdin' to ya'. Never forget that. You and Adriana have a good night. Give her my best."

"Good night, sir."

Chapter Twenty-Five

Rogers contacted his counterpart with the CIRG element at the airport to meet him at the Adventist church for transporting al-Jawhara, Franks and the others, including the dead, in more 'official' vehicles to the temporarily established base camp which had been established at the airport. To me he said, "We'll take care of things from here, Bruce. I can have one of my people escort you all and Joanie back to the Jeep. You can take it on home with you. Tomorrow, we'll stop by your B&B and pick it up to turn back in with the other rentals."

"Thanks but I think I'll just call my brother who'll pick us up here. My SUV is parked at his funeral home. It's our only transportation now that Adriana's van is a heap of ashes. *And* my Austin-Healey is in winter storage."

"You have a Healey?"

"British racing green, tan leather, totally redone."

Rogers grinned. "You see I'm standing here drooling."

"Come back here sometime next spring. I'll put the top down and take you for a spin."

"I'd like that." He then turned his attention to Smithers. "Will I see you again, Joanie?"

You know you will, Romeo.

"Absolutely," she said. "When this is all over, will look for your call."

Gee, how surprising is that?

I pulled my phone again from its holster and touched my brother's number.

"Bruce, what's going on? Where are you now?"

"Not far, Joey. You know the old church out on Harvest Road? The Seventh Day Adventist? We're there. Can you come pick us up?"

"You said *we*...who's we?"

"We were able to wrestle Adriana and the President's wife from the terrorists."

"Woo hoo!" he exclaimed. "Are they all right?"

"They're fine. Can you be here soon?"

"Leaving right now."

Within a half hour, the front parking area of the old church was filled with vehicles and flashing lights. Unmarked federal units, a couple of meat wagons, the rescue squad, two State Police cruisers and the county sheriff. And the Lincoln family car that the President and I had borrowed from Joey two nights before. Could be more vehicles in the lot than Preacher Hastings saw on a Saturday morning.

While standing in that parking lot, I shook hands with Chase Rogers and his magnificent six. Rogers then said "I don't know all of your history, Bruce, but I think I've been schooled by the master these last couple of days...not only in the area of tactics and leadership, but being methodical and keeping a cool head when things get hairy. The President and the entire country owes you. And when my report gets out there, everyone will realize..."

"Keep me out of it all, Chase. Remember, I'm now just a retired citizen helping my lovely wife operate a quaint B&B in the beautiful West Virginia hills. Nobody out there needs to know anything else about me. The rest of my days, I only want to stay in the shadows."

Adriana then slipped her arm inside mine and smiled. "That's right, Commander. He's just *my* ordinary, everyday hero...not the people's."

"Okay, I get it. Well, anyway, I hope to see you all again under, shall I say, less harrowing circumstances."

I smiled and nodded. "Take good care of the First Lady tonight. If you can send an agent by our place later, we'll be packing up her and the President's belongings to send on the flight with her. And make sure you clean God's house up good before you leave. See you fellows sometime."

Adriana and the First lady gave each other hugs and considering what they had been through together, I thought I may have seen a tear or two.

After the goodbyes, Rogers and Smithers clinched each other in a rather lengthy embrace that provided me an impression they would definitely do that again sometime...and often.

Joey held open the doors for Adriana, Smithers and Pastor Hastings. We would drop him off at his ranch. I slid onto the passenger's front seat.

When we pulled out, Joey was quick to tell me, "I noticed the damage on the car as soon as the agent dropped it off. You couldn't be more careful with it? See if I loan *you* any of *my* vehicles again."

I placed my hand on his shoulder and replied, "Hey, maybe the President will arrange to send you a brand new one."

"Yeah, one with extended seats that face each other in the back...and Sirius radio."

I grinned and shook my head. "Or maybe the government will just pay for the repairs."

* * * * *

We delivered Hastings back to his home and found that he was facing a severe scolding from his wife Wilma for "pulling such a thing. You could had got yourself killed." Apparently, he had not told his bride the whole truth when he left...that he was going to do more than just go with us to check about people breaking into the church. I was glad to shake his hand one more time and then get the hell out of there before skillets flew.

I asked Joey if he could take us back by McGowan and Sons (minus one) Funeral Home. He asked me what for. I told him I'd like to use his pickup he kept parked there and hardly ever drove. My Suburban was without a windshield and its radiator was full of bullet holes.

"You want my old pickup so you can wreck *it* too."

"I'll be careful with it."

"You might, but will everyone else. Seems like people enjoy shooting at you."

"Just a day or so. I'll be getting the old beast towed for repairs."

While I was on the subject, I mentioned to Adriana maybe it was time to get me something new to replace the Suburban...something with some bells and whistles on it. She was still so happy to see me and be out from under the terrorists, she actually agreed. I thought maybe the next day I'd go look around before she came back down to earth and regained her senses. But then I said I had such sentiments for the old beast, considering what the two of us had been through, maybe I'd sit it up in the front yard on blocks like some kind of trophy. But, I think I may have pushed the envelope a little too much with that idea. She grabbed hold of my ear lobe and gave it a twist. She hated it when I told people I met that I was from West Virginia where all the cars were up on blocks and the *houses* were on wheels.

When we got to the funeral home, Joey succumbed and handed me the keys to his truck, a seven year old Ford F-150 crew cab. But, before we left the rear parking lot, what he then mentioned to me took away my elation and put me in a somber mood. The medical examiner had just that afternoon released the bodies of Harlan Williams and his two troopers. They were lying under the sheets on his slabs. He asked me if I wanted to view the bodies and I told him I had seen enough of them back in Sam Black Church where they lay murdered. He also said there would be a triple funeral for them on Wednesday at the Methodist church. It would bring hundreds of local, county and state police officers from all over West Virginia. The funeral procession containing cars, SUVs and motorcycles could be the largest parade of law enforcement ever in the State of West Virginia.

Adriana noticed my surly mood on our way back to Wolf Laurel. "You suddenly look a little down. Do you dread going home to see that horrible sight that we left on Friday?"

I looked at her and gave her some semblance of a smile. "Yeah, that's it."

But that *wasn't* it. I had been thinking all the while just how I could go about finding Harlan's killer...and how I would kill him. It's not a Christian thing to have in your head a plan to murder someone. But then when I found him, in my mind it wouldn't *be* murder. It would be justice.

On the way home to Wolf Laurel, I noticed in the rear view mirror there was likewise nothing jubilant about Smithers. I thought she would be just a wee bit more sprightly. She had played a big part in the take down of the terrorist element and cultivated a friendship with a handsome dude that might just might take off into something else. She had not only uttered a word, but sat staring out her side window as though she was in some sort of trance."

"Joanie, you okay back there?"

"Yeah. Just doing a little worrying is all."

Now it came to me. "About your daughter of course."

"What's going to happen to her now? When it's learned that the jihadi leadership was captured, the people who have my daughter might just kill her." She obviously had been crying because I heard her snuffing back the mucus.

I intentionally didn't want her to know what Franks told the man on the phone, not just yet anyway. It might not happen. But seeing that she was suffering from worry, I went ahead.

"Joanie, after his takedown back there in the church, I appealed to Franks and his conscience to call your daughter's captors and have her released. After a little prodding, he went ahead and made the call. But, I didn't readily tell you because I didn't want you to get your hopes up in case they don't."

Her mood perked up almost instantly. "He did that? He gave instructions to have her released?"

"Let's just see if they will."

"I will *pray* that they will," said Adriana.

"Thank you, Bruce. I can't tell you what that means to me."

I gave her a nod.

When we turned off the road into the gravel driveway, it seemed to the both of us there was a kind of ghostly pall hanging over our house. I didn't feel that earlier in the day. But I was in there with other people and during the daylight hours. The last time Adriana was inside, it was almost wall to wall bodies. The last time *I* was inside, my stomach had been turned by what I believed to be the nauseous smell of death...whether it was real or not. I touched the brake pedal and brought the vehicle to a sliding stop in the gravel. We sat for a few moments just looking at the place. The interior of the house was dark, and in my mind, at least tonight, something terrible still lived in there. Something...cold. Colder than the coldest night in December. I looked over at Adriana. I thought maybe she felt it, too. There was a look of apprehension on her face. The agents had obviously cleared out. They hadn't stayed the night after all. I had told her they might still be there when we arrived. But as they weren't, even with me lying in our bed next to her, she would have felt a lot safer had one or two of them remained.

"Skip, what do you think about us just staying the night in a motel? I don't know if I want to..."

"Sure." I stroked her hair and allowed my hand to brush her cheek. "We never break out of this place and go somewhere for the night...just for the hell of it."

She smiled. "Let's do it. You pick the place."

But as Smithers was also with us, we had left her out of our conversation. I turned to her and asked, "How about you, Joanie? You want to stay here tonight or go with us?"

"I can understand your and Adriana's reluctance to go back in there tonight. If it were my home, I might feel the same way. I might just want to get a fresh start tomorrow. But I don't mind staying here. My stuff's here where I left it also. You all go on. I'll lock up."

"Okay. The key was supposed to be left in one of the flower pots on the veranda. I'll wait to see that you're able to get in."

She touched both Adriana and me on the arm. "See you all tomorrow and hope you have a restful night."

"There's plenty of food left in the fridge as I know you have to be hungry," Adriana told her.

Smithers said thanks and stepped out of the car. Upon reaching the veranda she searched through two flower pots before finally locating the door key. Once she was safely inside, I backed the pickup out and headed down the driveway toward the road.

Because I looked as though I had just crawled out of the woods after two days of hunting, I knew we wouldn't be staying at The Greenbrier; but I didn't want to take my wife to a fleabag motel either. So, we decided on a pretty nice little family-owned place in White Sulphur Springs...the Magnolia. The only thing was, we had no change of clothes or underwear, no toothbrush, comb or toiletries. On the way, we stopped at the Wal-Mart, finding it was getting ready to close. The greeter wanted to stop us, but the twenty I shoved in his hand made his night. "You've got ten minutes to make the cash register."

Adriana and I then split off and hustled into the women's and men's departments, respectively. I found my sizes and got what I needed in five. She got choosy and took a little longer. All the while, announcements were being made that the store was closing and everyone needed to go to checkout immediately. As I was standing near the clerk at the register, she was beckoning me to put my things on the conveyor belt, but I stalled. "Waiting on my wife."

"Well, she'd better hurry."

"Little lady," I said, "I've never known her to hurry about anything."

"If she doesn't get here in one minute you both will have to leave here empty-handed."

But she did make it...with fifteen seconds to spare.

The shower was steamy-hot ecstasy. One of the few pleasures of life the older we get. Another one is lying under clean sheets next to the woman you love and enjoying her body like you both were twenty one again and it was your first time. I think part of the sexual fervor that night was a quashing of what was left of the fear and uncertainty we experienced those two dreadful days...that we may never see one another again.

A light dusting of snow had fallen overnight and we woke the next morning to a golden sun trying its best to burn through a dense fog. Neither one of us had eaten squat the past two days and we were famished. After driving back to the west on Route 60, we stopped at the General Lewis for a breakfast of ham and eggs and some fluffy country biscuits with apple butter. For the first real time, we checked each other out over the breakfast table and shared some chuckles about our Wal-Mart wardrobe...me in a pair of jeans with a 36 inseam where I had to form a cuff down at my boots that made me look like I had just left the farm; and my fashion-conscious wife wearing slacks made in Bangladesh with a red and green Christmas sweater adorned with snowmen and reindeer.

"You spent all that time in the store last night only to come up with that?" I asked her.

"Maybe none of my friends will see me before we get home."

Before returning to our home, we swung by the Verizon store to get Adriana a new cellphone since Franks had smashed hers. Considering that her husband had been accused by the media of kidnapping the President and committing treasonous acts against the government, when her new phone was brought into service, she found at least a dozen missed calls from her friends. As she listened to them one by one on our way back to the inn, most of the ladies had expressed concern for her safety and a couple of others wanted to know where she was while all that was going on with me. Another of her societal acquaintances said she knew something like this would happen, her marrying an "uncultured scoundrel" like me. Adriana laughed out loud over that one.

But I had hoped by now that I was back in the community's good graces since the media had retracted those earlier reports about me and set the record straight. And even though I didn't want anyone to know about my former life as a counterterrorist operative and that it was me who led the assault that freed the First Lady, I *did* want my reputation back. I preferred not having women snatching their children off the street and fleeing for their lives when I showed my face in downtown Lewisburg.

As the story about Friday night's assault to kill or capture the First Family was certainly on everyone's lips, we were sure that for days to come Wolf Laurel would see a profusion of curiosity seekers and sensationalists driving by craning their necks and taking pictures. Something we would just have to contend with. But then as Adriana was always worried about having enough patrons staying at the B&B, would the adverse publicity keep people away? I told her, it might work in reverse...the number of customers might just balloon. Her rebuttal to me was that she wanted people staying at our inn for the *right* reasons...for its ambiance and romantic allure, not because of its recent shocking history.

The sun was now out in all its glory and when Wolf Laurel come into our view, its radiance reflecting off the windows seemed to be sending us a *welcome home* message. It was a different house from what we saw the previous night. The ghosts had dissipated and the old place was once again showcasing its warmth.

Smithers had heard us approaching and greeted us at the door with a smile and a pleasant "good morning." I allowed Adriana to go in first. But she stalled a moment and then took a deep breath. My guess was that she dreaded finding the place like we had left it on Friday evening. And I didn't blame her. When I was there changing clothes, except for the removed bodies, it *was* like we had left it.

However, when we entered our house, we had a bit of a surprise waiting on us. Smithers had done a lot to clean the place up. The furniture was upright and so was the Christmas tree. She had not only swept up its broken bulbs and pieces of the shattered fireplace stone, but had applied some type of solution to remove the blood stains from the flooring. In the air was an aroma of fresh potpourri, which at least for me, meant no more smell of death. She of course couldn't do anything about the scores of bullet holes in every part of the den and hallway. But after a good day of patch work and paint, one would never know what went down there. We would also have to replace our leather couch and chairs which had likewise fallen victim to both friendly and enemy rounds.

"You did all this?" I asked her.

"I got up early this morning to clean. After a lot of elbow grease, the stains finally came up."

Adriana gave her a hug. "Thank you, Joanie. I dreaded more than you could imagine what I knew I would find here today. What a nice surprise."

I noticed that Smithers also had her bag packed and it was sitting by the door. "You're leaving?"

"I was saving this news for last. It's great news. Whoever had my daughter called the D.C. Metro Police and said they could find her inside the Jefferson Memorial. They found her safe and unharmed. God answered my prayer."

"Great news!" Adriana exclaimed. She gave Smithers another hug. "I'm so happy for you."

"Yeah, I'm glad that worked out, Joanie," I added.

"And you made that happen, Bruce. I can't tell you enough..."

"I guess even in the worst of humanity, somewhere inside them there remains a little good."

"Well, I need to go. I don't know what I'll be going back to. The White House protection team is suspended pending a complete investigation. I talked to the Director this morning and he's expecting me back this afternoon for a debriefing about everything. I hope they'll keep me there at The White House and not put me back on VIP detail. They know that four, maybe five Secret Service agents were involved in the conspiracy with the jihad organization. One still remains out there and is being placed on the Most Wanted list."

"He's definitely on *my* most wanted list."

"So, can I get you to drive me back out to the airport? I can bum a ride on one of the Blackhawks that's been going back and forth."

"Maybe your buddy, Chase, hasn't left yet and you can hitch a flight with him."

She smiled. "Maybe I'll just see about that."

Adriana told me she'd stay behind, but would lock up. It wouldn't take me a half hour to be in and out of the airport. They hugged again. They were the huggingest bunch of women I had ever been around.

"I won't ever forget you, Joanie. You kept those people from hurting us...especially that al-Jawhara, who made it plain that all infidel women deserve to die. I thought a couple of times the First Lady and I were toast."

"You saw how he knocked *me* around."

"Anyway, you have to come back sometime. You can stay here anytime, our treat."

Let me get this straight. My wife is not charging someone to stay at Wolf Laurel. Since when? I wasn't so sure she wouldn't even send the White House a bill...certainly for damages.

"Maybe someday. I want to have better memories about this place."

Before I let Smithers out of the truck at the Bureau TOC (Tactical Operations Center), I brought up an old subject. "Joanie, the last time we were here at the airport, I didn't handle things very well with you. I jumped too soon to the wrong conclusion. And then when you told us that your daughter had been kidnapped to coerce you into being their spy, I think I was still unreasonably hard on you, not appreciating your situation. And for that I'm sorry. Just wanted to clear the air between us."

"I can't blame you for your reaction, Bruce. Legally and dutifully, I did the wrong thing. I was acting like a mother and not an agent of the U.S. Government. So, as far as I'm concerned, we're good with one another."

I gave her a smile. "We are. The subject ends right here. Neither your boss nor the President will hear about it. I had also told Chase Rogers to not put the matter in his After Action Report."

"Thank you, Bruce."

"And I'm sure you're anxious to get back to your daughter, so I'll let you go."

Her eyes glistened as she smiled. She leaned over to my side of the car and hugged me. Doesn't anyone shake hands anymore? "You're a good man, Bruce...deep down under all that machoistic exterior."

My turn to smile. "Goodbye, Sweetpea. Have a great life."

I sat with my arms crossed and watched her walk away until she disappeared inside the TOC. Yeah, in hindsight, I'm not sure what I would have done in her situation. But I did know she would go far in government service. And it would be kind of neat if she and Mr. Rogers got together some day. They would make a great looking couple.

Chapter Twenty-Six

It was a pretty neat thing communicating with the President where I could call him directly and then he might call me without detailing a member of his staff to tell me, "Please hold for the President." That arrangement of course wasn't going to last very long, considering he would be out of the White House in a little over a month. But as I was returning home from the airport, Eagle One dialed my number.

"Bruce, it's me." When the President of the United States calls and says "it's me", you don't ask "who?"

"Good morning, sir. How are things with you?"

"Wonderful, now, thanks to you."

"Let me pull off into a parking lot here." I took a moment to turn into a bank lot and find a spot to park the Ford. "All right, sir, I can better carry on a conversation. Did the First Lady make it back okay last night?"

"That she did. It's wonderful having her back in my arms, Bruce. And did you get some good rest?"

"Yes, sir. We both did. And after hot showers and a good breakfast, we're new people. I just dropped Joanie Smithers off at the airport. She'll be coming your way. She's worried she's going to be reassigned, considering the suspension of your protection detail."

"I'll make sure she has a job here as long as I'm in the Oval Office. I'll also tell the incomin' president about her heroics. In those desperate hours, Joanie made sure my wife was well-protected until al-Jawhara sent her off to that huntin' camp with part of his element. I'm not sure what that was about, do you?"

"I just think she was a distraction to him, even a threat, and he had too much else on his mind. I'm surprised he didn't just end her life."

"Well, I sure think a lot of her. By the way, I wanted to bring you up on some things. Late last night, after the Attorney General secured a search warrant from a federal judge, Bureau agents raided that Muslim safe house. Not only did they find a treasure trove of documents and plans that named the cities and dates selected for the detonation of dirty bombs, but also the names and locations of more than fifty Islamic radicals associated with this Stealth Jihad group. At this moment, more than a dozen FBI SWAT elements are on the move to locate and apprehend everyone on that list."

"Ah, great. With al-Jawhara, the apparent kingpin of this organization out of the picture, anybody not taken down in those raids and who are waiting for his attack orders, will hopefully never receive them. That says al-Jawhara has to be isolated and never given an opportunity to send out any orders from his prison cell."

"I'm way ahead of you on that, Bruce. I have ordered that he be given the full interrogation treatment, after which he will remain at Gitmo in solitary confinement indefinitely. In essence, he will suddenly disappear from all civilization."

"The ACLU is going to *love* you, Mr. President."

"They already do...*not*." That sounded like something a high schooler would say.

"You said you had some *things* to tell me. Was there something else?"

"Yes, something kind of heart-breaking. It was bad enough that the police found Arnie Kessler's body in the Potomac, but his wife, Mae, was also discovered further down river. Her body apparently floated away where Arnie's didn't. In those safe house documents, they not only found the names of the Secret Service conspirators, like Franks, Tyson, and three other Secret Service agents, but the Chief of Staff's name as well. Under al-Jawhara's direction, Franks was handling most of the operation and at the same time communicating with you, me, the press *and* Arnie. From what my Intel sources tell me, Arnie had apparently developed a case of conscience and told Franks he was turning himself over to the Bureau. Somebody got to him and Mae at their house. Apparently, they were both shot in the head there and then tossed in the river. Their blood was found in the bed where they slept. I've been knowing both of them for years and it grieves me not only that he would betray his country for a pile of money, but that he and Mae ended up like that."

"I'm sure it's personally distressing for you, sir. There is one loose end that I'm interested in wrapping up. We talked about it, Mr. President."

"Tyson."

"Yes."

"He's high on the Bureau's list for capture. All across the country, state and local law enforcement have his face and personal data on their radar. Unless he has arranged with some back alley identity vendor for a new set of ID credentials, he won't be able to use a credit card, withdraw money from an ATM or get on an airplane. He's either now a lone wolf out there hiding out on his own or has allies and friends putting him up. That could also mean there are more conspirators in this deal we don't know about."

"Probably the latter. But he's on *my* radar as well. I wrote down some notes while reviewing the history and personal information in his shield yesterday morning. He'll get nailed sooner or later. That's not to say I'll saddle my horse and go after him, but he'll continue to be on my target list until he's brought in."

"I saw how much your friend meant to ya, Bruce. You just enjoy your retirement. *We'll* get 'im. A matter of time."

We ended our conversation at that point and since our business with one another was basically over, I didn't know if I would hear from him again. In his official function as the President, anyway. Any further communication would probably be via his new Chief of Staff. But maybe we'd get a White House Christmas card. And I doubted that he and the First Lady would plan another mini vacation to Wolf Laurel anytime soon. I did think we would always have a special friendship and I hoped Adriana and I would somehow, sometime see the royal couple again.

That evening when I settled into my Big Easy with a bottle of Rolling Rock to catch the national news at six thirty, the White House Press Secretary issued a press release informing the country that *"the terrorists who had not only carried out the assault on an inn where the First Family was spending the weekend, but who had also abducted the First Lady and ordered the detonation of the bomb in Carthage, all in an effort to coerce the release of 24 prisoners in Guantanamo Bay, had been captured in a church in Greenbrier County, West Virginia by federal agents. Four subversives were killed and four taken alive. We have identified two primary suspects among the captured...former Secret Service agent Steffen Franks, a major player in the conspiracy, and Ameen al-Jawhara, the leader of the terrorist element, Stealth Jihad of America.*

The apparent command center for the terrorist faction in Washington, D.C. was raided by the FBI where more than fifteen Islamofascist were apprehended. Also discovered at the location were jihadist operational plans to detonate radioactive devices in a dozen cities across the United States including New York, Los Angeles and Dallas as well as the smaller cities of Charleston, South Carolina, Harrisburg, Pennsylvania and what was referred to in the documents as Sin City Las Vegas, Nevada. The CDC and Director of the ATF report that in the Town of Carthage, Maryland, outside of D.C., twenty seven people are now confirmed dead with another three hundred or more being treated for radiation symptoms such as skin sloughing, body tremors, debilitating fatigue and bloody diarrhea. We believe that with the arrest of the Washington-based terror group and the discovery of seven other jihadist nests uncovered in the aforementioned cities, any threat of further attacks has been quelled. The President not only credits the Bureau for gathering the Intel on the jihadists, but also one

> *of its CIRG HRT strike teams for carrying out the assault that took out these terrorists and freed the First Lady."*

I held my Rolling Rock up to the TV screen in salute. "Here's *to* you, Buck Rogers."

* * * * *

Wednesday morning, after my run through the frosted countryside, I showered, had a bagel with Adriana, and donned my only suit, a basic black Brooks Brothers bargain that Adriana had bought for me back last spring when we were in Boston (pardon the alliteration). She had also laid out on the bed one of my nicer-looking neck ties...not the aforementioned Scottish one.

She was gorgeous in her black, knee length dress that clung so delightfully to her svelte body, looking nothing like I found her three days before. Had it not been for the contractor repairing and repainting the sheetrock downstairs and the somber event ahead of us that day, I would have dropped everything and had my way with her.

Harlan Williams' funeral was at eleven in the Methodist church downtown.

As I expected, by ten thirty police units from all over the state were parked for blocks all the way up and down Washington and Lee Streets as well as along adjacent side streets. Because we had arrived a half hour earlier than that, we were able to find a spot in a bank parking lot a half block away. Funeral director Joe McGowan would have his hands full in determining how the procession would be organized. With the help of two other morticians from the county, using their hearses, he had taken the bodies of Harlan and his troopers to the church at 8:00.

The night before, at Harlan's visitation, Adriana and I had offered our sorrows to his wife of thirty one years and his two adult sons. I didn't know whether or not she knew the facts surrounding his murder or that I had something to do with his death. If she did, she didn't let on. We did talk briefly about all those memorable days of golf at the country club and his love of fishing. He had the honor and pleasure of being the only non-McGowan invited to fish at our camp, which sadly had also met its demise at the hands of al-Jawhara's killers.

Adriana and I took one of the few spaces left in the pews that Wednesday morning after which the sanctuary quickly became standing room only. By the time the service began, the town police were unfortunately turning away late-comers. They would have to pay their respects later at the gravesite service.

It was a long funeral. Each of the three officers was eulogized by a laundry list of troopers who had served with them. The minister himself took about forty minutes behind the pulpit praising their bravery and dedication to duty. But although many of the mourners eventually began squirming, I didn't mind those two hours. These heroes deserved to have every word about them heard.

Only Harlan was to be interred at Memorial Gardens. One of the troopers would be buried in his family plot in Hinton while the other was carried to his hometown in Covington, Virginia, where a second service and burial were to happen the next day.

As we stood on the hill at Harlan's gravesite looking out beyond the rows of tombstones onto the panorama of the

Greenbrier countryside...the picturesque hills and dells of the Alleghenies...the American Legion bugler sounded Taps. More than a hundred officers of the law and a handful of Marine veterans stood at attention with their fingertips touching their brows until the last somber note echoed throughout the valley. As an epilogue to that ceremonial tribute, the Methodist minister then read from the 23rd Psalm, followed lastly by the passage from the Anglican Book of Common Prayer:

"In sure and certain hope of the resurrection to eternal life through our Lord Jesus Christ, we commend to Almighty God our brother, Harlan Thomas Williams and we commit his body to the ground. Earth to earth, ashes to ashes, dust to dust. The Lord bless him and keep him. The Lord make his face to shine upon him and be gracious unto him and give him peace. Amen."

I had heard it spoken so many times in my life...most recently at the funeral of Lionel Byrd. It has remained in my brain as one of the most profound and poignant benedictions to life I have ever heard.

In all, there must have been over two hundred people standing there on that hillside, mostly huddled together in the cold and cutting wind. A few officers who would have been back six rows deep had they tried to stand in close proximity to the gravesite service, waited down on the cemetery road by their units. I also recognized a few faces in the crowd, none of them wearing uniforms...a couple of country club acquaintances, Alonzo down at the bakery where Harlan and I met occasionally for a bagel, and Jim Donnelley who ran the indoor shooting range where Harlan and I, two very competitive personalities, met every couple of weeks to see who could out-shoot the other. There might have been three or four other faces I had seen around town, but I didn't know who they were. Adriana, on the other hand, probably recognized several, being a long-time resident of the area, but she didn't acknowledge anyone. It wasn't the venue for socializing.

One man who looked to be in his mid forties, dressed in a long coat and an Indiana Jones style hat, stood down the hill a ways under a massive oak. I don't know why he caught my eye, but he just looked out of place. Occasionally, the wind picked up the tail of his coat and revealed that underneath it he had on a suit. I wondered if he was Bureau. Maybe the President sent a representative who not wanting to squeeze into the mass merely made his official appearance. But maybe he was someone who didn't want to be seen up close.

But for the most part, being not that close to the service, I was trying to listen to the closing words of the minister. Unfortunately, with the occasional gust of wind blowing into him versus in my direction, his voice would trail off. After a half minute, I turned my head back toward the outsider and he was gone. I looked in every direction around the tree for curiosity sake and it was as though he had disappeared.

When I thought the service was drawing near its end, I took Adriana by the hand and walked back down the hill. I wanted us to get out of there before the large throng of people broke up and the caravan of police units began clogging up the exit to the highway.

On the way back home. we stopped off at the local Chevy dealer to look at their SUVs. They were indeed a snazzy looking breed with all of the neat features and gee-whiz gadgetry. For me, the vehicle had to be large and brawny, not because we had a bunch of kids or friends to tote around, but the vehicle had to *look* the part. Had to be black and leave no doubt to the world the man behind the wheel was no wimp. Had to have a large rear storage compartment for my 'toys'...and I'm not just talking about my golf clubs. Something like a Tahoe or another Suburban.

Adriana thought that since she also needed to replace her fire-gutted van, why couldn't my selection be something that didn't leave us in sticker shock. Maybe we should look at replacing both vehicles with two that were pre-owned. Two vehicles for the price of one brand new one. She was right of course. We didn't have the need to shell out what could amount to $80,000. We did have comprehensive coverage on both units, but what little insurance payment we had coming, if the company would pay off at all considering how they were destroyed, would be a drop in the bucket against the high cost of today's new vehicles. But for now, I would take advantage of my brother's good heart and drive his pickup for a while.

Just before three thirty we turned off the road and into our parking lot where sat a Volvo SUV. Ordinarily, I wouldn't give a strange vehicle in our driveway another thought. But we had no one staying with us and expected none of Adriana's friends. And I didn't have any friends. Maybe another curiosity seeker taking pictures, I assumed. We had had our share of them already, but usually they just cruised by slowly on the road. However, for some reason, *this* vehicle bothered me. It appeared there was one head, a male, sitting inside the SUV behind the steering wheel.

"I wonder who that is?" Adriana asked me.

"I'm fixing to find out. Stay in the truck."

With one hand on the automatic occupying my shoulder holster, I exited from the pickup and walked cautiously like a good cop would around to the left quarter panel.

Wrapping my knuckles on the sheet metal, I yelled, "You inside. Put down your door glass and show me your hands." For several seconds there was no response, which compelled me to go ahead and pull my weapon. I stood a little longer behind the driver's door, waiting him out. I wouldn't wait long. Then I started thinking. Was this a set up? I might be checking out the Volvo while at the same time bullets came flying from the nearby woods. And was Adriana now vulnerable?

Slowly, the driver's door opened and the same mysterious character I saw standing off by himself at the cemetery came out with his hands in the air. Through the still open driver's door, I saw the hat he was wearing earlier lying in the passenger's seat.

"And just who the hell are *you*?" I asked him.

"Can I put my hands down?"

"No. Who are you and what are you doing in my driveway?"

"I'm...a friend of Steffen Franks."

With my left hand, I shoved the man up against the Volvo and then placed my pistol up underneath his chin. "You don't want this to go off accidentally, so don't even breathe."

"Uh, please. I mean no harm."

"You didn't come here to settle his score?"

"No. But I am here on his behalf."

"How so?"

"I can't talk with your gun in my Adam's apple."

"All right, sit your ass down in the seat and place your hands on the steering wheel."

He did as ordered. While he was getting in the car, I saw that Adriana had gotten out of the pickup. I motioned for her to go on in the house. She gave me one of those 'who is it and why did you have a gun on him' looks, but I gave her a nod and a thumbs up. She then continued up the steps to the veranda.

"I saw you at the cemetery. Why were you there?"

"Steffen. He of course knew that you and that state police officer were friends. He told me to check the paper and see when the cop's funeral was. Since I didn't know what you looked like and couldn't pick you out from all those people, I decided to ask around where you live. Hardly anyone knew you, but a good many know your wife. So, I just came by here to wait."

"Okay, so you're a bloodhound and a friend of Franks. What the hell do you want with me?"

"To talk."

"About what?"

"About Steffen. You see, he has no family, but he has *me*."

"And you are what to him?"

"His friend, his...significant other if you will. The feds allowed him to contact me because of our relationship. Of course they listened in on our conversation."

"Uh, *huh*. So, you're bosom buddies. I get it. Now, be more specific. Why are you here?"

"To...provide you with some information, and in exchange, ask for your help."

"I'm listening."

"Steffen did do wrong and unfortunately committed some regrettable acts. He not only killed or had people killed, but he betrayed his country for the promise of three million dollars. All he had to do was kidnap the President and hold him so that those prisoners would be released."

"And you had knowledge of that, which says you were in on the conspiracy. If you're here to give yourself up, you're at the wrong place. You can do that with the feds at the airport. It's still locked down by the FBI and NTSB until the plane that Franks or someone in his group shot down is removed."

"I'm not here to turn myself in. I'm just hoping we can make a deal to not only help Steffen but to keep me from being arrested for accessory before and to the fact."

"What's your name?"

"Darren Pavloski."

"You're talking to the wrong person, Darren. I can't help you. I'm a federal retiree with no authority. Go to the feds."

He was quiet for a moment and then turned his head away from me.

"You heard me, right?" I said.

"I heard you. Here's the thing, Mr. McGowan. As much as he despised you for trashing his plans last Friday night, he found out that the Muslim terrorist who offered all that money was not going to pay him or the others what was promised. The bastard held Steffen responsible for failing to deliver the President. Steffen betrayed his country and the guy he was in the conspiracy with betrayed *him*."

"And you were in touch with him all that time realizing what was happening."

"Not all the time. I just got bits and pieces and when this al-Jawhara found out Steffen was on the phone with me about what was going on, he flipped out."

"Okay, so they were all bad guys and you were just a choir boy sitting home ready to live happily ever after on the money Franks received for his services."

"I'm not here to talk about that. I'm here to see if you can use your influence to get Steffen a lighter sentence."

"And I would do that why?"

"A couple of reasons. You may not know this, sir, but Steffen on several occasions had to plead for al-Jawhara not to kill your wife and the First Lady. That was the man's plan all along. Steffen might have done wrong and needs to pay for his crime, but he does have a goodly amount of compassion in him. As much as he was pissed at you for spoiling all his plans, he said you struck a chord with him when you allowed him to surrender, then sat down with him about that agent's little girl. He said he saw a different side of you than what he pictured."

"You said you had a *couple* of reasons. What's the other?"

"Steffen knows you want to find Curt Tyson. I can tell you where he may be located."

"Now you have my attention. Of course, if this is just a ploy to get me to make the deal, I'll make sure you're under arrest for accessory, obstruction of justice and a ton of other things and then you'll be in the slammer with your boyfriend. The feds aren't too pretty with their interrogation techniques."

"It's not a ploy. I do have some information."

"What happens if I do appeal to the Attorney General, asking him to give Steffen a chance at a plea bargain, and then the court throws the book at him anyway?"

"Then I'll at least know you in good faith tried. So, are you ready to talk business?"

"All right. Twenty years is better than life without parole. You have my word on the matter *only* if the information you provide is truthful. If I'm sent on a wild goose chase, the deal is off and I'll be ecstatic when your ass is thrown into prison right along with his."

"Curt Tyson and his wife have an apartment in Falls Church."

"You think I don't know that?"

"Hear me out. What no one else knows is that he rented another apartment with another woman in Fredericksburg."

"Is the roommate Secret Service as well?"

"No."

"What's the address?"

"Do Steffen and I get a break?"

"I said all right. But I also said the information has to check out. If Tyson rented the place under his name, the Bureau's investigation team would have that information in two minutes."

"But he didn't. He rented it under an alias, David Sullivan."

"And how do Steffen and you know about that?"

"Another person living in that same apartment complex was there with Steffen when you took him down in that church."

"What's his name?"

"Bill something or other. Oh, yeah, Billy Younger."

The bell then rang inside my head. It was the name of the Bubba that I cracked on the head in the church rest room. If Darren's information wasn't valid, I didn't know how he could have known about Bubba. If Darren was lying, he'd be found out anyway. So, because he had made an effort to track me down and appeal to my good side, I supposed I would take him at his word.

"All right, Darren, I'm not turning you in. But, how do I get in touch with you?"

"Here's my card." It read *Darren Pavloski, The GQ Men's Store, Alexandria, VA*, etc. Both his work and cell numbers were on the card. Tyson's apartment address was written on the back. "Promise you'll do what you can for Steffen? It's not that important what's done with me."

"I said I would." I shoved the business card in my pocket. "Be talking to you, Darren. Stay accessible. Now get the hell out of here before I change my mind.""

He nodded, started his car and slowly pulled away.

I had some thinking to do. The right thing of course was to report this information to the feds who would either raid the place or stake it out. But as I promised Tyson *and* myself, I would personally be carrying out his death penalty.

Chapter Twenty-Seven

By Thursday afternoon, our contractor had patched up the sheetrock in the den, the hallway and one of the guest rooms, repaired two shattered blocks of the stone in the fireplace and replaced four pieces of batten and six outer matching boards on the rear of the house where MP5 bullets had penetrated clean through several walls all the way to the outside. Woodwork throughout the B&B damaged in several places was filled with wood putty and stained. The only thing left to do on that Friday was the interior painting. When done, the house was ours again. No more guests till after New Years. Adriana was mine and mine alone for the Christmas holidays.

I would neither have peace nor Christmas in my heart unless I went after Curt Tyson, alias David Sullivan. All I had to go on was his address and his file photo, an image that had been burned into my brain from the previous Sunday morning when I took nearly the entire night studying the material in both his and Franks' shields. By nature I am not a vindictive person. I have brought justice upon people on numerous occasions, especially during my tenure with the Bureau and afterward with Team Zulu as a counterterrorist operative. It was my job. Nothing personal. But as I have described before, I can count on one hand of fingers the times when I went after people who had hurt, kidnapped or murdered members of my family and friends. It was their time to die. For Curt Tyson, this was one of those times.

My dilemma? How would I explain to Adriana that all of this wasn't over for me...that I would need to take a couple of days to officially wrap things up. And that in doing so, I would leave her alone at Wolf Laurel when the nightmare of what happened there almost a week ago was still fresh in her mind. I could probably fix that last thing by having Joey and his wife Cora stay with her those days I was gone. But I wasn't going to lie to her about what that 'wrap up' was. In the past, I might have watered down the truth about what my previous job was about, what kind of missions I would be undertaking and where I was going. These things would involve considerable danger and contain a certain amount of associated risk. So, how would I explain my going after Tyson? If I told her we might have located him, she would merely say "good, let the police handle it. You are going to stay out of the picture, aren't you?" Or words to that effect.

I had to tell her. That last time when the President had sent me out to nail the number one terrorist in the world, the man called The Viper, it came very close to seriously damaging our marriage. She reminded me I was retired from the action game. There was no reason for an aging has-been like me to go hunting for danger anymore when there were hundreds of skilled, well-trained young protagonists out there in the alphabet agencies who were fully capable of doing what I used to do.

Over the dinner table, I told her. Told her I needed to have closure on a couple of things. There was one more terrorist running free...someone instrumental in the attack on our home and on the First Family. Someone who killed one of the best friends I ever had, certainly the best since I retired. I needed to go looking for him. Would be gone maybe two or three days, that's all. I needed her blessing.

What I told her brought no surprise. She laid her fork down gently and dabbed her lips with her napkin. But then I had trouble reading those eyes. They had something in them I had not seen before. Not angst, not anger, not alarm. Maybe something cognitive, I thought. Something between reason and volition. She had heard me, heard my passion, weighed carefully what I was saying. I had put my entire soul into the rescue mission, into getting her safely home, and I knew she was mad as hell at her captors. They had disrupted her life, not to mention *threatened* it. The President of the United States had been attacked in her own house. People's blood had soaked into her carpet and hardwood floor. And people had died there. She made no bones about wanting all the terrorists punished to the nth degree.

"If you do this, will you do it with federal backup? You won't go after him alone, will you?"

Who *was* this woman? Had a new wife risen like a Phoenix from her captivity with a desire for revenge? And was I really the person she wanted to carry it out? Her husband? I suddenly either needed a shot of Scotch or to slap myself and wake up since I had fallen asleep at the table.

I tried not to show my elation *and* surprise. "At this point, I don't know. We'll see."

"How about Commander Rogers?"

"I can send him an invitation."

Her mention of his name didn't totally surprise me. I may have caught her checking out the handsome dude once or twice the evening we threw down on the terrorists.

"When would you plan to go?"

"In a day or so."

"I guess I am not the voice of reason this afternoon. I must be crazy giving my husband my blessing to go get this guy. If something would ever happen to you, I..."

"Not to me. Tyson is small potatoes compared to the heavies I've taken down."

"I only saw him at our camp for a short time and then he took off. He was arrogant and condescending, especially to the First Lady. Joanie Smithers wanted to slap his face. I will say Franks stopped both him and that al-Jawhara from harming us. So, where is Tyson supposed to be hiding out?"

"Possibly hiding in plain sight in an apartment in Fredericksburg...under an alias."

"You didn't fully disclose what the man in the parking lot told you. Did he tell you where to find Tyson?"

I nodded. "He wanted to make a deal to save his boy friend, Franks, from a life term."

"Franks is gay?"

"All the way."

"Not that it matters of course. It just surprises me."

"I *am* glad he convinced his pals to keep their hands off you. You realize that al-Jawhara and Tyson planned to kill you all when you were no longer of any use."

"I suspected that and Joanie insinuated as much."

I smiled at her. "Glad you're sitting here with me tonight, sweetheart."

She smiled back and we clicked wine glasses.

I finished my soup which was now cold, walked around to kiss the cook and helped her clear the table. After pouring the both of us a second glass of wine, I went upstairs to do a little thinking. I needed to think about what I would say to Rogers. Would I offer him that invitation? I sat for a while in my Big Easy with the glass of Merlot in my left hand while pointing the remote at the TV with my right. I wanted to catch some news to determine if any of the commentators were still slamming me or had they now begun praising me. Coincidentally, the six-thirty news anchor was announcing that in a short moment the station would break away to the President's special news conference.

The President had been silent to the outside world for nearly forty-eight hours while in seclusion at Camp David with his staff, the Pentagon brass and various department directors of the law enforcement arena, primarily discussing any remaining terrorist and security threats. And although in a couple of days there would be an official White House press release, he just wanted to say a few words not only of thanks to the heroes who had hopefully shut down any future threats, but words of encouragement to all who continued to fear for their safety. I learned during those two tenuous days a hell of a lot of things about the man that probably no one else in the country or even his administration might ever see...some very *human* traits of his personality like his tempestuous anger, his stalwart courage and of course his warm and commiserate heart. But, I was convinced that considering all that had happened to him over this past week and how he handled the national crisis, he had the admiration of not only the American people, but the world. He certainly had mine.

The President stood stoically in the East Room of the White House in a plain black suit and blue tie facing the camera for scantly three seconds before given the cue to begin his speech. Remarkably, his eloquent and impromptu words contained not even a hint of his Texas drawl nor did he use a teleprompter.

"My fellow Americans. We have together endured a very difficult even harrowing time in our country's history. Not since 9-11 have we seen such resolve on the part of an enemy terrorist regime to not only attack and kill American citizens but a plan to leave our cities in ashes. As we know, the jihadists' primary goal has always been to disrupt the lives and liberties of our people and cause us to live in fear. This particular group, however, who called themselves the Stealth Jihad of America, had concocted a plan nearly mirroring that historic plot in 1864 devised by a sinister group, including John Wilkes Booth, to kidnap President Lincoln in exchange for Confederate prisoners. Likewise, these modern day terrorists schemed to take *me* prisoner to coerce the release of twenty four prisoners from the Guantanamo Bay facility. In conjunction with this plan, they intended to punctuate their scheme by exploding dirty bombs in several of our cities.

"Several weeks ago, my wife and I had decided that we would take a few days..."

In less than twenty minutes, the President provided the country a capsule of that fateful Friday night's events, making only slight reference to yours truly (at my earlier request). He basically conveyed that in spite of the relentless pursuit by the terrorists, I saw to his and his wife's safety, risking my own life to personally see to his return to the White House. For that he was eternally grateful. The only other thing he said about me was that he sorely regretted that I was initially pegged by his Chief of Staff as a co-conspirator in the plot. But he also praised the HRT element that not only so bravely and tactically rescued the First Lady but took down her captors. All of these heroic efforts cut short the plans of the jihadists. Again, at my request, he left out the fact that I was part of that HRT team.

"My friends, the threat will never be over until every jihadist faction and every terrorist bent on destroying America is located and annihilated. But with God's blessings along with the resolve and vigilance of every American, we will stand strong against these evil doers. I ask that you continue keeping the faith. This is especially the time of year we need to do so. With that, the First Lady and I wish you all a Merry Christmas, Happy Hanukah and a warm and safe holiday. God bless you and God bless the United States of America." He then turned and walked away from the podium. As the camera stayed on his departing form, I nodded and held up my glass to toast him. I held it high until he was out of sight. "And God bless *you*, Eagle One," I said.

I then looked over at the clock on our wall. Six fifty-two. It was time. Time to make my call and time to hit the road...with or without him. After pulling Rogers' card from my wallet, I touched the numbers to dial his cell.

"Hello."

"Chase, Bruce McGowan."

"Damn, didn't I just get rid of you?" He then laughed.

"Want another dose?"

"What's going on?"

"I think we found Tyson. He has a sometimes apartment in Fredericksburg."

"But he has an apartment and a wife in Falls Church?"

"That's correct. But you're certainly not going to find him *there*."

"Yeah. Our field agents had already been there questioning his wife last Sunday when they turned the apartment upside down. How did you find out he has a place in Fredericksburg?"

"A friend of Franks paid me a visit. Franks sent him to talk to me to see if I could arrange a deal for him in exchange for information."

"So you definitely know where Tyson is."

"If the information is correct, yes. I thought you'd like to join me for a takedown."

"*You're* going after him?"

"I *am* going after him. I told him what I'd do when I found him."

"Bruce, you were under presidential direction when we went after al-Jawhara and Franks. This is a different deal. It's now a matter for the Bureau."

"In other words, you're saying I shouldn't be involved."

"Anything from here on is the FBI's game. Where is he?"

"Why don't we meet somewhere off line and talk this out? Now that I have a clue as to where he is, no way I'm not going after him. I have a score to settle," I said.

"Don't take this the wrong way, Bruce, but we want to make an arrest, not keep score."

"Meaning you *don't* want to meet with me."

"You're good, Bruce. Damn good. A living example of what stellar law enforcement is. You could be a text book study for new recruits."

"But."

"But you have no authority to go after him or even be a part of the Bureau element that does. You and I worked together because the President ordered it. If the Director sanctions it, then...whatever."

"Then call the Director."

"Sorry, Bruce. Not something I can do."

"Then we're done here."

"Come on, Bruce. Where *is* Tyson? I have a responsibility to report this up the ladder."

"Sorry, Chase. I'll take care of business myself. You have an opportunity here. Would be another feather in your cap."

"You're obstructing justice."

"And I thought we played well, together."

"Will one more kill make any difference?"

"*This* one will."

"Let the Bureau handle it, Bruce."

"Goodbye, Chase."

"Bruce!"

I clicked him off.

Yeah, it was time all right. I decided that before Chase Rogers dispatched agents from the local field office to pick me up, I needed to go ahead with my plan and move out. So, I packed a quick bag, snatched up my Remington and strapped on the XD that Joey had returned to me. I also assured that my knife and cuffs were hanging from my gun belt.

"You're leaving now?" Adriana asked me.

"Time is of the essence. Tyson may decide to move out at any time. If he's static too long, he'll risk someone recognizing him."

"You *will* go in there as part of the FBI team, won't you."

"I sent the invitation."

"That's not the answer I was looking for, Skip."

"I'll be fine. I promise you."

She looked away for a moment, took a deep breath and closed her eyes. "Please make it a trouble-free takedown."

Then she smiled. "But if you have to bust him up a little bit, slug him a good one for me."

That's my girl. But I still didn't know who she was.

"I've done this before, sweetheart."

"In an official capacity." And then came the look I was afraid I might see. Reality was setting in. "Skip, I...think maybe I might have had a knee-jerk overreaction to some anger I've been feeling since this past weekend. In hindsight, I should have handled my wrath a little differently. Why don't you just let the FBI take out this guy?"

"Hey, not to worry. I said I'd be fine. You'll see. No bullet holes, I promise."

I kissed her deeply and then slung my bag over my shoulder. I definitely had to beat a path out of there before Adriana *did* change her mind. And if I had in some way pissed Chase Rogers off, he might just report my intentions of going after Tyson to the local FBI satellite office. I didn't think he would, but just in case, I wanted to vamoose before any feds started knocking on our door.

I had earlier filled up the tank in my brother's pickup, so I didn't have to stop for gas. No one should recognize the truck nor have any reason to stop it unless I was caught speeding. I would probably not make Fredericksburg until sometime after ten, barring any traffic issues or mishaps. Twice my cell went off with a 703 area code showing up, and as I knew it was Rogers trying to reach me, I let it go. Whether he would actually put someone on my trail, I wasn't sure. He was CIRG, HRT, a special assignment agent, not a mainstream, everyday government agent. He was a tactical mobility operator who answered to a laundry list of people up the chain, ultimately responding to orders from the Executive Assistant Director. A smackdown like this would not be considered a critical response operation or hostage rescue; agents from a field office would be the people who'd pull it off. In essence, he had no real dog in the fight.

I needed a cup of coffee badly and saw an IHOP sign advertised on I-95 a half mile before the Fredericksburg exit on Plank Road. I also needed to stretch my legs and not just pull into a drive-through. At the exit I turned left and drove the short distance to the restaurant parking lot. After getting out, I passed two working class men and a late night couple, all of whom had probably just filled their oversized guts with chicken and waffles or stacks of pancakes soaked with syrup. Just a little late to be shoving *anything* down the swallow pipe. Watching them waddle out with toothpicks in their mouths and lighting up cigarettes, I thought how tragic it was that they were killing themselves every way they could think of except putting a gun to their heads. For sure, there would be no donut with my coffee.

I thought about calling Rogers back to see if he had simmered down. He could meet me somewhere like that IHOP and talk about it. Maybe we needed to clear the air. But if he did meet me, being the good and responsible agent he was, he might call the local field office to have agents show up with him. I only called him earlier in the first place because Adriana expected me to have a horde of his Bureau types with me while taking Tyson down. But then I thought about it again. No, I wouldn't call him. I'd leave well enough alone. Actually, I wanted Tyson all to myself. I didn't want any witnesses to what I had planned for him. And I do my best work alone, anyway.

I got the coffee *to go* in a large Styrofoam cup. It would keep me delicious company while I took some time to stake out the apartment. 1743 Cherry Hill Drive was back across the interstate and just under two miles off to the left in a one building complex. Tyson, AKA Sullivan, was supposed to live on the third floor in Apartment H. I remarkably found a place to pull in at the edge of the curb directly in front of the complex where I could sit and closely observe residents going in and out. Residents entering the building keyed themselves into the front door while visitors were probably compelled to press the buzzer belonging to the apartment dweller for entry.

I didn't have a plan. I was just going to observe for now. There was no way I could tell if Tyson was even in his apartment. Once I knew for sure, a plan would quickly materialize. In checking out the windows on the upper floor, I saw that a couple of them were lit up; but my question was, did either of them belong to Apartment H? And then, just how was I going to get through the front door to make my way up there?

I thought I'd just sit patiently for a while and make love to what was left of my coffee. Anyway, if Tyson did make himself visible outside the apartment complex, I wasn't sure if I'd even recognize his face. Having only seen that face in a photo, I thought my committing it to memory would be a cinch. But a week after taking that mental snapshot of his face, the image in my brain had faded. And the fact that the street and outside steps to the apartment were not well-lighted would make it doubly difficult.

Pedestrian traffic had understandably slowed down considering the lateness of the hour, nearly eleven. In the past ten minutes, only two residents had climbed the steps and keyed in. One was an elderly lady with white hair who made her way up the short flight of steps with the aid of her cane and the other a short, balding man who was as wide as he was tall. Definitely not the likes of Tyson. However, if I did want to get into the building, it appeared the only way I could do so is waltz in behind one of the residents. After exiting the pickup, I pulled my cellphone out and stood on the sidewalk at the base of the steps, pretending to be talking with someone. I was neither a bad looking guy nor did I look threatening in my high dollar Greg Norman jacket that Adriana had bought for me the Christmas before. Unfortunately, I had to stand out in the bitter cold for nearly fifteen more minutes before a cute young thing about twenty five got out of her parked Nissan and made her way to the apartment building.

I finished my 'conversation' by saying, "Okay, sis. I'll see you next week. Tell the kids their Uncle Bruce says *hi* and give them my love."

The girl with the long brown hair gave me a nice smile which I returned. I allowed her to go ahead of me up the steps and then pretended to fumble around in my pants pocket for my plastic key. "Now where is it?" I mumbled loud enough for her to hear.

"Don't worry, I've got it, " she said. But then as she opened the door, she said, "But wait. You could be Jack the Ripper. I don't know that I've seen you before."

I smiled again. "Just moved in last weekend. I'm still trying to get this key thing down."

"I know," she said. "I've only lived here a little less than a month myself. Half the time the key won't work. It reminds me to call the management company."

Before I walked in behind her, I took notice of the name above the Apartment H door buzzer...Johnson. Had Mr.

Pavloski been straight with me about the occupant of Apartment H?

As it appeared the little fox lived on an upper floor, I followed her up the first flight of stairs past Apartments D, E and F and then we both continued on to the third floor.

"Oh, you're up here, too. Which apartment?"

I had three choices. Tyson was in H or at least supposed to be. The girl would live in one of the other two. It was like I was trying to make the right choice on *Let's Make a Deal* what was behind door number... Maybe I should be that gentleman in H. But for some reason I said G.

"Well howdy, neighbor. I wondered who was in G. I haven't seen anyone coming or going in G since I've been here."

We then reached the landing that led to the apartments. She held out her hand. "By the way, I'm Margie Johnson. I'm in H across the hall."

And then it started to ring clear. She was Tyson's Fredericksburg girlfriend.

"And I'm Uncle Bruce." But instead of taking her hand, I pulled my XD and shoved it into her ribs. I then placed my left index finger up to my lips. "Don't make sound. You cry out and you'll immediately be losing consciousness. Now open your door and go inside like you normally do."

She had that predictable stunned look of horror on her face. "Are you going to rape me?" she asked softly.

"That's not what I do, Margie. Is anybody inside?"

"No," she replied. She unlocked the door and opened it. And it *was* dark inside. I flipped on the wall switch.

Just in case Tyson was in the bedroom sleeping or waiting in the dark for a little action, I first swept my automatic around the room and then coaxed her with my left hand toward the hoo-ha room.

"I thought you said you wouldn't force yourself on me."

After checking the bedroom, bathroom and kitchenette, I was then convinced she and I were alone. I took her back to the living room and shoved her down in a sofa chair. I stood over her with my pistol hanging menacingly at my side.

"All right, Margie. Talk. Where's your boyfriend, Tyson?"

"Who?"

"Let's try this name...David Sullivan."

"Dave? Obviously, he's not home." Now I *knew* Pavloski hadn't been lying to me. I'd be sure to send him a *Thank You* card.

"When do you expect him?"

"I don't know. He said he'd be here sometime after midnight I think. Why are you looking for him...and with a gun?"

"How well do you know Dave?"

She eyed her purse. "Can I light a cigarette? You're scaring the hell out of me."

I picked up the purse and dumped it out. No gun. Just a few personal items and an opened pack of Kools. I tossed them to her. She lit one and expelled a long plume of smoke.

"I met him in a bar about ten days ago. We hit it off and he's staying with me for a while till he finds a place."

"What did Dave tell you he does?"

"He's a CPA."

"Another lie."

"And why would he lie to me?"

"Because he's not David Sullivan."

"What do you mean? Of course he is."

"You really *don't* know, do you?"

"I'm not sure what I'm supposed to know or what the hell you're talking about," she snapped.

"He has a wife in Falls Church."

"No he doesn't." She thought a moment and then took another drag. "Even if he does, are you some kind of freaking private detective hired to go around scaring the shit out of people's girlfriends? You probably also peek in people's windows and watch them undress. And you wouldn't just be here with a gun in your hand because a wife sent you."

I sat down across from her to explain the facts of life.

"You're right, I wouldn't. His name is Curtis Tyson and he is or *was* a federal agent. He kills people, Margie. You've probably seen him with a gun on him."

"Yeah, what of it. He says he has to go work in a bad part of D.C."

"Big gun, shoulder holster, the whole bit, huh?"

"Yeah."

"Does that sound like the kind of equipment an accountant would wear?"

She didn't answer.

I continued. "Margie, your boyfriend Tyson...and you'd better get used to calling him that,...killed three West Virginia state troopers and conspired in a plot with some terrorists to detonate that bomb up in Maryland."

The look of horror was back on her face. "I don't believe that. Not him. He's never even said a cross word to me and treats me nice."

"Of course he does. You've given him a place to hide out and female companionship. You probably have dinner waiting for him in the fridge. Believe me when I tell you he's not the man you think you know."

"So, who are you...the law?"

"No. I'm somebody who's looking to take him down. Personal reasons."

"That means you're breaking the law. Yeah, of course you are, breaking in here and threatening me with a gun.

Maybe I should dial 911 and tell them you're here trying to rape me."

"Maybe I should just tie you up and put duct tape on your mouth."

"You wouldn't do that," she snipped.

"In a heartbeat if you scream or give me any trouble."

She finished off her cigarette and tamped it out in an ash tray on the end table. "Say I believe you and cooperate with you. What's in it for me?"

"You get to go on with your life without fear of Curtis Tyson killing you when he's done with you."

"That won't happen."

"That *will* happen, Margie."

She now looked visibly shaken. "He'll be home any time. What should I do?"

"First of all, do you believe everything I told you?"

"I don't know...maybe. But how do I know he doesn't just owe some money and you're the mob. You just made all this up so you could kill him."

"I might kill him, Margie, but I'm not the mob. I'm retired FBI."

"If you're retired, how is it you're involved in this thing?" she asked.

"The state troopers he murdered were friends of mine. I'm only here for justice. And he's who I told you he was. If you went through his personal belongings, I'll bet you'd find the name, Curtis Tyson, somewhere...and maybe some documents that associates him with a foreign terrorist."

She nodded. "I did find a letter in his coat pocket one day with that name on it. I asked him who it was and he just said 'a friend.' I don't want to believe you, you know. But somehow I think I do."

"Margie, I want you to leave for a while. Go somewhere for a drink or to a friend's house. You don't need to be here when he comes in."

"I guess I could go downstairs to my new friend Colleen's apartment. She stays up till two or three almost every night and watches TV, then goes to work at one the next afternoon."

"Then go."

"What makes you think I won't just leave here and call the police?"

"Like you said, I think you believe me, Margie. I'm trusting you won't call them. He sees them coming and he'll find another way out of here."

"But you said you may kill him. He might be all those things you said, but I don't want to see him dead."

"Let's just say I'll be waiting here for him. Being dead is up to him."

Margie closed her eyes and pulled at her bottom lip for a few seconds. "All right. I'm pretty bummed out over this.

And my night was going so good. I'm out of here." She then picked up her purse and started toward the door.

"Margie," I called after her. "If he gives me any trouble and it gets messy here, I don't want you to walk in here and find him. Give it two hours with your friend. If she goes to bed and kicks you out, go somewhere else. Take your cell phone with you. If Tyson calls and says he's not returning tonight for some reason, you can come back up. I'll be here. Under no circumstances warn him about me. If you do, he'll turn dangerous. You'll know too much and you'll be dead."

"Are you still trying to scare me?"

"No, Margie. I'm trying to save your life."

Chapter Twenty-Eight

Twelve twenty. In the kitchen I found a silver tray on the bar that contained a three quarter bottle of Cabernet Sauvignon and four large upside down wine glasses. Pouring myself a half glass, I then turned off the lights and sat down in the same sofa chair Margie had vacated only ten minutes before. The fabric in the chair reeked of her smoke. The ashtray on the end table smelled even worse. It was quiet inside the apartment...so quiet all I could hear was the motor of the refrigerator humming. In my lap lay my XD. I had attached the suppressor.

Sitting there, I began thinking about the man I was sent to locate some time ago, a hit man of all people, a man with whom I was compelled to collaborate on that job that temporarily brought me out of retirement. The mission where together we killed the Viper, the most savage terrorist in the world. I wasn't thinking of the mission we pulled, I was thinking of the man who strangely became my friend. What caused me to think of him was something he had reluctantly told me.

Atticus Steed was a bizarre man...an enigma. A likable enough sort, engaging, mysterious, charismatic, yet a ruthless, remorseless killer. After pushing him six ways from Sunday to give me an example of a way he took care of business, over a carafe of wine he finally did. He told me that he might break into the victim's house and wait for the mark to come home. In generally all cases, he had never seen his victim. Steed was kind of like the Mission Impossible operative who received the order for the hit from a voice on the phone with no other instructions except to "make the kill." But, there was one thing about Steed that made him different from everyone else in his field. He had to know he wasn't killing an innocent person. In advance of the hit, he did his homework on his mark. Read the news articles, scanned evidence files and perused court transcripts. If the perp somehow got off because of a technicality or was found not guilty because of insufficient evidence, Steed would assume there was guilt. While waiting on his target, he might break out a bottle of the man's vino, sit in his chair and watch his TV. The door would then open and...bang. Was I any better than Atticus Steed? Maybe I had *become* him.

I suddenly heard footsteps on the third floor stairs and glanced at the digital numbers on the clock beside the stinking ashtray. Twelve thirty two. Quietly, I sat the wine glass down on the hardwood floor and then picked up the XD. The turn of the key and click of the deadbolt. The door opened and the lights came on. He actually walked in and turned around to close the door without checking the room out. And then he saw me.

"Shit!" he exclaimed. And then he made a move for his gun.

"Don't even think about it." I aimed the muzzle of my pistol at his forehead. "This is the part in the movie where you die if you pull that out."

He then raised his hands. "And just who the hell are *you*?"

"The guy who messed up your dreams and put the squelch on your big payoff."

"McGowan."

"Sit down on the floor and put your hands on top of your head."

Slowly, making no sudden moves, he did as instructed. And now I had my first real look at him. Tall, maybe two to three inches taller than me, strapping physique, dark close-cut hair, piercing dark eyes and a square face. He was definitely the man I recalled from the photo in his personnel shield.

I then picked myself up out of the chair and walked over to slip his Sig Sauer out of his holster.

"How did you find me when the entire law enforcement community is looking for me?"

"*Everybody* gets found, Tyson. I don't know how many nights this past week I laid awake designing, rather creatively I might add, all of the ways I wanted to kill you. Kill you on sight without hearing the first word come out of your mouth. It's taking every ounce of willpower right now for me to keep from putting a bullet between your eyes."

His smile was laced with a sneer. Impudent bastard. "My guess is that you're mainly here because I killed your police captain friend."

"So, it *was* you who did it."

"It seemed like the right thing to do at the time." And then he laughed.

In a flash of anger, I flipped my XD into my left hand and brought my fist down hard on the side of his head. He crashed into the floor like a brick. It was enough of a blow to put him out. I could have hit him with the butt of my pistol, but needed the feel of my fist on his skull. Of course, my knuckles were now smarting.

I walked back over to the bar and picked up the bottle of Cabernet. As he laid unconscious on the floor, I poured what was left of the wine onto his face. Its biting liquid rushed into his mouth and nostrils, causing him to cough and sputter. He then sat up and wobbled a bit trying to regain his balance.

I sat back down in the chair and faced him.

"Give me a reason I shouldn't end your life right now."

"I have some money."

"Let me guess. Al-Jawhara and company primed your pump with an advance on your payoff. How much?"

"Enough to make it worth your while. Six figures. I can get it tomorrow."

"Who were you planning to spend it on...your wife or Margie?"

"Where *is* Margie?"

"Safe. *You'll* never see her again...*or* your wife...or your money."

"Look, McGowan..."

"No, *you* look, you piece of shit. As much as I want to shoot both of your eyes out right now, I'm going to go against not only my better judgment, but the promise I made to myself that you would die immediately when I found you. You'll soon be joining your buddy Franks, who by the way turned you in."

He scowled. "That son-of-a-bitch."

I studied him a moment. I tried to see in him the likes of a Secret Service agent, but to me he just looked like John Dillinger in a pea coat and jeans. How he could have fooled Margie Johnson into thinking he was a CPA, she had to be blinded by his good looks and big penis.

"Tell me something, Tyson. You were not only a Secret Service agent with everything going for you, but the actual SAC on the President's protection team with an esteemed job and a ton of power. How does somebody like you ultimately end up a cockroach laying on the floor with a busted head staring down the barrel of my gun? Big comedown, huh maggot?"

He only glared at me without responding.

I popped open my phone to dial Rogers. Whether he would send some of his people down to pick Tyson up or just contact the Fredericksburg field office, whoever came would keep me from plugging the bastard. But they needed to hurry before I changed my mind.

"All right, stand up!" I barked.

Still apparently off balance from the blow to his head, he stumbled as he stood. Blood continued to ooze down the side of his head and around his left ear. I pulled the cuffs off my belt and ordered him to "Turn around and place your hands behind your back."

What happened next in retrospect seemed like a blur. As he was turning his body, still seemingly unsteady, he fell toward me. By instinct, I pushed out with my left hand to keep him from toppling into me; however, he suddenly lunged at me, upper body first, at the same time knocking me back into the sofa chair with his large frame, I inadvertently pulled the trigger. He screamed out in pain as the bullet entered his right side. But as the round apparently did not strike anything vital, with a sweep of his hand, he grabbed up the ashtray from the end table and clobbered me on the head at the temple. My second bullet penetrated his thigh. That caused him to stumble back and fall. It was now *my* turn to be woozy. The blow had dazed me to a point where my world was spinning and I had trouble focusing my eyes. Before I could regain my faculties and get a bead on him with my XD, he was already dragging his wounded body toward the door. When I fired two more quick rounds in his direction, not knowing if I hit him, I did see through my blurring eyes that he grabbed his shoulder. Unfortunately, he was already through the door before I could get to my feet.

Blood was now gushing from my head wound and running down my cheek. Grabbing a handkerchief from my pocket, I applied pressure to stop the bleeding while at the same time giving chase. I could already hear him stumbling down the stairs before I passed through the doorway. Finally, when *my* feet hit the stairs I found that both my vision and equilibrium were slowly returning. By the time I reached the lower staircase, Tyson was well into the street. Although he was already out of sight, even in the dim light I could see where large blotches of his blood were leaving a trail for me on the sidewalk. Would he continue on foot? The way he was leaking, he wouldn't make it far.

Suddenly, not fifteen feet from me, I heard a car start up and saw that Tyson was struggling to get his BMW out of the tight parking spot where he had parked directly behind my brother's truck. By the time I hustled to where I could empty my XD into his windshield, he was already pulling away. I fired three rounds into his back glass, but he kept going, apparently unscathed. Unfortunately, in making his getaway, his front bumper banged up Joey's rear bumper. My brother was going to kill me. I would be returning yet another one of his vehicles with damage on it.

Quickly, I jumped into the pickup and began giving chase. He was heading back toward Highway 3. The Beemer's taillights were easy to keep track of. However, after he turned right, he gunned it. I could hear its engine roaring at high RPMs a block away. I thought he may turn onto the interstate, but instead, he continued on across the bridge toward the west, toward historic Chancellorsville. And he was flying. I was surprised with all of the bleeding he was doing, he was able to maintain his speed. And I thought for sure he would come upon a police or sheriff's unit before long.

My speedometer needle approached 85 as I tried desperately to keep him in sight. Finally, about three miles further to the west, I saw him slow and turn off the road into a field. By the time I reached his car, I found the driver's door opened and his dark form limping across the meadow, clearly visible in the moonlight. Apparently, he had pulled from his car a second pistol. Seeing my headlights behind his BMW, he turned and fired three rounds. The bullets whizzed harmlessly over my head. It was time to end it.

From the back floor of the pickup, I retrieved my .308. Resting the barrel of the sniper rifle on the hood of the truck, I quickly zeroed in on his head and pulled the trigger. A second later through the rifle's NVD scope, I watched his body drop. It was a clean shot. The bullet which traveled on through his skull would have buried itself in the ground a hundred yards further down range. No one would ever find it to do a ballistics check against my Remington. The final nail had been driven. Paybacks are hell, Tyson.

* * * * *

Well, I wouldn't be returning home with any bullets holes in me. I did manage to keep that promise to Adriana. When I stopped off at an all-night gas station to fill up the tank on Joey's truck, I went to the restroom to wash the dried blood off my face. The ashtray assault had left a deep cut in my temple area merely an inch from my left eye. It was still oozing blood and I probably needed a few stitches. However, I bought some Neosporin and a box of band aids and doctored myself up. I'd have a scar there probably the rest of my life, but I was okay with that. Every time I looked at myself in the mirror, it would be a reminder that I had gotten revenge on the man who took my friend's life.

Tyson's body would probably not be found until the next morning...maybe by dogs, maybe by a farmer, maybe by hunters. But with half of a head, he wouldn't readily be identified. David Sullivan wouldn't come home to his girlfriend, either. I imagine after my little talk with her and especially finding out who he really was and that he had a wife up near D.C., she probably wouldn't care. And unless she decided to tell anyone about me, no one should be the wiser I was even on the premises. If the authorities somehow did find out, so be it. I'd own it.

Actually, I had performed an act of mercy by ending Tyson's life so quickly. Had he continued further into that field and then into the woods, he would have fallen, maybe laid on the ground for hours and either bled or froze to death. A slow, agonizing death. So yeah, I showed him compassion, whether he deserved it or not. What the hell. I figured if I kept telling myself that, maybe I'd start to believe it.

Chase Rogers would hear about Tyson over the wire and he'd know immediately who killed him. I had thought of Chase as a new friend, considering our shared mission. But if duty came first, he'd throw friendship out the window and report the telephone conversation we had to his superior. Perhaps in the interim, however, the President might hear that I had been pulled in for interrogation and would then make a phone call. He said he owed me big. Maybe I'd see how big that really was.

I was home at a quarter till five. Adriana had been sitting up most of the night and when she heard Joey's pickup in the driveway, she jumped up from her TV chair and ran out onto the veranda. There is nothing sweeter than having a woman wearing a beautiful smile and a white silk negligee waiting for you at the door. As cold as it was, she didn't stop to put on her housecoat before stepping outside to welcome me home.

"I was worried when I didn't hear from you," she said after warming me up with those velvet lips of hers.

"I thought you might be asleep and I didn't want to wake you."

"Fat chance of that. What happened to your head?"

"I bumped it."

"How?"

"It's not important. What *is* important is the feast of beauty my eyes are devouring right now."

Her smile widened. I was also compelled to notice what the freezing weather had done to her breasts. They stood up like they belonged to an eighteen year old cheerleader in a tight sweater at a thirty degree football game...perky, pointy and palatable. I think she noticed that I noticed and so she reached inside the door for her coat on the hall tree. She didn't have to be embarrassed on *my* part. Of course, it likely wasn't embarrassment on her part at all; it was self-protection. I sometimes get hungry that early in the morning...for a different kind of breakfast.

"Are you finally done playing James Bond?"

"Absolutely."

"That being the case, do you have anything to tell me?" In other words, had I located my target?

"The information was correct. I found him."

"And?"

"I spanked him good...just for you."

"I hope it hurt."

"It did."

"Do the authorities have him in custody?"

"He decided he wanted to resist."

"Then he's..."

"He is."

"Well, whatever happened, he had it coming."

"That he did. Why don't we talk about other things, my dear," I said. "Like both of us getting some sleep. I'm bushed."

"Promise no funny business?"

"I don't do funny when I'm doing business."

Monday morning, I went to the Ford dealership and bought a new rear bumper for Joey's F-150. It was also time I returned the truck to him, bit the bullet and bought some transportation. Both our vehicles, my Suburban and Adriana's Toyota van, were ten years old at the time they were destroyed. My frugal wife had just about convinced me that we needed to purchase pre-owned vehicles. It wasn't that we couldn't afford brand new replacements. After all, because several months before when I along with Mr. Steed had rubbed out the young jihadist that was in line to replace Usama bin-Laden, the President had arranged for some covert financial source to pay us both a cool million for our contract work. The dough we received had to be confiscated drug money or something.

Tuesday we talked with a sales guy at Barker Toyota. A real piece of work. Everything you would expect a used car salesman to be. Chubby, wearing a plaid springtime sport coat with a wide lapel, Army low quarter shoes and a comb-over that made him look like something between Donald Trump and a TV evangelist. And then he went on and on about a late model van that we found out he actually knew nothing about. A three year old ride with a hundred thirty thousand on the odometer...but it was "all interstate miles" borne out by the fact that it still had the original brakes. All for only a thousand over retail price. I whispered to Adriana, "should I just go ahead and shoot him?" She couldn't stop giggling. Needless to say, we left there and I went home to take an Excedrin. We said we'd maybe try a Nissan or Honda dealer on Wednesday.

And it was on that Wednesday morning the phone rang. It was Rogers. This time I answered the call. I was sure it was about Tyson. His body had been found and I was the suspect.

"Hello, Bruce. Things back to normal in your life?"

"Having all the fun I can stand. How about you?"

"Back to status quo. Training every day and I've been wrapping up reports on our little project we did together. Is your nose back in joint with me on the Tyson matter?"

"Absolutely," I replied.

"I hope you understood where I was coming from. Even if we *had* been tasked with the mission to go after Tyson, without specific approval from the Director or higher up for you to participate, you were a no go. Anyway, it appears it worked itself out. Somebody got to Tyson. His car was found just off the road near Fredericksburg. Locals then found his body out in a field. Yeah, somebody got to him all right."

He was baiting me. He was fishing to see how I'd react. But even if he was, his mission wasn't about chasing down murder suspects. That was for field agents or local law enforcement to do. But because I had called Rogers to tell him I was going after Tyson and then Tyson ended up dead just hours later, he *would* have a responsibility to report my call on up to his highers.

"Any ideas who?"

"Could be there are still remnants of the jihad group out there and since Tyson was no longer a player, he knew too much. Maybe the same thing happened to him that happened to the President's Chief of Staff. Of course, Tyson's murder could also have been a vengeful killing."

"Meaning me."

"Maybe. You said you had found out where he was and were going after him. *Did* you?"

"If you really thought that, there would have already been agents from Clarksburg or Charleston at my door. I'm thinking you didn't even report my call to anyone."

"If I did, by the time it went anywhere, your friend Eagle One would have any investigation on you shut down."

"My friend?"

"In *his* book, you do no wrong."

"He's a man of honor, Chase. That wouldn't happen."

"I'll prove to you how high you are on his list."

"What do you mean?"

"The President specifically singled me out to do yet another mission."

"To come after me."

"What are you doing this morning?"

"I just got back from a late morning run. Still sitting in my jogging clothes having a bowl of Wheaties. Why?"

"I'm five minutes out from Wolf Laurel."

"What? Why?"

"Just be ready out front in zero five." He then ended the call.

I wasn't sure it made any sense. The President sending a CIRG agent to pick me up? I thought my last conversation with the President was quite cordial. He had been immensely pleased I had gotten the First Lady back. And helped end a national nightmare. I do no wrong, remember? And then why would the order to pick me up have come from *him*? Furthermore, why was he dispatching Chase Rogers? Had my two newest friends gone south on me?

Adriana called out to me from the den. "Who was on the phone, Skip?"

"It was Chase Rogers."

"How is he doing?"

"He's on his way here."

"Coming here?"

"Appears so. Maybe he was wrapping things up at the airport with the CIRG and wanted to stop by, I don't know."

I then pushed aside my cereal bowl and leaned back in my chair. So, was he here to take me away after all? Was all of that dialogue about it not being his job to go after common criminals like me just a bunch of hoo-ha? And did I need to ready myself to go with him?

I poured myself a cup of coffee and walked out to the veranda. The morning sun had already begun warming the air and it was actually rather comfortable to sit out in the old rocker. When I had gotten settled, I heard the door close behind me. Adriana took the chair beside me. She would be watching with tearful eyes if Rogers and his people handcuffed me and placed me in the back of a Bureau unit. We had become friendly and had worked well together. I would have no hard feelings. He was just doing his job. But why him? And why did the President specifically send *him* to pick me up? I was still trying to sort out the pieces of our conversation that actually added up.

After I had downed a half cup of the coffee, three large, black official looking vehicles pulled into our driveway...two SUVs and a van. Two men in civilian attire exited the first SUV. Rogers was one of them. The drivers of the two trailing units then stepped out from under the steering wheel. I was unsure why it would take four agents and three vehicles to cart me off. I looked at Adriana. She had a look of worry on her face.

"I thought it was just Chase Rogers coming by," she remarked.

Only Rogers and his passenger approached the steps. I tried reading their faces, but found them stoic. I then set my coffee down on our wicker table and stood ready to face the music. There would be no resistance of course.

Chapter Twenty-Nine

Epilogue

"Good morning, Bruce, Adriana. Good to see you two again."

That greeting didn't sound like it came from someone who was getting ready to take me into custody.

"Hello, Chase." We shook hands.

Rogers then gestured toward the man with him who was of Asian ethnicity. "This is Terry Chan with the GAO. He rode down here with me this morning."

Now, big time puzzled, I shook his hand as well. "Good morning, Mr. Chan."

I then looked at the two men still standing by their vehicles. Rogers said, "They're with Terry here."

"Please have a seat, gentlemen." I pointed to the two chairs near ours. They took them. "Would you and your two cohorts out there like some coffee?"

They looked at one another and then both shook their heads. "We don't have a lot of time, Bruce. We need to get on back."

"Okay, Chase. Now that you've got me really confused, is this just a social visit because you're in the area or did you stop by for something official?"

"I told you on the phone I was here at the direction of the President."

"Yes, which doesn't make a lot of sense."

"Well, this *will*, Bruce." He then looked out toward the parking lot. "Bruce and Adriana, say hello to your new rides."

"What?"

"They're actually not new. Both the Suburban I was driving and the Chevy Savana van behind it are low-mileage three year old Bureau vehicles that are being replaced by current models. They were slated for trade or auction with a fleet of others. And these are the cream of the crop in the GAO motor pool. Merry Christmas from the President."

Both Adriana and I were speechless. We sat nearly motionless with mouths agape.

"Well, are you going to say something?"

"Uh...thanks?" I finally spit out.

"Your vehicles being destroyed like they were in your efforts to protect the President and First Lady, he felt badly about. Even he couldn't swing getting you current year models, but these are in near perfect condition. Enjoy them with his blessing."

"And we were only expecting a Christmas card from him," I said.

He and Chan laughed.

"Well, let's go down and see if they meet with your approval," Rogers said.

I thought maybe I was going to miss my old bucket of bolts which had over the years taken on a persona all its own. Like me, it had some miles on it, had been shot up a few times and was prone to breaking down in places. But before it lost its windshield and radiator, it was still starting up and running. Just like *I* start up and run nearly every morning.

Now this newer beast, a modern, masculine looking thing of beauty with leather seats, was loaded with bells and whistles. I would have to spend the better part of a day studying the owner's manual to learn all its features. And that neat hidden storage area in the rear compartment would more than adequately accept my .308, the NVD equipment and a couple other of my more dangerous toys.

Adriana's new Savana van was much larger than her old Toyota and it might be a bit more bulky for her to manage. But she wouldn't look a gift horse in the mouth. I always wondered who came up with that saying. And just what the hell did it mean, anyway?

"Ah, man," I said. "And we were just getting ready to go out and spend eighty grand on vehicles."

"Mmm, no we *weren't*," replied Adriana.

"Here are the titles, folks," Chan said. "They've been signed and along with the affidavit and odometer statement, you won't have any trouble at the DMV."

Rogers then dialed a number and handed me his cell. "He wants to talk with you."

"He *who*?"

Rogers didn't reply. He just nodded toward the phone.

A bit bewildered, I took it from him.

"Hello, Scorpion. Do they meet your standards?"

"They do indeed, Mr. President. I can't tell you..."

"Then *don't*. You saved my life and risked yours to go get my Mrs. You also saved the lives of a hell of a lot of people in America's cities. And in doing so, you lost your fishing cabin and had your B&B nearly destroyed. Then, both of your vehicles were totaled out. I can't do enough to show my appreciation for your loyalty not only to me but to your country. This gesture on my part is merely a small token."

"It's quite enough, Mr. President, I assure you."

"I have to go, Bruce. I hope you and Adriana have a wonderful Christmas."

"Be well...be safe, sir," I replied.

I handed Rogers' phone back to him.

He smiled. "It's not every day a common nobody like you gets to be friends with the President of the United States."

I grinned back at him. "Eat your heart out, Bullitt."

"Before I leave, is there anything about your little trip to Fredericksburg the other night you'd like to tell me?"

"What trip to Fredericksburg?"

Another smile. "That's what I thought. Okay, McGowan, be cool and keep your head down. See you around."

"Right. Give my best to Smithers."

"Uh...Smithers?"

"Uh...*yeah*." I gave him a wink.

His only response was a sheepish smile.

After watching all four men pile into the last SUV, Chase Rogers gave me a salute through the windshield. He then backed up, turned around and pulled onto the roadway. What happened just outside of Fredericksburg would stay between us. Apparently, it was one of Tyson's own terrorist consorts that had been ordered to kill him. That would be federal law enforcement's speculation, anyway. Former SAC Curt Tyson had gone renegade with the Stealth Jihad of America, selling out his country for an undisclosed amount of money. Money that never changed hands. And then there was that other renegade. Would I keep my promise to Franks and talk with the prosecution about getting some time cut off his sentence? After all, his information not only led me to Tyson, but Steffen Franks had done his best to keep al-Jawhara and Tyson from killing the hostages. Yes, I would. I would find out the date of that hearing and make the appearance. I *always* keep my promises. That's the reason Tyson was lying on a slab in some morgue.

The cellphone call that Wednesday was the last conversation I would have with Eagle One. He would leave the White House a month later, also leaving the responsibility for the security of our country with the guy coming in. And, it would be the last time I'd be summoned by someone as important as him to go do the job that people in all those alphabet agencies were trained and paid to do. Adriana McGowan and I were once again back in business as the innkeepers of Wolf Laurel.

www.ingramcontent.com/pod-product-compliance
Lightning Source LLC
Chambersburg PA
CBHW031153010826
48971CB00012B/73